SNOWED IN & SET UP

WHITLEY COX

Copyright © 2018 by Whitley Cox

All rights reserved.

No part of this book may be reproduced in any form or by any electronic or mechanical means, including information storage and retrieval systems, without written permission from the author, except for the use of brief quotations in a book review.

ISBN: 978-1687536068

*For my fantastic editor and friend, Chris Kridler.
You are an incredible person and I'm so lucky to have found you.
Thank you for all your help, kind words and support.
You are just one tremendously amazing human being.
xoxo*

PROLOGUE

Bcc: Dr. Will Colson, Amber Roth, Rowan Briggs, Juniper Davis, Dr. Austin Masters, Hunter Kingsley
Subject: Christmas in the Mountains!

Hey!

What are your plans for Christmas? Because Riley and I would love to have you join us at my family's cabin on Snoqualmie Pass. You can literally walk out the front door and up to the chairlift. Just a few friends spending the holidays together, eating good food, playing games, snow shoeing, skiing and snowboarding—you know, all that fun stuff!

We've got lots of bedrooms and all the amenities. I'll provide the food if you bring your favorite libations and a gift for Secret Santa.

There's not much parking so I'm going to hire a shuttle to pick everyone up in Riverbend. I'll email you later on with the address of where you can park so your car won't be towed.

Come celebrate Christmas in rustic but cozy style. The shuttle will pick you up on December 23rd and take you back down on December 28th. Five whole days of nothing but food, friends, festivities and flurries.

Please let me know by December 20th if you're able to come.

Kisses,

Daisy and Riley McMillan

New Message — x

CHAPTER ONE

Will

WILL Colson let out a big manly grunt as he heaved his snowboard bag out of the back of his charcoal-gray BMW M5. He still couldn't figure out why he'd agreed to this. He hated Christmas. Hated everything about Christmas. The music, the decorations, the idea that a fat man in a red suit could travel around the world in a flying sleigh and visit every home in the world in one night. It was all a big joke. So how in the world he found himself heading into the quaint little coffee shop in Riverbend, Washington, located at the base of Snoqualmie Pass, was anybody's guess.

But it was either this or sitting alone in his high-rise Seattle condo, nursing a bottle of Macallan 18 until he was numb enough to go to bed. His mother was down in Trinidad visiting her family, and his dad, *fuck*, his dad was off with wife number—was it four or five? —down in Palm Springs for the winter. And without a brother or sister to lean on or go visit, Will was left to his own devices. But he liked it like that. No one to answer to, no one to disappoint.

Because as far as Will was concerned, he was just a big disappointment to everyone. It didn't matter that he was a world-class doctor, having spent time in war-torn countries, repairing cleft palates on babies and treating the sick and wounded. He was a selfish man because he liked his job; he was good at it, and that was enough for him. He didn't want a family, he didn't need a family, and although Janice had said the same things when they'd first met, that her career would always be her focus, they weren't even a year into their marriage when the topic of babies came up. And that's when it hit the fan.

But why would Will want to bring kids into the world? Not when he was sure he would just be a huge disappointment to them, just like his old man had been to him. Like father, like son, right? When Will was eight, his dad walked out on his family on Christmas Eve. Left him and his mom crying on the couch as his dad announced he was leaving her for another woman, a nurse he'd fallen in love with. She became wife number two, but she didn't last long.

Of course, there was also the fact that years later, Janice handed Will divorce papers on Christmas morning as he poured his coffee and hummed *Jingle Bells* under his breath. She'd stated "irreconcilable differences and neglect," that his demanding job interfered with them starting a family. She'd called him "selfish and a psychopath." And by the news and ruckus on Facebook recently, she hadn't wasted any time on the baby front. They hadn't even been divorced a year, and already she was announcing her engagement to Will's *ex*-best friend and their pregnancy to the entire world. So, after that devastating revelation, Will replied "yes" to his co-worker's wife's email, more out of necessity to escape reality for a few days than a desire to get into the Yuletide spirit. He needed to get away.

Will slid into a vacant booth and ordered a coffee. Not really hungry but feeling like he needed to do something with his hands, he picked up a menu and began to read it. The door chimed, and he looked up, but all he could see was a tiny flurry of dark red hair and duffel bags struggling to get into the warmth of the café.

Amber

"You sure you don't want to join us and the kids?" Tim Roth asked his sister as he pulled up in front of the boring-looking coffee shop covered with a thick blanket of snow in sleepy little Riverbend.

Amber gave him a half-smile and an eye roll as she went to open her door. "As much as I would *love* to spend a week with you, Jillian and the kids driving down to California in a minivan, I'm going to have to pass."

He snorted a laugh as he put the van into park before opening his own door and joining her back near the hatch. "Fair enough. To be honest, I'm a tad nervous about it as well. Jill thinks we can just drive nonstop, switching drivers and sleeping on the way. I'd just as soon grab a hotel rather than listen to Harlow whine for eight hours."

Amber grabbed her duffel bag and snowboard bag and swung them both over her shapely shoulder. "You make it sound like *so* much fun."

He reached out and grabbed her by the shoulders. "Merry Christmas, sis. Enjoy your ski trip with your friends. We're definitely going to miss you." He pulled her close for one of his famous bear hugs. The Roth family bear hugs were legendary, and when it was just the brothers, the hugs often ended up in a wrestling match. But no matter how many times Amber said she wanted to roughhouse, too, the boys had always been very gentle with her. She was the baby, and they treated her as such.

"Merry Christmas, Tim. Give the kids a big kiss for me. And don't forget to give them my presents *before* you guys leave for California. I bought them all travel art kits, something to give you and Jill some peace and quiet for a least a few hours on the trip."

He finally released her but didn't let go quite yet. "Okay, will do. Merry Christmas." And with a final squeeze to her shoulder he let her go and wandered back around to the driver's side, before shooting her one last look. "You pack a dress?" Tim didn't even wait for her response as he opened the door of the van and hopped in. He chuckled before the door slammed shut, and Amber could see his body jostling in mirth as he started the engine and put the car into drive.

Tim could be such a dink sometimes. A tomboy to her very core, Amber hated dresses and makeup. She much preferred jeans and a flannel and to sit and drink a beer while watching the game than go out shopping for sparkly clothes with the girls or gab over martinis and tapas. It only took her parents a few years of wrapping up dolls and ponies and tea sets that never even made it out of the packaging for them to realize that what Amber really wanted was her own tool belt and tools. She wanted blocks. She wanted Tinker Toys, a train set, and Legos. Things she could really do something with. Toys that used both her mind and her hands to create. And those things came easily, seeing as all the boys ahead of her had these toys in excess.

After the initial shock wore off that the family's sweet little red-haired pixie was going to be following in her father's footsteps and joining the family construction business, everyone accepted Amber's decision and fully supported her. And she'd made a name for herself in the process, winning contracts her father would have never even considered bidding on. In the last three years, since taking the helm of Roth Construction Incorporated, she'd expanded the company exponentially and made a buttload of money in the process.

But despite her contempt for all things girlie, all things sweet, all things *sentimental*, Amber loved Christmas. She loved everything about it. The food, the decorations, the music, and the time spent with those she loved. With three older brothers, she'd been spoiled rotten at any gift-giving holiday, be it Christmas or her birthday. Even Easter saw her raking it in on the present front from every branch of the family tree. Being the only girl in the entire Roth clan for several years (until her niece Harlow was born five years ago), with nephews and boy cousins as far back as anyone cared to count, she was treated like the gem of the family, rare and delicate and prized.

When Daisy, a friend from spin-class, offered her a chance to come and spend the holidays in the mountains, surrounded by snow, friends, and holiday whimsy, Amber leaped at the chance. Her parents were across the country in Florida, visiting her aunt for the holiday, and all of her brothers were either in Hawaii, California or down in Arizona with their wives and kids. Not one of them would be experiencing a white Christmas. So, with a twinkle in her hazel eyes and holiday spirit in her heart, she packed her bags—even throwing in her one and only dress, a bright red lacy number that always dropped a few jaws—and headed for the mountains.

She made her way toward the door of the coffee shop but turned back to wave to Tim before she pulled the heavy oak door. She ducked inside, fumbling furiously with all her sacks and luggage, her hair flying around her as she battled the wind and hinges. When she finally popped her head up, the most gorgeous brown eyes were staring back at her from across the room.

Rowan

Rowan Briggs turned off the ignition of his Chevy pickup and reached for his phone, confirming the address. Yep, this was the right spot. Seemed like an unusual place to grab a shuttle, but then Riley had married an odd woman. Daisy was nice, sweet as pie and well-intentioned, but the woman was a tad eccentric. I guess that's what you get when you marry a Canadian.

Rowan chuckled to himself.

Crazy Canadians and their "eh, this," and "eh, that."

He'd only been over the border a few times in his life, despite the fact that he lived only fifty miles from it, and each and every time had been a blast—skiing at Whistler, a houseboat on the Shushwap. But by and large, Rowan found Canadians to be a bit odd. Overly friendly, overly happy, and what the hell was it with all the apologizing?

Reaching into the back seat, he grabbed his bags and jacket and double-checked that he had his knife case and spice set before he opened the door and headed toward the coffee shop.

When Daisy had sent her email a few weeks ago, Rowan had literally scoffed and shaken his head at the harebrained idea his old summer camp buddy's new bride had concocted. He had no time for such a holiday. He had no time, period. The man worked seven days a week, twelve hours a day as a sous-chef at the Rouge Oak Room in Olympia, and when he wasn't working, he was in the kitchen at home, coming up with new and creative dishes. Only those dishes never made it past his front door. His younger sister raved about them when she was over for dinner, telling him he should quit the Rouge Oak and open his own restaurant, but what Annie didn't understand was that to do that, you needed capital. And Rowan had none.

But now here he was, heading inside the coffee shop to meet up with whatever other suckers had RSVP'd "yes" to Daisy's invitation. Because as of three days ago, Rowan was officially unemployed.

Overlooked, yet again, for the executive chef position by the owner, Silvio, who decided that twenty-two-year-old Cindi, the little line cook who'd been dropping to her knees in Silvio's office for the past three months, was far more *skilled* and qualified for the job than Rowan, who had nearly twenty years in the restaurant industry. Who had a Red Seal, had attended Le Cordon Bleu, had worked in France under none other than the infamous Chef Lucien Lacroix, the temperamental but genius culinary mastermind who everyone and their dog ached to apprentice with.

When Silvio broke the news, Rowan had quit right then and there. He took off his apron, rolled up his knives, grabbed his recipe book and spice set, and walked out mid-shift. It didn't matter that he liked everyone he worked with and was sick to his stomach that he was leaving them in the lurch during the holiday season; it was a matter of principle. He'd earned that executive chef position, and he was done being overlooked and underappreciated. He was done not having his ideas and recipes considered. They were good, damn good, and he knew it. But Silvio wouldn't even taste Rowan's creations, claiming he possessed a "traditional palate" and Rowan's ideas were too "out there" for the Rouge Oak.

So, in a blind fit of rage as he stalked out to his truck, having flipped both Cindi and Silvio two giant birds, he pulled out his phone and punched in a big "YES" to Daisy's email. He didn't realize until he was home and the steam from his ears evaporated what he'd actually gone and agreed to.

He opened the heavy wooden door of the café and stepped inside, instantly greeted with the smells and sounds that comforted him the most. The clatter of utensils on plates, the sizzle of a grill, and the smell of bacon and . . . was that a Tuscan chicken panini on the press he detected? He took a second whiff. *Shit*, it was about to be overcooked. Standing there taking it all in, he knew what he wanted more than anything, and that was to one day run his own restaurant, with the freedom to cook what he wanted, when he wanted, with no limitations. He was about to ask the waitress if any other shuttle passengers were in the shop when he was slammed in the back and nearly knocked off his feet.

Juniper

JUNIPER DAVIS, OR "JUNEY" to her friends, glanced at the clock on the dash of her Lexus. She was late. Juney was never late. She left her house at four in the morning in order to get to the border crossing ahead of the holiday rush. But apparently, every other Canadian heading south for the holidays had the same idea, and she was stuck sitting in line for hours. But thankfully, that was where Juney did some of her best writing. In her car, driving, with her digital recorder. In those three hours, she dictated nearly four chapters of her latest fantasy novel, and in the process, created at least three new characters to whom she wanted to give spin-off series.

But, productivity aside, Juney hated being late, especially when meeting people for the first time. First impressions were everything. She hoped to God that she wasn't the last one to arrive, causing whoever else was heading up on the shuttle to wait for her. She would have to apologize.

It'd been an easy decision when Daisy, a childhood friend, sent her the email invitation. With both her parents on a Mediterranean cruise for the holiday, and her sisters off with their husbands' families, Juney was left all on her own. Which, in a lot of ways, was how she preferred it, at least for now.

And although there were always things to do around the family vineyard that she ran, or a new manuscript to write, or a completed one to edit, paperbacks to sign or fan letters to respond to, she hadn't seen Daisy in almost a year, and it was high time Juney did something for herself. She'd spent the last month interviewing chefs for the new tasting room and restaurant she was opening in the winery. A picture-perfect dining spot right on Okanagan Lake. But so far, she hadn't been wowed by a single person, and the countdown was on to their soft opening. She needed a chef—yesterday! So, instead of dwelling on her problems, she put them aside until the new year, packed up her laptop, her skis and a case of her family's finest, and hit the road. Ready to ski all day and roast chestnuts and drink wine all night.

She spotted the sign for the coffee shop on the right and turned into the parking lot. She didn't see anyone looming outside, appearing as though they were waiting for a shuttle. In fact, she didn't *see* a shuttle bus, either.

Crap!

Had she missed it?

Had it left without her?

She threw the car into park and leaped out. She almost forgot her digital recorder, but at the last minute, bonking her head in the process, she swung back into the front seat and grabbed it. Juggling her bags, she hustled inside, not bothering to look where she was going or what she was doing. She rammed face-first into a hard, warm, muscular back that smelled faintly of . . . was that oregano?

"Oh my God, I'm so sorry."

Austin

Austin Masters ran his hand down his face in exhaustion, his three-day-old ruddy stubble rough beneath his callused fingers.

He'd forgotten to shave.

He was forgetting a lot of things these days.

Had he remembered to brush his teeth this morning? Having been up until nearly 3 a.m. working, then awake at seven and out the door by eight, Austin was exhausted. Oh well, he was heading up into the woods, and this was how woodsmen wore their beards, right? He took a right into the coffee shop parking lot, then tossed his big red Dodge into park. His phone had been beeping incessantly at him since he'd hit the road, but he refused to answer it. Always another crisis. But he was on vacation, and the crisis could wait until the new year. Even Reggie had told him to go and relax, and that was a lot coming from a fellow workaholic.

Muttering several fucks under his breath, he ignored his earlier claim and grabbed his phone anyway, scanning the emails and then finally accessing his voicemail.

Shit, six missed messages.

"Dr. Masters, it's Fiona Allenby again. I'm sorry to bother you when you're away on vacation, but Mr. Smythe would *really* like those new modification plans on the zero-emission luxury car *now* rather than later. He's worried about our competitors beating us to the punch. So, please call us back as soon as you can."

Austin let out a weighty sigh. Their "competitors" would never be able to come up with the kind of innovations that Austin and Reggie were developing, and certainly not in the next five days.

He had time.

Besides, he hadn't quite worked out *all* the kinks yet, and he wasn't about to send Mr. Smythe the modifications until he knew they were foolproof. One more message, that was it, then he was going to switch his phone off.

"Sheldon!" It was Reggie. The eccentric Brit always called him Sheldon after the dorky, socially inept main character on *The Big Bang Theory*. The funny thing was, Reggie wasn't the only one. The moment the show aired, people started calling Austin "Sheldon," even though he looked nothing like the actor. Apparently, he had the awkwardness down pat.

"Sheldon! I'm assuming you got the message from Fiona Appleby or Allenby or whatever her name is? Look, we're fine. Smythe is fine. Go have some fun. Fuck knows you need some joy and excitement in your life. The project will be here when you get back. Anyway, don't stress about Smythe, it'll only piss off your ulcer. The project is coming along nicely, and we'll finish it up when you get back. Happy Christmas, mah boy."

Austin shook his head with a smile. He really liked his boss, the millionaire environmental genius with a well-known temper. Reggie had always been kind to Austin, despite the rumors that circulated about him being difficult to work with and prone to flying off the handle and walking out mid-meeting. Reggie had taken Austin under his wing, treating him more like a son than an employee or protégé.

And Reggie was right.

Austin needed some down time, so instead of calling back Fiona Allenby, he turned off his phone and closed his eyes. If the company at the cabin turned out to be subpar, he would sleep the week away, only coming out of his room to eat. He was exhausted.

A prodigy since he could walk, Austin had finished high school at thirteen, graduated college at seventeen, and been offered graduate student positions at both MIT and CalTech. He went with MIT, deciding that a change of scenery for a few years might do him some good. He loved the West Coast, but he wanted to see what the East Coast had to offer.

Which was not much, in the end. Well, besides snooty rich kids, Red Sox fans, frigid winters, hurricanes and cheap lobster (that was the only plus). So after finishing his master's in record time, he hightailed it back to the Pacific Northwest. He moved down to Pasadena to get his Ph.D. at Caltech, only to be recruited right back up to Washington state, before the ink on his diploma was even dry, by the oddball Reginald Caruthers.

But Austin couldn't remember the last time he'd done anything fun, done anything for himself. He'd been working so hard for so long; it'd become the norm. First school, then more school, then even more school. He was a grad student before he could even step inside a bar. And now, working on the new zero-emissions car with Reggie was just another job—a fun job, and one he enjoyed, but it was work all the same. His doctor had even warned him he was working too hard when he'd gone in complaining of stomach pain. Turns out he had the beginnings of an ulcer. His doctor had advised him to ease up, told him he would have a heart attack at the tender age of twenty-seven unless he slowed down and got a life.

So, when his childhood friend's new wife's email sprung into his inbox a few days before Christmas, he'd leaped at the opportunity to get away from the real world for a week and hang out with people who wanted to talk about more than just biofuels, solar panels and the world's depleting helium stores. Raised by atheist parents, Austin didn't celebrate Christmas; instead his family observed the winter solstice. But that didn't mean he didn't delight in the joy and whimsy of the holiday season, and he'd been known to treat himself to an eggnog latte and gingerbread cookie at Starbucks from time to time. He double-checked his truck was locked, grabbed his bags, then headed for the door, only to see a sexy-as-hell white Audi A3 pull into the parking lot, blonde hair and a black toque behind the wheel. The faintest sound of the Arkells' *Leather Jacket* drifted into his ears before the engine was killed. He loved the Arkells.

Hunter

HUNTER KINGSLEY TAPPED her fingers on the leather steering wheel of her Audi A3, her head bopping lightly to the Arkells on the radio. This was good, this was really good. Hunter needed to get away. She needed to regroup and take some time to think. She switched lanes, then stopped at the red light. The sign for the coffee shop was up on the right, just past the gas station. Daisy would know what to do. Daisy was like a big sister to Hunter. Having met on the beach one summer when Hunter was seventeen and Daisy twenty-two, Hunter, a lost and lonely soul, selling her clothes and Daisy peddling ice cream as a summer job, the two had hit it off and been like sisters ever since. Daisy was the one to encourage Hunter to go sell her clothes at music festivals and art fairs. Yes, she would definitely help Hunter figure out where her future lay, what was next in store. Because right now, Hunter was, once again, feeling lost.

Having bounced around the system as a foster kid, Hunter hadn't had the best life. With an absent dad and a teenage mom, she wound up a part of the system before her third birthday. But somehow, despite having dropped out of high school at fifteen, then backpacking across the U.S. with a girlfriend for two years, working odd jobs and living in hostels, she'd managed to pull up her bootstraps and start a business.

Small at first, stalls at local craft fairs and bazaars, cajoling the odd store to sell her stuff, she'd set up her old VW hippie van on the side of the road down by the beach in the summertime and sold the odd piece. Then there was Etsy and other online stores, which did all right. But it was at the Sasquatch music festival where her bamboo, hemp and organic cotton clothing really took off. She sold out the first day and had orders coming in nonstop for over a month afterward. She had to rent a bigger apartment to accommodate all her supplies and eventually hire an assistant to help her with production. And from there, Breathe, Babe, Breathe clothing line was born.

Now, after nearly six years in business, she had five stores in Washington state, three in Oregon and two in California. And there was talk of another two going in L.A. and San Francisco in the new year sometime, as well as one in Vancouver, Canada. Yes, she was living the life. The little foster kid who hadn't finished high school was now a successful businesswoman and had recently been named one of *Forbes's* thirty under thirty.

But now what? She'd done it. She'd reached the pinnacle of success. Where to now? Get her GED? Nope, she did that two years ago. Start another business? Nope, that was last year. Curiously Kinky at-home romance parties were growing like wildfire in a windstorm. She had more employees than she could shake a stick at, more people signing up to be representatives and consultants than she could keep track of and people booking parties left, right and center. So much so that there was now a wait list for the coming year until September (wedding season was HUGE). And they'd just recently expanded to virtual parties, where you could log on and do a Skype or Facetime party with your representative, then place your order online.

So, where to now?

Could she go any higher before she touched the sun and got burned?

Turning into the coffee shop parking lot and putting the car in park, she quickly slathered on some lip gloss, adjusted her toque and turned off her phone. She was powering down this week. She needed to. It was as if she had been wandering around in a fog for the past six months. A creative block of sorts. No new designs or business ideas had come to her in ages, and that alone was alarming. She was never without her sketchbook, never without a new idea rattling around in her brain. And yet, over the last six months, she hadn't sketched more than a pair of shorts or had one new business idea.

Things were getting a little worrisome.

Things were getting stale.

She needed to regroup and talk to Daisy. Daisy would help her figure out the next step, she always did.

After making sure she had her snowboard bag and suitcase, she rolled up to the front door, but not before admiring the sexy red Dodge parked out front. She had a thing for big manly trucks, and as she pulled the door handle, she caught herself wondering if there was a big beefy man inside to go along with the big beefy truck.

THE RIDE UP to the cabin was not nearly as awkward or uncomfortable as Amber had feared. Six strangers headed up into the snowy mountains to spend Christmas together, their only connection being the spritely host who waited at the top for them, hopefully with a tray full of rum and eggnogs, heavy on the rum, light on the nog.

After realizing who was who, mainly through weird wordless conversations with curious eyes and head tilts, they all made their way out the front of the café and met their shuttle. They did the quick, get-to-know-ya questions as they traversed up the highway, the twenty-one miles to the summit.

"Do you need a hand with your bag?" Will asked Amber

once they were at the cabin and unloading the van in the driveway. She struggled to toss her ski bag over her shoulder while not letting go of her other luggage.

She narrowed her eyes to a glare. "I think I've got it, thanks." Her eyes fell to his enormous hands and how dark they were. The skin beneath his nails was a soft pink, and his nails were perfectly trimmed. She was used to looking at gnarled and filthy hands, hands with cuts and scratches, calluses and bruises.

She liked his softer hands.

She liked them a lot.

Having those hands on her body, in her hair . . . inside her . . . the thought made the blood pumping swiftly through her veins begin to sizzle.

He shrugged, not seeming to care one way or another. "Okay." And with the kind of graceful ease that made Amber seethe inside, he swung his own bag over his big muscular shoulder, flurries landing in his black, close-cut hair as he sauntered up the freshly shoveled path of the driveway.

"Has anyone been here before?" Juney asked, her cerulean eyes taking in the impressive entirety of the log cabin, mimicking Amber's feelings about the gorgeous home away from home.

Amber shook her head. "It looks more like a log *mansion* than a cabin."

Hunter hummed quietly. "Even though Riley and Daisy have made their own fortune, Daisy's parents are *loaded*. Her dad invested in Microsoft at the right time. I think he went to school with Bill Gates or something. Had the inside scoop." She flipped her flaxen hair over her shoulder before rubbing her hands together from the cold.

"This your bag?" Austin asked her, eyeing the unusual fabric.

Hunter nodded. "Yep."

Austin handed it to her out of the back of the shuttle bus. "What's it made out of? It's really soft."

Amber leaned in to feel the fabric for herself as Hunter went on to explain. "Bamboo. Same with my board bag. I actually made them myself. Bamboo breathes and dries really quickly. The faster things dry, the less likely they'll start to stink. And that musty smell that fabrics get when they haven't dried properly is actually mildew and can be harmful."

Amber frowned as she let go of the silky fabric. It was nice but seemed like it would tear easily.

Austin simply nodded. The guy looked stupefied as he stood there staring at the blonde. "Oh, really?" he went on.

Amber shook her head and made a rude noise in her throat.

But Hunter seemed to be into him and nodded with a genuine smile, following Amber and Austin and the rest of the crew up the path and the big cedar staircase to the front door. "Yeah. We also toyed with the idea of weaving silver into our fabrics as well, as silver has antimicrobial properties, but after reading some studies about how the silver content depletes over time after washing and ends up in our water systems, we decided to nix the idea."

"Daisy! Riley!" Will shouted, his big, dark hands pounding on the door. They were met with silence.

"Is there a doorbell?" Rowan asked.

Amber looked around. She spotted one under a bough of cedar tied festively with a big red velvet bow and pressed it several times. It chimed sweetly in the cabin. Nothing. Not a peep from inside the house.

Will's lips curled up into a wily grin. "They're probably in bed. I think Daisy mentioned they were on the baby train express."

Snickers and half-hearted chuckles drifted around the other five.

"Maybe we should try the door?" Amber suggested, elbowing her way forward and trying the knob. It swung forward, and the smell of cloves, oranges, pine tree and cinnamon hit her in the face like a roundhouse kick. She took a quick inhale and smiled.

It was the smell of Christmas.

"Do we go in?" Austin asked behind her. Hesitation colored his tone.

Amber shifted foot to foot, that sudden feeling of being a part of some horrible prank or a Christmas horror film creeping its way up her spine. Was a psychopathic man in a cheap velour jumpsuit and scraggly Santa beard going to come murder them all in their sleep with an ax? Chanting "HO, HO, HO!" as he hacked off their limbs?

Will moved forward into the house, his big frame taking up the entire doorway. "May as well. Maybe they ran back into town for supplies. Or they're out skiing. Let's check for a note or something."

Everyone nodded, a series of murmurs both for and against the idea of wandering into the empty house filling the air, along with the shuffle and stomp of heavy boots and bags being brought across the threshold.

"Here's a note!" Amber announced.

"What's it say?" Juney asked.

"It says, 'Hit Play.' What the hell? Hit play where?"

"Here," Will said, holding up the remote for the big-screen television mounted above the beautiful fireplace.

"So, hit play, then," Rowan said, letting his bags clunk to the ground and wandering over to stand behind the couch, his trusty knife kit tucked under his arm as if it might suddenly jump up and run away. Everyone spread themselves out around the room, some sitting, some standing.

It was an enormous space, with plush dark brown leather furniture, cream shaggy rugs, green-and brick-colored tapestries and dark stained logs. But despite all the darkness, the big picture window next to the ten-foot-tall tree decorated in red, white and gold let in so much light, the place seemed massive and bright.

Will pointed the remote, and the television flashed to life.

"Hi, guys!" It was Daisy. "You're probably wondering what the hell is going on. Well . . . I have a little confession to make: Riley and I won't be joining you this week. Sorry."

"What the fuck?" Rowan blurted.

"See . . . I'm a matchmaker. Like literally. I do it for a living, you all know that. *Daisy's Chain Attraction Match-Making Service* is how Riley and I are able to afford the four-week Caribbean catamaran cruise we're on right now. But in the spirit of the season, I decided to play matchmaker for free for some of our nearest and dearest friends. You're all single, you're all lonely, and you all are incredible people. I wouldn't have invited you up if you were subpar. No, Daisy's Chain Attraction only matches the best with the best."

Rowan snorted.

Austin gulped.

Will made a manly noise in his throat that Amber couldn't quite put her finger on.

"You've all been carefully selected, put through my computer, and your perfect match is here." Wary and intrigued gazes drifted around the room, sizing one another up. Wondering, hoping, *fantasizing*. "But . . . " Daisy raised one crimson painted nail in the air. "I'm not going to tell you *who* you've been matched with. That's up to you to figure out."

"You can't be serious?" Amber muttered under her breath.

"Amber, you're probably rolling your eyes right now. You're probably getting ready to leave. Well, why do you think I had you take a shuttle? Give it a week. Enjoy the cabin, go skiing, snowboarding, snowshoeing. Just get to know one another. The fridge is stocked, there's lots to drink, and you even have a doctor on site in case one of you sprains an ankle. Right, Will?"

They all turned to look at the big doctor with the bright white smile, but he wasn't in his spot. The sound of ice being cracked free of the tray drew everyone's eyes. Will started pouring scotch into six glasses.

"If you don't find love," Daisy went on, "well, so be it. But my algorithm has resulted in over thirty marriages, nineteen babies, and that was only in the first two years."

"She never said how many *failed* matches," Rowan added snidely.

"I have an eighty-seven percent success rate, Rowan, the eternal pessimist."

Rowan spun around. "Fuck, is she here? Does she have hidden cameras somewhere? Are we on a nanny cam?"

"You're not on a nanny cam, don't worry. I just know you all very well and know who's cynical and who's not."

"Well, fuck," Rowan grumbled under his breath.

"Now, have a holly jolly Christmas, enjoy getting to know one another, and . . . here's hoping you get some use out of that mistletoe. Merry Christmas, everyone. The shuttle will be back to pick you up at noon on December 28th."

The screen went black.

The sound of ice rattling around in glasses caused heads to swivel toward the noise. Will wandered back into the living room, his arms bogged down with a tray. "Who wants a drink?"

CHAPTER TWO

AMBER PUT her phone back in her pocket. She'd texted Daisy almost as soon as the screen had gone black. What on earth was her friend thinking? Putting six complete strangers in a cabin on Christmas? That was nuts, and certainly not how Amber wanted to spend her favorite holiday.

But then, where else did she have to go?

Rowan sipped his drink before talking. "Well, I'm not sure about everyone else, but I'm starving." He gauged what was left in the glass, shrugged and then tipped it back up and drained it. "If y'all don't mind, I'm going to head into the kitchen and rustle up some grub. Anyone for grilled cheese?"

Juney smiled at him. "That sounds perfect. Do you need any help?"

He nodded. "If you'd like."

"I'm going to start a fire . . . in the fireplace," Austin said with a boyish grin, as he wandered over to the enormous round stone hearth and opened up the cover.

"So, we all agree then?" Will asked, making his way over to the big bay window that looked down onto a small, snow-covered gully. "We're going to try this harebrained idea of Daisy's and spend Christmas together?"

Amber lifted one shoulder and brushed her red bangs out of her eyes. She needed a haircut. A moment ago she'd been against the idea, spending her favorite holiday with a bunch of people she didn't know. No way! But the longer she looked at the gorgeous tree, took in all the decorations and Mr. Sexy-Doctor-Man and his sexy doctor throat and sexy doctor hands, the more she didn't think Daisy was that off her rocker anymore.

What was the worst that could happen? She'd spend five days and her favorite holiday eating food, drinking booze, snowboarding and hopefully getting ploughed from here to kingdom come by the M.D. over there? Where M.D. stood for Mighty Delicious.

"Why not?" she said, shaking her head and peeling her eyes away from Will's taut derriere. "All expenses paid, essentially. A beautiful place to spend Christmas. Might as well. I know I have nothing better to do. It was either this, or a road trip down to California with my brother's family, and he has three kids under five."

Out of the corner of her eye she could have sworn she saw Will shudder.

Ha!

Her sentiments exactly.

Once the fire was roaring, everyone wandered through the living room into the kitchen, and sidled up to the bar that hung over the island in the rustic-meets-modern kitchen. It was an open concept designed cabin, so even from their perch they could still feel the warmth of the fire and see the snow falling outside. Everyone watched as Juney and Rowan, two people who had never met before that day, worked seamlessly together preparing a late lunch. With dark red brick, dark cherry wood cupboards and copper pots hanging up over the range, the kitchen was definitely cabiny and extremely homey. But then toss in the stainless steel top-of-the-line appliances, and suddenly the rustic wasn't so *rustic* anymore.

"This is some pretty gourmet grilled cheese," Juney joked. "I was thinking cheddar between two slices of whole wheat. But this, wow!"

Rowan's grin was wide and warm. "I like to ramp things up . . . especially food." He handed her one of his knives and a couple of shallots. "Be careful, please, these knives are incredibly sharp."

Her lips curved faintly with the subtle hint of a smile. "Got it!"

"Let's get to know one another." Hunter beamed, pulling a barstool up next to Austin and accepting a drink from Will. "See if we can figure out who Daisy thinks belongs with whom."

"Are you willing to start?" Austin asked, turning to face her.

Hunter swayed where she sat, and Amber chuckled softly to herself. Yeah, the dude was hot. Not as hot as the big black alpha-doctor, but hot. Austin's eyes were the most intense green she'd ever seen. Dark like fern or red cedar bow or something, but with vibrant specks of gold. And that dark red scruff that hugged his chiseled cheeks and jaw made him look roguish and rough.

Pink dashed across Hunter's cheeks. "Sure."

A smirk tugged at the corner of Austin's mouth. "Okay . . . and go."

She rolled her eyes. "All right, well, I'm Hunter. I'm twenty-six and own Breathe, Babe, Breathe clothing line."

"Wait, you *own* it?" Austin asked. "I know this company. I like this company. I'm pretty sure I'm wearing your...I mean *their* underwear right now."

Hunter bit her lips and nodded. "Yeah."

Austin's eyes, along with everyone else's, were growing wider by the second. "As in *all* the stores?" he asked, a slight crack to his voice.

She nodded again with a smile. "Yeah. I started the company. It's my baby. Anyway, I own Breathe, Babe, Breathe and Curiously Kinky at-home romance parties. I enjoy snowboarding, yoga, running, and when I can find the time to actually sit down and pick up a book, reading historical romances, particularly ones about ancient Europe, 1700s era."

Austin's eyebrows nearly shot clean off his head. "Holy crap," he muttered, the pep in his voice suddenly disappearing. "I—I didn't put two and two together when you'd been talking about your snowboard bag. I thought you'd gone and bought some eco-friendly fabric and knew your way around a sewing machine. But *own*." He swallowed and he pulled his elbow away from Hunter's. They'd both been resting their arms on the granite counter, less than an inch between them. Even though he hadn't moved, based on his facial expression alone, it was as if the man had grabbed a big blanket and pulled it over his head.

He was shutting down.

"You said you're twenty-six?" Will asked, his biceps flexing as he crossed his arms in front of his well-defined chest. Dear God, the man wore dominance and sexy like most people wore T-shirts. Amber's nipples tightened against her bra as his strong throat undulated when he swallowed his scotch. What did that throat taste like? Will must have caught her staring, because his gaze roamed to her face, lingered on her lips, which she hadn't realized until that moment she'd been licking, and returned to her eyes. One dark eyebrow slowly, sexily drifted up half an inch on his handsome face. His eyes darkened to the color of warm whiskey. Amber tightened her jaw to keep her mouth from dropping open.

"Yeah." Hunter nodded. Her answer snapped Amber out of her erotic reverie.

"And you started this company all on your own?" Will continued, his gaze flicking back to Hunter and appearing genuinely curious. The blood in Amber's veins suddenly started to run hot.

No. No. No! He can't be interested in the little blonde.

Hunter nodded again, looking down at her knotted fingers.

"What's your name again?" Amber asked, curiosity taking a front seat, despite her building jealousy.

"Hunter Kingsley," she whispered.

"Hold the phone!" Amber raced back over to the living room and sifted through a few random magazines, coming back a second later. "Is this you?" She held up the magazine and Hunter cringed, burying her face in her glass but not actually taking a sip.

It was an image of her standing next to a bunch of bamboo stalks, wearing one of her popular bamboo dresses and holding up a sign that said, "Organic, Fair Trade and Competitively Priced," a subtitle below said, "Hunter Kingsley, turning the clothing industry on its head, one sexy hemp dress at a time."

"Oh God, I hate that picture. I hate that article," she grumbled. "That is *so* not me. I'm not a bragger like that. But it was good for business, and my PR rep set it up before I could say no."

"Holy crap," Austin said again, rubbing his whiskered chin as he stared at her in awe.

Hunter rolled her eyes. "Yeah, anyway, I'm up here because as successful as my businesses are, I'm in a funk. You know how authors get writer's block? Well, I've got designer's block. Or entrepreneur's block, or whatever you want to call it. I usually have a sketchpad full of ideas, but right now it's empty."

Will rested his hand on Hunter's shoulder, humor in his deep brown eyes. "I find drinking helps. Not that I'm creative, but it helps get the ideas flowing, whatever they may be."

Hunter nodded and took a sip of her drink. "Ah, yeah, that helps."

Will grinned at Hunter. "Beautiful, successful and someone who appreciates good scotch. I guess the only question left to ask is . . . Stones or Beatles?"

A wash of invisible flames danced up Amber's neck and cheeks. Was he flirting? Damn it, he was. Will liked Hunter. *Shit!*

Hunter's amber eyes sparkled up at him and she grinned wide. "Stones, of course."

ROWAN DREW out the big knife from his knife set and placed it on the cutting board. He picked up a couple of the bell peppers Juniper had washed and started to slice into them.

"All right, who's next? Juniper?" he asked.

She flipped the grilled cheese in the pan as Rowan opened jars of olives and pickles. "You can call me Juney. Everyone does."

He nodded. "Okay, Juney . . . what's your story?"

Will, who appeared to be on his third or fourth drink, snorted where he sat, a cocky grin on his face. "Yeah, Juney, what's your story?"

Rowan fought the urge not to glare at the man. Whether conscious of it or not, everyone seemed to be deferring to Will. An air of authority percolated the air around him. Maybe it was because he was a doctor, or appeared to be the oldest of the bunch, or that he was the biggest, tallest and most muscular, but either way, when Will spoke, everyone listened. Rowan wasn't particularly bothered by that, either. He was cocky when it came to all things food-and kitchen-related, but as far as bravado went, he left that for the bigger guys. His skills, his expertise, his *bravado* were with a knife and a skillet. He didn't need to seep alpha-juice from his pores to be considered a worthy adversary or person worth getting to know or admiring. No, Will could have the limelight. Rowan would earn their love through his food.

Juney let out a big sigh. "Well . . . I'm Canadian."

Rowan's head snapped up from where he'd been watching his blade slice through the peppers. "Really?"

She chuckled awkwardly. "Yeah, is that going to be a problem?"

He quickly shook his head, admiring her knife skills and the expert way she julienned the carrots. "No, not at all. And now that I think about it, that totally explains your incessant apologizing earlier in the coffee shop. When you ran into my back, you said 'sorry' like eight times."

Juney rolled her eyes, a pretty flush racing up her slender neck and into her cheeks. "I did not. Maybe only five."

Laughter surrounded them.

"Well, you don't seem as weird as some Canadians I've met," Rowan chided. "But the jury's still out."

"Thanks?"

"What do you do?" Hunter asked her, coughing slightly as she took a big sip of her scotch.

"I run my family's vineyard," Juney answered. "Golden Sunrise Vineyard in Mission. We're getting ready to open a restaurant and a new tasting room as well. And I'm a writer."

"Wow!" a few voices murmured. Bellies grumbled at the sight and smell of what was currently sizzling on the grill.

"What do you write?" Rowan asked as he put together a plate of pickles, olives, cocktail onions and raw veggies. "Sappy romances? Women's fiction? Books about finding yourself and being happy with the life you have? I mean, I have no problem with those kinds of books, but they're definitely not my cup of oolong."

Juney's mouth twisted wryly as she sipped of her scotch. "Uh . . . mostly, paranormal and fantasy novels."

"Really?" Rowan finished plating everyone's grilled cheese and began passing them out. "Like what books?" He was a big fantasy nerd. His latest series kept him up until the wee hours of the morning, and he was growing rather impatient for the author to finish the next book. He was dying to know what happened when Turprol the Shefling rogue had gone into The Temple of Forbidden Life. The book ended with him walking in unarmed and alone. Rowan normally hated cliffhangers, but his favorite author knew how to do them just right.

"Have you heard of the Envious Souls Series? Not a lot of people have, so it's okay if you haven't."

Smash!

Rowan dropped the plate he was holding, and his food splattered to the floor. The ceramic shattered into a dozen or more sharp pieces. "Shut the fuck up!"

Everyone stared at him wide-eyed, but he didn't care. He didn't even care that his lunch was currently in a mangled heap on the floor and covered in plate shrapnel. He took off to his room at a dead run and was back less than ten seconds later.

"*You* wrote this?" he asked. Well, more like accused. He held up the latest book in Juney's Envious Souls Series, *Nothing but Ashes*. "*You're* J.J. Davidson?"

Juney knelt down and began to collect Rowan's meal off the floor. Hunter, who'd run and located a broom, stood next to her, waiting to sweep. Everyone else in the room was dead quiet.

"*You're* J.J. Davidson?" Rowan asked again, this time with less accusation and more awe in his tone. Like a child who was finally getting to meet Santa, or their favorite sports hero or something.

Juney stood back up and opened the cupboard beneath the island to toss the sandwich into the trash. "Yes," she said finally, lifting her head and meeting his gaze. "Juniper Jane Davis. But I tweaked my last name because Davidson has a better ring to it."

"And you're a *woman*?"

Will gave Rowan an incredulous look. "What does that have to do with anything?"

Amber glanced up at Will and grinned at him. "Exactly," she said. "What does being a woman have to do with it? Women can do *anything* men can do. In fact, they can do *more*. And often do it *better*."

Rowan shook his head, realizing how he must look and sound. "Sorry. It's just, well, I *love* your books. They're amazing. I have them all in hardcover, and I pre-order everything. I subscribe to your newsletter, follow you on Facebook. I just had no idea you were a woman. The way you're able to write men. Do you have a bunch of brothers or something?" He was blathering like a fool, but he didn't care. Some people want to meet celebrities or great scientists, politicians or religious figures, but Rowan? His list consisted of world-class chefs and J.J. Davidson.

Juney shook her head as she started making him another sandwich with some of the leftover ingredients. "Nope, two older sisters. Rose and Fern."

"Are your parents into botany or something?" Will asked with mirth in his tone.

Juney rolled her eyes and laughed through her nose. "Or something."

"Alliteration too?" Austin asked.

"Yup. Rose Renee and Fern Fiona," Juney said with a snort.

"Well." Rowan coughed, having finally regained some semblance of composure. "You're definitely able to get into the head of men better than a lot of female writers. You're . . . you're one of my favorite authors, and I can't believe I'm meeting you. It's . . . " He looked down at his feet at the sudden realization of how *fanboy* he was behaving. Embarrassment prickled along his skin, and the temperature in his face began to climb. "It's an honor," he said quietly.

Juney's lip twitched. She put the spatula down and held out

her hand, waiting for him to hand over the book. He did so, but with the excitement of a groupie or fan finally meeting their idol and getting their autograph. She reached into her purse and pulled out a fancy pen, flipped the front cover open and scribbled. A few seconds later she closed the book and handed it back to him with a faint smile.

"There you go. Now don't ask me when the next one is coming out, because I haven't even finished it yet. I've been so caught up trying to find a chef for this new restaurant that my manuscript has taken a back seat for the past month." She flipped the sandwich and gave him a shy but genuine wink.

"Hey, has anyone noticed the mistletoe hanging overhead?" Hunter asked, pointing one long slender finger to the copper pots above Juney and Rowan's heads.

Everyone's eyes drifted upward to the small clump of foliage hanging by a red satin ribbon.

Juney's eyes met Rowan's, and she smiled sweetly at him.

Rowan was in love.

WILL SIDLED up next to Amber, the sexy redhead, and took a healthy sip of his drink. God, he loved scotch. Amber had switched to wine at some point and was cradling her glass of red as they all sat around the island in the kitchen and watched Juney and Rowan tidy up.

"Holy Hannah!" Juney announced, her eyes going wide as she stopped wiping up crumbs from the counter and stared out the big picture window next to the tree. "When did that start?"

Everyone turned around to look out the window. The ground was covered; the limbs were covered. There was no denying that it would be a white Christmas for the six strangers, and now, by the way it was coming down in unrelenting buckets, not only would it be a white Christmas, but a snowed-in Christmas as well.

"Snowed in and set up," Amber said with a half-laugh half-snort. "I wonder if Daisy planned the weather as well. That sounds like something she would do. Get a bunch of unsuspecting people in a secluded place, make it dump snow like there's no tomorrow so they're all forced to sit and stare at one another until they either hump like bunnies or throw on snowshoes, brave the blizzard, and hike back down the mountain to freedom."

"Two choices, huh?" Hunter said with a smile, turning to Austin. "What would you choose?"

Austin's throat bobbed as if he'd just swallowed a whole lemon, and his face shone a bright red. But he didn't answer.

Will grinned. The genius had it bad for the little blonde, that was noticeable from space. He turned to face Amber. She'd been ogling him earlier, and he wanted to see if he could fluster her again. Her hazel eyes twinkled, and a sexy flush crept up her chest when she was rattled. "Well, I don't know about you, but I've never been much of a snowshoer myself."

Amber's gaze zipped up to him. He gave her a challenging glance back and lifted one eyebrow.

"Too soon to say," she said blandly, though her eyes held a gleam to them that said "the former sounds much more appealing.". Question was: did she think the former would be more appealing with Will? Was she his match? He certainly found her attractive and a little spitfire, with sass, attitude, and a bit of a chip on her shoulder. But he liked chips. A health nut because he had to be, Will numbered chips among his few vices. He liked salt and vinegar the best but would settle for dill pickle if forced to

"I know what I'd choose," Will replied, flashing her his

biggest smile and giving her a quick lone eyebrow lift for good measure.

Amber rolled her eyes, but the heavy swallow of her throat and slight twist of her lips betrayed the composure she was fighting to keep. "I'll see if I can find some board games or something around here. It's only three o'clock in the afternoon, and we need to pass the time somehow." Her gaze drifted down to her drink. "And it can't just be getting hammered."

She disappeared down the hall, and Will couldn't stop himself from checking out her ass. All firm and tucked tight in those sexy black skinny jeans, while a soft brown checkered flannel shirt covered her petite frame. He took inventory of the other four people as they chatted softly with one another. So figuring he'd found his match, or so he hoped, he wandered off down the hallway. He'd found her sexy from the beginning, but that ass, that ass had sealed the deal. He needed it beneath his palms, between his teeth — and fast.

"Need any help?"

Amber jumped at the sound of Will's voice behind her. She'd been muttering to herself about this and that and the other thing, mainly the other thing, Will's *thing*. He'd heard her. He fought to hide his smile, but knew it was a futile attempt. The woman was feisty. Spunky and cute, all wrapped up in a neat little freckled package.

Amber swallowed hard and licked her lips. "Uh, sure."

Will's eyes fell to her mouth. She slowly slid her tongue across the plumpness before sucking that fully cushioned lip between her teeth. He wanted those lips. He wanted those lips against his. He wanted those lips wrapped around his shaft as he buried his hands in her dark red hair and pulled, bucking fiercely into her face as she hummed and rammed him to the back of her throat.

Amber peeled herself away from his gaze and started opening cupboards.

She was flustered.

Good.

"Linen, linen, linen, towels, cleaning supplies. There has to be a games cupboard around here somewhere," she murmured, continuing to make her way down the hallway.

Will stalked after her.

"Ah-ha!" she announced after about the hundredth or so door. She flung it open to reveal a treasure trove of games: floor-to-ceiling shelves stocked with nothing but board games, chess sets, tins of dominoes, et cetera. "All right, *doctor*, come pick your poison. Which game would be less brutal on your ego losing to me? *Operation*, perhaps?"

He growled low and stepped up behind her. They were less than twelve inches apart now.

"Wh-what are you doing?"

"Do you think we were matched?" he asked softly. Desire heated the air, and hunger glowed bright in her amazing hazel eyes. He let his free hand come up and run down the length of her soft plaid shirt. The top few buttons were left undone, and he could see a white tank top peeking out, along with the fully rounded mounds of her creamy breasts. His cock twitched in his pants, and his pulse thundered through his veins.

Eyeing him with intrigue, she lifted one shoulder cavalierly and boldly reached out and grabbed his glass, tipping it up and draining it before wiping the back of her wrist across her mouth. "*Ah*."

His eyebrows rose half an inch. She was ballsy. He liked that —a lot!

"Do you think we're matched, *Little Red?*" He took a half-step forward until there was scarcely enough room for air between them, and Amber was forced to crane her neck to look up at him. He liked the way her eyes went wide as they slowly climbed the length of his body, only to finally stare at him, her face flushed and her mouth in a sexy little O.

"Fuck, you're tall," she muttered.

He chuckled. "You're short. How tall *are* you?" Was she over five feet? He was going to guess no. Or just barely. Will was six-three, and at the moment Amber was eye-level with his chest.

Swallowing, she puffed out her sexy chest, and if he wasn't mistaken, rose an inch or so. Was she on her tiptoes? "I'm four-eleven."

He fought the urge to smile.

"And a half."

He lost the battle, and his mouth split into a giant grin. Damn, she was something. "Do you think we're a match?" he asked again, wanting to get back to the topic at hand. If Amber wasn't interested, he needed to know now. Needed to either make the switch to Hunter or Juney, or make arrangements with his hand for the rest of the week.

She was nervous. But then some kind of resolute sureness washed over her. He watched it happen. Her back straightened, and her chin lifted so she was looking him square in the eye, nerves gone, replaced by nothing but pure and sultry confidence.

"Maybe. Would you like that?" Her fingers were right in front of his belt, and all he wanted was for her to reach out and unbuckle it, pull it through the loops on his jeans, then hand it to him and ask him to spank her.

His hand came up next to her ear. He let one finger graze her cheek. "I'd like a lot of things." Slowly, he wedged his knee between her legs, and he dipped his head. "For starters . . ." His mouth was inches from hers when they were suddenly thrown out of the moment by heavy stomping and a booming voice.

"You guys find a game yet?" Austin asked, his greenish-gold

genius eyes taking in the moment. A big stupid grin took over his face. "Or are you playing your *own* game?"

Will shot him an irritated scowl. "We'll be there in a second. Go stoke the fire, you little puppy." He flicked his head as if to say, "Now git!"

Austin spun on his heels and loped back down the hall to join the others in the kitchen.

Amber chuckled low in her throat, wrapped her arms around his waist and pulled him against her. "For starters?" she prodded

Something overhead caught Will's eye. They both looked up.

"Where the hell is all the mistletoe coming from?" he asked.

Amber lifted one shoulder. "Elves?"

He hummed and turned back to face her. "Hmmm. For starters, right." He tilted his head to the side and captured her mouth with his. Her lips were soft and warm, and the way they drifted across his sent red-hot shards of longing coursing through his body. His tongue darted out, coaxing her to part her lips and grant him access. She did so willingly, allowing him to wedge his way inside, teasing her, toying with her in long, lascivious licks until he could feel her body relax beneath his touch, smell her reaction. It was visceral, primal. He wanted to dip his hand beneath her waistband and check to see if she was wet, too. What did she taste like? His cock had ached inside his jeans as he watched that delicious ass of hers swish back and forth earlier. He'd been a fucking goner the moment she turned her back on him. And now, tasting her, feeling her, he knew if he didn't stop soon he would punch a hole right through his pants.

Eventually, he pulled away. She whimpered in refusal, her hands tightening around his back. Her tight little fists gripped his shirt. Amusement flowed through him, and he laughed low and deep in his chest as he pulled her bottom lip between his teeth. She whimpered again, this time pressing her hips against him for a half a second.

Oh, fucking Christ, the woman is going to kill me.

Will swallowed, then looked down at her. "Even if Daisy didn't match us . . . for the next five days, you're mine, Little Red. Got it?" Then, leaning forward and deliberately brushing his bicep across her breast, he grabbed *Operation, Risk,* and *Scrabble* before heading back to the living room.

CHAPTER THREE

Amber let out a loud and long exhale as she rejoined the group sitting on the floor next to the fire. She'd broken the seal and found herself having to get up nearly every thirty minutes to use the washroom. Curse that Juney and her family's to-die-for cabernet sauvignon.

They'd been playing games and drinking for hours, only stopping to eat again after Rowan and Juney, who had ducked back into the kitchen while the others continued to play games, re-emerged a short while later with tapas galore. They'd all gorged themselves, washing it down with good wine and good scotch.

"Dr. Will," Amber said with a slight slur, propping up a pillow behind her and leaning back against the hearth.

Will's head slowly lifted from where he was busy putting away all the Scrabble tiles, having been narrowly beaten by just ten points by the wordy vixen Juney. The firelight danced across the handsome planes of his face, creating sharp angles and bold edges. "Yes, Little Red?" His voice was dark like the purr of a lithe jungle cat.

Amber's whole face ignited. "Uh . . . " She took a sip of her wine. Allowing the dark taste to warm her belly. The looks Will had been giving her all night set her body to scorching hot and made her brain forget words. Those eyes, dark brown and full of passion had stripped her to down nothing and were ravishing her six ways from Sunday.

Hunter eyed Amber and offered her a knowing grin before turning back to Will. "What's your story, dude?"

Oh thank God for Hunter.

Will's face flashed reluctance, as though he was looking for a way to divert the attention from himself or change the subject. But instead he shrugged, tipped back his drink and let his shoulders sag an inch or two. "Well, I'm a doctor. I'm thirty-seven, divorced, and . . . that pretty much sums me up."

Amber fought the urge to snort. She highly doubted that *summed* him up.

"What kind of a doctor are you?" Hunter asked, grabbing the deck of cards from the coffee table and opening it up. She began to mindlessly shuffle them. Meanwhile everyone else's eyes flew to her fingers as she spun and flipped the cards around in her hands like some Vegas dealer or street performer.

"Emergency, mostly," he said.

"Any kids?" Hunter asked. Clearly, she had no problem asking all the questions Amber wanted to ask but was either too drunk or too timid to bring herself to say out loud. Here she was interested in the guy, he'd already kissed her and laid claim, and yet she was too shy to ask him anything. She'd hardly even made eye contact with him since that kiss. What the hell was her problem? Probably the fact that Will hadn't been able to *stop* looking at her all night and that rattled her something fierce.

Will scoffed. "Uh, no."

Hunter made a slightly indignant face as she wrestled her long blonde locks up into her fist and drew a hair tie from her wrist up and over, fixing her thick waves into a ponytail. "What does that mean?"

"It means I have no kids. And I will never have kids. I don't want them."

"You don't want them?" Juney asked, looking at him as though he'd just sprouted another head, and this time it was far less attractive than the one he currently had. "Why?"

Will's jaw clenched and a muscle ticked in the corner. He lifted one shoulder. "I just don't. I don't think my job or lifestyle is conducive to having children of my own. My dad was a doctor, and I hardly ever saw him. I don't want to do that. I like kids well enough. I actually did a pediatrics fellowship and really enjoyed it. But I just don't want my own children. It kind of sucks I'm an only child, because I think I'd be a pretty cool uncle."

Amber's jaw dropped at the mention of Will not wanting kids. She didn't want kids either, and she'd been hard-pressed to find very many partners who shared her sentiment.

They had to be paired.

Daisy was no fool. She knew what she was doing. He was her match, he had to be.

Will's eyes flew up to Amber's face. "What?" he asked. "Do you think I'm some monster?"

Amber shook her head, her mouth suddenly very dry. She looked at her wine glass. It was empty. Boldly, she reached out and grabbed Will's stocky tumbler of scotch and took a healthy sip. It burned down her throat, but she refused to make any kind of face of discomfort. "No. Not at all, actually. I—I don't want kids either."

WILL'S JAW DROPPED. He lifted one eyebrow at her. He'd been down this road before. Enough women he'd been with *claimed* they didn't want children, only to jump head-first on the baby train the moment he made any kind of commitment, thinking they could change his mind and sway him toward wanting kids. A couple of serious girlfriends and Janice, his ex-wife, had even gone so far as to drag him along to a few baby showers and thrust a baby into his arms, thinking that the sight of the wrinkly little human would suddenly make him want one of his own. It hadn't worked. Instead, it only prompted him to book an appointment for a vasectomy.

"You just saying that?" Will asked finally.

Amber shook her head, her bright hazel eyes wide with honesty. "Not at all. I've never wanted them. My brothers all have kids, and I'm a great aunt. I take the kids for afternoons when I can, and I spoil them rotten. I've even taken them for entire weekends so my brothers and their wives can go spend the night at some hotel and find their mojo again. But my own? Nope."

"Why?" Juney asked again, looking at Amber with the same open curiosity she'd had for Will.

Amber shrugged. "I like my job. I'm the boss. I'm busy. My life isn't conducive to kids, and call me selfish, but I'm not willing to adjust or make compromises to *make* it conducive. Plus, I'm not overly *maternal*."

Rowan scratched the blond whiskers on his jaw. "Well, you two are *definitely* matched then. Because I want kids. Not sure any woman out there wants to have kids with *me*, 'cause I'm a miserable fucker. But I'd like to be a dad one day if given the chance."

Amber and Will locked eyes and a small, knowing smile passed between them. Oh yeah, they were totally matched.

"I'd like kids, too," Hunter said. "But if you don't want kids, that's cool, too. No sense giving in to the pressures of society only to wind up miserable. There are too many kids out there who were unwanted, me included. Good for you two for being honest with yourselves and us. I certainly don't judge you."

"Me either," Austin added. He'd been rather quiet through all of this, his eyes focusing on the back of Hunter's semi-bare shoulder. Will had noticed the hint of a tattoo peeking out from her white shirt. He was sure he'd see it, eventually. But Austin, the boy's eyes were glued to the back of the poor woman's shoulder as if hypnotized. He had it bad for the little blonde.

"Well, I definitely want kids," Juney said with a sad sigh. "I'm not judging you guys either, but I know I want them. I'm thirty-four, and the clock is ticking. Rather loudly I might add. Right now, it's just me and my books and my wine. And although they are both a *legacy* of sorts, I want more. Neither of those things keep me warm at night, despite the joy they bring me."

"You could pour the wine on the books, then light them on fire," Austin said with a nerdy grin.

Everyone gave him a weird look.

" 'Cause then they'd keep you warm," he added, his face falling when he realized his attempt at a joke had fallen flat. He clammed up. Hunter snorted and gave him a hint of a smile. Will shook his head. Nice enough, but damn the kid was socially awkward. Did Austin ever think before he spoke?

Amber stood up and stretched her arms above her head. Will's eyes followed her lithe body as she bent it back, pushing her breasts toward the sky.

"Well, I think I'm going to head to bed. I'm exhausted." She teetered where she stood and reached out to stabilize herself on the arm of the couch. "And, apparently, a tad drunk as well." She shot Will a look that said a million words, all of them dirty. Then bidding the rest of them a good night, she padded softly down the hallway to her room.

"Yeah, I think I'm going to go to bed, too," Juney said with a yawn and brief glance at her watch. "Holy Hannah, how is it eleven o'clock?"

"Good food, good company, and good booze makes time fly." Hunter chuckled. She tilted her head at Austin, her hands still playing with the card deck. "You want to play cards?"

His eyes flashed up at her. "Totally."

"I'm off to bed, too," Will said, standing up and laughing at Austin's enthusiasm.

Rowan's lip twisted wryly. "Me, too." He stood up and clapped a hand on Austin's shoulder. "Remember to wrap it up you two. No glove, no love." And with an almost sinister snicker, he and Will took off behind the women toward the hallway full of bedrooms.

AUSTIN GROUND HIS MOLARS TOGETHER. Fucking Will, *fucking* Rowan.

"I, uh . . . " He let his gaze slowly drift up to Hunter's sweet round face. "I . . . I'm sorry for him saying that."

Hunter laughed, her amber eyes glittering the color of warm honey. "Isn't that why we're all here? To hook up?"

His eyes went wide. "I thought it was *more* than just that."

"Well, yeah, but ultimately we're all meant to hook up at some point, find a spark, find our match." She adjusted herself in her pile of pillows and blankets on the floor, tucking her long, tanned legs beneath her and pulling the big, brick-red cashmere throw over her knees. Once she appeared more comfortable, she began to deal out the cards. "Do you know any cool games? I figured we'd play Blackjack if nothing else sounded good."

He swallowed. "Blackjack is cool."

She dealt out the cards. Austin's eyes fell to her fingers, his mouth opened slightly in awe as she continued to spin and slide and shuffle the cards like a professional dealer. She had such beautiful hands. Long slender fingers, beautiful narrow nails, trimmed perfectly with a pretty and understated French manicure, and a tiny little thin white gold band around her left pinky finger, just girly enough, but not too girly to scream high-maintenance or pretentiousness.

"W—where'd you learn to shuffle like that?"

Her smile was wide, and it made a dimple wink in her left cheek that he hadn't noticed before. "When I backpacked across the country, I spent some time in Vegas. I wasn't old enough to go into the casinos, but I hung out with some street magicians, and they taught me a few things. It's more of a fidgeting thing, though. Keeps my hands and mind active. Plus, I used to be a nail biter. Cards helped me kick the habit."

Austin knew all about the need to fidget and be constantly moving. He had one of those fidget spinners at work, one in his truck and several scattered around his house. They helped him focus, kept his mind clear and his hands occupied.

"So, tell me about yourself." Her sexy voice startled him. He'd been so busy staring and fantasizing at her hands and the cards, he must have zoned out. His head snapped up to her face. An almost knowing smile passed across her plump lips, but she didn't say anything to call him out. Instead she just continued on with the conversation.

"We know you're this super genius child prodigy who's working with the environmental mastermind Reginald Caruthers. But what else? Besides that giant brain of yours, what else is there about you that's interesting? What do you do for fun?"

"Uh..."

She was incredible. Friendly and easygoing, sweet as could be, and she was giving him the time of day, asking him about himself and his interests, yet he couldn't form a complete sentence in his giant genius brain to answer her.

"Cat got your tongue?" She giggled.

No, more like a gorgeous entrepreneur of the year who owns a sex toy and fetish company has rendered me speechless with how intimidatingly beautiful and so out of my league she is. It hadn't taken long, just the rest of the afternoon and early evening, for Austin to come to the horrible realization that Hunter was beyond his grasp. The woman was virtually untouchable. He'd Googled her when he'd ducked back into his room briefly after lunch and found out she was not only a successful entrepreneur, but a millionaire to boot. Toss in the fact that she was the most beautiful woman he'd ever laid eyes on, owned a sex toy company, and the pictures on her Facebook page and Google images had her linked with some of Seattle's most eligible and handsome bachelors, and he didn't have a snowball's chance in hell. There was no way they were matched. Despite the fact that Will didn't want kids, he would bet dollars to donuts Daisy's algorithm had paired the hot, successful doctor with the hot, successful entrepreneur. Or maybe she was supposed to be with Rowan? They looked the part. Both blond and tanned, fit and happy, as if they'd just come in from catching that perfect wave off the coast of Big Sur. Beautiful people.

She made a noise in her throat, and he snapped back to reality once again.

Shit! What the hell did she ask?

He shook his head. "I uh . . . no . . . I dunno. I don't really *have* any hobbies. I work ALL THE TIME. Seven days a week, twelve hours a day. Sunup to sundown, I'm working."

Hunter nodded, the curled end of her ponytail bouncing and bobbing around her slender shoulder. "I hear ya. I work all the time too. I can't tell you how many times I've wanted to say 'fuck it all' and take off with a backpack to go see the world. I've got all this money now, and I've never even left the continent. I want to travel."

Austin nodded his head fiercely. Well, at least they had one thing in common. "Right? I've never even been out of the country."

"Not even across the border?"

He shook his head.

"Wow! Yeah, you definitely need to travel."

"I have a postcard of Angkor Wat on my fridge," he started. "When Daisy and Riley went a few years ago, they sent me a postcard. I started doing some research on the place and slowly became obsessed. So much history and tragedy. Each site tells its own story. I'd love to go one day."

She stared at him.

He started to feel uneasy, as if he'd said something horribly wrong. A thick coat of sweat slicked his palms, his eyes darted around the room and his heart hammered in his chest.

What did he say?

"Did I say something wrong?" he finally asked, worried he'd somehow stuck his foot in his mouth or blacked out for a moment and said something heinously insensitive or politically incorrect. Given his current exhaustion level, anything was possible these days.

She shook her head with what sounded like an almost nervous chuckle. "No, it's just that, well, I have a postcard from Daisy and Riley on my fridge too. And it's from Angkor Wat."

He let out a relieved sigh. "The one at sunrise?"

She nodded. "I became infatuated with the place. Read up on it, watched documentaries. If I ever get the chance to travel, it's the first place I'm going."

Holy shit!

They had something in common. He worked his jaw back and forth to relieve the tension.

"I'd love to go to Cambodia in general," she went on, obviously feeling the sudden intensity of the moment and needing to make light of it.

He was feeling the same way. Each and every moment he spent with her, Hunter was proving to be equal parts incredible as she was intimidating. Unobtainable, and yet he was drawn to her.

"I mean the culture, the beaches, the history. Beautiful, humbling, and inspiring. At least that's what I've heard."

"Yeah," he whispered, his eyes raking across the planes of her face. "Beautiful."

She licked her lips, her perfect little tongue running along the seam. Austin licked his own lips and swallowed. His Adam's apple wobbled heavy in his throat as he stared at Hunter's lips. Those beautiful, plump lips.

And now they were wet.

Was she trying to kill him?

Silence ticked deafeningly loud around them, and a new tension filtered into the room. There wasn't even the crackle and pop from the fire, as it had burned down to no more than orange glowing coals some time ago. The only real light in the room came from the enormous Christmas tree in front of the big picture window and its reflection.

Hunter cleared her throat. "One day, maybe. One day I'll make it to Cambodia."

Dread, fear, inferiority, incompetence. They all flooded him. He wanted to be matched with Hunter so badly, but the more he found out about her, the more he worried she was untouchable. The more he figured they couldn't possibly be matched. She was so full of life. Had achieved so much, and what was he? A smart nerd with a photographic memory, seven Facebook friends and an ulcer in his stomach because he was under so much stress at work. What did *he* have to offer *her*?

Reluctantly, he let his eyes drift away from her, and he shuffled toward the fire. "I should, uh . . . I should probably put this out so we can go to bed. Wouldn't want to set Daisy's family cabin on fire."

Hunter giggled. "No . . . no, we wouldn't." She went about putting the cards away and cleaning up the boxes of games. She took all the empty glasses to the sink and gave them a quick wash. She was drying her hands when Austin approached her from behind. She spun around full throttle to face him. They stood only a few feet apart. Austin's eyes shifted upward, and Hunter's gaze followed.

More mistletoe!

Where was it all coming from?

A little smile clung to her lips. That Daisy was a crafty one. But her heart was in the right place. Her eyes fell back to Austin, and the look he was giving her mirrored the feelings that stirred deep and warm in her belly.

Please kiss me. I like you.

The light from the tree in the corner glowed in his eyes while the scruff on his chiseled chin and jaw screamed at her to run her tongue, her lips, her thighs over it. It took her breath away how handsome, how drop-dead sexy he was. And yet, he had absolutely no idea.

Hunter couldn't remember the last time she met a man as attractive as Austin who didn't have any clue of his sex appeal. Who walked with slumped shoulders and no swagger to his gait. She'd dated a lot of Type-A alphas lately, and she was over them. Sure, they were commanding in the bedroom, but they were also controlling in the relationship, telling Hunter what to do, ordering her meals for her when they went out. If there was one thing Hunter hated more than anything, it was a control freak. In the bedroom was one thing, but she was her own goddamn boss once the bed was made and her clothes were back on.

But Austin seemed different. She'd never dated a shy guy before. All her previous relationships had been with life-of-the-party show-boaters; a football player for the local team, Wes had been a linebacker and a pushy bugger. Then she briefly dated one of the outfielders for a minor league baseball team down in Oregon. She'd been around the block once or twice. But one thing all the guys so far had in common was they were all in your face, braggarts and party animals. Even the other two guys in the house seemed more "in your face" than Austin. Will, he knew he was good-looking, with his dark hair, dark eyes, dark skin and bright white teeth. The man was sex and confidence with an M.D. You could tell by the way he carried himself, there was a cockiness about Will. He was well aware of his looks and how damn fine they were. And Rowan, he was good-looking too, almost like a pretty boy with his surfer-boy blond hair and deep dimples. But he had a darkness about him that Hunter found slightly off-putting. He'd confided in everyone that he'd recently been slighted and overlooked at work and in a fit of rage quit on the spot. He still carried that anger, and it buzzed and fizzled around him like a red crackling ball of angry energy. The man needed to do some yoga.

But she'd been through her fair share of arrogance and broodiness and was done with it. She wanted a change. She wanted wholesome. She'd never had wholesome growing up, so it had a certain *appeal* to it. Safety and security. And Austin not only screamed wholesome and safe, but the guy could be a model, an underwear or billboard model, wearing a three-piece suit or a flannel shirt and jeans with an ax in his hand or a Stetson on his head.

Oh God, a Stetson!

Austin swallowed again and nodded. "Well, goodnight, then." He thrust his hand forward.

A fucking handshake? Is this a joke?

Hunter's eyes went wide, and tears burned in the corners. He obviously wasn't attracted to her the way she was him. Maybe he wanted to be matched with one of the other women. Juney was beautiful and so smart. Amber was sassy and feisty. An intellectual or a woman with a big family, and she was neither of those. Her heart crumbled.

She stuck her hand out and took his. It was warm and callused, strong. She wanted that hand on more of her. She wanted him to pull her forward into his arms and crash his lips down onto hers. It didn't matter that they'd just met. Attraction could be instant. This entire week had been designed to set them up with someone they were supposed to be compatible with. Daisy had put them all through a program. Her match was here. And she wanted it to be Austin.

But he didn't pull her forward and obliterate her doubt in his attraction. However, he didn't let go of her hand either. Their eyes locked again, and a sizzle of electricity flew through him into her. A spark, almost like getting shocked when you scuff your feet across a carpet and then touch something metal. Heat flared in her abdomen, and a shudder slid down her back. Hunter's chest tightened and suddenly, for no other reason than to relieve the strain, she wanted to take off her bra. She was big-chested, and carrying around Double-D's all day got painful.

The kitchen was dark, the house quiet. The only light came from the beautifully lit tree that stood tall and bedazzled behind them, a constant red, gold and green reminder of the holiday, of why they were all here. It was Christmas, and they were being given a shot at happiness, during a time of the year when miracles happened and love was dense and heady in the air.

But Austin finally pulled his hand away and broke the spell.

"Goodnight, Hunter." He gave her a curt nod, his eyes focused somewhere around her knees, before taking off past her toward the bedrooms, leaving her standing there winded and crestfallen in the dark kitchen.

Several minutes later, after quickly visiting the bathroom to wash away the day, Hunter pulled the duvet up to her chin and rolled over onto her side facing the door. She could have sworn she heard someone outside in the hallway. A creak in the floorboards, followed by a moving shadow beneath the door, but it was probably someone up to get a glass of water. She let out a melancholy sigh and closed her eyes.

Boy, had she been wrong. She couldn't remember a time when she read the signs with a guy so incorrectly. The way he looked at her. The way he'd inched his chair closer to hers. He jumped at the chance to hang out and play cards after everyone else had gone to bed. They were both young and successful, desperate to travel and see the world. Had the entire attraction been all in her head? Was she matched with anyone here? Or was she destined to be alone for Christmas? For the rest of her life? A lone tear trickled out of her eye and onto the pillow as she clutched the covers tight and begged sleep to take her. Wished for the week to be over before it even really began.

"Fucking moron," Austin muttered under his breath as he closed his bedroom door and his back collapsed against it. "Fucking moron." What the fuck had he done? Did she want him to kiss her? She did, didn't she? He wasn't exactly an *expert* in reading the signs when it came to women, but it didn't take a genius to pick up on the vibe he was getting from Hunter.

She wanted him.

Hell, she'd been talking about "hookups" from the get-go. Instead, the night had ended with a handshake.

A fucking handshake.

He could sense her hurt the moment her hand had clasped his. Defeat, nearly as strong as his own, pulsed through her into him. But there wasn't anything he could do. He had nothing to offer her . . . nothing worthy of her, anyway.

Fucking moron.

Pacing the length of his room, he ran his hands across his face and up into his hair, pulling on the ends until his scalp ached, punishing himself for his stupidity. She wanted him, and he blew it.

In a fit of rage at no one but himself, he flung the door open and stalked down the dimly lit hallway toward her room. The light was on, he could tell from the crack beneath the door, and he heard her shuffling around inside. She was probably getting ready for bed. He lifted his fist to knock; he was going to kiss her. She wanted it. Hell, he wanted to kiss her within the first five minutes of meeting her.

He was going to kiss her.

He was going to push her into her room and see where the night went. However far she wanted it to go, he'd go, willingly. Even if in the light of day, she realized he was just this huge, inexperienced disappointment.

But then the light from under the door flicked off, and he heard her bed squeak. His fist fell to his side in defeat, more like surrender, and he gnashed his molars together until his jaw hurt. Letting out a shaky sigh that rattled through his bones and made his stomach churn in adrenaline-fueled fury, he spun on his heel and headed back to his room.

Fucking moron.

CHAPTER FOUR

Rowan paced back and forth in his room, the signed copy of his *Envious Souls* book in his hand. She'd signed it! He'd met J.J. Davidson. Hell, he was staying in a log cabin with her for an entire week. The author Rowan thought was a he, wasn't a he at all. *He* was a SHE! A gorgeous she. A funny she. A *single* she. And she could cook!

Well, Daisy, you weird little Canadian, you may have just found me my dream woman.

"But what now?" he muttered.

Were they matched? They had to be. Will and Amber were two childless peas in a pod. Hunter and Austin . . . fuck, those two better be fucking by now, the way the pheromones were bouncing off the walls between them earlier. They were probably rolling around naked on the rug in front of the fire at this very moment.

So, that leaves me and J.J. I mean me and Juney.

He opened his bedroom door. Luck was on his side. Her room was right next to his. Was she up? Light peeked out from beneath her door, and he heard the random shuffling of papers.

Oh sweet baby Jesus, was she writing?

His fist came up before he could think twice, and he rapped lightly with a knuckle. More papers jostled, and he heard the floor creak. The brushed brass knob jiggled slightly. The door opened, and there she stood, illuminated like a pajama-clad angel from the lamp on her nightstand, wearing a skimpy little white spaghetti-strapped tank top, black shorty-shorts, thick black-framed glasses, and a messy bun. His cock jumped in his flannel pants. Fuck, she was hot in glasses. He spotted a laptop on the bed behind her. She *was* writing.

Rowan swallowed. "Hi."

Juney lifted one eyebrow in interest. "Hi."

"Whatcha doing?"

Nooooo, no more dorky rhetorical questions. That was your last one. Otherwise you are no longer allowed to be around people, especially women. And most definitely not gorgeous women.

She huffed a laugh through her nose. "Writing. I had a sudden surge of inspiration, and when the characters are talking, it's best to let the voices speak than attempt to silence them until morning. I've had many a sleepless night trying to ignore the voices in my head."

"Well, as long as they're not telling you to kill." He chuckled at his own mirth. Juney grinned. "Unless of course they're telling you to kill Lord Dorfell of the Second Command, then by all means, murder, woman, murder, and the more violent the better. I hate him."

A ghost of a smile coasted across her face. "Did you knock on my door for spoilers?" She pushed the door open and invited him inside. He went in without hesitation. The laptop sat on her turned-down bed, while a notebook and a pen perched on the nightstand and a scattering of papers quilted the bedspread. He was witnessing his favorite series in the making.

Rowan shook his head. "No. Well, maybe. I . . . I wanted to

thank you for the autograph and apologize for my dorky hardcore fan behavior. I hope it didn't embarrass you at all. I also wanted to thank you for helping me in the kitchen today. You've got some mad knife skills."

She chuckled. God, how he loved her laugh. Husky and low, a little throaty. Not a high-pitched girly giggle. No, Juney laughed like a woman.

"You're welcome. And no, you didn't embarrass me. It's always nice to meet a fan."

She wandered back around to her side of the wrought-iron framed bed and climbed on, pulling her laptop onto her lap. She nodded at the vacant side of the bed, inviting him to sit down. Rowan licked his lips and swallowed, but he didn't waste any time deliberating on the decision.

"What are you writing?" he asked, nestling in among the cream-colored pillows and trying to read her chicken scratch on the pieces of scattered paper.

"The latest *Endless Souls*."

His jaw dropped. "Really?"

She nodded and nibbled her bottom lip, giving him the side-eye. "You want to read a passage or two? I don't normally let anyone read it before I send it to my two trusty beta-readers and my editor, but . . ."

His eyes went wide. "Will it spoil anything? Wait! What I mean is, fuck yes, but . . . Will it ruin the book for me? I—I love the surprises. The complete one-eighties you throw in, the suspense. I don't want to ruin the experience by reading something that will tell me too much. But yes." He ran his hands through his hair and shook his head, letting out a nervous, breathy laugh. "Oh God, I'm torn."

She chuckled and passed her laptop to him. "It won't ruin anything. In fact, I could use a second opinion on this passage. I'm wondering if it's too passive. Let me know what you think."

Rowan's hands trembled slightly as he took the computer from her and settled it on his lap, the words of his favorite story, raw and fresh from the mind of the creator, laid out before him. Was he betraying himself, sneaking a peek before the masterpiece was finished? But he also couldn't look away. As much as he wanted to, he couldn't. Like a moth to flame, his eyes were drawn. He began to read.

JUNEY STUDIED Rowan as he read her latest work. Would he know that the character she'd created, the personality that had kept her from being able to fall asleep, was based on him? An under-appreciated, talented, slightly ornery half-man half-Shefling who, although his father was the commander-in-chief of the Shefling army, his mother had been a lowly handmaid. And thus, *Rowarn* as she had named him, had been forced to live a life as a cook in the castle kitchens. Even though his dishes were known and praised throughout the kingdom, he was still looked upon as no more than a half-breed and castle staff scum.

Rowan's eyes drifted across the screen. He finished the six paragraphs, scrolled the page up and read it again. He did this twice before handing the laptop back to Juney. Her pulse pumped hot and quick through her veins at the thought of someone reading her unfinished work.

Rowan looked at her, his mouth open in awe. "You . . . you based a character on *me*?"

She pursed her lips for a moment before smiling and glancing down into her lap. "Maybe. Your story earlier about how hard you've worked in the industry, only to be continuously overlooked . . . it spoke to me. I've only eaten two of your meals so far, but you're incredibly talented. Innovative. I like that."

She could tell he was excited. The rapidly throbbing vein in the side of his neck was proof. But he hid it well and simply offered her a raised eyebrow. "*Rowarn?*"

She snorted. "Well, none of my characters' names are conventional. Medila, Yolgo, Starklan, you get the drift. I thought *Rowan* might be a tad *too* obvious and not fit with the fantasy made-up name theme. Are you mad?"

"Mad?" His eyes flew open wide.

Damn, he was handsome, with longish curly blond hair that wrapped around his ears, dark brown eyes and dimples on either side of his face so deep it was as though someone had taken push-pins to his cheeks.

"I'm not *mad* at all. In fact, I'm . . . " He was shaking again. Suddenly, caught up in the excitement of it all, he leaned forward in a flurry of enthusiasm and kissed her.

When Rowan's lips found Juney's, she was surprised. Surprised, but not the least bit upset. She'd invited him in, after all. Invited him to climb onto her bed, read her work. No one read her work.

No one.

Not until she finished her first draft, then she'd give it to her father and her sister, Rose, for beta reading. They were the only two people she could rely on to be the most honest, tell her when something was good or absolute garbage. Only then, after some re-working, would she send it to her editor.

She'd shocked herself when she allowed Rowan to read her work. But she liked Rowan. She liked that he cooked, that he was an artist of sorts, like herself, and that he, too, felt under-appreciated. Because even though Juney was essentially at the top of her game, running a thriving winery and was a *USA Today* and *New York Times* best-selling author, in a lot of ways she was still "Little Juniper Davis," the ugly duckling of the Davis family, with buck teeth, frizzy hair and braces on her legs until she was seven. It wasn't until she was in her early twenties that she had finally "blossomed," as her mother called it. And by that time, she had two novels and six short stories written, along with the outline for the first two books of her *Endless Souls* series.

While her sisters and high school friends were out getting drunk, high and finger-banged on Friday nights, little Juniper Davis was at home wearing her headgear and writing her stories. Needless to say, when it came to men, Juney wasn't exactly beating them off with a stick. She'd had relationships over the years, a boyfriend here and there. She almost got engaged to Marshall Tanner, who'd taken a keen interest in the family vineyard and even made noise of clear-cutting some of his own family's land in Tanner Ridge to build a vineyard of his own. But the long distance had been what killed them. They'd met at a big wine tasting event in Vancouver, hit it off immediately, dated for almost three years. But Juney wasn't willing to move to the tiny town of Tanner Ridge, and Marshall wouldn't leave his family home or property for anything, so they'd ended things.

Marshall had been her last relationship, and that had ended over a year ago. She was ready to date again. Ready to find Mr. Right. Otherwise, she decided, if she didn't find him by the time she turned thirty-five, which was in September of this coming year, she was going to make an appointment with the sperm bank and do it on her own.

Juney wasn't sure what to do. Should she wrap her arms around Rowan's neck and pull him down on top of her? Open her mouth and invite his tongue inside? He hadn't really initiated anything past the hard, fast, and startling peck. She was about to make a move, a move she still wasn't entirely certain about, when Rowan pulled away, his eyes glassy and his cheeks an adorable rosy pink.

"Sorry," he muttered, licking his lips and swallowing.

Damn, he was handsome. Never in her wildest dreams did

Juney ever think a man as good-looking as Rowan would find her attractive.

She shook her head. "Don't be."

His eyes flashed up to hers. They were hooded with arousal, and the pupils had dilated so wide, she was having a hard time seeing any of the beautiful light-brown iris.

"I like you, Juney," he said. "And not only because you're one of the most talented writers ever, or that you can julienne a carrot like Bobby Flay. You're cool, you're beautiful, and you let me read your work. That . . . It's an honor and one I won't take lightly. Thank you."

Juney's lips parted with rapid breaths. Her skin was hot. She liked him too and had all but determined, after their big group discussion earlier, that she and Rowan were matched by Daisy's algorithm. They were so much alike, wanted the same things, shared similar interests. He was her match; she was certain of it.

Then she did another thing that night that shocked the hell out of her. She began tidying up her papers, the papers that held plans and doodles, random thoughts and quotes that she wanted to use. She had everything in a file on her computer, but sometimes she preferred to refer to the hard copy rather than bounce between windows on her laptop.

Rowan quietly watched her, one eyebrow drawn up sexily in mounting confusion. She loved the smirk he sent her as she snagged his gaze out of the corner of her eye. She gave him one right back. Once everything was put away on her nightstand, she grabbed his hand and pulled him on top of her, shivering beneath him, even though her skin felt feverish. But his desire for her soothed her own raging need.

He went willingly but not without a sincere look of surprise on his face. She spread her legs, and he settled between them while he braced himself, his arms on either side of her. He wasn't huge, but he was still bigger than Juney, and the man had muscles. As he held up his weight, she could see his biceps and forearms bulge and strain.

"A—are you sure?" he asked.

She smiled and lunged forward with her mouth, dragging his bottom lip down with her teeth. His excitement and heat pressed eagerly into the apex of her thighs. Only their pajamas got in the way of skin-to-skin. The friction was nice, but she wanted more.

"I'm sure," she whispered. "I like you too, and isn't this what this week is all about?"

Rowan swallowed hard. "I didn't bring a condom." Panic enveloped him. "Fuck, how could I have been so dumb as to leave my room without protection?"

Laughing, she reached over and opened the drawer of her nightstand. "It would appear Daisy thought of everything." She drew out a strip of condoms.

"I've always liked that nutty Canadian," he said with a chuckle, finally finding his confidence and offering her a big, mischievous smile.

Juney liked him. He liked her. There was no need to be nervous anymore. They had this.

Gentler than before, Rowan's lips brushed hers. She opened for him and his tongue pushed inside, sweeping around her mouth as his lips softly sucked on her tongue. She mimicked his movements and kissed him back, swirling her tongue around his and enjoying the taste of him.

She was breathless when he lifted his head, his smile turned wicked, and her heart rate ripped into a gallop. "Now, I'm all for using those condoms, but . . . I've never tasted a *New York Times* best-selling author. In fact, I'm not sure I've ever tasted a *Canadian*. A double treat. Do you taste like maple syrup?"

"Oh, fuck!" Juney laughed, her entire body shaking with laughter at that ridiculous statement. Her belly ached from how hard she was laughing and the weight of Rowan on top of her. A couple of tears trickled down her cheeks.

Was this guy for real?

"Is that your idea of dirty talk?" She couldn't let that line slide. Even if it killed the mood, stopped it in its tracks, she just couldn't let it go.

Rowan blanched slightly and lifted his head to look at her. "Maybe. Not good?"

She was still laughing, her tight and achy nipples pressing against him as her body shook with continued laughter. "Uh, no. Funny . . . but not hot."

His bottom lip jutted out into a fake pout. Damn, he was cute.

Rowan's eyes narrowed, and he cocked his head. He deserved that mockery. There wasn't much blood left in his head to function properly and filter out the nonsense before it spewed from his mouth. He was just glad she was laughing at him but hadn't pushed him off and pointed to the door.

He ground against her, and her breath hitched in her throat.

Oh yeah, he had this.

"Well then, perhaps I shouldn't talk at all." Slowly, he inched his way down her body, planting warm wet kisses on her neck and chest, the swell of each luscious, perky breast. Juney wasn't overly big-chested, but what she did have was perfect. Soft and creamy, with dark ruddy areolas and perfect scarlet nipples barely visible through the white of her ribbed tank top. They were so hard and tight, standing up and pressing against the thin material. He couldn't wait to make them ache from the warmth of his mouth.

He drew her tank top up and swirled his tongue around her navel, watching her with hooded eyes and open fascination. She was beautiful, and when aroused, the woman was fucking stunning. Bright sapphire-blue eyes sizzled, big and so full of life and intelligence, with thick dark lashes that fell against her cheeks like raven feathers when she closed them. Her back arched as she pushed her body into his. He continued on his descent, drawing her shorts and thong down past her thighs, tossing them to the side, leaving her bare and exposed.

He took one final look at the woman before him. Her eyes were closed, and she was biting her lip, waiting for him.

My author. My beauty. My match . . .

He spread her lips with his fingers, flicked his tongue out and grazed her clit. She inhaled sharply, and Rowan grinned.

He dove in.

Up and down through her soft pink folds he swept his tongue, reveling in her little mewls and need-driven moans, in the slight tilt of her pelvis as she shamelessly pushed herself further onto his face, desperate for more pleasure. And he gave it to her. He drew Juney's clit into his mouth and sucked before lashing hard and fierce at it with his tongue, until it swelled and hardened. She was wet, so wet for him. He took the opportunity and pushed two fingers inside her, pumping and scissoring, feeling her rippled walls contract and squeeze him.

He wanted her to come. He wanted her to come hard, to fill his mouth with her sweetness. He needed to taste her, all of her.

"You're close, Juney, I can feel it. Come for me, baby," he said in between lascivious licks, getting a serious high knowing her fingers were bunched in the sheets, her knuckles white as she grappled at the fabric and squirmed beneath him.

Then she let go. He alternated between circles and quick flicks. She seemed to like the quick back-and-forth flicks more, so he stuck with that. She swelled against his tongue as her wetness poured hot and sweet into his mouth.

"Oh . . . God!" she cried, bowing her back and pushing into

his face. He dove in again and went to town on her clit, sucking harder and harder, drawing the nub deeper into his mouth as his fingers continued to pump. Her walls contracted around his fingers, and another warm, silky gush filled his mouth. He lapped up her juices and hummed softly, loving the feminine and delicate way she came.

Once he knew her orgasm was over, he rose up onto his knees, shucked his pajama pants and boxers to the floor and knelt in front of her, waiting for her to open her eyes. She just lay there, her chest heaving and a small, contented smile dancing across her heart-shaped mouth. He leaned forward to kiss her lips, his cock laying thick and heavy between them.

Finally, she fluttered her lashes open and looked at him.

"Hi," she said softly.

His balls tightened, and his chest clenched. This woman would be his undoing, he knew it.

"Hi." He flashed her a big grin.

"Wow."

"Yeah?"

She stretched beneath him, appearing sated and thoroughly devoured. Her nipples, still perky and tight under her white tank top, pushed up toward the ceiling. He wanted to draw one into his mouth and flick it with his tongue until she gasped. Only then would he bite it, not too hard, but hard enough to make her gasp again and moan.

"Mhmm," she hummed, looking up at him all doe-eyed and sleepy.

"You're beautiful, Juney. Gorgeous. Sexy, stunning."

Her eyes opened wide at him, the placid laziness on her face from a moment ago gone.

"I mean you're also smart and funny and creative and stuff. But . . . well, call me a superficial jackass if you must, but, *damn*, woman, you are hot."

. . .

Juney's voice caught in her throat as she gazed up at Rowan. His grin was wide and playful, and at that moment he reminded her of some surfer-dude beach bum. His skin was bronzed and tanned as though he spent countless hours shirtless at the beach, while his hair had that sun-kissed shine and windswept inhibition to it. Never in a million years did seven-year-old Juney, twelve-year-old Juney, hell, twenty-five-year-old Juney think a man that looked like Rowan would ever call *her* hot.

Tears burned the corner of her eyes as she reached for him, a swell of emotion engulfing her. She'd been called smart and funny, creative, and responsible her whole life. But never *hot*.

"Please," she said softly, her hips instinctively lifting up and brushing against him. His quick inhale made her smile. Brazenly, she lunged at his bottom lip with her teeth again, her hands grappling behind him, nails raking his muscular back, eager to feel his weight on top of her again.

He stilled and lifted up, grabbing the strip of condoms off the nightstand. With a Cheshire cat-like grin, he waggled his eyebrows at her. "We both want kids, but not yet, right?" And like a prophylactic savant he tore open the foil and rolled it on. The sight of him touching himself, holding his big, thick length in his hand, stroking the silky flesh as he brought the latex down to the base, left Juney speechless. Not to mention the fact that he'd used not only the *K* word but also the *H* word. He wanted kids. He'd called her hot. There wasn't a doubt left in her mind that they were matched.

Rowan lowered himself back down on top of Juney and smiled, their faces mere inches apart. Her arms floated up to rest on his shoulders. He probed her cleft, and she shimmied her hips on the bed to draw him in, eager to feel him inside her.

Their gazes locked. Desire heated the air in the room, and hunger glowed fierce in his beautiful brown eyes.

"Please," she said again, the polite Canadian in her betraying the animal inside, the feral beast that roared to be let free. With a smile akin to a snarl, he drove home hard and swift, sheathing himself to the hilt in one solid thrust that made her eyes fly open and her whole body ignite. She hadn't been this full, this desired, this content in forever.

Rowan picked up his cadence. In and out he pumped. Her pussy clenched around him, wanting to feel every thick inch of him as he grazed her walls and claimed her. His pelvis battered her clit relentlessly with each thrust. She let her head tilt back, her eyes threatening to roll into the back and never return.

"Open your eyes, Juney," he said, the rough timber of his voice low and commanding. She flashed them wide. He was staring down at her. A cocky grin of triumph floated across his pouty lips. "I want you on top, woman." With that, he snaked one hand beneath her, rocked them side-to-side a couple of times, and suddenly she found herself on top.

He peeled away her tank top, letting her breasts spill free, her nipples diamond-hard and aching for his hot mouth. Sitting up, Rowan propped himself up with a few pillows against the iron-barred headboard before drawing one of her crimson buds into his mouth, sucking hard before nipping the tip with his teeth, sending lightning strikes of longing zinging through her body. All the while, Juney continued to move, riding him, bobbing up and down on his lap, feeling the tip of him hit her deep, deep inside.

"Oh, God," she cried again, another orgasm brewing inside her like a tumultuous winter storm. Her heart thundered against her ribs, and her breath panted out in ragged gasps.

Rowan pulled his lips from her, and she groaned. His hands came up, and he buried them in her hair, pulling until the hair elastic that held up her messy bun snapped and her dark brown tendrils spilled across her bare shoulders.

"I—I'm close," she whispered, her chest heaving and her blood pumping hot. She hoped she could hang on for a few more moments. She wanted them to come together; she wanted to watch him come undone.

"Me too, baby, me too," he breathed. His teeth tugged on the other nipple, and his tongue flicked it until she sucked in a breath from the sudden rush of pain. Feelings raw and real ripped through her. He tugged again and she gasped. Pain, delicious, delicious pain hinting at an edge of pleasure made heat flare in her abdomen and a shudder blitz down her spine.

"Rowan."

He shoved his hands back into her hair and pulled her head forward, hard, demanding, until their lips locked and he drove his tongue forcefully inside her mouth. Plunging rough and quick, twirling around hers in an evocative dance, fucking her as thoroughly as his cock was fucking her pussy. In and out, in and out. She was done for. Her climax was right there. Pounding at the door like a ferocious beast. Demanding to be unleashed.

Rowan grunted against her lips, then stilled. Juney broke with a sharp cry as the climax speared through her like a javelin, impaling both of them at the same time. Bright lights flashed behind her closed lids. The only sound that seemed to fill her ears was the loud thrumming of her own pulse and Rowan's feral growls and moans as he spilled himself inside her. She opened one eye briefly to look at him, but their lips were still locked, and he had a tight grasp on her hair, so she couldn't see much beyond his closed eyes.

He was holding on to her tight, his grip unrelenting, pulling her hair just hard enough it hurt. But it also felt good, really, really good. He was taking what he wanted, and what he wanted was Juney.

Slowly, she opened her eyes. The orgasm had ended, but her body still hummed alive and on fire. Every nerve ending was awake and screaming for more. Pulling his lips from hers, Rowan blinked his eyes open. He grinned as he twitched his cock inside her. She laughed, shaking against him. He laughed with her, and soon there were tears in both their eyes as they sat, still connected, smiling and shaking with clear heads and full hearts.

A few moments later, when she felt like he was going to slip out and reality had settled back upon them, she spoke. "Rowan," she said quietly, loving his name and how much it suited him. His hands were still in her hair and her head on his shoulder. He slowly pulled them free, sweetly tucking a strand behind her ear for good measure.

"Juney . . ."

"Stay the night." It wasn't a question. It was a hope.

He smiled and helped her climb off of him, then she quickly ducked into the en suite bathroom, having been one of the only two people to score a bathroom *in* her room. Amber had the other one.

Juney returned to bed a few moments later, and her heart did a little hippity-hop. Rowan was bundled up under the covers, his arms tucked behind his head and a placid smirk on those talented lips. She didn't bother putting her PJ's back on and simply climbed into bed, turning the light out as she went.

She rolled over to face him. A hand came out, wrapping around her waist. Grinning with glee and complete and utter contentment, she went into his arms willingly, resting her head on his chest, his heart beating solid and true beneath his ear.

"So, can you make *Rowarn* have a girlfriend or something?" he asked into the dark, his voice a deep and masculine rumble in his chest. "Maybe a super-sexy wine or mead merchant's daughter. You could name her . . . *Junella*."

She laughed. "*Junella?*"

He motioned to switch positions, and soon they were spooning, her naked butt pressed tightly into the crook of his body, right against his cock. His hand came up around her chest, and brazen fingers fiddled and tweaked her nipples. They were already comfortable with each other. It all felt so natural, so right. Juney let out a happy sigh and melted into him. Rowan responded in kind and pulled her more firmly against his chest.

"Well, I'm not very creative or good at naming things. *Junica?*" His breath was like a zephyr against her ear. She sighed inwardly from the overwhelming moment of happiness that was forming a mantle around her wildly beating heart.

"I'll think about it," she said, still giggling. "You think he *needs* a girlfriend?"

"I didn't think he did," Rowan said with a yawn, pulling her even more tightly against him. "Mind you, you only just created him. But when I read that passage you wrote about him, he sounded cool. Like a lone wolf. Busy in the castle kitchens. No time to be tied down to a maiden or anything. His days were in the kitchen, but his nights were spent with one of the willing wenches down at Corishwell's Tavern."

She snickered in his arms. His fan-boy was showing again.

He continued to talk. "But now . . . Now *Rowarn* definitely needs a girlfriend. And I think a wine merchant's daughter by the name of *Junica* would be perfect." And with that, he kissed her neck, pinched her nipple and fell asleep.

CHAPTER FIVE

"Shit," Will muttered under his breath as he stalked down the dark hallway toward Amber's door. He hadn't had this much to drink in months. Maybe years. But he also hadn't had this much consecutive time off in years, either. And each scotch had tasted better than the last, until before he knew it, the bottle was empty. It hadn't been all him, though. Little Red finished a glass or two, not to mention the others. Jesus, though, how many had he had? He stumbled half a step but caught himself on the wall, blinking back the spots from his vision, his legs suddenly feeling like lead weights filled with Jell-O.

Get it together, Colson!

His eyes flicked across the hall to his own bedroom door, and he quickly ducked inside to grab a condom. Couldn't be too prepared. And although he couldn't actually *have* children anymore, he didn't know Amber's history, and she didn't know his. If things got serious, they could have the chat later. He was clean, but condoms were just a part of the process.

He ran his hand over his face, took one last look at himself in the mirror. Damn, that forty-eight hour shift he'd finished the night before was hanging on under his eyes in thick bags. They looked more like freaking suitcases. He needed sleep. But Amber was waiting for him. He needed Amber.

Amber first, then sleep.

She was petite and feisty, and he wanted every inch of her beneath his lips before the night was over. He wanted to taste her creamy skin, bite those sweet nipples. He bet they tasted like raspberries. The woman had him by the balls, and she didn't even know it. He vowed to do practically anything he could to get her under him, on top of him, in front of him. Fuck, he would take her any way he could.

Yes. Amber's body beneath his first, then they'd curl up together and sleep.

Yeah, that sounded good.

He closed his bedroom door, took the two and a half strides across the hall, then pushed her door open, not even bothering to knock.

AMBER HADN'T COMPLETELY CLOSED her bedroom door when she heard it squeak open. Big warm hands landed on her biceps from behind. He lifted her up and plunked her feet on the bed, spinning her around in the process, bringing the delicious smell of him, manly cologne and scotch. It circled around her like a twister. She swayed slightly, but he held onto her and kept her in place.

"What took you so long?" She giggled, feeling the effects of the alcohol and enjoying how bold it made her. She wasn't one to shy away from sex or relationships, and in her thirty-two years she'd had the odd one-night stand. But Will flustered the bejesus out of her, so she was happy about the booze in her system. It was calming her nerves.

His smile sent a shiver of longing straight up her back and

back down again, pooling into a warmth between her legs. She bet most women dropped their panties for that smile, and she couldn't blame them one bit.

He didn't say anything, though, but moved his hands up her back. One grabbed the base of her neck hard and rough, while the other slowly drew the sleeve of her flannel shirt off and down her arm. His mouth fell to her bare shoulder. Her skin was searing hot. Was he going to kiss her?

No.

Instead, he dug his teeth into her flesh.

She moaned and arched into him, her own hands beginning to wander. Down his shoulders to his big biceps and forearms, past the muscular span of his chest, down his abs.

Holy mother of God, those abs!

Finally landing on his belt.

"Little Red," Will purred, his mouth moving up her neck. She tilted it to the side to give him better access. He moved along her jaw and down the other side to her collarbone, licking along the ridge. His deft fingers made quick work of the buttons on her shirt.

She pulled his belt free, then started on the zipper and button of his jeans.

Her body was on absolute fire. Scorching hot for this smoking man, and the heat coming off of his rock-hard body didn't help. Peeling the soft fabric of her shirt away, he dropped more sultry kisses down her arms and across her chest. Amber pushed his pants to the ground and heard his cell phone and wallet *thunk* to the wood floor. His shirt was next. She wanted to see, wanted to feel, wanted to lick and taste each one of his abs. Feel the rigid lacing beneath her tongue. She drew the hem of his shirt up his torso, and he pulled away so she could lift it over his head. There he stood, looking like a fucking god in white boxer briefs, with the biggest, most beautiful bulge at the front she'd ever seen.

She licked her lips, unable to move her eyes away. It . . . *he* was mesmerizing.

Will's chuckle was low and wicked in his throat as he reached for her. The joy he got from flustering her was evident in his smile. Her mouth parted just so, and she swallowed. Dear lord, he was beautiful. So dark, and the way his skin practically glowed from the dim lamp on her nightstand, he was polished onyx in the moonlight.

He brought his hand up and slipped the strap of her tank top slowly down her arm. The fire in her belly ignited into burning flames from his touch.

Amber knew she was tipsy from the wine and scotch, but add in the uneven surface of the mattress, and her knees were getting ready to buckle. His lips fell to her collarbone, and her entire core clenched. Her nipples hardened to achy pebbles. Could Will see them? She glanced back at him. His eyes were focused on her chest. Oh, he could see them all right!

"I uh . . . I'll be right back," she blurted out before pulling herself from his grasp as if he'd just shocked her. She moved away from his body, her own body screaming out "why?" so loud she was sure he and everyone else in the cabin could hear it. She stepped down off the bed and ducked into the bathroom, shutting the door behind her maybe a tad too abruptly, cursing under her breath at the loud *slam* it made and hoping she hadn't woken up anyone else.

Holy shit! Holy shit! Holy shit!

The man wasn't just sex on a stick, he was pure sex. There was nothing stick about him. Was he a branch? Sex on a branch? Sex on a log? No, log sounds wrong. Fuck, the guy was the whole damn tree. He was a sex tree. And he wanted her. And boy, oh boy, did she want him.

Hump like bunnies.

She'd said so herself. Will had chuckled when she'd said that.

He said he wasn't a snowshoer, that had to mean something. Then he'd followed her down the hallway, pinned her against the wall, wedged his leg between hers and kissed her. The man had staked his claim on her for the entire week.

So, why on earth was she in the bathroom when he was out in her bedroom with the biggest boxer bulge she'd ever seen in her life, and an eight pack of abs that was practically screaming at her to be licked?

Because I want him so badly it scares me.

Shaking her head at her foolishness and ridiculous second-guessing, she splashed some cold water on her face, gargled with Listerine, then took a wet washcloth to her downstairs business, just to be considerate. She had no idea what Will planned, but that tongue of his as he laughed and ate tapas earlier that night had mesmerized her. And if he planned on using it, she wanted to be ready. She pulled her hair out of the no-nonsense ponytail she'd been sporting all evening and pinched her cheeks.

What the fuck am I doing? I don't do this. I've never pinched my cheeks before for a man in my life, not ever.

But she pinched them anyway, fluffed her wavy red hair down around her shoulders, flashed a big "come hither" grin in the mirror and opened the door, ready once more to be ravished by the hot doctor in tight white boxer shorts.

Will was lying on her bed, his head up on the pillows and his arms tucked casually behind. His eyes were closed, and his bare chest rose and fell, deep and even. A low, barely discernible rumble filled the room. He was snoring.

She gaped at him. How long had she been in there? Not too long, it couldn't have been that long. A minute or two? But long enough, apparently, because the sexy tree who'd barged into her room and made her entire body spark to life like never before had managed to fall asleep half-naked on her bed, still sporting a very impressive tent in his boxers.

Letting out an exhale of what could only be described as a confusing mix of disappointment and relief, she pulled the dark red chenille throw off the foot of the bed and draped it over his big body. It scarcely covered half. She opened up a couple of drawers and a closet and found another blanket, covering him up with the two from neck to toe. Then, with an ironic huff and quick look of longing at the gorgeous man "in" her bed, she climbed in next to him and flicked off the light.

THE NEXT MORNING found Juney and Rowan in the kitchen preparing breakfast while the rest of the house slept. It'd only been one night so far, but that night had rocked her world. With both of them used to getting up with the sun because of their busy work schedules, their eyelids had flown open, as if set to a timer, at 5 a.m. They'd made love again—twice, then put on a pot of coffee and cuddled on the couch talking. Juney couldn't remember a time when a man made her feel this special, this beautiful. And to know she made him happy, too, it was the perfect Christmas present. It was all she'd ever wanted.

"Saskatoon berries, huh?" Rowan said with a chuckle, whisking pancake batter in a big glass bowl. "Never had 'em."

A smile crept to her lips. "They're *so* good. And they make an incredible jam."

He came up behind her and spun her around. "Yeah? Do *you* make an incredible jam?"

Rolling her eyes but unable to hide how happy he made her, she looped her spatula clad hand around his neck and smiled up at him. "Why yes, in fact, I do."

"Hmm," he hummed, bending his head low and dipping her in the process, his mouth capturing hers, his tongue demanding access. She moaned against him and opened up, welcoming him, dancing with him.

The faint *scuff-scuff* sound of slippers coming down the hallway filled the air, competing heavily with the sizzling of the skillet and griddle and quiet gurgle of the coffee maker in the corner.

"Oh, uh . . . sorry," a groggy feminine voice mumbled. Juney opened her eyes and turned just in time to see Hunter knock her hip into an end table. She winced from the pain but recovered quickly, her hand shooting out to catch the lamp that teetered back and forth. She managed to catch it, thankfully, right before it crashed to the ground.

"Good morning." Juney smiled, having pried her lips from Rowan's, and righted herself. She needed to check on the sausages in the oven.

Rowan flashed a cocky, handsome grin Hunter's way before taking up his post next to a frying pan full of vibrating bacon. "Morning."

Hunter pulled up a seat at the kitchen bar and cupped the reindeer-painted mug of coffee Juney poured and placed in front of her. "Thanks."

"Rough night?" Rowan asked with a smirk. "Were you up *all* night with the mega-genius?"

Hunter shot him an irritated glare that for some reason made her natural beauty seem even more fierce. "No."

"Good morning," came a yawn from down the hall.

The three of them turned to find Amber padding lightly on tiny bare feet down the hallway. She was wearing no more than a black tank top and red and green plaid pajama pants. Her red hair was in a messy, messy bun, and pillow creases looked like a botched facelift on her porcelain skin. She sidled up next to Hunter and thanked Juney for her coffee.

"What about you?" Rowan asked, blotting the bacon he

removed to a plate with a paper towel. "You and the grumpy doctor *play* doctor?"

Juney snorted and gave him an eye roll. "You're ridiculous."

"I'm happy."

She couldn't help the rush of pleasure that jolted through her and into every limb from his words, from his smile. He was happy because of her.

HUNTER CUPPED her mug to her chin and blew on her coffee, secretly hoping that she hadn't been the only one to strike out last night. Apparently, Juney and Rowan managed to figure out Daisy's algorithm in record time. Had Will and Amber gotten their groove on, too?

Amber rolled her eyes and shook her head. "Uh, no. We tried, but he fell asleep before anything started. I'm choosing not to take it personally. *Yet.*"

"Shit!" Rowan said, a dumbfounded look on his face. "Well, at least you know he's interested."

An icy wash of dread swamped Hunter, making her shiver, the sudden need for a cardigan or blanket all-consuming. She leapt up off the barstool and snatched a cashmere throw off the couch, wrapping it around herself like a baby-soft cocoon. Jealousy escaped her on a long sigh as she avoided everyone's curious eyes and reached for her coffee again. Yes, at least Amber could take solace in the fact that Will was interested in her. Austin apparently wanted nothing to do with her; he'd made that abundantly clear last night. Friend-zoned before she'd even had a chance.

Guess there's a first time for everything.

"What about you, Hunter?" Juney asked, her eyes full of motherly concern. This woman was a nurturer to her core.

Hunter could practically hear the woman's biological clock ticking from where she sat.

Hunter shook her head, her teeth gritted out the words. "Nope, nada. Not even a kiss. I don't think he likes me like that way. Maybe not at all. Maybe I'll try to find a ride back down the mountain to my car. Leave you lovebirds to your snowy love nest. Because obviously you two figured it out, and quickly, and Amber and Will need to get busy sooner in the evening."

Amber made a noise in her throat that wasn't quite a laugh.

"And if it's all the same," Hunter went on, "I'd rather not sit and watch you guys make use of the mistletoe while Austin and I avoid eye contact with each other for a week."

Juney leaned across the counter and rested a hand on Hunter's arm, her slow, understanding smile attempting to alleviate Hunter's uncertainties. "We haven't even been up here twenty-four hours. We have five days. Give him time. He seems shy. He might just be waiting to get to know you better. Or for you to make the first move."

Not freaking likely. Hunter never made the first move.

Hunter's lips trembled into the parody of a smile, but it was quick to vanish. The corners of her mouth were just too heavy. "Yeah . . . maybe. It's not like I was expecting sex last night. That would have been great, or even a kiss would have been cool. But he didn't even flirt. Nothing. I can't get a read on him. What's wrong with me? I'm a nice person, right? I'm successful. Sure, I don't have a college degree, and I just got my GED a couple of years ago, but I'm still pretty smart. Do you think it's the degree thing that's holding him back? That I'm not educated enough? Or maybe we're not *matched*. Maybe we're all attracted to the wrong person."

Rowan and Juney paused for a moment, their gazes locking in mild panic.

"Uh, no," Rowan finally said. "I think we all figured it out pretty damn quickly. Some *work* faster than others, that's all."

Juney beamed at him from where she stood, peeling an orange.

Rowan moved the berry sauce he'd been stirring on the stove over to a hot pad. "You're a fucking self-made millionaire, Hunter. At twenty-six, I might add. I'm pretty sure college degrees and whether you finished high school are irrelevant at this point. You're beautiful, smart, funny. I honestly have no idea what the guy's deal is. Maybe Juney's right. Maybe he's shy. Or gay." His eyes took in the women he hardly knew, gauging their response. And then he rapidly added, "Not that there's anything wrong with that. My older brother happens to be gay. I don't care who you love or who you fuck. I'm simply making an observation, is all."

Juney rolled her eyes, then gave Rowan a small grin to let him know she wasn't taking offense to his response. Amber nodded and muttered something about not being offended either.

But Hunter was off in her own little world, her lips flattened into a thin line in thought. "The millionaire thing then, maybe? He's intimidated by my wealth? My success? I'm not that different from everyone else. I still do my own laundry, put my pants on one leg at a time. And like everyone else, I'm incapable of folding a fitted sheet."

"I can fold a fitted sheet," Juney cut in.

"Well, then you're obviously a witch."

Amber burst out laughing next to her. "Nobody *normal* can fold a fitted sheet. You must be a witch."

Juney's face fell for a moment, but then she quickly plastered on a big grin. "Can *you* fold a fitted sheet?" she asked Rowan.

He gave her a dubious look. "What the hell is a fitted sheet?"

Soon they were all laughing, the debacle of the night with Austin soon forgotten. Hunter found herself smiling and joking with the others. It was nice to smile, especially after last night. It wasn't until their banter about how hot the griddle should be for pancakes—Rowan and Juney couldn't agree on a temperature setting, she said he was burning them—that they were interrupted by more slipper-scuffing from down the hall. All eyes turned to see who it was, and lo and behold, out trudged Austin looking as rough as Hunter felt. She quickly averted her eyes and stared down into her coffee mug, watching the steam rise up into her nostrils.

"Morning," Austin yawned. There were two choices: either take the other empty seat next to Hunter or walk around to the other side and sit next to Amber. He chose to sit next to Amber. A move that was noticed by everyone. Juney shook her head and went back to whisking the whipping cream. Rowan gave Austin a quick once-over, then shook his head as well. Amber got up and poured him a cup of coffee, which he took willingly and thanked her.

Hunter turned her head to look at him. His dark brown, wavy hair stuck out in every direction on his head, and an even thicker layer of auburn scruff covered his chin and cheeks. He looked better than ever. Disheveled and raw. Different from the guys she normally dated, who were chiseled and fit in all the right places, but screamed bravado and "look at me" from the rooftops with the way they carried themselves. Hell, her last boyfriend spent twice as much time primping in the bathroom as she did.

And even though she was coming to the conclusion that Austin didn't share her feelings, she couldn't deny the pull she had toward him. He had an understated magnetism, and she was drawn to his quiet power, drawn to his intelligence and tenacity. The more she thought about it, the more she was attracted to the fact that he *wasn't* attracted to her. How fucked up is that? But she couldn't deny it. The fact that the brainiac wasn't interested in her, was practically ignoring her, was turning her on. Never a nerd herself, because she just didn't have the attention span or drive to try in school, she was in awe of those who could.

Once her company started to take off, Hunter tried a couple of online and night business classes, but even those she struggled to sit through, didn't find them engaging or overly helpful. Her time could be much better spent forging relationships with suppliers or hunched over a sewing machine making the next great hemp skirt. So, even though she had zero education, not to mention no business knowledge, she managed to build a small empire, relying solely on her gut instinct and a few loyal and honest friends and co-workers. But that didn't mean that she didn't admire those who went to school. It said a lot about a person and how they valued themselves, how they valued intelligence. A never-ending quest for knowledge, always wanting more of it, always wanting to know more. Hunter found it hot. Abs, pecs, lips, eyes, they had nothing on a big, sexy brain.

"We're all going to hike up to the chairlifts today and get some runs in, earn the extra calories we'll consume tonight. You in?" Juney asked, snapping Austin out of his funk. The guy had been staring straight ahead at the little Santa and Mrs. Claus salt and pepper shakers perched on the island. Hunter only knew this because she'd been staring at Austin.

Get a grip, girl. He doesn't like you that way.

He pulled his eyes away from the salt and pepper shakers, the faintest of smiles tugging at his mouth. "Oh. Uh, sure, that sounds good. I'm game."

Rowan gave him a look and snorted, shaking his head with an eye roll. "At least you're game for *something*."

Hunter coughed and shot Rowan a dirty look.

Shut up, man!

He gave her a smug smile back and flipped a flapjack. She wanted to flip it onto his face. Just because he was happy and having multiple Christmas orgasms didn't mean he had to go rubbing it in and make the rest of them feel like lumps of freaking coal.

"Good morning."

All eyes whipped around to the deep and sleepy voice that was coming down the hallway. Will had pulled his jeans back on, but he hadn't bothered with his shirt, and the ridges of his chiseled abs flexed with each long stride.

"Morning." Hunter yawned, moving over so Will could take up a perch next to her. He offered her a sleepy smile, then thanked Juney for his coffee.

WILL WAS thankful that there was no seat left next to Amber. He was a total ass for falling asleep on her last night. And even though for the first time in forever he woke up feeling rather rested, he also felt like an idiot. Why hadn't she woken him up? Sat on his face or straddled his waist to snap him back to reality? He had closed his eyes for a brief second, bagged from the day and the days before. It'd been nonstop busy at the hospital, and he'd only managed all of thirty minutes of sleep in the on-call room.

He was pissed off at himself for dozing off last night, but he wasn't the least bit surprised it had happened. He hadn't had a solid eight hours in what was beginning to feel like forever. But there she was, avoiding his face and staring down into her coffee mug like it was a fucking Picasso or something, and rightfully so. She was probably either (a) pissed off at him or (b) feeling insecure about where they stood. He hoped it wasn't either of those but would take pissed off over insecure. He wanted Little Red to know how badly he wanted her; he just had to figure out a way to show her.

"You coming?"

Hunter's voice and cocked head pulled Will from his

thoughts, and he snapped to attention, nearly knocking his coffee mug over in the process. "Coming where?"

Rowan snorted in the kitchen and shook his head. "Not too many people *coming* in this place."

What was that prick's problem?

Will glared at the cocky chef as Rowan wiped his hands on the front of his apron and pecked Juney on the cheek at the same time.

Fuck, had Rowan sealed the deal last night? Jesus, where had that prowess come from?

Now Will was an even bigger dumbass because he'd fallen asleep on Amber, but Rowan had managed to get Juney to give it up on the first night.

The little blonde smiled at him. Hunter was cute, super cute. And normally he would have gone for her. She was totally his type. He liked blondes. Always had. Probably because as a teenager he'd been obsessed with *Baywatch*. I mean, come on, you can only watch Pamela Anderson run in slow motion down the beach so many times before a mild obsession and dreams of bodacious blondes with heaving bosoms start to infiltrate your dreams. Day and night. And he'd been with his fair share of flaxen-haired bombshells. His ex-wife had been black, but Will liked all types. But here, now, he wanted Amber. She was a ball-buster and spritely, and he liked that . . . a lot.

"Sorry, where?" he asked again, ignoring Rowan's smug smile and turning back to Hunter.

"We're all going to hike up to the chairlift and do some runs," Hunter said, lightly drumming her fingernails on the side of her mug.

Will nodded as he ran his hand down his face and scratched his whiskers. He needed to shave. "Yeah, sure."

"All right, you sexually frustrated weirdos," Rowan said with a chuckle, his arms loaded down with plates as he made his way over to the long, live-edge dining room table. "Breakfast is ready!"

He plopped an enormous platter of pancakes down in the center, followed by a plate of bacon, a plate of sausages, and enough scrambled eggs to feed an army. Juney followed hot on his heels with whipped cream, berry sauce, what looked to be toast, cut-up fruit, and maple syrup. Once they set everything down, the two of them stood up straight and smiled at each other. Something passed between them, something intimate, an inside joke or a wordless conversation. Whatever it was, it did not go unnoticed by the other four, who pried their sorry asses off the barstools and went to take their seats, incredibly annoyed with how chipper and sappy the Christmas lovebirds were.

CHAPTER SIX

HUNTER GIGGLED and took an awkward step out of the way to avoid the big dip in the packed snow. The sound of snowboarders and skiers filled the crisp mountain air. "When was the last time you boarded, dude? You're like a runaway train out there."

"Did you see that?" Will had come to an abrupt stop in front of her, his board carving nicely into the packed snow and sending up a confetti of flurries. "That was insane! I nearly bailed but righted myself just at the end, only to avoid hitting that tree. Fuck, I'm a fucking danger to myself and everyone else out here."

She ungloved her hand for a moment and dug into her pocket for some lip gloss. "Been awhile, then?" She hurriedly slathered it on, stowed it back in her coat and put her shivering hand back into its downy shroud.

"Uh, yeah." His smile was wide and carefree, unlike yesterday when every look, every blink had been with heavy eyelids and dark bags beneath.

"It looked like it."

"Hey!" He shot her a pretend glare, but then reached out and shoved her in a brotherly way. She responded by shoving him back and giggling. He might come across as a bit of an ornery ass, but she liked Will—not the way she liked Austin, but in more of a sibling kind of way. Like how a little sister might like or admire a big brother. She was an only child and grew up in the system, so although from time to time she had "brothers and sisters" when she was in foster homes, she never really found anyone she truly connected with on a level she would call "familial." Not until Daisy anyway.

Maybe it was because he was an only child, too. Who knew? But something in Will spoke to her. The man screamed alpha to his very core, not to mention slightly arrogant and a tad conceited, but there was also a protective element about him, nurturing and fiercely loyal.

Hunter gave him another hard shove in the shoulder, and he fell back on his ass into a big drift of snow, a carefree chuckle rumbling up as his big gloved hands started collecting snow and forming it into a ball. Hunter was laughing so much with her head tossed back, blonde locks pulled into a French braid over her shoulder, that she didn't notice the giant snowball headed for her face.

It caught her dead center and knocked her back until she fell on her own ass into some untouched powder.

"That'll teach you, brat!" Will laughed, scooping up more snowballs and throwing them at Hunter as fast as he could.

She started doing the same, and soon the two were caught up in an all-out snowball fight.

Austin swallowed hard. "Damn it."

"You're an idiot!" Juney said.

He hadn't blinked. His eyes were glued to the scene below. Had he just said that out loud?

Crap.

He and Juney were on a chairlift heading up to the top of the run, and he'd caught sight of Hunter down below. Her bright pink ski jacket was hard to miss against the pristine snow.

"She likes you. You obviously like her. I know it's only been a day since we all arrived up here and decided to embark on this ridiculous setup of Daisy's, but come on, man, what's your deal?"

Austin slowly peeled his eyes away from the scene of Hunter and Will and their cozy little snowball fight and looked at Juney. Finally, he let out a big huff, his shoulders slumping. "How'd you and Rowan manage to figure it out so quickly?"

A smile so serene and placid crossed her face, Austin wondered if the woman was already in love, or if it was just the orgasms and endorphin boost.

"We both know what we want," she said. "I was attracted to him right away. He went a little fanboy about my books at first, but I found it cute and endearing. And when he knocked on my door last night to talk and apologize for being weird about my books, he felt the pull, the attraction too. We just kind of . . . hit it off, and one thing led to another."

Austin shook his head. "But Hunter is so intimidating."

"She is? How so?" Juney cocked her head to the side.

Austin's lip twisted, and he looked back out over the ski hill. "Well, she's fucking beautiful, for one. A millionaire. Men probably line up to date her. Would I simply be joining the queue? Annnd . . . " His gloved hands knitted together only for him to pull them apart in a dramatic exhale. He glanced back up to Juney. "I haven't been with a lot of women. If you haven't already figured it out, I'm a socially awkward nerd. My nickname for years has been *Sheldon*. Can you guess why?"

"Because you're a super genius, socially awkward nerd?" Juney said with a chuckle. A slash of pink raced across her high cheekbones from the sudden gust of icy wind that swept over them and made the chairlift sway.

Austin lifted both eyebrows and nodded. "Bingo. Besides being a mechanical engineer instead of an astrophysicist, *The Big Bang Theory* is my life. Well, kind of. I don't have nearly as many friends as Sheldon. But I can pretty much guarantee you that Hunter has way more experience than me. I'd be this giant disappointment. Plus, she's into kink. I've never even spanked a woman, let alone tied her up or blindfolded her."

It was therapeutic, getting these things off his chest. And Juney was an easy person to talk to. Aside from being beautiful, she was also very sweet. Sapphire-blue eyes, big and bright with mile-long lashes, dark hair that fell down around her shoulders in elegant waves, and nice, albeit older angles to her face. Even though she was only seven years older than Austin, she held a quiet wisdom, intelligence that went beyond her years. Motherly and caring, she had a calming presence that made you want to tell her all your problems—and your secrets! Like a big sister. Austin's own sister was nearly twelve years younger than him—a "beautiful *whoops*" as his mother called her—and although he adored Madeline more than anything, the two were not close. She was only three when he left for college, and he hadn't lived at home since. So, although they saw one another most weekends when he went over to his parents' for Sunday dinner, she was only fifteen, and he couldn't very well talk to her about this kind of thing.

"And what makes you think that's a make or break thing with Hunter?"

He gave her a sardonic side-eye. "She told us her side business. How can she sell the stuff without knowing about it? Without enjoying it herself? You don't see too many Audi car salesmen driving Chevys."

"Well, are you *curious*? Perhaps she would be willing to teach you. You're assuming a lot right now and ruining your chances with a pretty great girl, from what I've seen so far."

He let out another long and loud sigh. "I heard her saying she's thinking about leaving."

"Mhmm."

"I just . . . I don't even know *how* to make a move. I've been with three women in my entire life, and that was a few years ago. And each and every time, the women threw themselves at me. They were grad students or co-op students who thought I was hot, invited me over for dinner to discuss 'work,' and then the next thing I know I'm naked on my back being ridden like an unbridled, unbroken pony, with no idea what's going on, no idea what to do, but not exactly hating the way things feel."

Juney tossed her head back and burst out laughing. "If the engineering thing doesn't work out, you could certainly try your hand at writing. You have a gift for painting a pretty hilarious picture." Her body continued to shake slightly as her laugher slowly subsided. "It's not that hard. Especially in this situation where you know the girl already likes you. Talk to her, the way you're talking to me. Ask questions. Get to know her. *Date,* so to speak."

"Yeah, but I can talk to you because you're more like a sister and she's . . . well, she's . . . "

Juney's eyebrows flew up beneath her toque.

"Oh, fuck! Oh, sorry. I didn't mean it like that. You're hot too. You're just, well . . . I just don't look at you like *that*. I can talk to you because, fuck . . . shit . . . Now you hate me too, right?"

Juney rolled her eyes and patted his shoulder with her gloved hand. They were nearing the top and needed to get ready to slide off the lift. "I get it. And for the record, I don't look at you *that* way, either. But you're going to need to talk to her eventually if you want something to happen."

The bar on the chair started to rise, and snow replaced air

beneath their feet. They both slipped off and down the small incline, making their way to the precipice to wait their turn.

"Start slow. Ask her how her day was today. Ask her where she's been boarding before, what her favorite restaurant in Seattle is." Juney set herself straight and dug her poles into the snow to stabilize, preparing to push off and head down. "You don't have to *start* talking about kinky sex and the fact that she's a millionaire right off the bat. Most dates don't."

Austin's lips pressed into a thin line before he spoke. "Yeah, but this setup isn't like most dates. You and Rowan have already slept together."

She shook her head with a smile. "Some dates end that way, but not all of them." With a wink, she drew her goggles down over her eyes, pushed off on her ski poles and headed down the hill, leaving Austin standing up at the top with his board, more confused than ever.

———

ROWAN SPIED Juney's dark hair cascading down over her white coat as she and Austin rode the chair lift. It was easy to spot, while the red bottom of Austin's board appeared like a ketchup-colored beacon among the eggshell landscape. He and Amber passed Will and Hunter as well. They were calling it a day and heading to the lodge to grab coffee. How did Amber feel about that? It was weird how they'd all paired off. It'd happened organically, but it made Rowan wonder if they'd paired off that way for a reason?

Naw. Juney's mine, no doubt about it.

Shaking his head at the asinine notion that Juney might be paired with Austin, Rowan chuckled inwardly and turned to Amber, determined to take his mind off the fact that Juney might be snuggled up tight next to Austin at that very moment. "So, you and the hot doctor man didn't get your freak on last night because he passed out?" he asked with an amused chuckle as he and Amber waited in line for the chair lift.

The little redhead nodded reluctantly. "Yes."

"But were you guys going to do it?"

"Yes."

"Ah, so it's not like he's lost interest or anything?"

She shot him a "what the fuck?" look. "Well, I fucking hope not. Jesus, filter much of those thoughts there, man?"

Rowan glanced down at his feet, struggling not to grin. "Sorry. Sometimes it turns off on its own."

Amber snorted. "It's okay." She jutted out her lower lip and huffed warm breath up into the chilly mountain air. "At least I think he still is. The way he behaved last night told me he was interested. I just think he was really tired. I mean he *is* a doctor, and they work long-ass shifts."

Rowan nodded, feeling a tad shamefaced for lacking tact in his earlier comment. He needed to make amends and lay on the charm. "Super long-ass shifts. And why wouldn't he be interested in you? You're beautiful. There aren't too many women out there who run their own contracting and construction company. That's pretty hot."

She gave him a light punch in the shoulder, unable to hide the small half-smile on her lips. "Nice apology."

Rowan's grin was big. "Thanks."

"What about you and the *New York Times* best-seller? Seems Stella got her groove back before the week even started. You two were all sickly sweet and making googly fucky eyes over the breakfast table. I nearly barfed up those delicious, super fluffy pancakes Juney made."

Rowan shot her a look. She smiled sassily at him. He deserved that jab. It'd been a tie on whose pancakes were fluffier, and he had to admit it, his woman—*holy shit, did he just think of*

Juney as his *woman?* —made some pretty mean and mighty fluffy flapjacks. He didn't have the balls to admit it, maybe one day he would, but he actually preferred hers over his. When no one was paying attention, he took an extra two from the platter heaped with her pile and flipped them on to his plate, dousing them quickly in maple syrup and fresh whipped cream before anyone could notice.

He shook his head, and his chest jerked as he snorted. "Well, you're certainly the hearts and flowers sentimental type, aren't you? You got a heart in there, Tin Man, or is it just an extra oil can for when you get rusty from working out in the Seattle rain all day?"

AMBER STOPPED short and didn't move with the line, her playful grin vanishing as fast as it'd come. Tin Man, or more accurately Tin *Woman*, was the nickname the men on the job site had given her behind her back. They didn't know she'd overheard them talking about her. One had called her an emotionless robot, while the other said she was Tin Woman. Everyone laughed and agreed Tin Woman suited Amber just right. Because she was all business, and they weren't sure there was even a heart beating inside her chest, let alone an emotion besides "fierce."

Was fierce even an emotion?

At kickboxing class that night, she'd nearly incapacitated her sparring partner with all her pent-up anger. Fortunately, the guy she was sparring with was nearly twice her size and, in the end, he'd pinned her to the ground, sat on top of her and told her to "Calm the fuck down." She did, apologized to Dwayne, then the two went and grabbed a beer. Dwayne wanted to talk about Amber's snap, but she called him a "pussy" and told him to drop it. Instead she switched gears and asked him how he and his partner, Leif's, adoption process was coming along. Fortunately,

Dwayne took the hint and backed off. Amber did not talk about her feelings. Not ever.

Growing up with three older brothers and the profession she was in did not allow for emotions and feelings to be on the surface or expressed with more than passing excitement over the Seahawks making the playoffs.

There were rarely any tears, any malaise expressed in Amber's world. Hell, she had gotten so good at tossing on the mask that she was becoming indifferent toward practically everything, even the happy parts of life.

Was she Tin Woman?

"Whoa, where'd you go?" Rowan asked, having to give her a light shove in the shoulder so they were no longer holding up the line.

Amber shook her head and swallowed down the lump in her throat. "Uh . . . nowhere. Sorry, I spaced out for a second."

"You sure? You don't want to sit this run out? Go find Hunter and Will and grab a coffee?"

She shook her head again. "No, no, I'm fine. What were you saying?"

Rowan snickered and motioned for them to move forward in the line again. "I was more or less asking who pissed all over your notion of forever? Why so cynical about romance and love and all that 'googly fucky eye' stuff? Isn't that why we're all up here? To take part in Daisy's cockamamie algorithm Christmas matchmaking?"

They were next on the lift, and a part of Amber dreaded having to ride all the way up to the top with Rowan and his stupid grin. Sure, *he* was happy. He got laid last night. *He'd* found his match. *He* could express his feelings and not be called an "emotional woman," "crazy bitch," or be asked if it was his "time of the month." He could be whatever emotion he wanted to be, feel whatever he wanted to feel, and he wouldn't be labeled for it based on his gender by the people he worked with or his asshat brothers.

Yes, over the years Amber's brothers had softened toward women after they started having girlfriends and eventually married, but growing up with them had been brutal. She hadn't even started having her period when they'd toss the "Aunt Flo" remark her way whenever she shed a tear or expressed a feeling. She had learned pretty quickly, once "Aunt Flo" finally showed up, how to hide her feelings. It also helped that by the time she was sixteen, despite her size, she could drop-kick every one of her six-foot-one brothers without breaking a sweat. They may not have let her roughhouse with them when they were younger, but joining the wrestling team and kickboxing after school had made her tough as nails and a worthy adversary.

She gnashed her molars together until a flash of pain ran up her jaw. She liked the pain. It was a distraction from the pain in her heart. "I'm just a cynic, I suppose. I'm not sure I believe in forever. Not sure I believe in happily ever after. Isn't it the Buddhist thing to say we are all just *suffering*? Is happiness really even a thing?"

His eyes flared wide. "Are your parents still together?"

They got ready for the next chair, did a little simultaneous hop up onto the seat as it swept up under their legs and settled in as the bar came down over their thighs.

"Yes, and all three of my brothers are happily married."

Rowan scratched his chin. "Why are you so cynical, then? Bad past relationships?"

Amber scanned the ski hill. The mountain was alive with skiers and snowboarders. Everyone careened and moguled around one another and the setup flags like ants wearing brightly colored jackets. "I've had a few crappy relationships in my life, but nothing too traumatic. No violent exes or harsh breakups. Just your run-of-the-mill dating, I guess."

"So then, why so cynical?" He asked that last part like Heath Ledger as the Joker in the *Dark Knight* says, "Why so serious?" and Amber caught herself smiling. No tact and no filter but Rowan was fun, and he definitely got Amber thinking *and* talking. And the guy wasn't bad to look at either, like a fit and chiseled California beach bum. Big dimples, unruly blond hair and a cheeky grin she was sure got him out of a lot of jams and into a lot of women's beds. But even though he was attractive—she most certainly would have *swiped right* if he'd popped up on a dating app, and would have probably agreed to a second date—he was no Will Colson. Rowan was your typical boy band good-looking. Straight white teeth, probably a six-pack under that ski jacket and the softest light brown eyes that any warm-blooded woman could get lost in. He was what teeny boppers decorated their bedroom walls with. But Will, Will had a raw animal magnetism that ignited a visceral urge inside of Amber, set her body to bubbling hot and made her want to rip off his clothes and tackle all six-foot-three of him to the floor.

"How many women are in the kitchen at your restaurant?" she asked.

"Well, zero, but I don't work in a kitchen anymore, remember. I quit. I'm officially unemployed."

She let out an impatient sigh. "Work with me here, you dork."

He smiled and wrinkled his nose. "I dunno, maybe five. A dishwasher, one on desserts, one on cold-side, another sous-chef who was below me, and one of our expediters is also a woman. Why?"

"Because I work with zero women. I'm the only one. I oversee twenty men, some almost twice my age, and I'm their boss. I took over the family business. I'm exactly like my dad. 'Roths don't show emotions. Emotions are what make you weak. Roths aren't weak,' " she said in a deep and booming voice to mimic her father. "I've developed the family chip on my shoulder and the art of tossing on a mask, putting my head down and getting shit done. All without the annoyance and interference of emotions. They just get in the way and make the situation cloudy."

Rowan's eyebrows met his hairline. "But you don't work twenty-four seven. Can't you be happy or sad and angry once you're off the job? I'm all for professionalism, but we all need an outlet. Me, my outlet is running . . . and reading. I get lost in Juney's books, lost in another world where the character's problems seem far more dire than my own."

Her temper left her on a sigh. "I kick box."

"Well, there you go. But what else? What makes you happy?"

"Can we not talk about this anymore? Please?" she asked through gritted teeth. The top of the ski hill came into view, and suddenly she was itching to jump off the chairlift. Rowan was nice, but he asked too many questions.

He shrugged. "Whatever, but I think you need to relax. Let the *magic* of Christmas and the bizarre setup that nutty Canadian got us into sweep you off your feet and open up your heart." They were almost at the top, and Rowan pulled his ski goggles back down over his eyes. "It's not every day someone finds you your match, presents them to you on a silver platter and then gives you a week, uninterrupted, to see if there's any chemistry. I'm not saying you're not up for the challenge or that Will isn't interested in you. I'm saying, be fucking *happy* about it, and lighten the fuck up. Smile, cry, laugh, scream. Do whatever you gotta do, but it's fucking Christmas. You're allowed to have some feelings."

The bar came up off their thighs, and thanks to what Amber could only assume was a poignant look behind Rowan's masked eyes, she was forced to stare at her own reflection. She was scowling. He gave her a curt nod and a friendly slap on the thigh before taking off down the small incline and off toward the run.

Amber glared after him.

Asshole.

But, damn, that asshole was right. She needed to lighten up. She loved Christmas, loved every part of it, but she wasn't sure a single person in the world knew it. Not even her family.

Rowan groaned as he stretched both arms above his head and let one fall around Juney's shoulders. They'd all headed into the ski lodge, after a couple more runs, to join Hunter and Will. Achy muscles, rosy cheeks and bright eyes met around the well-worn wooden table of the ski lodge restaurant while hands cradled Baileys-spiked coffees and everyone chatted animatedly about their afternoon.

"Hey, look," Juney said, pointing at a flyer on the wall just beside the mounted deer head. "It says they're having a big Boxing Day party next door at the pub. I didn't think Americans celebrated Boxing Day the way we do."

"We don't," Rowan answered, rubbing her thigh affectionately with his other hand. "To us it is literally a day where you box up all your Christmas presents and gorge yourself on turkey leftovers. But it's not a holiday. Back to the grind and usually hung over from too much eggnog."

Juney's chuckle was throaty and breathless, and her sizzling blue eyes twinkled at him while the corners crinkled up in a smile. Rowan's cock was getting ready to burn through his ski pants.

"Well, I think we should all come. It says they'll have a live band, karaoke and prizes. What do you guys think?"

Everyone besides Austin nodded around the table.

"Sure," Hunter agreed. "Sounds like fun. It'd be nice to get out and mingle, dance and hear some live music. I can't remember the last time I went out for something that didn't involve PR for work or drinks with a buyer."

"I could go for a couple of rounds of pool," Will chimed in. "Haven't played since college. I was pretty good."

Hunter shot him a sassy grin. "Care to make it interesting, doc? Winner buys the booze for the group for the rest of the night?"

Will's smile was wide and genuine. "You're on, *brat*," he said.

Suddenly, Amber's head swiveled around from where she'd been watching the football game on the big screen in the corner. Her eyes bore into the side of Hunter's skull as if she were Superman and Hunter's head was a piece of steel she was trying to sever in two. Rowan snickered to himself and shook his head. Clearly, Amber did not like the way Will was looking at Hunter, or that he'd given the other woman a nickname. Thank God he and Juney had figured it out last night. Add in the way Hunter and Austin were behaving, like tweens at their first sleepaway camp playing spin the bottle, he just couldn't handle the tension. It filtered thick into the room and took over the atmosphere.

His eyes fell on Austin. The guy was down to a dark green sweater and his ski pants and looked like he was going to puke. Was that because he was touching elbows with Hunter on the table? Austin inched his elbow away and swallowed. Rowan snorted.

Oh dude, get it together or move on.

Austin's gaze whipped up to Juney, who was sitting there next to Rowan, sweetly sipping her blueberry tea. The way he was looking at her didn't appear to be altogether innocent, and suddenly Rowan sympathized with Amber and her look of wanting to take Hunter to the mat.

Rowan tugged Juney closer.

I didn't mean move on to my *woman.*

CHAPTER SEVEN

Austin closed the cover on the fireplace and sat back on his heels, admiring the flickering flames and how with each new twirl they grew bigger and brighter. They'd all arrived back at the cabin a short while ago, weary-eyed and achy, flopping onto couches and nests on the floor. Not much had gone down since they'd trudged their way back through the dense falling flakes from the lodge to the cabin, but for some reason, an unsettling fog had floated down over top of everyone. Maybe it was the fact that it was Christmas Eve and they were all away from family. Perhaps it was that another night was upon them and no one knew what was going to happen behind closed doors once they'd all muttered "goodnight." Austin certainly couldn't get last night's awful debacle out of his head. Was he doomed to repeat it? Probably.

Fascination filled him, and he struggled to keep his bottom lip from dropping and his groin from tenting as Hunter's whole body stretched and tightened with a big yawn in front of him. Her arms drifted up above her head, and her mouth opened wide while her feet flexed in her slippers. The hem of her shirt escaped the top of her tight black yoga pants, revealing a tanned patch of soft skin. She continued to stretch, and the shirt continued to hike up. A glint of something sparkly made Austin's pulse thrum. She had her bellybutton pieced.

Damn!

He licked his lips, unable to look away from the ring on her midriff. Her big, beautiful breasts pushed demandingly against her baby blue T-shirt, the fabric stretching and straining with the pressure. At that moment Austin was desperate to have them in his hands, in his mouth. What color were her nipples? Were they as red and perfect as her lips? Hard and achy and desperate to be touched? He shifted uncomfortably and inconspicuously brought a pillow over his lap. But Will caught him, and the cantankerous doctor just shook his head and snorted.

Shut up! You struck out last night too. I don't see you playing footsies or holding hands with Amber.

His eyes fell back to Hunter. She'd repositioned herself on the floor and was busy playing cards with Amber in a bunch of blankets and pillows. Austin was working up the courage to ask if he could join them when a knock at the front door had everyone jumping. Had Daisy and Riley decided to come and celebrate with them after all? Abandon the sun, sand and surf for food, friends and flurries?

Rowan was the closest, puttering away in the kitchen, so with a quick wipe of his hands on the dishcloth over his shoulder, he went to see who could be coming by on Christmas Eve.

"Hello and Merry Christmas!"

Everyone's eyes flew to the door to see who owned the deep and confident voice.

Big amber eyes went wide and blonde hair flipped around. "Sam!" Hunter cheered, springing up from the floor and beelining it to the attractive man on the threshold. The hackles at the back of Austin's neck sprung to life.

Who the hell was this guy?

Hunter invited "Sam" in, but he didn't take off his coat or shoes.

"I'm not going to stay," he said with a chuckle, letting Hunter go after she'd practically tackled him in a hug.

Austin's face was on fire. No, seriously, who the fuck was this guy?

"What are you doing here?" Hunter asked, her eyes sparkly and darkening to the color of warm bourbon as she glanced up, practically swooning over the tall redhead with rugged good looks, chin scruff and rosy cheeks. "Did you bring the kids?"

Sam smiled. "They're with my parents down the road at our *other* cabin. My parents just bought another one, so we're spending Christmas at the new house. Though I think they intend to fix it up and rent that one out. This one has been in the family much too long to not call it our home away from home."

Slowly, the rest of the houseguests put down their drinks and stretched tired and sore limbs, prying themselves up off the couch and wandering over to greet the newcomer.

Juney leaned in and hugged Sam as well, the two chuckling low as they pulled apart, smiling. A move that did not go unnoticed by Rowan.

"Good to see you again," Juney said, moving to the side so the others could say hello. "It's been a while. Years, I think."

Sam's bright blue eyes glowed. "Would have been nice if we could have caught up at the wedding, but when your sister elopes, there's not too much you can do."

"I'm still not sure I've forgiven her for that, yet," Hunter grumbled.

Sam shook his head with another warm smile. "Me either." His eyes took in the people who obviously didn't know who he was, and he extended his hand toward Will. "Hi, I'm Sam, Daisy's brother." Slowly Sam's hand made the rounds. "Daisy sent me to check up on you guys, make sure you have what you need and that no one has killed anyone or braved the weather and tried to head back to their car because the company wasn't to their liking. Her words, not mine."

A few uncomfortable guffaws drifted around the group as they continued to stand there and stare at Sam.

"No, I think we're all grownup enough to make it work," Will said finally, rising to his full height and simultaneously taking a half-step closer to Amber.

Sam nodded and smiled. "Good, good. I figured as much. But I'm doing my brotherly duty and checking in. If you guys need anything, my number is on the side of the fridge. And we're all only a few doors down the way."

Rowan had suddenly appeared next to Juney, and his hand was rhythmically kneading her hip. "We're all good, man."

"So, how is it going?" Sam asked, a sly and understanding grin curling his full lips as he took in the way both Will and Rowan had staked their claim on two of the women.

Austin clenched his fists and jaw. Hunter was not his. As much as he wanted her to be, she wasn't, and he couldn't do the same thing. He couldn't touch her, couldn't even take another step closer.

"When my sister told me what she was up to, I called her crazy, but by the looks of things, Daisy's algorithm is proving fruitful."

Hunter made a noise in her throat before answering. The noise was not lost on anyone, especially Austin. "Crazy Daisy and her harebrained ideas. What about you, Sam? Any lucky lady won the heart of one of Vancouver's most eligible bachelors yet?"

Sam grinned. "No, not yet, I'm afraid. But I'm not really looking. The kids keep me busy. Landon is determined to walk before he's one, I know it. And Gemma, well, Gem is a spirited one, that's for sure. The kids are going to give me gray hairs before I'm forty. I've already found a few in my beard."

Sam's gaze flitted to Austin, and he shook his head. Austin shifted awkwardly foot-to-foot, standing behind the rest of the Christmas lovebirds, glaring, yes, glaring at him. He took in the way Hunter ogled Sam, the way her eyes glimmered, her cheeks flushed, and how her smile slipped when he mentioned he wasn't looking for anyone.

Sam drew his gloves from his coat pocket and pulled them back onto his hands; something above him caught his eye.

More *fucking* mistletoe. Had that always been there? The ulcer in Austin's stomach burned as he hoped Hunter wouldn't feel compelled to lunge forward and kiss Sam on the cheek. Or worse, the lips.

Sam smiled and stepped out from under the hanging twigs. "Well, looks like you're all set here. Things seem . . . *interesting.* I wish you nothing but love and happiness on this joyous holiday, and I hope you all find what you're looking for. What you want." And with a curt nod and the flash of a grin, followed by a very poignant look at Austin that lasted no more than two seconds, Sam spun on his heel and was out the door.

Rowan snapped his fingers as he headed back into the kitchen. "I bet you any money that's how the television is turning on on it's own. Sam has one of those universal remote phone apps. He was probably sitting out in his car with his phone and turned the television on earlier."

Everyone nodded. Made sense. Austin had the same app and used it daily at home.

"I didn't know Daisy had a brother," Will said with a shrug, not appearing to care about how the television was turning on and off on it's own.

Hunter followed them into the living room and found her way back to her cocoon of blankets on the floor. "Yeah, older brother. Sam is great."

"Divorced?" Amber asked.

Hunter nodded. "Yeah, but it's not what you think. His ex, Meegan, just up and decided one day that being a mother and wife wasn't what she wanted. I think their little boy was only a few months old at the time. She gave Sam full custody, signed over her parental rights, divorced him and moved across the country."

Juney, who had resumed her post in the kitchen with Rowan, stopped what she was doing, sending a big metal ladle clattering to the floor. "She did WHAT? I knew Meegan was out of the picture, but Daisy has never filled me in on the details. I thought it was just a run-of-the-mill separation."

"There's nothing *run-of-the-mill* about a separation. Especially when children are involved," Will muttered under his breath before he tipped up his scotch and drained it.

Hunter's brows pinched for a moment and she studied Will before nodding and turning back to face Juney in the kitchen. "Anyway, yeah. She just took off. Now Sam raises both kids alone. I mean both sets of grandparents are in the picture and help out a lot, but he's a single dad."

"A hot single dad," Amber added, making sure to catch Will's reaction. His green-eyed monster was out, that much was obvious.

"You two . . . ever?" Rowan asked innocently, his bicep bulging slightly as he hinged forward and started grinding herbs in a mortar and pestle.

Hunter's head jerked up as though someone had delivered her a swift uppercut. "Did we ever *what?*"

"You know . . . " he said, waggling his eyebrows. Juney

snorted next to him. Austin's face and ulcer burned hot and painful.

"Did you and Daisy's big brother ever bone?" Will asked, clarifying things. "Apparently, all of a sudden, we're back in middle school and Emeril Lagasse over there doesn't think he should say the word *sex*."

"I'm trying to have a filter!" Rowan snapped, but not without the hint of a grin. "I've been told I lack a filter. Besides, you just said 'bone.' How old are *you*?"

Will's mouth split into a big smile. "Touché."

Hunter's face turned a beautiful shade of pink, like the peonies in Austin's mother's garden. "No!" she finally said. "No, Sam is quite a bit older than me and has never been anything but a gentleman."

Rowan snickered. "I noticed you never said that you didn't *want* to."

"Filter!" Juney chastised.

Will and Amber chuckled while Austin just sat in the La-Z-Boy fuming.

"New topic, please!" Hunter sang. "I've never slept with Daisy's brother, ever, thank you very much. Yes, he's attractive. Yes, I've always had a tiny crush on him. But, no, we've never had sex. Never even kissed. Drop it."

Suddenly all eyes fell on Austin, who sprang to his feet and took off at a brisk stalk through the living room and down toward his room, his door slamming seconds later.

He needed to get a fucking grip. Hunter wasn't his. He had no claim. Yet the way she'd looked at Sam, giggled and blushed at his words and jokes, it'd sent Austin's blood boiling, and steam threatened to rush out of his ears. Such feelings had never plagued him before. But he also wasn't an idiot and knew that it was jealousy. The cannoning thoughts in his brain, the sweat on his palms, the heat in his face and the tightening in his chest. The burning in his gut. When Hunter lunged at Sam and hugged him, Austin saw nothing but red. This was jealousy.

Then fucking do something about it, you ass. She's been looking at you that way, too, only you're too big of a Sheldon to make a move.

Austin ran his hands through his hair and over his face, dragging it across the stubble a couple of times before stopping in front of the vanity to give himself a hard once-over. Dark brown hair, a tad long and curling over his ears, auburn beard with six days' worth of growth, greenish-gold eyes that everyone always commented on and said how beautiful and unique they are. He wasn't a *bad*-looking guy. In fact, some, excluding his over the top complimentary mother, had even called him handsome. Only when Austin stared at himself in the mirror, all he saw was the gangly teenager bumbling awkwardly through the quad looking for his classroom as big, scary college students, adults in comparison, glared down at him and wondered if he was lost, if he'd been separated from his mama.

It hadn't been easy to make friends in school. The age gap, the intelligence gap, neither had done him any favors with his peers. He was always the smartest and always the youngest. There wasn't anything people hated more than the young wise-ass in the corner with pimply cheeks and a squeaky voice correcting their equations. If he was honest with himself, Austin would say that Reggie and Riley, Daisy's husband, were two of his only real friends. However, Reggie was his boss, and Riley had been his next-door neighbor since they were kids. He was the only person who, despite their slight age gap, seemed to tolerate and enjoy spending time with Austin. And over the years, through high school, and Austin moving back east to do his masters, while Riley went to med school down at Stanford, the two had always remained friends, and he was grateful for that.

Frustrated that he would have to leave his room again to use the washroom and splash some water on his face, Austin took a couple of calming deep breaths, swallowed a few times, then put his hand on the doorknob. His gut ached. It had to be the ulcer, not just the jealousy. It had to be. He snatched the Tums bottle off his nightstand, tossed two back before swinging open the door only to find Hunter standing there, fist poised, ready to knock.

"You okay?" she asked, her cheeks burning an even brighter and more beautiful pink than before. The way it offset her golden curls made Austin want to grab her by the back of the neck and smash his lips against hers and taste every luscious inch of her warm skin.

Instead, he only nodded. "Yeah. I'm fine. Just . . . work stuff. I had an idea, and I had to run in here to send myself a voicemail message so I wouldn't forget it."

Liar!

She didn't believe him. He could see it in her eyes, the skepticism, the hurt. Fuck, the last thing Austin wanted to do was hurt her.

Her lips pursed, and she gave him a tight smile, one that didn't even make it close to her amber eyes. "Oh. okay, then. I guess. I just came to tell you that dinner is ready."

Busy chastising himself for his behavior, Austin's head snapped up from where he'd been studying his feet. "Oh! Uh . . . all right, then. Thanks."

She gave him another nod, then spun on her heels before turning back. "You know, you can talk to me. I'm not a bad person. In fact, some people have even gone so far as to say I'm *nice*. If something's bothering you, we can talk about it. I'm a pretty good listener. If it's work problems, maybe I can help. I'm no engineer with a fancy degree, but I'm a pretty good problem solver. First to get out of the escape room. I find Waldo before anyone else." Her lips turned up into a smile that made Austin's heart swell in his chest.

He licked his own lips, wondering how hers might taste. "Thanks. I will keep that in mind."

Taking a step forward she rested her hand on his arm. Austin's temperature ratcheted up, and his cock leaped in his jeans. "We could be friends," she said.

Did her eyebrow just lift a little? Was she implying something besides friendship? Lord knows Austin wanted more, even if he knew it was impossible.

Even if she wasn't implying anything sexual, Austin's head immediately went there, and paranoia swamped him that his erection might now be visible beneath his jeans. "I don't have a lot of friends," he whispered.

Her smile grew wider and warmer as she squeezed his arms a little harder. Austin's insides dissolved to mush. "I'm a good friend to have."

"I bet you are. You're incredible. You seem like the sweetest, most caring and genuine person I've ever met. I didn't know they still made them like you."

Where the fuck did that just come from?

Her eyes went wide.

His mouth dropped open. Oh God, what must she think of him?

"Uh... what I mean is, yeah? Discounts on organic clothes and handcuffs?"

Hurt clouded her face.

Fuck. Filter, Austin! Think before you speak.

Her lips pursed again into a thin white line before she spoke. "Yeah, discounts. Call me when you need new underwear."

Austin opened his mouth to say something, but snapped it shut. Hunter eyed him suspiciously, sadness and disappointment coming off her in waves.

She let out a loud, long exhale that said *so* much. "All right then, well. Dinner's ready." Then, wringing her hands in front of her, she turned around and softly scuffed her cute little slippered feet down the hallway back toward the kitchen.

Austin smacked the heel of his palm to his forehead and closed his eyes.

Stupid, stupid, STUPID!

CHAPTER EIGHT

Will set his empty drink down on the arm of the chair, the ice rattling gently, reminding him he needed to get up and get another. He stared aimlessly into the fire crackling in the hearth. Austin might be a nerd unable to close a deal with a cute little blonde who was into him, but he could build a mean fire. Had Will ever made a fire before? Had he even been camping? He couldn't remember.

"It's really coming down out there." Juney yawned, snuggling up tight next to Rowan on the couch. He wrapped an arm around her and pulled her close, planting a smacking smooch on the side of her head. The other four watched the two lovers, envying how easily the intimacy between them seemed to have emerged literally overnight. Sure, there'd been looks and smirks between the two as they all got to know one another last night, but if Will were going to put his money on any couple hooking up on the first night, it would have been him and Amber. It certainly hadn't been Hunter and Austin. Those two were on different planets, they were so far apart at the moment.

"Oh, yeah," he muttered, tipping back his scotch. "Total

whiteout." Will turned around, unable to watch the mush in front of him any longer. That should be him and Amber, but he'd stupidly gone and fallen asleep last night, and then the rest of the day had been awkward as all hell.

"Isn't there a hot tub?" Hunter asked, biting her lip before taking a sip of her wine, her cheeks flushed and eyes bright as she sat in front of the fire. Austin was next to her on the floor among a bunch of pillows, but he managed to keep his distance, having childishly created a wall of cushions between them.

Amber nodded. "Yeah, there is, right off the patio. Did everyone bring a swim suit?"

There were nods all around.

Her smile made lust roar into his cock. "Well then, what are we waiting for? Let's top off our drinks, suit up and get wet."

Will groaned under his breath at her choice of words. He wanted Amber to get wet all right. He wanted her fucking saturated, and before the night was through, he would make damn sure she was, his name on her lips as she filled his mouth with her release.

It was no more than five minutes of grabbing towels and changing into suits before six half-naked bodies stood outside with chattering teeth, goosebumps chasing across their skin and Will hopping back and forth on his feet. The deck was freezing. Although the little dance wasn't exactly *manly*—he felt like a bit of a garden fairy—somehow it felt right and staved off the frosty bite.

"Brrrr." Hunter shivered, pulling her towel tight around her bare shoulders as they all stood on the freshly cleared patio, waiting for Rowan to lift the hot tub cover.

Austin had busied himself earlier that day when they'd first gotten back from the ski hill and shoveled the driveway, clearing a path to the woodshed and around the deck. So even though it was frigid outside, they weren't ankle-deep in snow and close to losing a toe or two.

Juney and Rowan had prepped dinner, and Hunter and Amber had set the table, swept the floor and hung up everyone's wet clothes over the heater in the garage. Will had grabbed a scotch, sat in the living room, and read a book. He loved being on vacation.

"Ah, there we go!" Rowan said with a satisfied smile, flopping the big cover over and sending fluffy snow flying all around as it landed on the deck with a loud *thud*. Steam rose quick and thick up in the air, but no one wasted any time admiring it. They all slid in.

There were "Ahs" all around as chilly and sore bodies slipped into the warm water and found a seat and jet to soothe overworked muscles.

"I'm going to feel it tomorrow," Amber drawled, tipping her drink and taking a healthy sip. "I haven't boarded in years. I'm not sure I'll be able to move in the morning. My quads were screaming at me on that last run. I might even sleep in tomorrow."

Hunter smiled through clenched teeth as she sucked in air. "Oh, yeah . . . sleep in. I guess we can do that, can't we? We're on vacation. I can't remember the last time I truly slept in. You know, wake up closer to lunch than breakfast. God, it's been years."

Juney shook her head. "Me, either. It's up at the crack of dawn, off to yoga, then work, and then I write until midnight. Only to do it all over again the next day."

The girls yawned and nodded in agreement. "Yeah, I run," Hunter said sleepily, "yoga on Wednesdays and Sundays."

"I prefer kickboxing, myself," Amber added. "Helps get out my frustrations with some of the bone-headed men I work with. I can't exactly lose my shit the way I'd like to and be taken seriously, so I envision their ugly mugs when I'm sparring with a partner or hitting the bag. They'd all tell you I'm a super *zen* boss, but in reality I want to drop-kick at least one of them daily."

Will snorted.

Damn, she was tough.

He loved it. He studied the little redheaded pixie in the corner as she clutched her wine glass in her hand and closed her eyes from the pleasure of the jet behind her. He only managed to catch a glimpse of her body in her bathing suit before she sank down beneath the bubbles, but that glimpse had been enough to make his cock start to rise in his shorts. He was thankful for the water and the secrets it kept.

No-nonsense, just like Amber, her bikini was small and black. Three simple triangles, but damn if those triangles didn't turn him on. And the rest of her body was like alabaster, with peachy freckles across her chest and on her arms. He wanted to find out what each one tasted like. And tonight he would. Will had stopped drinking and traded his scotch for water. The others were still imbibing on wine, beer and scotch, but he wanted to be alert and present for Amber. He wasn't going to miss another opportunity to hear the little red kitten purr his name.

Amber rolled her bottom lip between her teeth. Was she even conscious of how damn sexy, how sensuous and seductive she was being right now? Probably not. She glanced out into the ravine below, and Will took a moment to watch her. An unencumbered view of the beauty. Slowly, her little pink tongue darted out and ran between the seam of her lips.

Oh, fuck me now.

He wanted to lick those lips. He wanted to bite them. Fuck, he wanted to lick and bite more than that lip, he wanted every goddamn inch of her beneath his hot tongue as he savored her taste. He wanted to sink deep inside her sweet pussy lips and apologize profusely for his stupidity of the night before. Never again would he choose sleep over fucking Amber.

Never.

Now, if only the puppies would leave so he could take his little redhead right here and right now, under the stars. His cock jerked in his shorts again. Yes, he needed to get rid of the others.

AUSTIN HAD BEEN RATHER quiet since dinner. He'd ducked out twice since tidying up to shovel the driveway or make sure enough wood was in for the fireplace. Having designated himself the house pyro, he was diligent in his responsibility of ensuring there was always fresh wood on the fire and lots of newspaper crinkled up and ready to go in the event the fire did go out.

He had a lot to think about, and the monotonous tasks helped. His little temper tantrum after Sam's departure and his chat with Juney on the chairlift had been eye-opening. But at the same time, it made him worry more than ever that he wouldn't be able to hold a candle to the other men Hunter had been with. That she would grow bored with him within months, if not days. What was the point of even trying? It'd been like a knife in the gut watching her laugh and chat it up with Will earlier, though, as the two goofed around on the hill, pushing each other over and smiling. He wanted that. Why couldn't he have that? And wasn't Will interested in Amber? What the hell?

He peeked over at the curvaceous blonde, who sat in one of the shallower seats, her breasts bobbing near the surface.

Jesus Christ, why the hell'd she have to go and wear *that*? Was it even a bathing suit?

It looked like three of his grandmother's doilies. Crocheted sage-colored patches that covered (just barely) her breasts and cleft. His doctor had warned him that overworking could lead to a heart attack. But the man hadn't bothered to mention that a vexatious blonde with a fetish for leather, lace, and lascivious sexual proclivities, with breasts so perfect he couldn't help but wonder if they were real, might also cause him to have a jammer. Or at the very least a stroke from a blood clot as his veins fought to pump enough blood up to his brain, because at the moment, it was all between his legs. Might as well call the EMTs now, because sharing a hot tub with Hunter in those scraps of fabric was surely going to kill him in some way.

He sipped his drink, enjoying the way the alcohol numbed his limbs and brain. His big brain that never stopped thinking, never stopped *overthinking*. Could he go to Hunter's room tonight? Knock on her door and kiss her? Could they start off slow? Did he want to start off slow? Did she?

"You look like you're trying to solve the world's energy crisis over there," Juney said with a laugh, her head resting on Rowan's shoulder as the two snuggled up sickly sweet in one of the corners, both of their hands hidden beneath the bubbles. Austin could only imagine the debauchery going on under the water right now.

Hunter snorted. "He probably is."

Austin's eyes flicked up to Hunter's, and she gave him a big, genuine toothy grin. Was that her third or fourth glass of wine?

"Are you?" she asked. Apparently she'd forgiven him for his comment earlier. Or the wine was numbing her frustration.

He glanced down into his glass and swirled the ice around for a second. "Sure. Maybe not the *world's* energy crisis, but a crisis for sure."

"I bet I know what the *crisis* is," Rowan said under his breath against Juney's temple.

She elbowed him, and he just snickered.

A warm tingle wormed its way into Austin's cheeks, and the tips of his ears prickled with heat. He averted his gaze and instead glanced up at the dark gray clouds. It had stopped snowing. But not for long. The forecast was calling for another eight to twelve inches.

Snowed in and set up, indeed.

Only now it was starting to feel like snowed in, set up, and slowly suffocated.

"Hey, you've got a tat, too," Will said lazily, noting the ink on Hunter's shoulder.

Austin sat up straighter. Oh yeah, that tattoo he'd been ogling the corner of all last night. Finally, he was going to get a glimpse of the whole thing.

Hunter contorted her body around so everyone could see. "Yeah, it's a flock of birds. A tad morose, but each bird represents a foster home I was in. There are seven in total."

Will whistled. "Jesus."

She shrugged. "Ah, it wasn't so bad. Made me tough and independent. I've heard some foster home horror stories, and I don't have any of my own, so I consider myself lucky. I bounced around the system a bit because families couldn't keep me for very long. Either they moved, had their own kids' issues to deal with, or couldn't make ends meet even with the subsidy they got from the government for me. A couple of families were a little neglectful, using me as a cash cow and spending the money meant for my needs on themselves. I didn't last long with them."

"So, the birds are more like a badge of honor or a symbol of freedom?" Juney asked.

Hunter nodded. "In a way, yeah. I wouldn't be who I am today without each of those foster homes, each of those birds. But at the same time, they don't really define who I am, you know? I'm not a foster kid. I'm Hunter Kingsley, owner of Breathe, Babe, Breathe. I'm my own person, free of my past, free of it all. I dunno. I saw the sketch when I was seventeen and carried it around in my wallet for nearly six years before I finally got it put on me permanently. I love it."

Everyone nodded.

"It's beautiful," Juney added.

"Thank you. You have tats, too?" Hunter asked, turning back to Will.

He nodded and then stood up, the water sluicing off his body in dark rivers. He spun around and showed everyone his calf. It was the head of a proud male lion with a shaggy mane and open mouth, exposing ferocious sharp teeth. Because Will was so dark-skinned and the only light from inside the house was from the Christmas tree, it was tough to make out. But you could see enough to know what it was.

"That's cool," Rowan said. "You a Leo or something?"

Will made a noise in his throat and sat back down in the water. "No. I got this right after my trip to Africa. A lion came into the local village I was working in and started to drag away a kid. There was a drought; everyone was hungry, including the animals. And the lions were getting desperate."

Gasps echoed around the hot tub.

"Holy freaking shit," Rowan said, his mouth just hanging open and his eyes bugging out. The rest held similar expressions.

Will nodded and lifted one shoulder. "Yeah, anyway, I'm not entirely sure what happened. I think I blocked a lot of it out. But somehow in my sleep-deprived, thirsty, heat-stroked brain, I thought it would be a good idea to go after the lion. I leaped onto him, and he released the kid, then went after me. But by this time, the game warden had arrived. They ended up putting the cat down. He was getting too comfortable and used to humans. It would have happened again at some point."

"Jesus Christ," Hunter muttered. "So, you decided to get its face tattooed on your leg?"

"To cover up the scars of its teeth marks, yeah."

"Isn't there a movie like that out there?" Austin asked.

Will took a sip of his water and lifted one eyebrow. "Yep.

Watched it on the plane ride back. Talk about reliving a nightmare."

Everyone continued to shake their heads, new admiration and a dash of awe on their faces.

"See, I don't hate kids. I saved one from being eaten by a lion, for crying out loud. I just don't want any of my own." A nervous chuckle bubbled up through his chest. Austin gave the man an appraising look. Normally Will came across so confident, almost to the point of being cocky, but right now he seemed downright uncomfortable. What was going on?

"That's a pretty crazy story," Austin finally said, his eyes taking in the way Amber was looking at him, as if he'd just saved *her* from the clutches of a starving jungle cat.

Will shrugged. "Not really. You hear all kinds of tales like that in Africa. I honestly don't even like talking about it." He swirled his empty scotch glass around, letting the ice tinkle. He'd switched to a big bottle of water after he drained his drink and had been nursing that for the last ten minutes. "But when I'm in the sauce, I tend to share a little more. Loose lips and all that."

Austin grunted and finished off his drink. "Loose lips."

Eventually everyone fell into a bit of a companionable silence. Juney and Rowan huddled up tight in the corner, hands beneath the frothy water. Amber and Will sat on opposing corners, avoiding each other's eyes. Hunter was in the remaining corner, and Austin was left to sit awkwardly in the middle on the bench, between the two lovebirds who were undoubtedly doing hand stuff under the water and Hunter, whose breasts were practically heaving out of her tiny and tight crocheted bikini top. He didn't know where to look. So rather than looking anywhere, he closed his eyes, tilted his head back and sank down into the heat as deep as he could, until nothing but his face was visible. Yeah, that ought to solve *all* his problems.

. . .

AMBER'S HEART beat wildly in her chest. Jesus Christ, the way Will was looking at her—she knew she was in a hot tub, but damn, she was wet. Those eyes . . . they said so much. And everything they said was downright filthy.

"Well, I think I am sufficiently pruney," Rowan said with a yawn, standing up and stretching, a noticeable bulge at the front of his shorts, especially since they clung to his wet legs. "I'm going to go have a shower and head to bed. Are you pruney, Juney?" He snickered at his silly rhyme and smiled down at her, offering her his hand. Juney took his hand and stood up, her hot pink bikini doing all kinds of justice to her lithe and dripping frame.

"I think I'm ready for bed, too," she said, following Rowan over to the step and allowing him to help her out. He wrapped a towel around her shoulders and rubbed the sides of her arms several times.

"All right guys, well, Merry Christmas Eve and goodnight. We shall see you all tomorrow. Hopefully Santa Claus brings you what you want." Rowan winked at Austin, then at Will and finally grinned wickedly at the other two girls before placing his hand at the small of Juney's back and ushering her toward the French doors.

"Cocky fucker," Will grumbled.

Amber snickered. "Wouldn't you be?"

Will's eyes flashed from the door to her face, his dark brown eyes blazing pure fire. "Abso-*fucking*-lutely, but at the moment I'm just a dumb fucker who fell asleep when I should have been wide awake."

She sucked on her bottom lip. The way Will stared at her was pure animal, and if it wasn't for the other two sitting like slack-jawed mutes in the other corners, she would be on his lap already, with her hands down his shorts, stroking him, the way she knew Juney had been stroking Rowan. They may have tried to hide it, but Amber was no innocent little virgin. She recognized the rhythmic twitch of Juney's shoulder and the slanted looks the two gave each other. Not to mention the quick inhales and sudden hard swallows of their throats as they fought the urge to orgasm in front of everyone. A part of her wished they had. She wouldn't have cared. Hell, it may have galvanized the rest of them to act on their urges.

She also couldn't deny the stab of jealousy that swamped her as Will and Hunter goofed off up on the hill earlier that day, or their comfortable chit-chat about tattoos. Amber had always wanted a tattoo; she just hadn't found the right image yet. Things between Will and the curvy blonde just seemed so easy. Hunter made Will smile, she made him laugh, and they were able to talk the way Amber only wished she could talk to Will. She and Rowan had chatted on the chairlift with such ease. Why couldn't she have that with Will? And yet, you couldn't deny the attraction between Austin and Hunter. The way he looked at her, the way she looked at him. What the hell was the blonde hottie's angle? Was she trying to string both men along until she decided which man she wanted? Which man was her *match*? Amber ground her molars together at the memory of seeing Will push Hunter over on her board and then, in retaliation, Hunter throwing snowballs at him until he fell over laughing.

"All right, you two," Will finally said, donning his best *boss-man-doctor* voice. "I think it's time the *kiddies* went to bed."

Hunter gave him a petulant look but rolled her eyes and motioned to stand up.

"I think the grownups need to have some *grownup* time. I ain't saying you have to go to bed . . . unless that's your *plan*." He waggled his dark eyebrows at Austin. Austin shot laser beams from his eyes, trying to blow off Will's head. "But we'd like the hot tub to ourselves now."

Amber's mouth was suddenly like a sand pit, and the heat

from the hot tub was nothing compared with the raging inferno inside her.

Yippee!

Apparently Will hadn't given up hope. He wanted to try again tonight. And from the looks of things, he had stopped drinking and had switched to water. The man was on a mission, and that mission was to give her holly jolly orgasms. Did this mean he had no interest in Hunter? He'd just shooed her and Austin inside, which meant he was choosing Amber. Amber's heart rate picked up and heat and moisture pooled between her legs. No wonder her mouth was so dry.

"All right, all right," Hunter grumbled, but not without flashing a big grin Amber's way. She ducked her head next to Amber's ear as she sat up and crossed to the steps. "At least one of us is getting lucky tonight. Enjoy." Then she sashayed her curvaceous hips over to the stairs and climbed out, wrapping a towel around her body before heading to the door.

Austin continued to sit there like a goober. What the hell was up with him? Did he have snow in his ears and didn't hear Will's "request"? Amber's gaze followed the younger man's eyes, which were glued to Hunter's backside, and then it dawned on her.

Will chuckled low and deep in his ripped chest. "Need a minute, man?"

It hadn't bothered Rowan in the slightest to stand up and leave the hot tub with a bulge in his pants, but Austin didn't seem nearly as confident or carefree. Maybe if he was getting laid, he wouldn't care. But the fact that he still hadn't made a move on Hunter probably left him feeling as though showing the rest of them his raging hard-on was a bit of a faux pas.

Austin's eyes swiveled from Hunter's back to Will's head. His glare was enough to melt steel.

A man on a mission, and that mission was to fuck Amber silly under the shifting clouds and peeking stars, Will reached for her hand, pulling her across the bench seat and settling her into his lap.

"There, dude. Now the lady can't see your shorts. And here, I'll distract her even more for you." Will grabbed Amber's ponytail and roughly pulled her head toward him, capturing her mouth with his. Amber's belly did a giant somersault as his hot velvety tongue swept inside and began to explore.

Finally, dude! Finally!

She let her hands float up to rest on his broad shoulders, brazenly pushing the juncture of her spread thighs against his shorts. He was already hard.

Not caring one iota that Austin might still be in the water, she rocked against Will's length, unable to hide or control the moan that escaped her from the rush of pleasure that sparked inside her as the fabric of her suit and his erection brushed her clit. He felt so good, so right. His body, big and hard, warm and strong. And when he kissed her, damn if those butterflies didn't multiply and start going off in a million different directions. The man's lips were like soft, pouty pillows, taking her own lips on a dance so erotic, so evocative, they sent her imagination running wild. What would these delicious lips of his feel like lower down her body? She could only imagine: satiny smooth, just like his tongue. Wet, warm, plump, sensuous. Oh so sensuous. The man had a mouth that could kiss like nobody's business, and when he smiled, when he said her name, that mouth was begging to be sat on.

The gentle *click* of the door barely even registered with Amber, but she knew they were finally alone. She decided enough was enough. They were alone now. Clothing was completely optional. With a whinge of reluctance, she pulled her mouth from Will's and brought her hands up around her neck to untie the halter of her bikini. He went to work on the strings at her back, and within a matter of seconds, her breasts tumbled free, bobbing in the water between them, against his titanium chest.

With a rough growl, Will dipped his head low and drew a nipple into his mouth, biting the tender nub and tugging hard enough to make her arch her back and moan softly. Pleasure shot fast and fierce through her body like a lightning bolt, hitting the target between her legs with overwhelming accuracy. He moved his mouth over to the other side and delivered the same delicious torture to the other one, drawing the nub into his warm mouth, sucking hard and then quickly flicking his tongue back and forth until she groaned again and wilted further into his arms.

He was rock-hard now, and Amber wanted nothing more than to feel Will, to feel all of him. She wedged her hands between them and fished him out of the hole of his shorts, bringing his length into her palm and stroking him. He was big, like *really* big, and a slight wave of panic swam through her at the idea of taking him inside her. She was no virgin, but she also wasn't a very big person.

Would it work? Would they fit? God, she hoped so.

WILL's hands made their way down Amber's body, resting on her rocking hips and encouraging her to continue to press her cleft against him. It felt so good having her on his lap. Her skin beneath his palms, her delicate frame perched in his lap, it felt right. Deftly, without even missing a moment from suckling her sweet nipples, he released the ties of her bathing suit bottoms, pulling the fabric out from between her legs and tossing it onto the deck. Now the only thing between them was his shorts, and that was quickly going to change.

Snatching her ponytail and lifting his head from her breast, he crashed his mouth down on hers once again, shoving his tongue into her mouth, sweeping around and claiming her. She responded in kind and opened her lips, stroking her hot little tongue against his in encouragement. Nipping his lip, she pulled with her teeth, grinning against his mouth. A girly giggle bubbled up in her chest.

That giggle was music to Will's ears. So sweet, so sultry. But it also had a roughness to it. Throaty and mature. The perfect definition of Amber. She was a complex woman, not a simple coin with two sides, no. There was so much more to Amber than met the eye. She came across all stubborn and aloof. Unaffected by the issues that plagued most people—most *women*. When Hunter had moaned about breaking a nail earlier, Amber had snorted in derision and then laughed. Or when Juney mentioned her favorite guilty pleasure was a manicure followed by a hot bubble bath, Amber had rolled her eyes and said she couldn't remember the last time she had paint on her fingernails and wouldn't dream of wasting time in a bath.

Determined to play the part of the tough-as-nails boss, because that's who she was all the time, Amber had a shell nearly as hard as Will's. He didn't like letting people in either. But Will saw past that. He saw that behind the understated ponytail at the nape of her neck and the flannel shirt and black jeans, she had a softness to her. Many layers. Many sides. He hoped as the days went on, she would let him see more of those sides, and not just the hard-headed foreman with girl-next-door freckles across her nose that she was showing everyone else.

He still had her by the hair, so pulling again, he separated them. Smiling wickedly, he scooped her up and placed her on the edge of the tub, making her sit out in the cool December night air. She was exquisite, her skin almost translucent in the light from the Christmas tree. Her eyes shone brightly back at him, full of lust as he took her all in. She was bare, and the sweet, plump, pink lips of her pussy drew his gaze like a beacon.

A quick tear of Velcro and the loosening of some string, and he was out of his shorts, tossing them onto the deck next to her suit. He had a condom in his pocket, so he needed to keep them close, but right now he wanted to taste her. Figuring she wouldn't mind if he was a bit rough, he knelt down on the bench beneath the water, palmed her thighs and spread them wide. He cupped her butt and drew her to his mouth, humming when he found her sweetness. She was wet and ready. Dripping. For him.

One long, slow lick into her, and she was groaning, her hips jerking up into his mouth. He hummed softly as he swept his tongue again up through her folds, sucking fiercely on her swelling clit and reveling in the way it hardened against his lips as she bucked into his face. But he took it as an invitation and rammed his tongue into her cleft, feeling the ridges of her walls contract around him as he fucked her, hard and swift. Her soft cries and girlish moans spurred him on. He slipped a finger inside her, resuming circles and sucks on her clit.

She was tight, really tight. Would she be able to take him? Fuck, he hoped so. At this point, he would settle for just the tip if he had to. Any bit of Amber he could get, he would take. An internal quake inside her grabbed his fingers in an unreal heat, and his cock grew long and thick, aching for some action.

She was sweet like honey. Her juices were unlike anything he'd ever tasted, and her skin was pure silk against his lips as he lashed at her clit and nipped her inner thighs. She tugged on his ears, pulling him deeper between her legs, making his nose knock her mound. So feisty, so in command of what she wanted and willing to take it.

He loved that.

Will didn't want a submissive partner, he wanted an equal, one who challenged him, who was her own boss, independent and fierce. Amber was proving to be all those things and then some.

"Fuck . . . Will . . ." she breathed, pushing even harder into his face, thrusting forward, her legs trembling.

He lifted them up and put them on his shoulders. She sighed from the reprieve and then shoved into him again. So greedy, so willing to take everything he gave her.

"Will . . ."

"Come for me, Amber. Come hard, baby." He wanted to hear her, feel her, taste her as she came. How loud, how wild could his Little Red get? How senseless could he make her? He wanted her to lose her head, hear his name from her lips as he made her lose control.

Her fingers tightened around the ends of his hair, and she threw her head back. Her chest, illuminated by the glare of the Christmas lights inside the house, glowed as it rose and fell with her quick and shallow breaths.

Parting her lips, she broke with a sharp cry. "Will . . . oh God . . . Will . . . fuck . . . yes!"

Her pussy gripped his fingers like a fist as she filled his mouth with a sweet warm gush, her clit swelling hard against his tongue as he continued to feast, loving the sounds she made as she came.

She was his.

Even if it was only for the week, Amber was his. This little sprite had him hypnotized, and the way his name flowed off her lips made him wonder how he could keep her saying his name like that for the rest of his life.

Ignoring her frozen butt cheeks and the chill that sprinted up and down her limbs, Amber flopped back onto the deck, her arm draped dramatically over her eyes. Her chest rose and fell as if she'd just run a marathon.

Holy mother of God, that tongue, that man.

He was relentless, absolutely relentless. Right when she

thought she was going to tumble over the edge, he would nip her thigh or suck her clit like it was a fucking lollipop, dragging her back from the precipice. She'd been teetering there for so long, she had no idea how long Will had been eating her out. Was it a few minutes? A few hours? A few days? Had the new year come and gone? She had no idea; time no longer existed. All that mattered was the man in front of her and the incredible pleasure he was delivering.

Two big, strong hands came up under her arms, and she suddenly found herself back beneath the water. The rush of heat made her body tingle and sting, her senses waking up again from the sudden coma they'd been fucked into. She fluttered her lashes open and looked at Will. He was all smiles, his chin and lips still glistening with her arousal.

"You're gorgeous," he said softly, setting them back down into their original spot, her straddling his lap, while his cock bobbed hard and ready at her sensitive center. "And the way you come . . . Oh, baby. So beautiful. I could watch you come every day."

She squirmed uncomfortably at his words, but she also couldn't deny the heady rush she got from knowing how he felt about her. She let her hands graze his incredible abs; powerful muscles filled her palms, and heat pooled in her abdomen. She wasn't the only gorgeous person in this hot tub. Will was a goddamn work of art.

"I want to fuck you, Amber," he said, his eyes sobering and snagging her gaze.

She blinked from his honesty, and a sudden bubble of uncomfortable laughter shot out through her mouth before she could stop it. "Okay . . . I want to fuck you too."

He shook his head somberly. "I just don't want to hurt you. I'm . . . I'm big."

She swallowed and brought her hand back down between them, wrapping her fingers around his length. Sweet baby Jesus, he was big! Huge. Could she take him? She wanted to try. God, how she wanted to try.

"I want to try," she said, biting her lip. "I'm tough."

A smile tugged at the corner of his mouth. "Oh, I know you are. I think you might be the toughest woman I've ever met, and damn feisty. I don't want to hurt you, though."

Swallowing hard, she lifted up, the crown of him probing her cleft, demanding sanctuary. She motioned to drop down, but he stopped her with a hand on her shoulder.

"Condom."

"Oh. Right."

In less than twelve seconds, Will had fished the packet out of his pocket and sheathed himself, sinking down into the water and helping Amber climb back up on his lap. "Go slow, baby. Real slow, okay?"

"Okay," she breathed.

"You don't have to take it all just to prove something." Affection and concern colored his voice.

A smirk tickled her mouth. She lunged forward and snagged his bottom lip between her teeth, simultaneously starting to take him inside her. "I'll prove whatever the fuck I want to." She growled, releasing his lip. She gasped when she started to feel the stretch. Another quick inhale had her gritting her teeth and shutting her eyes. Damn it, the hot tub had washed away all her arousal. He was going in dry.

"Breathe."

"You are *fucking* huge."

"You are also *really* tight."

"Yeah. Well, it's been a while," she muttered, her teeth still clenched.

"Breathe," he said again.

"Shut up."

Will chuckled softly, his hands coming up and kneading her

breasts, tweaking and pulling on the nipples until they were hard and practically screeching for his mouth. Amber continued to sink down on to his lap. Inch by glorious inch she took him, and the more she took, the better it felt. He was stretching her, pressing against the walls of her channel so hard she was able to feel everything, all of him.

With a final low belly groan, she dropped that last inch, and her eyes nearly rolled into the back of her head.

"You are the sexiest fucking woman I have ever met." His voice a low and feral growl. He released one hand from her breast and brought it down between them to rub her clit. "Go as slow as you need, baby."

She shook her head. "I'm okay." She didn't want slow; she didn't want gentle. Now that she knew she could take all of Will, she wanted hot and dirty, hard and fast. She wanted to be fucked senseless, the way he'd been promising.

Resting her hands on his shoulders, she began to bob up and down in his lap, first slowly, just to establish a rhythm, but then quickly picking up speed and vigor, loving the way he split her open, the way he grazed her walls and knocked her cervix. She felt everything, every hard, powerful inch of him, and it all felt incredible. Water sloshed all around them, a tsunami of their making, up over the sides, melting the snow that had frozen to the deck and sloshing down between the planks to the ground below.

Will snarled against her breast as he pulled a peak into his mouth and lashed at it with his tongue. "You feel so good," he mumbled. "Fucking tight."

"Harder," Amber demanded. "Faster." Bliss, jagged and hard in its reality, hovered just inches out of reach. She needed a new position. She needed him deeper.

Their eyes locked for half a second, blazing hazel to a raging brown fire. Will bucked into her harder. She had proven she could take him and wasn't in pain, and she was asking for it, demanding he take her hard and fast, so he was going to oblige.

"D-doggy style," she stammered, her eyes suddenly glazing over when he pinched her clit.

Will's eyes flashed back up to her face. Holy mother of God, she was his perfect woman. The last few women he'd been with hadn't been able to take him in this position. It'd been too painful for them. His heart thudded in his throat at the possibility of taking Amber from behind and her enjoying it. But he had to be careful, too. He didn't want to hurt her.

"Are you sure, baby? This position isn't easy with a big dick."

Ignoring him, Amber quickly slipped off of his lap and stood up, planting her knees on the bench seat of the tub, her hands on the upper ledge.

"Take me, Will," she breathed. "I want you like this, now."

She's fucking perfect.

With a low and primitive growl, Will ducked down and rammed his tongue into her pussy. He needed her sopping wet and on the verge of a climax if she was going to take him in this position. She mewled and pushed back into his face, her sweet heat softening and swelling against his lips. Around and around he swirled his tongue, only to plunge it deep into her quivering channel. She trembled against him, and her wetness poured over his tongue. He lapped it up and hummed, enjoying her flavor. Once he knew his Little Red was good and ready, he stood up, chuckling at her grumble of protest. He positioned himself behind her, gripped her hips and then slowly, carefully wedged himself inside.

"Faster!" she demanded.

Oh dear sweet lord, yes.

But he quelled his excitement. "You okay?"

"Yes," she gritted impatiently. "Deeper, Will, please." He sank the last couple of inches into her luscious heat, both of them groaning in satisfaction. Amber pushed back into Will and he bucked into her. The muscular rounds of her sculpted ass beckoned for him to grab them. One day, if this lasted more than the week, he hoped she'd let him take her there, let him fuck her sweet ass as he teased her clit with a vibrator.

His balls ached from how full they were, and the way her snug little pussy grabbed his shaft and refused to let go had Will doing everything in his power to stave off his release. But Amber's moans and grunts grew louder, fiercer, and the way she squeezed herself around him, he wasn't going to last much longer.

Fuck, he needed to get her there.

Reaching around under her, past her belly, he delved two fingers between her slick lips. Her clit was hard, and with each brush of his fingers, he felt it swell. She was close, too.

"Get ready, Little Red."

"Will, please," she begged, her voice husky and hoarse from lack of use.

He brought her clit between his thumb and forefinger, and as he pulled out, he pinched her slick bud and then drove home one more time. Amber shot off like a rocket, her body stilling and then rippling around him as the orgasm took hold, gripping her body and thrashing her around as if she were not more than a rag doll. Will stiffened behind her, and his fingers dug wells into the plump flesh of her ass as he found his release. The sweet contractions of her core milked him, drew him in as he spilled himself inside her. He tilted his head back and let out a low and surly roar, continuing to move, thrust after thrust, hammering into Amber until every last morsel of him was inside her. One day soon they'd have the birth control conversation and he would find out if she meant what she said about not wanting kids. He wanted skin-to-skin with Amber. Nothing between them. Ever.

CHAPTER NINE

Juney blinked. Once, twice, three times, a slow, placid smile spread across her face as she took in the man next to her. Rowan was awake, wide awake. And he was watching her.

"Good morning," she yawned, reaching out from under the covers and cupping his scruffy blond chin.

"Merry Christmas, Juniper," he said softly. His hand came up, and he covered hers, leaning into her touch and briefly closing his eyes.

Juney's chest tightened. It was such a simple act, and yet it meant so much.

"Merry Christmas, Rowan."

"What were you dreaming about? Book stuff?"

"Was I dreaming?" She yawned, pulling her hand away and instead scooting in close to him and draping her arm across his chest. He helped her tuck her head into the crook of his arm and draped those sexy muscles around her. She snuggled right in.

"Yeah, I think so. Your nose would wrinkle now and then, and you mumbled a few things."

"Damn, was I giving you spoilers in my sleep?"

His deep, warm chuckle wrapped around her like a cashmere throw. "I didn't hear any specifics. I'd plug my ears if I thought it would ruin the book for me."

"Oh, good. I can't remember what I was dreaming about. I rarely can."

"I had a great dream." His free hand came up and tucked under his head.

She lifted her head and swiveled her neck to look at him. "Oh, yeah? What about?"

"You, buck naked wearing nothing but an apron, a chef's hat, and black stilettos. You were sitting on the stainless steel counter in a big restaurant-style kitchen, holding a wooden spatula and patting it against your palm."

Juney swallowed. "And what were *you* doing?"

"I was finishing up a crudité."

She laughed. Of course he was cooking. He was *always* cooking. But she loved that he had a passion. Something that woke him up in the morning, drove him to succeed, to excel, to strive for the top. Rowan's tenacity was incredibly sexy, and his food was damn good, too.

"Ah, but then once I cleaned up and you tried my meal—you loved it, by the way—you begged me to toss you down face-first onto the counter, hike up your apron and fuck you from behind. Then you handed me the spatula and ordered me to spank your ass."

"I did not!"

That smile. Those dimples. They would be the end of Juney.

"My dream, baby. You certainly did." Rowan removed his hand from behind his head and grabbed Juney's. He drew it down beneath the sheets to where his cock lay long and thick against his taut belly. She gripped it, and he moaned. She gripped it harder, and he moaned louder.

"You'd like that, wouldn't you?" he asked, his voice a rough timber as she slowly snaked her hand a tad lower and cupped his balls, squeezing ever so slightly, earning the quick inhale from his lips she was seeking. "Me tanning your sweet ass as I pleasure you from behind. Taking you hard and fast."

Licking her lips, Juney brought her gaze up to meet Rowan's. There was no iris left in his eyes; it was all pupil, all lust, all need. Her hand moved beneath the sheets; back and forth she stroked him, loving the way he continued to grow and harden in her palm. Silky-soft, but so very hard.

"Tell me, Juney. Tell me your fantasies. I'd like to make them a reality if I could. Make you feel as special and wonderful as you truly are."

Her heart did a little *pitter-patter* inside her chest as the man she'd only known for a few days said all the right things to her, made her feel like she was the most beautiful woman on earth. A woman he wanted to cherish and spoil until death do they part.

His free hand pulled on her nipple, and she gasped from the bite of pain that set her neurons alive and sent a building pleasure sprinting through her body, ending between her legs and unfurling into a divine heat.

"Tell me, Juney. Tell me your fantasies."

Her breath audibly caught when he tugged even harder on the nipple. She closed her eyes for a few seconds and inhaled deeply. "Well, I like the dream you described. That sounds super-hot."

"Mhmm . . . and?"

"And . . . I guess I've never really had sex in too public of a place. I'd like to get it on somewhere a little risqué, maybe a bar bathroom or the backseat of a car on the ferry or in an empty movie theater. Not *too*, too public. But you know . . . "

Rowan's hand slipped down Juney's body, his fingers trailing fire along her skin. A finger pushed between her slick pussy lips, and he brushed her clit. "Yeah? Those all sound awesome. What else?"

Juney swallowed. "I . . . I've never been tied up before. That could be fun."

"It certainly could be. We might have to ask Hunter if she recommends a certain silk rope or shackles."

Juney's leg twitched when Rowan rubbed that secret spot on her clit. The spot that made her whole body quake and her brain shut down. "Yeah," she sighed, spreading her legs a little wider for him and pushing her pelvis into his inquisitive fingers.

Rowan's hand slipped away, and Juney almost reached for him. "Well, we can definitely do *all* those things and more, Miss Davis. But right now, right now I think I'd like a sweet, old-fashioned Christmas morning fuck. What do you say?"

He rolled her onto her back and covered her, his eyes holding so much more than just lust, and for a moment Juney was tempted to say something. She was tempted to tell Rowan how much she already cared for him. How he made her feel beautiful and special, that he didn't need to fulfill any of her fantasies, he was already fulfilling so much more for her than he could ever know. But she resisted the urge. It was too soon. Instead she let him settle in between her legs and wrapped her arms around his neck. They'd had the birth control conversation last night. He was clean, she was clean and had an IUD. They were good to go. Skin-to-skin.

"Get ready, baby." Rowan chuckled. "Santa's about to come down the chimney."

"Oh, you did not just say—"

But she didn't get to finish teasing him. His lips slanted over hers and his tongue wedged inside, silencing her while at the same time giving her exactly what she wanted for Christmas. Romance, the possibility of love, and hope for the future.

Juney yawned and snuggled in tighter against Rowan on the couch. It was later that morning, and they were all lazing around the living room, swaddled up tight in flannel robes and chenille throws and cradling spiked coffee. She was about to close her eyes. The Baileys in her coffee and the early morning orgasms were making her sleepy, but suddenly the television flicked on over the mantle.

"What the heck?" she asked, her eyes darting around to see who had snatched up the remote.

Heads shook and curious eyes wandered across curious faces, and then suddenly, Daisy appeared on the screen. Her loose strawberry-blonde curls jostled boisterously as she grinned at them.

"Hi, guys!" She waved. "I'm not live, so don't bother asking me any questions. But I just wanted to wish you all a big Merry Christmas and see if everyone brought their Secret Santa gift."

Groans echoed around the room, but slowly heads nodded.

"Good!" She clapped, continuing to bounce in her seat. "All right, first things first. I want everyone to put a number tag on their gift. There are gift tags in that drawer on the side table closest to the hearth. Once you've done that, put the *other* numbered tags into the velvet bag, and then everyone pick a number. Obviously, if you pick your own, try again. Got it?"

"Yes, mom," Rowan said. Nobody had to see him to know he was rolling his eyes.

"That's enough out of you, Rowan," Daisy scolded.

Rowan's back went ramrod straight and he snapped to attention, spinning around in his spot on the couch. "Okay, seriously, either we're on a nanny cam or the woman is a mind reader."

"My guess is on the nanny cam," Will said with a snort. "She strikes me as a bit of a voyeur. All sweet and innocent on the outside, but on the inside she's got some real twisted proclivities."

Amber and Hunter both laughed and nodded. Austin's face slowly turned the same color as his holly-red coffee mug.

"Yeah." Rowan nodded. "My money is on that."

"Anyway," Juney interrupted. "Moving on."

"Has everyone done what I've asked?" Daisy said on the television.

Both Rowan and Will, who were mighty comfortable all snuggled up with their women on the couch, both said "No" at the same time.

"Good!" Daisy clapped again. "Well, I'll leave you to the gift opening. You all know how to do that. Just a reminder, the shuttle is coming for you at noon on December 28th. Until then, have a wonderful time, make memories, make friends and make . . ." Her smile was sassy, and the twinkle of mischief in her bright blue eyes made everyone groan. "The most of your free matchmaking. Normally this kind of thing would have cost you a pretty penny." She giggled at her hilarity and then wished them all Merry Christmas one more time before the screen went black.

"My present is in my room," Will said with a yawn.

Amber nodded. "Mine too."

"Mine too," Austin said. He'd been rather quiet throughout the entire thing, as had Hunter.

She had shrouded herself in at least three blankets and was sitting against the hearth clutching her mug, her eyes fixed on the leg of the coffee table. "Me too," she said absently.

"Well, mine is under the tree," Juney said, getting up from her spot on the couch to go and grab a beautifully wrapped parcel with a green velvet bow.

"Of course it is," Will said cheekily.

Juney shot him a look of mock irritation as she wandered back over to the coffee table. The gift was long and narrow, and the brushed gold wrapping paper reflected the lights on the trees as she brought it over and set it on the coffee table. She hoped that whoever wound up with her gift would like it. Even though she hadn't given it a ton of thought, simply because she was just too busy with work, it was still a very nice gift. She sat back down next to Rowan with an audible huff.

"Mine's in my room too." Rowan gave Juney an affectionate rub on her thigh before hoisting himself up out of the soft, warm leather and, just like Amber, Will, Hunter and Austin, headed off to his room for the gift.

Her skin tingled where he'd touched her, and she wanted him to put his hand back.

"You're such a keener." He winked before he rounded the corner and headed down the hall.

Juney got up from her spot on the couch and went to go putter away in the kitchen. She and Rowan had been the first up, just like the day before, and they had nearly a third of Christmas dinner prepped before another Shanghaied vacationer poked their pillow-creased face into the kitchen.

Austin was the first back out to the living room, followed by Hunter. They avoided each other's eyes as best they could, but when they plopped two identical gift bags down on the table, their gazes locked.

HUNTER'S BREATH caught in her throat. Despite the fact that Austin didn't want her, the attraction she had for him wasn't going anywhere. Last night had been brutal. Between Juney and Rowan doing hand-stuff beneath the bubbling water and Amber and Will pretty much kicking them out of the hot tub so they could have sex, Hunter had had just about enough. And then there was that incredibly awkward, make you want to crawl into a hole and die, slow agonizing death moment in the hallway with

Austin, and Hunter was pretty sure this Christmas was making its quick ascension to the top of the crap pile as far as Christmases went. A bunch of people she hardly knew, love in the air for everyone but her, a man she was interested in but who clearly wanted nothing to do with her, and to top it off, she'd woken up with a headache clawing at the nape of her neck and a zit the size of Jupiter's biggest moon on her chin. Normally she wouldn't have cared, but today she did, so before she joined the masses, she troweled on the concealer until the puss geyser was covered and no more than a slight peachy bump.

Undoubtedly the zit was probably from her need to make haste the night before in the bathroom. She cringed into her coffee mug at the horrible memory . . .

"Oh. Oh, sorry," Hunter had mumbled, suddenly feeling her wine in her toes and bumping awkwardly into Austin's hard, broad chest. She hadn't been looking where she was going, her mind off in la la land and her eyes on her feet as she made her way to the bathroom, eager to shower, brush the booze off her teeth and climb into bed. Hot tubs always made her sleepy, and Santa didn't bring presents to kids who weren't in bed with visions of sugar plums doing the foxtrot through their heads and all that. She heard a faint moan down the hall from Juney's room, and a stab of envy speared her heart.

"No, uh, it's me. I'm sorry," Austin grunted, taking a step back, his toiletries bag clutched in his big palm.

Hunter's gaze drifted back down to her feet, then to the door, then the ceiling. She paused. Austin's eyes followed hers.

What was with all the mistletoe? That hadn't been there earlier in the day, had it?

Her eyes landed on Austin's lips. They were beautiful lips. Shiny and red, plump and perfect. A primal urge attacked her, and she ran her tongue between the seam of her own lips.

Austin's eyes were like laser beams, watching her every move. Had he even blinked?

She didn't move an inch, not even a millimeter. Hunter's chest rose and fell in shallow, rapid breaths. Austin's nostrils flared and his green eyes darkened to the color of red cedar boughs.

"I, uh, I don't think that was there earlier? Mistletoe seems to be popping up everywhere." She chuckled uncomfortably and rolled her bottom lip between her teeth. "Like there's a sneaky little elf somewhere hanging them in the most random places. Desperate to make everyone around here kiss."

Austin's eyelids fell to half-mast, and his Adam's apple jogged heavy in his throat.

Jesus Christ, man, fucking say something. Anything!

"Y-you go first," he finally stammered, pushing the door open for her before bringing both his hands down to the front of his pants. He held his toiletries bag in front of his lap and gestured with his head for her to go inside.

Hunter glanced into the washroom and then back to Austin's face. The man appeared terrified. She followed his gaze. He was staring at her chest.

Shit!

She had already changed into her pajamas, taken her bra off, and was in nothing more than a peachy pink tank top with the words "Breathe" over her breasts. But there was no mistaking her dusky areolas beneath the thin fabric, and her nipples had hardened to tight, painful points. She suppressed the desire to cup her breasts and relieve their sudden, heavy ache. She wanted Austin's hands on her. Austin's lips on her. Austin's body pressing hers up against the wall as he rammed his cock inside her, swift and sure.

What was his problem? He was clearly attracted to her. All the physiological signs were there. So, what was it? Did he just not like her? Was it her personality? Was he not into blondes? Had he hoped for Juney or Amber to be his match?

More importantly, what was *her* problem? She'd never lusted after a man like this before. And certainly not one who continued to treat her this way and show her little interest. But despite it all, she was drawn to Austin. He was unlike any man she'd met before. Unlike any man she'd been attracted to before. His big brain, his shyness, his awkwardness, they were refreshing and appealing. She was intrigued by the quiet introvert, saw something special in him. He didn't say much, but she knew there was probably a heart nearly as big as his brain inside that sculpted chest of his. Hunter had always gone with her gut in business, but never love, and look where that had landed her. Maybe now, maybe Christmas was when she should start listening to her gut . . . and heart.

But when he quickly averted his gaze and clenched his jaw, disappointment and melancholy flowed icy-cold through her veins. Biting her cheek until she tasted blood, she nodded. She would not cry. Not here. Not right now. With a hard swallow and a tight smile, she ducked inside the bathroom, shutting the door quickly, and even though she knew he wouldn't come in, locked it.

Remembering last night made fresh tears burn Hunter's eyes as she sat in the living room avoiding Austin's face the best she could. She'd been quick in the bathroom, not bothering with a shower, and cutting in half her normal length of time to scrub her face and brush her teeth, floss and apply her night cream. She knew Austin needed to use the washroom too, and she didn't want to make him wait too long. Well, that haste had resulted in a big ol' Christmas pus volcano on her chin and a night of endless tossing and turning and restless sleep.

In the end, Hunter knew what the problem was. She was sexually frustrated. Austin's eyes, his body, his hands and images of them doing despicably wonderful things to her flitted through her mind as she reached for the battery-operated boyfriend beneath her pillow and brought the wand down beneath the sheets. It didn't take long; Hunter knew how to pleasure herself, knew how to get the job done so she could sleep. A few minutes of pressing on her G-spot, a couple of flicks with her finger on her clit, and she was sighing and sinking into the mattress, her lids slowly closing while Austin's eyes, those beautiful goldish-green eyes, were the last thing she thought of before sleep finally claimed her.

"You okay?" Amber asked, Will in her wake as they rejoined everyone in the living room, wrapped parcels and gift bags in hand.

Snapping back to reality, and leaving last night where it belonged — in the past — Hunter let out a pained sigh and sipped her coffee, inhaling abruptly and wincing when it burned her tongue. "Just peachy."

AMBER's whole body vibrated as she plunked the perfectly wrapped present on the table, then flopped back onto the sofa. Her eyes sparkled as she secretly patted herself on the back for her beautiful gift-wrap job. Her family assumed she paid a professional to wrap her presents for her, especially given how clean the lines were and intricate the bows. But no. Amber did it all herself. She loved wrapping presents, especially Christmas ones. There was just something so therapeutic and relaxing about hearing the sound of the scissors gliding through the glossy paper, or pulling the single blade along a stretch of ribbon, only to watch it curl. Then add in the joy of watching someone unwrap that gift, marveling and commenting about how beautifully it's wrapped, then light up even more when they found the treasure inside—it made Amber's insides turn to goo and her heart do a happy *thumpity-thump*.

Will's gift took its place next to hers, and he pulled her against his firm body, tucking her small frame under his arm. "What's up with you?" he asked, an amused smirk tugging his sensuous and cushiony lips.

"What do you mean?" she asked.

"You seem different. Giddy or something. You like Christmas?"

Amber made a noise that was somewhere between a snort and a scoff. "No. I mean I don't *hate* it. But I'm . . . I'm *whatever* about Christmas. Never had a particularly bad one if that's what you're asking. But . . . whatever."

Dear God, why did she feel that it wasn't okay for her to divulge her true obsession for the holiday? That when she left work every day between December 1st and December 25th, she stopped in at Starbucks, bought an eggnog chai tea latte and a cranberry bliss bar and then cranked up the carols and sang along on her drive home. Only to toss her keys into the hand-painted (by Amber) snowman bowl by her front door, flick on the lights of the giant Christmas tree in her living room and bake Christmas cookies until bedtime. She brought the cookies to work with her on occasion, saying her mother or sisters-in-law made them, but no, Amber was the one who used pretzels as reindeer antlers and mini marshmallows for snowmen. Christmas meant the world to her, and yet no one in her world knew it.

Will shrugged. "Okay. You just seem . . . happy."

Desperate to change the subject, she let her hand fall to Will's thigh, and inch by inch, her fingers crept along until the middle one brushed his crotch.

Like a groggy poked sleeping bear, it twitched beneath her finger.

"I am *happy*," she said. "After last night . . . and this morning."

I'd say that's one of the best Christmas Eves and mornings I've ever had. What a way to fall asleep and wake up."

He hummed so deep in his throat that it sounded more like a purr. "My head bobbing up and down between those sweet thighs of yours. Little Red, I'll wake you up that way every morning on this trip if I can."

Amber's nipples tightened beneath her tank top, and she licked her lips. She wanted more than this trip with Will. She wanted every morning and every night to be like the last they'd shared, with nothing but hot, sweaty sex and talking. They actually talked a lot, to Amber's surprise. Before joining the rest of the group in the morning and after Amber's TWO wake-up orgasms, they'd snuggled a bit in bed, and Will spoke more of his time abroad working with Doctors Without Borders and his current job at the hospital.

He was sweet, funny, and kind, and the way his tongue and fingers made her toes curl and her body quiver, Amber knew she wouldn't be ready to let go of Will when December 28th rolled around.

No.

Now she had to figure out a way to make that clear.

"All right, everyone," Juney sang, swaying her soft curves around the island in the kitchen and back into the living room. She was clutching a fresh cup of coffee in front of her nose, the steam rising up and quickly fogging up her glasses. "Let's do this."

She took a seat next to Rowan, who had rejoined the group, and he casually draped an arm around her shoulder, planting an ephemeral kiss to her temple. She smiled from the touch of intimacy. That only prompted Amber to give Will's thigh another squeeze, enjoying her own new intimacy and how it set butterflies all aflutter in her belly.

Hunter drew the tags out and quietly labeled all the gifts

with numbers. Once she was done, she put the matching number tags into the small bag Daisy had mentioned minutes ago. "Who wants to go first?" she asked, waving the bag toward Will while deliberately avoiding eye contact with Austin. His eyes hadn't left the side of Hunter's head since she'd sat back down.

"Oh, all right," Will said with a grunt and an eye roll, leaning forward and taking the bag. He dug around for a bit, making a show of it; his tongue stuck out the side of his mouth and his lips twisted up in feigned effort. "Let's see here."

Amber chuckled to herself. See, even the surly doctor had a fun side.

Will's big, sexy hand emerged from the bag, and he held out the number. "Four," he said, bending forward and checking to see the number on each of the gifts. His hand stopped on Amber's perfectly wrapped package, and he picked it up. "This yours, Little Red?"

She swallowed and nodded. "Yes."

"Hmm." He grinned at her as he slid one of those long, capable fingers along the perfect seam of the paper, prying the tape up just right so as not to ruin the wrap job.

"Wait!" Juney said, making Will stop his torturously slow unwrapping. "Let's all pull numbers, and *then* we can open them together."

Will nodded. "I like that. Less time wasted. Here." He passed the bag of numbers to Amber. "Your turn."

Amber's heart sank.

No.

This was not Christmas. It couldn't be rushed. She wanted to watch each person open their gift and express joy. But not wanting to go against the rest and reveal her true love for all things Christmas, she kept her mouth shut and drew out a number.

"Two." She leaned forward and sifted through the gifts, grabbing the bright silver bag with red tissue paper sticking out. It was heavy.

Will made a manly noise in his throat. "That's mine."

Amber's pulse quickened in her veins. What were the odds? She passed the velvet bag to Juney.

"One," Juney said, wasting no time and immediately extracting a number. She found the package labeled one and settled it into her lap while passing the bag of numbers to Rowan. He was just as speedy and leaned forward, mumbling "five" under his breath.

Rowan passed the bag of numbers to Austin, and he plunged his hand inside. He only had two more to choose from. Austin pulled out his number, then passed the bag to Hunter, his eyes never leaving her face. She continued to avoid his gaze.

"Everybody got their number and their gift?" Juney asked. "And you've made sure you didn't grab your own?"

Heads bobbed up and down in nods.

"Okay, awesome." She looked down at Rowan's lap. "Hey, you have mine."

Rowan grinned. "Do I?" His gaze fell to her hands. "And you have mine."

"And I have Amber's," Will added. "And . . ." He glanced her way. "She has mine."

"That means . . . " Juney went on, her mouth turning up into a big grin, "that Hunter and Austin have swapped too."

"Spooky." Rowan chuckled.

Amber's insides slowly warmed and turned to happy mush. No, Christmas magic.

"Okay, everyone . . . and . . . unwrap," Juney announced, her eyes falling to Rowan and drinking him in, as if his gift was something purposefully selected just for her and not a secret Santa gift that could have ended up with anyone.

Paper rustled and tape tore while bows were pulled and bags gently pried open.

"Wait, a second," Hunter hummed, opening up her gift bag. Everyone paused. "I think I got my bag." Her eyes zipped up to Austin just as he pulled out a bottle of Patron tequila and what looked to be two concert tickets.

Austin's eyes went wide.

Hunter reached into her bag and pulled out the exact same thing. A bottle of Patron and two concert tickets.

"What the heck?" Hunter said.

Austin was shaking his head.

"Did you guys give the exact same thing?" Rowan asked with an amused chuckle.

Hunter nodded. "Yeah. Tequila and concert tickets."

Austin continued to shake his head.

"How'd you both score concert tickets?" Juney asked.

Hunter answered as if on autopilot, "I love the Arkells and bought thirty tickets when they first went on sale. Gave them to my staff as Christmas presents. I had a few left over."

"I love the Arkells too and my boss has connections and got me some tickets. I'd asked him for two, but he scored four," Austin said with awe in his tone, still staring at the tickets and tequila and shaking his head. "Though your seats are better than mine."

"And I love tequila," Hunter said.

"Me too," Austin muttered.

"Wow," Rowan said, exhaling loudly. "That's pretty crazy. *Match!*"

Juney elbowed him.

He gave her a mock look of mortification. "What?"

"What did you get, Amber?" Juney asked. It was obvious she was trying to take the focus off of Hunter and Austin and their awkward pre-teen drama.

Amber had been busy getting a secret high from the intense Christmas whimsy and magic unfolding before her as Austin and Hunter, two people who were so meant to be together, opened up the same gift. Great minds. Common interests. Attraction. Why couldn't they just act on it? Let the spirit and wonder, the joy of the holiday envelop them.

"Huh, what?" Amber asked, shaking her head and turning to Juney.

"What did you get?"

Amber dug around inside the bag she knew to be from Will and slowly pulled out the heavy object. Her breath caught in her throat as she gasped.

Will rolled his eyes. "Corny, I know. I'm sorry. There's a bottle of scotch in there too, to make up for the ridiculous snow globe. I just saw it at the store the other day when I was out grabbing booze, and it reminded me I needed a secret Santa gift. But it's kind of cute, right? A snowman with a tool belt building a snow fort." He snorted a laugh through his nose. "Why does he need a tool belt? It's snow. He doesn't need a hammer or saw or screwdriver. And it fits, 'cause you're in construction."

Now it was time for Amber's head to shake.

The magic of Christmas at work again.

She'd seen this snow globe in the grocery store the first week of December. She hadn't bought it then, deciding she would go back and buy it the next time she was out getting groceries. Only it hadn't been there. And it hadn't been there the next time either. She'd asked at customer service and even put in an order, but they'd claimed the warehouse was out. Even eBay and Amazon had resulted in zilch. Crestfallen, she'd come to terms, although not without a few choice words once back inside her car, that she just wasn't meant to have this adorable snow globe. Wasn't meant to add it to her collection that sat on her coffee table for six weeks during the holiday season and then got carefully wrapped up in paper and tucked away for the other ten and half months of the year.

Tears stung the corners of her eyes and her throat threatened to close up. Her head was still shaking. "No," she finally said. "No. I . . . I lo-like it. I like it. It's . . . it's super cute. Thank you. And scotch . . ." She chuckled to hide the emotion roiling inside of her. "Well, scotch this expensive is always appreciated. Thank you."

Will's smile was small but genuine. "You're welcome."

"Your turn," she said.

Will's finger plunged back in between the pristinely wrapped paper, and the tape popped free. Amber sat there on pins and needles, watching as he gently unfurled and then folded the paper, the plain green box sitting on his taut thighs waiting to be opened. Would he think it was stupid? Corny? Lame? Hopefully not. Like all Christmas gifts, including ones for strangers, Amber had put a lot of thought into this gift. Along with the gifts for her parents, a new fly-fishing rod for her dad and a gift certificate for pole dancing lessons for her mother (yes, pole dancing lessons; Muriel Roth was a free-spirited woman with an open mind and a zest for adventure and the kinky side), as well as presents for her brothers, their wives and children, Amber had spent nearly an hour wandering around the mall searching for the right gift for the secret Santa.

Will opened the box to reveal a bottle of rare twenty-one-year-old scotch, a box of gold-leaf-flecked chocolate truffles and a four-pack sampler of Puget Sound Potato Chip Company's newest flavors: habanero cheddar and chive, rice vinegar and kelp, balsamic and basil, and honey mustard with roasted garlic.

His hand paused, and his eyes drifted up to Amber's face. "H-how . . . how did you know?"

She cocked her head to the side, her heart beating wildly in her chest. She couldn't get a read on his reaction. He didn't seem upset, but there wasn't a smile on his face either. More than anything, the man seemed confused, if not a tad spooked. "How did I know what?"

"Th-that I *love* potato chips and this is my favorite scotch? The liquor store was out when I went, otherwise it's what I would have given you, too."

Her pulse thudded loud and quick in Amber's skull. She could barely hear him or anyone else. "I—I didn't know. This was secret Santa, remember? I just bought some nice things. This is my dad's favorite scotch, and I really like potato chips, they're one of my vices. And, well, chocolate with gold, how can you go wrong?"

Big, beautiful brown eyes twinkled back at her. If she wasn't mistaken, Will's eyes even teared up a bit. The irises darkened and appeared glassy, and his sexy throat bobbed heavy and thick. He nodded once, twice and then closed the box.

"Thank you, Little Red. This is a great gift."

If it were possible, Amber's heart inflated and deflated at the same time. He loved her gift, but he suppressed his reaction. What was up?

"Me next," Rowan said, having patiently waited for Will to open his gift. He tore off the paper like a fervent kindergartener then opened the box. "What the hell?" he practically hollered.

Juney sat there biting her lip.

Rowan turned to face her. "A St. Maurice Lefebvre knife? How the heck did you get your hands on this?"

Juney's teeth slowly slipped off her bottom lip as her mouth drew up into a big, infectious smile. "I, uh . . . I know the rep. We've set the kitchen up in our new restaurant with all St. Maurice Lefebvre knives and kitchen accessories, and the rep tossed in a couple of extras because, well, he likes me, our order is going to pay for his kid's first year of college, and I gave him a case of wine as a Christmas present."

Rowan shook his head. "These knives . . . Holy shit. These knives make Henckel look like Ikea. I've been coveting. No, coveting is an understatement. I've been dreaming, worshipping, *obsessing* over these knives for ages. I just . . . Well, they're not cheap, and I'm not exactly employed at the moment."

Juney lifted one shoulder. "It's not the whole set, but it is the biggest blade. Hopefully it works to chop things like carrots and celery and stuff. The rep said they're sharp, so be careful."

Had the man blinked yet? Amber wasn't sure.

"I'm not sure I can even bring myself to use it," he said.

Will snorted. Hunter chuckled, and Austin made a noise Amber couldn't quite discern; was it a scoff? A hiccup?

"No, you should probably use it," Juney said with a laugh. "And I tossed in a bottle of my family's finest as well. A 2007 merlot, so don't drop that bottle. It's worth almost as much as the knife."

Rowan's gaze zipped to Juney's face. Amber's own core clenched, and her nipples tightened again against her tank top. The way Rowan was staring at Juney was enough to make anyone feel the heat and longing. So feral, so lustful. Was anyone else seeing this? The man was ready to take the little novelist right then and there on the couch. His eyes flashed pure need, while his nostrils flared and his pupils dilated.

"I can't believe you managed to get your hands on this knife," he said softly, gently running his finger along the side of the blade, having removed it from its velvet casing. "My gift isn't going to be nearly as amazing. At least not *now*. And not with *you* as the recipient."

Juney's lip twisted. "I'm sure it's going to be a great gift." She opened the bag and lifted out a hardcover copy of a book. "*Endless Souls: Book 1, Ravens Will Cry*. By J.J. Davidson. Oh, I hear she's good." Her body shook lightly with merriment as she opened up the front cover. "And it's signed. Wow, a limited edition. This wasn't cheap."

Rowan's lips wiggled sheepishly. "I have two copies. I bought two, just . . . because, and then I didn't get my ass in gear to buy a secret Santa gift, so I tossed this in last minute and stopped and grabbed a bottle of wine."

Juney put her hand back in the bag and lifted out a bottle of pinot noir. "Mmmm, Unbridled Passion Vineyards. I love their wine. This is wonderful, thank you."

Rowan looked down at his lap. "I'm sorry, Juney. It's nothing compared to your gift."

She shook her head and placed her hand on his, giving it a gentle squeeze. "No, it's fine. It's better than fine. I love my own books, and I *love* this wine. Thank you. Besides, you didn't know you'd be spending Christmas with the author, or that she would be opening your gift." She chuckled softly. "The universe has a funny sense of humor sometimes."

More like the magic and wonder of Christmas. But Amber didn't say that out loud. Instead, she lightly shook her beautiful snow globe and watched all the flurries flutter around.

"Isn't it crazy that we ended up with one another's gifts, *and* that we all love what we received, *and* we all gave the same kind of booze? Wine, scotch and tequila." Juney turned the bottle of wine over and read the label. "I mean, it's nuts."

"I think it's kind of funny that all six of us bought alcohol," Will said with a laugh.

"Anyway," Rowan said, stretching his arms above his head and groaning lightly, "I better get in that kitchen. That turkey isn't going to stuff itself." And then as if a light flicked on inside his brain, he paused and perked up. "Would you guys object to having only turkey breast for dinner with baked stuffing? I have an idea for the dark meat. I noticed a meat grinder in the cupboard and was thinking about making turkey burgers for our last night here."

Heads shook and shoulders shrugged.

"Not at all," Hunter said with a yawn. "That sounds good." She stood up from her nest of blankets on the floor and picked up her gift bag. "I'm going to go and have a shower. Then I'll come out and help with breakfast."

Juney wandered into the kitchen behind Rowan, her hand lightly grazing his back as he peeled his new knife out of its casing and gently ran it under the faucet. "I'll get going on breakfast. Everyone good with fruit salad, soft boiled eggs, and toast? Something light before a big meal."

Now heads were nodding.

"I have to go shovel the driveway," Austin muttered, getting up from where he sat. He'd been quieter than normal since they'd all opened their gifts. Amber wanted to reach out to him, but she wasn't sure how responsive he would be.

Amber began cleaning up the mess of wrapping paper and gifts, grabbing a plastic bag from under the sink and collecting everything that could be burned later in the fireplace.

"I'm going to call my mom," Will said blandly, getting up from his spot on the couch. "It's already Christmas afternoon in Trinidad, so she's probably at my granny's getting the goat ready for dinner." With a wink and a smile at Amber, he took off to the bedroom.

"Has that guy lifted a finger since he arrived?" Rowan asked, the blade in his hand gliding through a raw carrot as if it were no more than a warm stick of butter.

"Not unless it's topping up his drink," Juney said with a chuckle. "He's taking this whole *vacation* thing seriously."

Amber's cheeks caught fire. It was true. She'd been noticing it here and there, but hadn't really given it much thought. But Rowan was right, Will was totally freeloading. Everyone else did something around the cabin to carry their weight. Rowan and Juney always jumped into the kitchen, she and Hunter were usually on cleanup, sweeping and tidying and doing dishes, and Austin had designated himself the keeper of the fire and official driveway shoveler. He was out there multiple times a day, keeping the walkway ploughed and the driveway clear. But what was Will doing to pitch in? Besides that first night, where he'd grabbed everyone a drink, the man hadn't done a thing to help out. He was sitting back and letting everyone else do the work, while he reaped all the benefits.

Hmm. Was this something she could bring up with him? Were they close enough yet? She folded the wrapping paper from her gift to Will and continued to think. Maybe she could ask him to help her do the dishes? Shoo Austin and Hunter out of the kitchen to go avoid eye contact with each other in the living room while she and Will scrubbed pots together. Yeah. She nodded and smiled to herself. That sounded like a great plan.

CHAPTER TEN

Hunter cringed as she, Austin, Will and Amber trudged their way into the garage from the side door. And the award for the most awkward afternoon goes to: Austin and Hunter! They were all damp, with rosy cheeks, runny noses and snow on their lashes, having been accosted by a brief storm and dump of the white stuff on their way back from snowshoeing. It'd been Amber's idea. She said she was feeling restless and fat. Eating food all day long, drinking booze all night but not exercising nearly as much as she was used to. The woman apparently went to kickboxing five nights a week. Hunter had giggled at the image of the tiny redheaded sprite be-bopping around swinging punches and trying to kick guys twice her size in the head. Tiny person, *big* personality.

After digging around in the garage for nearly half an hour, Amber and Hunter had uncovered four sets of snowshoes, which all seemed to be in working order. Juney and Rowan were elbow-deep in preparing dinner and had declined to venture out into the wilderness with "tennis rackets" on their feet, which meant unless Austin and Hunter wanted to sit around the cabin all afternoon watching the two lovebirds cuddle and giggle in the kitchen, flaunting their lust, they needed to get out.

Only it'd been like a goddamn double-edged sword. Because Will and Amber were equally disgustingly affectionate, holding hands, laughing, pushing each other playfully. It was enough to make Hunter sick ... with envy.

"All right, you two little lost lambs," Will said with a chuckle as they had made their way through the snow. The trail was eerily quiet. Nothing but the sounds of their feet in the snow and their breath making warm fog in the air. The clouds hung low and gray too, threatening more snow. "We're going to go, uh, walk ahead over here for a bit. Check out this part of the trail. You two ... " He grunted. "You two stay put."

Hunter rolled her eyes as Will grabbed Amber's hand and pulled her down a side trail. They disappeared around a bend. The heavy snow-laden branches of the evergreen trees quickly hid their bright ski jackets.

"They're not going to ... ?" Austin asked from behind her.

Hunter spun around to face him. "Yes, I believe they are."

"B-but ... "

"I hope his dick gets frostbite," she said heatedly.

"If they're having sex, that's unlikely. The friction alone should generate enough heat to ward off any frostbite. And then there's the fact that he would be *inside* Amber, and the human body, even when outside in the cold, is ninety-eight point six degrees, give or take."

Hunter's mouth hung open.

Austin noted the look on her face, and his eyes quickly fell to his feet. "You were kidding."

"Yes."

He kicked at a clump of snow. "I wonder if Juney and Rowan are engaged in the exact same thing. Though hopefully not on the counter where they're making our dinner. I know it's not a restaurant, but that's a huge health-code violation."

"Do you think about what comes out of your mouth before you say it?" she asked. There wasn't exactly accusation in her tone, but Hunter was finding herself a little irritated with Austin. He was so awkward around her, and yet she hadn't given him any reason to be.

He swallowed. "Sometimes."

"Hmm."

"But not all the time."

"Hmm."

"I'm sorry."

She shook her head and let out a defeated sigh. She needed this guy to see her as normal. See her as the girl next door, not some untouchable millionaire bombshell. She rested her gloved hand on his arm. "Don't be. It's who you are. And I happen to think who you are is charming. A little dorky, but charming. Honesty can be refreshing."

Austin's gaze flew back up to hers. Even through all the layers, Hunter knew her nipples were tight, and the heat that generated low in her belly made her chest break out into a sudden sweat. Without even trying, the man could give her the most scorching looks. Stripping and penetrating.

"So . . . " He cleared his throat. "Like Juney's real name is Juniper, but she goes by Juney, do you have a nickname? Do people call you Hunny?"

She exhaled a laugh through her nose. "Nope. You're the first."

"Oh."

Tired and not wanting to stand any longer, Hunter plopped herself down into the snow. It sucked that things with Austin were so uncomfortable. That first day when they were all sitting around the kitchen and living room getting to know one another had been the best. He'd clammed up later that evening when they were alone, then there was that awkward bit in the hallway after Sam had left. And he rarely smiled, at least not at Hunter. But when he did, he took her breath away.

Austin sat down in the snow across from her, and the silence between them grew to a deafening shriek. Should she say something to him? Ask him more questions about his life, his work? Ask him about his family?

"So, um, any siblings?"

He nodded. "A sister. She's twelve years younger."

And . . . ? Come on, dude, give me something. Add to the conversation.

"And are you close?"

He shook his head. "No. Age gap is too big. I left home when she was four."

"Oh."

Nothing.

"Which car company are you working for? You mentioned earlier you and Reginald Carruthers were working on a project for a big car company. Or is it top secret?"

"It's top secret."

Warm breath wafted out and up into the ether as she let out a big huff through her nose. The guy was killing her.

Come on, dude, talk to me.

"But if you're good at rhyming . . ."

Hunter sat up straight. If her butt wasn't slowly starting to freeze, she might say she was on pins and needles. She loved puzzles and poems, riddles and mysteries.

His lip turned up at the corner into a naughty little smirk. Like a high school girl or devoted church parishioner getting ready to dish the dirty deets. "It might . . . I'm not saying it *does*, but it *might* rhyme with *Howdy*."

Her mouth twitched and then finally the smile broke free. "*Howdy*, hey?"

He nodded, his green-gold eyes glowing even though the rest of his face remained stoic and innocent. "But I'm not saying that it *is* for sure. Only that it might be. It could also rhyme with Ward, or Moyota, or Wee Nem Bubble Screw."

Hunter burst out laughing. "Wee Nem Bubble Screw?"

"Yeah, you've heard of it?"

"Perhaps. Is that who your project is for?"

Austin's smile made the butterflies in her belly wake up. "Maybe. Or it might be *Howdy*."

"Hmm. Well, I drive a *Howdy*. I traded in my Wee Nem Bubble Screw earlier this year, loved it."

"I've always wanted an M5."

"Oh, does Wee Nem Bubble Screw label their cars the same way as BMW?" she teased.

Another big smile.

Why couldn't he be this charismatic and fun all the time? They were chatting, laughing, teasing. Was it all in Hunter's head that they had chemistry? Was she deluding herself?

Suddenly, Austin's smile faded, replaced with immediate panic, and he lunged at her. "Look out!" He leaped across the trail in the snow and tackled Hunter to the ground, falling on top of her. Less than a second later the *whizz* and rumble of a snowmobile going Mach-1 filled her ears as she fought to breathe beneath the big hunk of a man on top of her. The frigid rush of air from the speed of the vehicle brushed across her face, and a rampant chill coursed through her body. She'd nearly been hit. Austin had saved her.

"Y-you okay?" he asked, pushing himself up on his hands and gazing down at her.

She took a couple of huge breaths; he'd knocked the wind

right out of her, and now she was struggling to get enough air in again. His eyes squinted, and then horror streaked across his face.

"Hunter! Are you okay?"

All she could do was nod and blink.

Using his gloved hand, he gently wiped snow from her face, his own face still in full-on panic mode. She gazed up at him, allowing him to take care of her, and despite the circumstances, his weight on top of her felt good. Really good.

When he finished clearing off the flurries, his eyes fell back on hers. "You're all right?"

She nodded again and blinked a few times. "I think so. Thank you."

"All right, you two," Will's voice behind them boomed. "Well, that's a start. Though it'd be nice if you were only partially dressed."

Austin helped Hunter sit up. She was still panting, and her heart was threatening to pump itself clear out of her body. Will stalked toward them on the side trail. He pushed a big branch out of his way and held it up so Amber could duck under. Color infused her cheekbones, and her hazel eyes were bright.

"And here I'd hoped we'd come back and find you two tangled up half-naked in a snow bank. Melting the flurries with your fiery passion. We can give you more time if you need it," Will teased.

Hunter shot him a look that said, "fucking drop it." "I was almost run over by a snowmobile," she said. "Austin pushed me out of the way in the nick of time."

Amber's mouth dropped open. "Holy crap. You okay?"

She nodded. "Yeah, a little rattled, but otherwise, I'm okay."

Flurries fluttered down around them. The flakes were huge and thick. Will looked up into the sky, the white flakes stark against his dark skin. "I think we should head back. It's getting dark, and if it starts to cover our tracks, we could be in trouble."

Everyone nodded, and Hunter pushed herself to her feet and fell in line behind Amber. She turned around to face Austin. "Thank you. I could have been a frozen pancake."

He smiled, his lip lopsided and kind of sad. Then he quickly averted his gaze and looked down at the back of Hunter's boots. "You're welcome."

The butterflies in Hunter's belly, the ones that had been laughing and dancing when they'd been joking earlier about car companies, suddenly all dropped into a frozen heap, their wings covered in frost while their little jaws chattered and trembled as they kept asking, "Why?"

"Well, that was fun!" Amber said with a contented sigh as she shrugged out of her ski jacket and hung it up over the heater Will turned on once they all got back to the cabin. "I didn't think I'd like snowshoeing, but . . . " Will flashed her a big grin. "I think it might be one of my new favorite sports."

Will growled, then reached over and cupped her face. "Mine too, Little Red."

"Oh, for fuck's sake," Hunter grumbled, ditching her boots, snow pants and finally her coat, hanging them up on the rack. She stomped toward the garage door and opened it, her good mood from earlier having flown the coop. She'd been having a great time with Austin. They'd laughed and chatted. Granted, the conversation had been rather one-sided, with her asking most of the questions, but at least he'd answered them. It was a step in the right direction. Then she'd nearly died, and he'd saved her. Another plus (well, kind of). And then all of a sudden, as soon as Amber and Will returned from their frozen backwoods tryst, Austin had zipped his lip and hadn't said a peep to her since.

Merry *fucking* Christmas.

Amber was tight on her heels as Hunter exited the garage, followed by Will.

Shaking her head and muttering the word "wine" under her

breath, Hunter headed toward the kitchen, only to stop short at the sight before her.

"Oh, shit! Fuck! Oh, sorry!"

Rowan's bare ass and one of Juney's nipples were visible between his teeth as he pushed her up against the fridge, hammering hard and fast. Juney's eyes were closed and her head thrown back as she bit her lip and pulled on the ends of Rowan's blond hair.

Amber bumped into Hunter's back. "What? Oh!"

"What?" Will asked. "Damn."

"What is it?" Austin asked.

"Nothing for you to see, little man," Will said, turning around and ushering Austin down the hallway toward the bedrooms.

But the lovers' trance was broken.

"Oh crap!" Juney's voice, hoarse and sexy and full of remorse—and pleasure—chased them all down the hallway. "Sorry, guys."

"It's okay," Amber called back. "Finish what you were doing."

"You heard them," Rowan said with a throaty chuckle.

"Oh, be quiet." Juney laughed.

But Hunter didn't hear anything else. Amber and Will retreated to Amber's room, Austin to his, and with one last look of longing at Austin's closed bedroom door, Hunter ducked inside her own room and shut the door.

CHAPTER ELEVEN

Amber smoothed down the front of her lacy red dress and checked herself out in the full-length mirror on the back of her bedroom door. She'd decided to abandon her customary ponytail and instead leave her hair down, falling around her shoulders in gentle red waves. Not one for makeup, she didn't really have much to work with. A bit of lip gloss and some bronzer for those days she was feeling extra ghostly. She'd snorted, scoffed and rolled her eyes when her sisters-in-law, Jill and Penny, had taken her shopping and tossed bronzer into the basket. "By January you're practically translucent," Jill had said. "Just brush some on in the morning. No one will even know. But at least you won't look dead." She'd been right, of course. And even though Amber didn't bother with bronzer most days, it was never *not* in the center console of her truck, just in case.

Those girly-girls had also helped her buy the dress. It had been for her other brother Tyler's Valentine's Day wedding. She hadn't had a clue what to wear. The other women had taken pity on her, and the three of them had gone shopping for the day and then hit up the spa. Not exactly Amber's idea of fun, but in the end she'd managed to enjoy herself. Despite how much estrogen and Nina Ricci perfume wafted off her sisters-in-law, she did love them.

She studied herself in the mirror again, then against her better judgment, pinched her cheeks.

Damn, this is the second time I've pinched my cheeks. What is the hot doctor doing to me?

Then, digging in her bag, she pulled out something, walked to her door and turned off the light. A quick peek out proved no one was around, and noises from the kitchen revealed the majority of the houseguests to be drinking and laughing and getting ready for dinner. Perfect!

Wandering over to the hall closet, she pulled out the stepstool, then carried it over in front of Hunter's bedroom door. She put her ear to the solid wood. Good. She wasn't inside. It was only one step up, but that wasn't even enough, and Amber found herself teetering on her tippy toes trying to stick the pushpin into the doorjamb. You'd think by this time she would try to find another, higher stool.

"What are you doing?" came a deep masculine rumble from the head of the hallway.

Amber spun around and lost her footing. Suddenly, there was nothing beneath her feet, and the ground was looking awfully close and hard.

"Whoa, whoa!" Will said, lurching forward and grabbing Amber at the last second. His strong arms braced her awkwardly as she toppled against him. "You okay?"

She nodded. His big chest had knocked the wind right out of her. "Yeah, you just spooked me."

Will set her on her feet, then took the object she was trying to hang above the door from her hand. "Mistletoe?"

Amber looked down at her feet, and she curled her chocolate-plum-painted toes. It'd been Amber's birthday two weeks ago, and Jill and Penny had insisted the three of them go get pedicures. She would never admit it, but the foot massage had been decadent, and she kind of loved how nice her feet looked once the esthetician had buffed, scrubbed, and painted them up.

"Are *you* the one who has been hanging up all the mistletoe everywhere?" he asked, shock taking over the tone of his voice. There wasn't really any accusation there, more bafflement than anything else.

Amber nodded solemnly as heat filled her chest and cheeks. It reminded her of the time she'd been caught trying to shave her face, like her dad and brothers did. She'd made a godawful mess in the bathroom and nicked herself something fierce. Her dad hadn't been upset, more just surprised at how big of a tomboy Amber really was. It was then he and her mother stopped buying her tea sets and dolls and let her play with her brothers' toys and bought her things like Legos and Kinex.

"Why?"

She lifted one shoulder. "Just to be funny. Nobody has any idea. I dunno. Add a bit of whimsy and mystery to the week."

She couldn't bear to look at him. But she had no choice when his knuckle came up under her chin. "Look at me, Little Red. Do you *like* Christmas?"

No! I fucking LOVE it!

She rolled her eyes and gave him an irritated scoff. "I don't hate it. It's just a prank, though. Let it go. If this were Halloween, I'd be hanging bats or spiders. Relax." She shook herself from his grasp and looked away. "Besides, Hunter and Austin need all the help they can get."

"You're not wrong there," he muttered, taking the pushpin from her hand. Without a grunt of strained effort or needing to stand on tiptoe, Will reached up and pushed the pin into the doorjamb, then hung up the mistletoe bundle.

Amber picked up the stool and put it back in the closet. "You're not going to tell everyone, are you?"

That smile. A smile that big, that white, that sexy, shouldn't be legal. He grabbed her around the waist and pulled her body against his. "You look gorgeous tonight."

"Thank you." Amber's breasts ached from how hard they were pushing against the tight fabric of her dress with each ragged gasp. Her nipples tightened to stiff peaks, and her panties were growing wetter by the second. The man knew how to seduce without even trying. "You promise not to tell anyone?"

Will's eyes darted up to the mistletoe. They were standing directly below it. "Your secret's safe with me, Little Red, so long as *we* get to test it out first." He dipped her low and brushed his lips against hers, the heat from his big body flooding her. She melted into his arms. Christmas was freaking awesome.

ROWAN PULLED the twin turkey breasts from the oven. His mouth flooded with water from the decadent smell and the sight of the bacon, sizzling bright red, which he'd draped overtop to keep in the moisture. He placed the pan with the breasts on the counter, covered it in foil, then reached back inside the oven and pulled out the pan of stuffing, followed by a pan of his mother's sweet potato casserole. It didn't matter how many years in professional kitchens he'd worked, who his mentors had been, or the red seal from Le Cordon Bleu, Mrs. Johanna Briggs' sweet potato casserole recipe was the best in all the land.

"Mmm," Hunter hummed, pulling up the barstool in front of the counter. She'd been on the phone in the library, something about checking in with her birth mother. Apparently the two still spoke. "That smells incredible." Her eyes darted down to a skillet on the stove. "What the heck are you doing to the Brussels sprouts?"

Rowan's eyebrows bobbed up and down, and he gave her a wicked grin. The only thing that made these foul little green bouncy balls edible. "I'm sautéing them in butter, a little bit of truffle oil, copious amounts of fresh garlic, a bit of bacon, salt and pepper, with a dash of chili flakes."

She shook her head. "I've only ever had them steamed, and they tasted like feet."

"Trust me." He smiled. "You'll love these. I also do them in a killer mustard sauce, but today I'm going with garlic and bacon."

"I haven't had a bad dish from you yet," Juney interjected, joining him at the counter and spooning the fresh cranberry sauce she'd made into a delicate crystal dish. "And using cornbread instead of regular bread in your stuffing—genius!"

Heat rushed to his cheeks as he flashed her a sexy smile. "What can I say? I'm a genius in many places, the kitchen . . . the *bedroom*." He hip-checked her, and her laugh made his chest tighten.

"Gross," Hunter said dryly. "Way to rub it in."

"That's what she said." Rowan chuckled.

Juney rolled her eyes, which only made Rowan laugh even louder.

"Where's Austin?" he asked.

Hunter shook her head, then blew her bangs from her eyes, one shoulder casually bobbing toward the front door. "Out shoveling the driveway, where else?" The woman's frustration was coming off of her in heated waves.

Jesus Christ, what the hell was Austin's deal?

Rowan turned up the heat on the stove. "What happened to you guys out in the snow?"

She shook her head again. "Definitely nothing as exciting as what was happening in *here*. At least not to *me*."

Rowan growled low in his throat, and out of the corner of his eye, he saw the tips of Juney's ears turn bright red and her pale cheeks burn. That impromptu kitchen sex had been incredible. He hadn't even known what had come over him, but suddenly he had to have her. Maybe it was the dusting of flour she'd accidentally wiped across her forehead, or the cute tendrils that had escaped her ponytail and were peeking out around her temples, but whatever it was, he'd needed her then and he'd needed her badly.

Hunter cleared her throat, and that snapped him out of his daydream, but it wasn't enough to temper the surge of need between his legs. The color in Juney's cheeks made him lust for her again something fierce. The woman was fucking stunning. He tried to adjust his pants, but it was no use. He was rock hard again and painfully pressing against his dress slacks. Thank God for aprons.

"The sexy doctor and Amber took off to go screw against a tree," Hunter continued, "while Austin and I sat in the snow and froze our butts off and then I nearly got run over by a snowmobile. He saved me, and I thought we had a moment. But—" Her throat wobbled, and she let out a weighted sigh. Were those tears in her eyes? "Apparently, that moment was all in my head. He clammed right up again. Then it started snowing, and we all headed back."

"Maybe tonight," Juney said softly, giving Hunter one of those motherly looks she was becoming known for.

Rowan's heart did a little *thump-thump*. He loved how genuine and sweet she was. Such mother material. And although the idea of children wasn't out of the question, he never really thought of himself as a dad, at least not until Juney said her clock was ticking and she wanted kids. Now Rowan couldn't stop thinking about kids. Kids with Juney's eyes and brains and coloring.

"Mistletoe seems to be popping up everywhere," Juney went on. "And it *is* Christmas. You might get lucky. I know both of my sisters got engaged over Christmas. It's definitely a magical holiday."

"What? Christmas?" Amber asked, joining Hunter at the bar. Will was in her wake, and they both had that look on their faces as if they'd just been making out. Bright eyes, swollen lips. His hand brushed the small of her back. When she went to sit down, he sat next to her and draped his arm around her shoulder. He had to be touching her. Rowan felt the same way about Juney.

Juney nodded. "Yeah, don't you think it's a magical holiday?"

Amber lifted one shoulder and then tipped the decanter of wine up and filled her glass. "I'm not saying it doesn't have its whimsical merits, but I wouldn't go so far as to say it's *magical*."

Will snorted next to her. Did he know Amber's nickname at work?

Not much of a betting man, but Rowan would bet dollars to donuts Amber wasn't being honest. She was tossing on her "tin woman" armor and not showing anyone her true colors. She had been like a barge of fireworks when they'd all exchanged gifts that morning, teeming with excitement. She'd practically had an aneurysm of joy as she pulled that snow globe out of the bag. And as much as she tried to hide it, a smile that real was tough to cover up completely. The woman liked Christmas. Hell, she probably loved it, but for some reason she didn't think it was okay to show.

"Well, I think it's magical," Juney said with a smile. She pulled the roasted potatoes out of the oven and, with big tongs, began plating them. "I've always only done mashed for Christmas dinner, but roasted potatoes are a great idea. So crispy."

Rowan winked at her as he pushed the browning Brussels sprouts and bacon around in the pan with the garlic. The smell made his stomach rumble. Everything was better with bacon. "I like mashed well enough too, and I did a small bowl of it as well for the diehard traditionalists who need to make their volcanoes, but there is something so satisfying about hearing the subtle crack of the crispy outer layer of the potato as you cut into it and then watch the steam rise up into the air. A pad of butter or some gravy . . . " He kissed his fingers and then quickly pulled them away. "*C'est magnifique!*"

"Well, *Chef* Briggs, everything you've made so far this week has been *c'est magnifique*. I'd let you cook for me anytime."

That was the second compliment she'd paid him about his food in a matter of minutes. As much as his big chef ego was enjoying the praise, Rowan couldn't help but wonder if there was more to it. He knew his food was good, damn good, but was she simply being herself, sweet, complimentary Juney, or was there more to her admiration?

The door from the garage slammed, and everyone turned to see Austin, a scowl on his face and pink in his cheeks, stalking in. He glanced at Hunter and the vacant seat next to her but instead chose to stand next to Will. Both Will and Rowan rolled their eyes and made rude, but very obvious noises in their throats.

"Shit or get off the pot, man. You've got two days left with her. Make a move."

Juney's mouth dropped open, followed by Hunter's, then Amber's, and finally Austin's. Will burst out laughing.

Oh, for fuck's sake! That wasn't in my head? I said that out loud? That was not supposed to be out loud. FUCK! FUCK! FUCK!

If it were possible, Austin's cheeks turned an even darker shade, and his chest started to rise and fall as if he'd just come in from a gruesome hike.

"Filter!" Juney whispered, batting him on the hand with the tongs. "In your head. Say those things in your *head!*"

"I thought I had," he said under his breath.

"Oh, man." Will chuckled, getting up from his seat, but not before running his hands along the back of Amber's neck. "I need a drink. Austin, man, drink?"

Austin nodded. "Ah. Maybe a double?"

Will's dark chuckle rolled through the kitchen. "Is there any other kind?"

CHAPTER TWELVE

JUNEY LET out a contented sigh as she finally allowed herself to sit down at the head of the table. Rowan was at the other end, and the two of them shared a look of camaraderie and joy over the expanse of decadent food they had lovingly prepared. It was impressive. *He* had been impressive. Authoritative in the kitchen, confident and capable, but also calm, cool, and collected.

He knew what he was doing, but at the same time, he still valued her help. Every time he sought her out for consult, allowed her to taste his dishes as he prepared them and offer critiques, her heart soared. He made her feel needed and that her opinion and presence at his side were appreciated. And even though he could have easily prepared the entire meal himself, he never once made her feel as though she wasn't an integral part of the Christmas dinner preparation. When she said he needed more sage or salt or another dash of pepper, he heeded her feedback with a smile and nod. Unlike many of the other chefs she'd worked with and interviewed, Rowan didn't come off nearly as cocky or conceited. He was confident, but that confidence was tempered in a way that appealed to her. Content and at ease in his surroundings; sure in his abilities but also humble enough to accept help and the opinion of others.

"Wow!" Hunter said on an exhale, draping her linen napkin over the lap of her beautiful dark-green sheath dress. She'd confessed earlier, when Juney had asked, that it was indeed one of her own creations, a simple but flattering bamboo frock with a boat-neck and a subtle stitching embellishment along the cap sleeve and hem. It enhanced Hunter's amber eyes and, when she pinned her hair up on top of her head in a casual twist, accentuated her long, slender neck. "This all looks fantastic. I don't know what to try first."

"The Brussels sprouts first, for sure," Rowan said with a wink, passing her the bowl where they steamed crispy and caramelized among the crunchy bacon and fragrant garlic. "And then the turkey, the stuffing, and the roasted potatoes." He reached forward and speared a big slab of sliced turkey breast, and even from her place at the other end of the table, Juney could see how juicy the meat was. Not an easy task. The breast almost always ended up being too dry, no matter at whose house she spent Christmas.

"Mmm," Hunter hummed, scooping out a big heaping spoonful of sprouts. "I'll take your word for it, Chef Briggs. But if I don't like them, I'm blaming you."

"Don't wait," he said. "Pop one of those bad boys in your mouth now and try it."

He watched patiently as she speared one of the little half-spheres with her fork and popped it into her mouth. Juney could practically feel Rowan's apprehension. Had he blinked?

Hunter chewed methodically, her face a mask. She swallowed before looking at Rowan.

"I fucking love them," she said with a big smile, puncturing another one with her fork and then stabbing a bit or two of bacon as well. "You've converted me, Chef Briggs."

Rowan let out a sigh. It didn't matter how confident he was in his dishes, he was still human, still humble, and he wanted Hunter to enjoy his food. Juney's heart melted from how relieved he appeared. He really was the whole package.

Once everyone had filled their plates and topped off their drinks, they all sat around the table, gripping the Christmas crackers that Juney had found earlier that day in a box beneath the tree. It had been addressed to "Everyone" and had said "Love, Daisy!"

"Is this Christmas cracker thing a Canadian tradition?" Rowan asked, looking at Juney with a curious smile.

She nodded. "It must be, if this is the first time you Yanks have ever done them. We do them every year in my family. And Daisy *is* Canadian."

"They originated in the U.K. and are primarily used for Christmas celebrations by members of the Commonwealth," Austin put in.

"Huh," Will said with a slight head shake. "Thanks, Einstein. Much obliged. Everyone ready? My arms are getting tired." His big arms were awkwardly crossed in front of him as he held on to Amber and Juney's crackers.

"One . . . two . . . three, pull!" Juney announced. Snaps and sparks filled the table as everyone pulled their crackers. Will pulled so hard on both women's that they'd torn in two, while Austin had jerked so hard he pulled it right out of Hunter's hand, but it hadn't gone off. She was then forced to do her own afterward as Austin's face turned fifty different shades of red.

Crackers were cracked, flimsy colorful paper hats were unfurled and placed upon heads, and trinkets and toys were unveiled. Juney draped her new whistle necklace around her neck and gave it a light blow, and Rowan went to work at the other end of the table assembling his small six-piece puzzle of a dinosaur.

"Did everyone get a fortune in their cracker, too?" Amber asked, pulling out a piece of paper and unrolling it.

Heads nodded.

"Who wants to read theirs first?" Juney asked, searching inside her cracker for the small piece of paper.

"I'll go," Rowan said with a smile. His grin made her belly do a happy flip-flop. The man was full of surprises. He hadn't struck her as someone who liked Christmas. He wasn't as ornery or anti-holiday as Amber, but when they'd first arrived, his cynicism and sarcasm had been a tad off-putting. But perhaps that was just nerves? Or residual anger from his lack of a job. Whatever it was, it seemed to evaporate the moment he stepped back into the kitchen, and since then he'd been in a fantastic mood. And, in turn, so had Juney.

"Have at 'er," she said, giving him a coquettish smile.

He cleared his throat. "Letting go of a bad attitude and a big ego can be its own reward. Release the past and humbly but openly embrace the future." His eyebrows buried themselves beneath the chunk of blond hair that tumbled over his forehead. "Hmm, that's rather fitting. I've been trying to be less of a cocky ass. Figure that might have been what killed my chance at the promotion."

She loved his honesty. And unlike a lot of men she'd met, men she'd *dated,* Rowan recognized his flaw and was consciously trying to make a change for the better.

He took a healthy sip of his wine and sobered, the introspective look on his face gone. Now he was all smiles again. "Your turn, Amber."

Amber's lips twisted, and her cheeks turned a vibrant pink as she read her slip of paper a couple of times before saying it out loud. "Express your true self to experience great joy and find your inner peace." An awkward cough caught in her throat, and she used her napkin to muffle it. "These things are lame," she finally said, taking a healthy sip of her wine. "I'm surprised it didn't start out with 'Confucius says . . . ' "

Will eyed her suspiciously but didn't say anything. Instead he glanced down at his own paper and read. "Not all flat stones skip the same distance on the water." His nose wrinkled. "Huh?"

"I think it means, not every situation is the same. Don't judge one moment by the failure or success of previous moments," Juney said solemnly. "I think that's advice we can all take to heart. Just because we may have had one crappy relationship or a bad first date, or awful Christmas, doesn't mean every first date or relationship or Christmas will be terrible."

"Hmm," Will hummed in thought, adopting Rowan's pensive look of introspection. "I suppose. Your turn, Austin," he said, taking a sip of his wine, clearly eager to deflect the attention away from himself.

Austin's eyes went wide as he held the paper up. "You are more than what you believe yourself to be. Do not let fear hold you back from finding happiness."

The guy's face kept going through the whole paint swatch of red hues. What was he now? Cherry tomato? Fire engine, perhaps?

"Damn, these fortunes are rather spot-on tonight," Rowan said. "What's yours say, Juney?"

Juney read the slip, then re-read it, and then read it again. And with each re-read, her mouth dropped open wider and wider.

"What's it say?" Rowan asked again.

"True love is finding your biggest fan."

Will scoffed. "I bet you Daisy made these up herself."

"And we all just *happened* to get the one that corresponds best to us?" Rowan said blandly. "They're not labeled or designated to anyone in particular."

"You think it's Christmas magic or something stupid like

that?" Will asked with a head shake as he reached into the center of the table and pilfered some butter from the dish and started slathering it onto his roll. "You believe in that crap?"

Rowan shot him a snide look but didn't say anything. "Dinner is getting cold. Everyone eat. Hunter, I think you're last."

Hunter had already started eating; all the Brussel sprouts on her plate were gone. With a bashful smile and a quick swallow, she picked up her strip of paper. "Let go of your burdens, spread your wings and soar into the unknown."

"Well, that could be for anyone," Will said.

Obviously, he didn't buy the mystery or the fact that fate alone had bestowed each fortune into the lap of the person it best suited. Oh yeah, no way in hell was Juney a match with Will, he was much too cynical. And even though she prided herself on her practicality and pragmatism, she wrote fantasy and fiction for a living. She couldn't help but believe that some form of magic, be it fate, kismet or some other universal or otherworldly involvement, may have had a hand in delivering the right fortune to the right person. Elves perhaps? Mischievous sugar plum fairies?

Juney shot Will a look, and just then, the lights in the kitchen, living room and on the tree flickered, off, on, off, on, and from out of nowhere a faint gust of wind swept down across the table and blew out the three tapers in the center.

Six mouths hung slack-jawed.

"I-is there a window open somewhere?" Hunter asked, her eyes darting back and forth between Rowan and Juney.

Juney shook her head. "No."

"There aren't any windows in the dining room," Rowan said slowly.

Austin drew a lighter out of his pocket and stood up, leaning over the table and re-lighting the candles.

"Well, believe what you wish, Dr. Colson," Juney said

smugly. "But *I* believe we were all meant to receive these specific fortunes. Get us thinking at the very least."

Will made a face that only men with very little patience and big egos can make and then snorted as he took a bite of his roll, tucking it into his cheek. "Pass the roasted potatoes, please."

A SHORT WHILE LATER, Juney rubbed her belly as if a chubby baby kicked inside and it wasn't just the monster food baby that gurgled happily. Letting out a contented sigh, she leaned back in her chair. "Well, I dare say that was one of the best Christmas dinners I've ever had."

Rowan beamed at her from the other end of the table. She wished he were closer. Will's arm was draped around Amber's shoulders as the two sat cozily at the table sipping wine. Hunter and Austin buried their awkwardness in more pie and wine.

"It's all about the bacon on the turkey skin," Rowan said with a yawn. "And the sexy helper in the kitchen. Nothing lights a fire under your ass to put out a good spread like a beautiful co-chef."

Co-chef. She liked the sound of that. And she liked even more that he hadn't called her a sous-chef. Even though she'd totally been his lackey and wouldn't have been offended if he'd even demoted her title to line cook. But the fact that he considered her his equal in the galley meant a lot.

She pushed herself away from the table and stood up. "Come cuddle with your *co-chef* next to the Christmas tree, Chef Briggs. I'm tired of sitting this far away from you."

Hunter grimaced in her seat and upended the wine bottle into her glass while Austin stared into the candle flame as if hypnotized. Will and Amber followed Juney's lead, as did Rowan.

"I like the way you think," Rowan said, coming up behind her and looping an arm around her shoulder. "And I love this dress."

She grinned up at him as they sauntered into the living room. She was wearing her favorite holiday cocktail dress. It was shimmery gold with long sleeves, a scoop neck and a back so low she had to buy special low-cut underwear to wear underneath it. Only tonight she wasn't wearing any, something she'd yet to confess to Rowan.

It was dark outside, and the tree reflected magically against the window pane. The fire in the hearth flickered low; Austin from his perch at the table took notice and was over in a flash bending down, removing the protective glass and poking at the flames with the poker. He put on a couple of new logs, then sat staring at it for bit longer. He was an odd guy.

Amber made her way into the kitchen and plunked down a couple of bowls of food. Earlier in the day, she'd mentioned to Juney that she would try to get Will to help her do the dishes. It was beginning to irritate her that the hot doctor wasn't pulling his weight around the cabin. It didn't really bother Juney, but she figured there was no harm in Amber asking Will to pitch in a little more, earn his keep, just like the rest of them.

"Well, that was absolutely wonderful," Amber said as she opened up the dishwasher.

"Yes, I agree," Hunter replied, bringing in the plate of turkey and a bowl of stuffing. "I'll have to do some back-to-back yoga sessions and an extra mile or two on the treadmill when I get back home to work all that pie off, but it was well worth it."

"It was mostly Rowan," Juney said from her spot on the floor next to Rowan. They'd gathered a bunch of pillows and blankets and were cuddled up in a cozy little nest next to the Christmas tree and up against the big picture window. "He's the brainchild behind the Christmas feast for kings. I only stewed the cranberry sauce, mashed the potatoes, and made the rolls."

"Well, the rolls were one of my favorite parts," Will said, coming in behind everyone in the kitchen, clutching nothing but his scotch and scratching his hard belly with his other hand.

Hunter went to tie an apron around her waist, but Amber stopped her. Her eyes quickly flicked to Juney and then Will before landing back on Hunter. "You go sit down. I'll do the dishes. Will, you want to help?"

But he was already staring down at his phone. "I've gotta go call my aunt. She just texted me. Says the whole family is together and they want to Skype." Without another word, and still staring at the screen, he wandered off in the direction of his bedroom.

Juney lifted one shoulder. Dr. Colson, master avoider. "What can you do?"

She could see Amber clench her jaw and let out a big huff.

What could she do? They weren't boyfriend and girlfriend. They'd known each other for all of two days. It didn't matter that they'd been intimate. There were some things in a relationship that took time. Sex, no, that one could often be immediate, but calling someone out on their shit, depending on who they were, that took skill, time and less alcohol down the hatch. Not that she had any issues with Rowan so far, but she wasn't sure she'd be ready to point out his faults to him yet, either. Despite the mind-blowing sex and instant chemistry, they were still getting to know each other, and she didn't want to go and piss him off or worse, scare him off.

But Amber was also a ballsy little thing, unlike Juney. She was a boss in her own right, a boss at work. She held rank over twenty men. She must know how to get men to do what needed to be done without wounding their egos in the process. But instead of saying anything to Will's back, she just watched it disappear down the hallway, a look on her face that Juney couldn't quite place. Was it anger? Sadness? Fear?

"I'll help," Hunter said, coming in and taking the apron from Amber. She placed it over her neck and then tied it around her waist. "I love your dress, by the way, Amber. Where did you get it?"

The two women started chatting amicably in the kitchen about this, that and the other thing, while Austin took off toward his room, muttering something about calling his sister, leaving Rowan and Juney to their own devices on the floor beneath the beautiful tree.

"I really do love this dress," he said with a low growl, running his hand down her back and leaning in to kiss her shoulder. "The back is incredibly low, though. Do you have to wear special underwear or something?"

She licked her lips and shifted on the blankets until she straddled him. "Or *something*." Reaching for his hand, she guided it down to her lap and beneath her dress.

Rowan's eyes went wide as his fingers grazed her cleft. "Juney..."

Boldly, having never done anything like this before and turned on by the naughtiness of it, she pushed her hips into his caress. At first, she'd been mortified when she was caught earlier that day, pinned up against the fridge as Rowan hammered into her, but it'd also been exhilarating. She was a grown woman, a sexual being, and it was high time she got a little dirty now and then.

A salacious smile curved up Rowan's mouth as he cupped her mound with possession and his thumb rubbed her clit. His other hand wrapped around her waist, and he pulled her close until she was straddling his lap. Juney shot a look behind her at the two women in the kitchen. They both stood at the sink, their backs to her and Rowan.

Rowan snagged her bottom lip between his teeth and tugged as he pushed two fingers inside her. A moan fled her before she could stop it, and she bucked into his hands.

"Shh," he scolded with a chuckle, releasing her waist and scooting them backward toward the big floor-to-ceiling window, hiding them behind the enormous tree. "Don't want to get caught now, do you?"

She closed her eyes and mewled softly when he rubbed his thumb back and forth against her bud again.

"Unless that's your thing now, you dirty girl?"

He chuckled low in his throat, a sound that stirred something hot and needy deep in her belly. She was starting to crave his touch. Even when he was near, she was starved for it. The way Rowan looked at her, with such adoration, such awe. The way he cherished her, worshipped her body. She couldn't remember the last time a man had made her feel so wanted, so desired.

"Rowan," she whispered, frantic for breath, frantic for an orgasm, frantic for more of him inside her.

"Shh."

"Rowan, please."

"Oh baby, I love it when you beg. You're going to come for me, aren't you?"

"Yes."

"You love it when I'm inside you, don't you? Pumping your hot, tight little pussy with my fingers."

"Oh God, yes . . . so much."

"You're close. I can feel it."

"Rowan . . ."

He drew his tongue up the side of her neck. She let her head loll to the side to give him better access and closed her eyes. The way his fingers pushed and grazed her walls, his thumb brushing back and forth against her needy clit, it was all too much. She tensed, squeezed, held her breath and let go. Quiet as could be, she let the climax flood her veins, pooling deep and warm in her core, and spreading out into her limbs until everything was a divine tingly heat and Juney was exhausted.

"Where is everyone?" Will's deep voice rumbled into the room, causing Juney to snap out of her post-orgasmic daydream. She didn't move or bother turning to look. Her body was in well-earned atrophy. She would move when she had to.

"Austin's off in his room," Amber said dryly. "And Rowan and Juney are having sex over behind the tree."

CHAPTER THIRTEEN

THE FOLLOWING day was Boxing Day. After a sleep-in, followed by a day of hard skiing and snowboarding, hot tub time to ease achy muscles and some killer turkey pot pie made by Rowan and Juney, the group hiked their way back to the ski lodge and into the Tipsy Moose. Rowan heaved the solid well-worn wooden door open for everyone, and they were all immediately slapped upside the face by loud laughter, even louder music, and the warmth of more than four dozen bodies and a dancing fire in the hearth. Making their way inside, with Will at the front and Austin at the back, they all took in the show.

Pool tables, a Keno board, a dart board were off in one corner, and a couple of slot machines took up another. There was a stage for live music next to the hearth and what appeared to be a very old but well maintained jukebox between the doors to the washrooms. Various mounted animal heads lined the log walls, with a big elk overtop the fireplace. A few stuffed birds sat perched in various positions on small ledges, and the odd big trophy fish hung on a wooden plaque with a gaping mouth and curved tail. The wooden tables showed serious signs of wear, with moisture rings and knife marks, and the dark green carpet was heavily trodden, but the place was clean. A handful of neon signs for mass market breweries like Labatt and Molson hung behind the bar, while a few more, for local Washington state breweries, were poised between the animal heads on the wall.

Rowan reached for Juney's hand and tugged her through the moguls of tables and chairs. "Here's a free booth. Let's grab it quick."

She grinned at him and gave his hand a tender squeeze back. "Sounds good."

Hunter and Austin followed them, while Will and Amber walked up to the bar and ordered the first round.

"The poster said they have karaoke," Juney said. Well, more like slightly hollered as the music from the sound system was a tad too loud to carry on a decent conversation at a reasonable decibel.

"Oooh, I love karaoke," Hunter said, bouncing in her seat and rubbing her hands together. "A few of my employees go out to this cool after-hours Korean karaoke bar a block or so from Pike Place. I've tagged along half a dozen times. It's nothing like this though. You get your own room, pick your songs, read them on the screen and go crazy."

Juney giggled. Rowan loved her laugh. Even her giggle was throaty and sexy, and it made his prick twitch inside his pants and his heart rate go into overdrive. Just like Will was always looking for a reason to touch Amber, Rowan couldn't get enough of Juney. He draped his arm around her in the booth. The look in her eyes said it all. Sapphire flames and lust danced hot and bothered back at him, and at that moment, he knew he was going to fulfill another one of her fantasies tonight.

"My sister, Fern, and I traveled to Japan for work, years ago," Juney started, "and we went to one of those karaoke room bars as well. It was intense. Each room had a different theme. We got the 'green' room. Everything, and I mean *everything* was green. Even the doorknobs, the microphone, the keyboard. There was a giant Granny Smith apple on the wall behind us. It was sensory overload, and when we left, we were drunk on Japanese wine, and rather than pizza, we were craving apples. We ran to the nearest grocery store and bought a five-pound bag."

"It's the same at the Korean one downtown," Hunter said with a nod. "I've been in the black and white room, the Elvis room, the Michael Jackson room, and the Boyband room."

"Libations!" Will announced, sauntering over with two beers and a scotch for himself in hand. Amber was behind him cradling a beer and two glasses of wine. She handed the wine to Juney and Hunter and then took a seat next to Austin. He thanked Will for his beer and quickly tilted the bottle up to drink.

A man with a clipboard and crisp white T-shirt over what could only be a six-pack beneath walked over and flashed everyone at the table a big toothy smile. Rowan was pulling Juney tighter against him before he even knew what he was doing.

"Howdy, y'all! Merry Christmas and Happy Boxing Day. Welcome to the Tipsy Moose. I'm Hank, and I'm passing around the sign-up sheet for the karaoke, if any of y'all are interested." He set a scuffed and torn green binder on the table. "These here are the songs. We've got pretty much everything. Take a peek, find something you like, and then sign up on the form here and when you're done, bring it over to me at the stage there."

His eyes roamed around the table and across everyone's faces, but he stopped and held his stare a little longer when he passed over Hunter, and then again when he passed over Juney. Will was busy nuzzling Amber's neck, staking his claim like the red-blooded alpha that he was. Shit, should Rowan be doing the same? Should he lean over and shove his tongue down Juney's throat? He'd have to wait to do that kind of thing once he had a couple of beers down the hatch.

Hunter picked up the binder and smiled back at Hank. Since that afternoon, something in her had changed. She no longer seemed to care that Austin wasn't paying attention to her; if anything, she was avoiding him as well. She batted those long eyelashes of hers at Hank and leaned into the table, the edge pushing up her breasts until they practically spilled out of her tight black V-neck T-shirt. Rowan heard Austin gulp next to him.

"This is great," Hunter said, thumbing through the binder. "Do you have anything by the Arkells?"

Austin's back stiffened to the point where he jostled Rowan. Rowan shot him a dirty look, but the guy seemed oblivious. He was too busy grinding his molars and trying to pop Hank's head off with his geeky mind power.

Hank's eyes were fixated on Hunter's chest. "We do. 'Leather Jacket,' 'Whistleblower,' '11:11,' and 'Ballad of Hugo Chavez.' "

Deliberately making sure to push her breasts up even further, Hunter leaned across the table and reached for the pen. " 'Leather Jacket,' please," she said sweetly.

Hank winked at her. "You got it, sweetheart. I've got copies of the binder, so I'll leave it here in case you guys want to make more selections. There are about ten people ahead of you, but when it's your turn, I'll let you know, okay?"

She flipped her blonde hair back over her shoulder, and her mouth stretched out into a big closed-mouth smile. "Sounds *perfect*," she purred.

Rowan and Will both coughed, Amber and Juney averted their eyes, and Austin, well, Austin looked like he was about to suffer an apoplexy or challenge Hank to a duel.

"There'll be dancing a bit later too. Save one for me?" Hank asked. He flipped his brown hair back off his eyes and flashed another big smile at Hunter. The rest of the table could have been empty, the occupants naked or all suffering from dysentery, and he wouldn't have noticed. He only had eyes for Hunter.

Dear lord, was this flirting? It was awkward to watch. Rowan could only imagine how awkward and forced it felt to those immediately involved. Thank God he and Juney had skipped that. Well, except for his random comments that made her cringe, laugh, and then shut him up with her delicious little lips. She really was the perfect woman. He squeezed her hand again and let his other hand draw light circles on her sculpted shoulder. He had to wonder, though, was Hunter actually interested in Hank, or was she simply behaving this way to piss off Austin? Because either way, it was working like a hot damn.

Hunter lifted one shoulder and took a dainty sip of her wine, her lashes falling against her cheeks as she savored the malbec on her tongue and swirled it around for a few moments before swallowing. Both Hank and Austin's eyes were riveted on her face and then her neck as it undulated softly with her swallow. He could only imagine what those men envisioned her swallowing.

"Maybe. I've never been much of a dancer. I have to have quite a few glasses of wine coursing through my veins before I'll step out on to the dance floor. And even then, I always seem to have two left feet."

Hank leaned over, putting his elbow on the table, not giving too hoots that he was popping Austin's bubble and essentially partitioning him off from the rest of the group. "Don't worry, darlin', with me, your feet won't even hit the ground." Then he grabbed her hand, turned it palm up and let his lips fall to her wrist. "I'll come find you when the right song is on."

"So, the chicken dance?" Rowan said, before he could stop himself.

Hank's eyes left Hunter and fell to Rowan. Both men smiled uncomfortably before Hank stood back up. Well, that seemed to have broken the spell that Hank had cast upon the table. The intruder chuckled softly in his chest as he nodded. "Slower than the chicken dance." He winked at Hunter again and took off toward the next table.

Was that the sound of a train? Rowan looked over at Austin. Nope, just steam coming out of the guy's ears as his face turned bright purple and his eye did this weird twitchy thing.

Seriously, dude, what the hell is your problem?

JUNEY HEADED off to the washroom to go freshen up. She'd been trying so hard not to break the seal, but in the end it was a futile attempt. Excusing herself, she finished her wine, nodded at Hunter that she'd split another bottle with her and then took off toward the door marked "Does."

Two bottles of wine, three shots of tequila, a few hours, and *several* beers later, everyone was feeling good. Hunter had kicked Will's ass at pool, twice, and now the doctor was on the hook for picking up the entire bar tab for their group. And it didn't matter how many wine or beers the rest of them were drinking, three fingers of Will's scotch cost the same as one bottle of the malbec Juney and Hunter had split. The doctor had expensive taste.

Besides the awkwardness at the table when they'd first arrived, things had been going well. Rowan was affectionate and sweet, keeping them all laughing, while Amber and Will told stories about work and Hunter filled in the gaps with tales of her time spent backpacking and hitchhiking across the country. The only wet blanket was Austin, and even he, as the night went on and the booze started to flow, seemed to loosen up. He still wouldn't really talk to Hunter, but she seemed resigned to that fact and ignored him, too. It broke Juney's heart that the two of them weren't connecting. She knew how they felt about each other, and they knew it, too, but for some reason, Austin lacked the confidence to even speak to Hunter, let alone woo or pursue.

Juney was glad that her match had the cojones to knock on her door that first night. As much as she liked Austin, she wasn't sure she could be with a man who had such insecurities, when she herself had insecurities up the wazoo.

She checked herself in the mirror and used a tissue from her purse to blot her forehead and beneath her eyes. It was warm in the bar, and no matter how good of a makeup artist you were, things changed under the fluorescent lights.

The music outside started up again, and she could hear voices singing to the karaoke. They weren't terrible, but they weren't great, either. You could tell whoever was singing the duet, they had both been drinking for a while. Gaps in the song were filled with giggles and random "ahs" as the singer took a drink.

She took one last look in the mirror. It didn't matter that she was in the wine business; a whole bottle of wine and tequila shots in the span of a couple of hours, and she was feeling it. In her toes, her fingers, her eyes, her head. Juney was drunk.

Grabbing the brushed brass handle to the bathroom door, she swung it open and came face to face with the image of Hunter and Rowan on stage singing. Their arms were looped around each other, each had a microphone, and they were belting out the words to the song at the top of their lungs with enormous, happy smiles plastered on their drunk faces.

And they looked like the perfect couple.

Both blond. Both with million-dollar mega-watt smiles. Big beautiful eyes, killer bodies. Where Rowan had pecs, Hunter had breasts. Breasts Juney only ever dreamed of having, rather than the modest B-cup bee-stings she hid beneath the padded push-up she was wearing now. Hunter's breasts were perfect. Hunter and Rowan were perfect. They were a match.

How could she have been so foolish to think that Rowan was her match? That Daisy's algorithm had deemed Juney and Rowan soulmates? She was probably matched with Austin. They were both insecure. Both smart and nerdy. But he looked at her as more of a mother or sister, and despite the fact that he wasn't acting on it, he only had eyes for Hunter. Did all the men want Hunter? Was Will settling for Amber too? Or maybe Juney was matched with Will? No, he didn't want kids. Daisy had to have put that into her computer.

Juney's mouth went slack and despair chilled her veins to the point of pain as she stared at the couple on stage. She could feel the blood drain from her face. Their smiles were so natural as they glanced at the screen with the lyrics, then at each other, then back at the screen, then out into the crowd.

Rowan was not her match.

She wanted to move. Wanted to run back into the bathroom or down the road. Run away so that the tears could fall where no one could see them, but she couldn't. Fear, despair, sadness, they had cemented themselves inside her, in her feet, in her heart. She was immobile. Forced to watch them until the song was over. And then of course, Rowan, being Rowan, pulled Hunter close and planted a big kiss on her temple before tipping his beer up and draining it. It wasn't until he pulled it away from his mouth that he noticed Juney standing there.

Thoughts, so many of them, scattered across his face, along with fear and confusion.

Juney made to turn away. This time her feet cooperated and left the floor, aiding her in her quest to flee. She couldn't watch what she knew in her heart to be a match made in blond-bombshell, California beach-bum heaven. They were meant to be. She'd been deluding herself these last few days that Rowan could be her match, possibly be interested in her. Not when Hunter was there and available. No. She needed to leave. Let them discover their attraction organically, without her broken heart in the way. She pushed the bathroom door open again, but before she could duck inside, Rowan was behind her.

"Juney!"

"Leave it, Rowan. I'm such an idiot!"

He pushed her into the washroom and spun her around to face him, his hands on her shoulders. "Why are you an idiot? What's wrong?"

She shook her head and bit her lip. Tears stung the back of her eyes, and her throat threatened to seize up. "It's nothing. Just forget it." Sadness hollowed out her stomach.

He shook her gently, his eyes pleading with her to open up. "Tell me why you looked so terrified when I saw you standing there a second ago. What the hell happened?"

Swallowing hard, she continued to shake her head. "I—I'm not your match!"

"What?" His brows pinched until an adorable wrinkle formed between them.

"You and Hunter. Up there. You are the perfect couple. Both blond and beautiful. I can't compete with her." Oh fuck, now she was a blubbering mess. The tears were coming down, hot and rapid. She bunched the sleeve of her long-sleeved gray shirt in her fist and used it to wipe her eyes and cheeks.

"What?" he asked again. "Where is this coming from?"

"Seeing you two up there, I realized I'm nothing compared to her. You're beautiful people. You're supposed to be together. Make beautiful babies, live in your beautiful house, have a beautiful dog. I'm not like you."

"You're not beautiful?"

She shook her head. *No. I'm an ugly duckling. Forrest Gump.*

"Juney . . ."

The man was at a loss.

"Y-you're right, you're not beautiful."

Her head snapped back up to his face from where she'd been looking at her feet.

"You're not beautiful. Beautiful is an overused word. Baby,

you're . . . you're fucking stunning. Gorgeous, breathtaking, striking. You're not beautiful, because beautiful isn't a good enough word to describe you. I wish you could see yourself as I see you, because when you're in the room, you're all I see. Are you upset I was singing with Hunter?"

She didn't know what to say or how to react. Suddenly her head was bobbing. Her stomach hurt, and her temples pounded. No more booze.

He let out a sigh. "I'm sorry. She'd actually asked Austin to go and sing with her. Looks like booze hits us all in different ways. I apparently sing karaoke, Hunter doesn't give a shit and gets ballsy, and you . . . "

"I turn into a jealous, emotional lunatic."

"You turn into sweet, adorable, *slightly* more emotional Juniper Davis. A woman who in only a short amount of time has managed to make me crazy . . . and in a good way. I'm not interested in Hunter. She's like a kid sister. And I felt bad for her when Austin turned her down. As for the peck on the cheek, well, I give that same kiss to my sister, Annie, when I see her. I'm sorry, though, if it made you second-guess my feelings for you."

Her face was on fire, and her throat was raw. But the ache in her heart was slowly receding, and although everything seemed blurry at the moment through all the tears, Juney was seeing Rowan more clearly than ever.

"And for the record, I kind of like the jealousy." His grin was wily. "Lets me know how crazy you are about me, too."

She hiccupped, then quickly covered her mouth with her hand. "I'm sorry."

"For what?"

"F-for thinking you wanted Hunter simply because you were singing up there. You're allowed to be friends with her. You're allowed to sing. I'm not a jealous nut job like that, I swear. It's gotta be the booze. Stupid Hunter and her shots of tequila."

Rowan chuckled as he stepped forward and let his hand fall to her waist. "You're not a nut job. And I happen to think you're an adorable drunk."

She sniffed. "Even when I'm flying off the handle and turning green with jealousy?"

He nodded. "Even then, because it happens to be a lovely shade of green. Like romaine lettuce or fresh arugula."

A hiccupy laugh bubbled up, and she finally smiled. He always knew how to make her smile. She looked up into his eyes but found no humor there. They were smoldering, lightning hot. The lighting in the bathroom was terrible, fluorescent and almost yellowy, but even then, fire seemed to dance in his soft brown irises as he looked down at her. She bit her lip. That look, it turned her insides to mush and made her heart palpitate so fast she feared it would beat right out of her chest and sprint its way across the floor. Not to mention the tingle that drifted across her skin, down her spine and belly to seat itself between her legs.

His hand released her waist and shifted up to her face. A knuckle gently ran down her cheek, collecting the last of her tears. His gaze flew to the door, back to her face, then the door again. Suddenly, he released her and stalked the three strides to the deadbolt.

"Locked or unlocked?"

She shook her head. "Huh?"

"Do you want me to fuck you in this bathroom with the door locked or unlocked?" His eyes darkened to the color of warm bourbon.

All the moisture left her mouth.

"Juney?"

"Uh . . . l-locked. We've already been caught once."

Grinning back at her, he switched the lock. He returned, cradling her body in less than a second. "I want you and only you, Juney. Let me show you." He sank to his knees and let his hands trail up her black leather boots, continuing up her legs. Along the stretchy fabric of her . . . His eyes flew up to hers when he reached the top of her thighs. "These *aren't* tights!"

Her lips pursed, and she shook her head. They were thick, dark gray, cable-knit thigh-high socks. Juney wasn't even sure where she'd got them—her sister Fern, maybe? But on a last-minute whim she'd tossed them into her suitcase, figuring they'd pair well with her black pleated skirt and long-sleeve gray shirt. She'd nearly frozen her ass off on the walk up to the lodge, but the expression on Rowan's face had been totally worth it.

"Holy fuck," he whispered, his fingers making their way up to the waistband of her underwear and pulling it down.

Juney hadn't been foolish enough to wear a thong *and* a skirt with the socks, but lacy boy-shorts weren't out of the question.

Rowan slid her panties down her legs, his eyes going wide as he took in the red lace.

She stepped out of them.

"Juney," he purred, inching forward, his hands wandering back up her thighs. He helped lift her leg and place one foot on the counter so she was even more exposed to him. The cool air was a welcome balm on her scorching skin. He ran his finger back along her legs and then beneath her skirt. One hand cupped her butt, and the other one came forward and dipped into her folds. "You're so wet." His breath was warm on her sensitive skin as he ducked his head beneath her skirt and planted hot, searing kisses on her inner thighs and lips. "Wet for me."

Juney's knees wobbled and threatened to buckle beneath her, but Rowan kept a tight grip on her ass as his lips encircled her clit and sucked. She wasn't going anywhere. He hummed softly, and the gentle vibration sent new shards of pleasure swirling through her.

This man wanted her.

Not Hunter, not Amber.

Her!

She closed her eyes and pushed into his face, her hands coming down to rest on the top of his head. His face was buried beneath her skirt, so all she could see was the nape of his neck, but even that was dead sexy. He swept the flat of his tongue up through her folds, and Juney let out a low moan.

Damn, that felt good.

And only when he knew she was close, shamelessly pushing into his face, would he mix it up and suck again or twiddle her clit with his finger. She was on the edge, riding along that inch-thick ledge like a damn circus clown on a unicycle, and every time she thought she was going to topple over and fall, Rowan would bring her right back.

But this wasn't all she wanted. She wanted him to take her, all of her, in here. In the dirty bar bathroom with dozens of people outside. They all probably knew what she and Rowan were up to, but she didn't care. A part of her liked that. Juney had never done a spontaneous or wild thing in her life, and that had to change.

She pulled on his ears. "Not like this," she said breathlessly. One last flick to her clit that made her knees nearly buckle and Rowan stood up, his knees popping like an old man's as he brought himself to his feet with a slight groan.

His eyes were glassy, and his hungry lips glistened with her arousal. Juney lunged forward and tasted herself on him. She'd never tasted anything so erotic before. His need pressed hard and long into her hip, and the desire to taste him, to have him in her mouth, pleasure him the way he'd pleasured her, took over and she sank to the floor in a crouch, pulling Rowan's zipper down along with her. She freed him from his boxers and cupped his balls, giving them a gentle tug.

Rowan watched her from above. With a smug smile, their gazes locked as she took him in her mouth.

. . .

Rowan had never met a woman like Juney before. So unbelievably amazing, sexy, gorgeous, smart, and yet, she had absolutely no idea she possessed any of those qualities. They hadn't really talked much about their childhoods yet, or what it had been like growing up, but based on a few things she'd said in passing, Rowan guessed childhood hadn't been easy for poor little Juniper.

But the woman had certainly made up for it in her adult years. Highly successful author and vintner, entrepreneur extraordinaire. And the fact that she was one of the most gorgeous women he'd ever laid eyes on made her the whole damn package. It'd broken his heart to see her face when the song with Hunter had ended. He thought someone had died. And now, his jealous blue-eyed beauty was on her knees in front of him, with his shaft in her pretty mouth as she cupped his balls and swirled that talented tongue of hers around and around.

Did she know what she was doing to him? Making him hers. He would do anything for this woman. Walk across hot coals, jagged glass. He barely knew her and yet she already had him by the balls, literally and figuratively.

His hands dove into the satiny strands of her dark brown hair, and he let his fingers comb through until he reached the base of her skull. Then he gathered it in his fist like a ponytail and guided her deeper. This wasn't the first time she'd taken him in her mouth; he knew she could go deeper. He wanted to feel every inch of her hot little mouth, feel those plump lips at the base of his cock as her tonsils tickled his crown.

She blinked up at him and smiled with her mouth full of him. Jesus Christ, he nearly came on the spot. When a beautiful lone tear sprung from the corner of her eye as she deep-throated him again, her hand guided him to the back, where her throat muscles contracted around him. He was hitting her so deep, he could barely stand it.

Before it was too late, he reached under her arms and lifted her off the floor. "Fuck, Juney, that was incredible. That mouth . . . Dear God."

"In-inside me, Rowan," she panted, her eyelids hooded. "Now . . . please!"

He growled as he spun her around to face the mirror. He flipped up her skirt. Dear sweet baby Jesus, those socks, those boots, her delicious ass. It was all too much. With his hands on her hips, he angled himself at her core. Their eyes locked in the mirror ahead, and she smiled back at him. It was a wicked smile. A dirty smile. A smile that said, "Take me, big boy, and make me scream."

She gripped the edge of the counter and lifted her hips up to help him. He notched himself at her center and drove home. A sharp cry fled her lips as he impaled her, hitting her deep on the first thrust. Damn, she felt good. Hot and slick and tight. And the way she gripped him like a fist, her pussy pulsing and squeezing him on every draw, begging him to come back deeper inside, desperate to hold on to him. She was pure sex, and she didn't even know it.

"Rowan," she said with a kittenish mewl. "Oh God, Rowan."

Yes.

"Rowan . . . oh God. Don't stop."

I won't. Not ever.

He bared his teeth and picked up the pace, hitting her deeper, hitting her harder, hitting her faster. The sound of flesh slapping flesh ricocheted around the small bar bathroom, competing with their groans and sighs. He was already close. She just felt so good. So right.

He wanted to feel more of her beneath his palm. Wanted to feel her clit swell and harden in his fingertips as he took her to the brink and then tossed her over. Releasing his grasp on her hip with one hand, he hunched over her body and wrapped his arm around her, lifting her skirt up to explore her folds. He felt himself sliding in and out of her, his shaft rock solid and soaked from her dripping pussy. He found her clit and tugged on it. She gasped, followed by a low and erotic moan as she pushed down into his ministrations. Begging for more.

Another tug followed by a sharp pinch.

"Rowan . . ." She sighed. "I'm close."

"Me too. Come, babe."

She pushed back into him and let her head hang down between her arms, her hair falling in front of her face in dark chunky tendrils. He drew his tongue up the vein in her neck and nipped her earlobe. "Come, Juney."

"Oh G-od . . ." Her body went stiff, her clit swelled and hardened, and her cleft pulsed around him in unbelievable heat as she let go, her whimpers and sighs music to his ears.

"Yes."

"Rowan . . ."

"Juniper." His balls tightened and drew up. He stilled, let out a loud grunt into her shoulder as he clamped down hard with his teeth, and allowed the climax to claim him. Blood rushed through his veins like a flooded river as the orgasm unfurled inside him and pleasure radiated out from his center in waves. He spilled himself inside of her, her sweet little pussy milking him, squeezing him, capturing his seed.

Yes.

No one but Juney.

Seconds later, she let out a sated sigh, and her back slumped beneath him, her breathing coming out in slow, ragged gasps as she fought to rejoin reality. He felt the same way. It was a euphoric experience being with Juney. Ethereal. Unreal.

He slipped from her, and she stood up. Like a gentleman, he

ducked into one of the bathroom stalls and came out with a wad of toilet paper to help her clean up.

"Here," he said, picking her sexy red underwear off the counter. "I'd love it if you kept them off for the rest of the night, but it's probably safer if you didn't."

She smiled demurely at him and took them from him, her lashes fanning out against her rosy cheeks as she glanced down at her feet. She was embarrassed. It was sweet.

"I, um . . ."

"I'll leave you to freshen up," he said with a chuckle, tucking himself back into his boxers and pants, taking extra care not to catch his slowly deflating johnson in the zipper. "But when you're done, come back out. I think we should do a duet together. And I definitely want to spin this sweet ass of yours around on the dance floor." He grabbed her hand and spun her around right there in the bathroom.

She looked up at him and smiled. It was a smile that said a thousand words and made Rowan's heart beat a thousand times and his stomach do a thousand somersaults.

"I'd like that."

CHAPTER FOURTEEN

"So, turkey burgers tonight?" Juney asked the following morning as she and Rowan grabbed their coffees from the kitchen and wandered over to the couch to cuddle. The house was still quiet, and they were enjoying the solitude and view of the snow falling in big, thick, clumpy flakes as the sky slowly grew lighter.

"That's the plan," he yawned. "I'll grind up the dark meat. I found a package of ground turkey in the freezer, too, so we'll add that as well. And I'm thinking a mango salsa and papaya slaw with some brie melted onto the patties. I could whip up some Kaiser rolls, make some yam fries and potato chips. Sound good? I'll call it 'I like it when you call me Big Papaya. What do you think?"

Juney stared at him in awe as she brought her mug up to her chin and blew over the top, sending the steam coiling up and out into the air. "Sounds decadent for a burger." Her lips lifted at the corner in a small smile. "And the name is hilarious. I can't wait. Your culinary visions and creations amaze me. You're exactly the kind of chef I've been looking for at my restaurant at the winery. Not afraid to take a classic and give it a classy and upscale twist, but without making it pretentious or unidentifiable. I swear every chef I interviewed wanted to do something *deconstructed*. What's wrong with the constructed version as long as it's done right? I don't want a deconstructed filet mignon. I want a damn filet mignon!"

Rowan's eyes lit up with laughter. He took a sip of his coffee. A sexy grin caught on his mouth as he swallowed. "What can I say? Food is my life. And I think that deconstructed nonsense is overrated and overdone." He let out a defeated sigh, and his shoulder slumped ever so slightly. "Though, based on my current predicament, I'll deconstruct the shit out of something if I have to to pay the bills. I'd love to have my own restaurant, but that takes capital, and with the way the country is going, I'm not sure I'll ever be able to afford to own my own restaurant. I'll just have to start hitting the pavement when I get back to Olympia. Or maybe move to Seattle." He shook his head. "Yeah, I'll probably have to move to Seattle. Silvio's probably blacklisted me in Olympia. The guy has connections, and I didn't exactly leave on *good* terms."

She rubbed his thigh, letting her hand slowly trail its way up to the V of his legs. She could feel his heat, and it was making her head loopy. Removing her hand quickly, she cupped her mug again in both palms.

But Rowan grabbed her hand again and put it back with another big, sexy smile. He ran his finger along the back of her hand, encouraging her to begin rubbing. She did, but her head wasn't in it.

Juney pursed her lips together and gazed out the window again for a moment. Was it too soon? Could she ask him? Should she wait a bit, see if he finds something here in Washington? Would he think it was weird, her asking him? She spun back to face him. "I'd like to offer you a job."

That smoldering look he'd been giving her a second ago, the same look he'd given her in the kitchen Christmas day and again in the bar bathroom last night, a look that said, "I'm seconds away from stripping you naked and taking you here and now — hard," was gone. And a look she hadn't seen before, didn't recognize and couldn't place quickly enveloped him. When he removed his hand from hers, she stopped rubbing and slowly withdrew.

"You taking pity on me?" he asked with such accusation, Juney's eyes went wide and her skin prickled. Red shot across his cheekbones, and anger alighted in his eyes.

"N-no. Th-that's not it at all."

"Then why are you offering me a job? Trying to hang on to me any way you can?"

A fist. An enormous, callused, muscular fist gripped her heart and squeezed while a boot, a filthy steel-toed boot, pressed hard on her lungs as the heel swiveled relentlessly, grinding out the air from her body in ragged gasps. What was happening? She couldn't breathe. Was she having a heart attack?

He sneered at her and stood up. "I'm no one's pity hire, Juniper. I'll find my own way. Find a new restaurant or take out a loan from the bank. Do a food truck or something. But I don't need you, someone who barely knows me, offering me a job in motherfucking *Canada* out of pity. Jesus . . . " He ran his hand through his hair. "Is it pity or desperation?"

Tears, hot and plentiful, burned the corners of Juney's eyes as she stared up at the man she thought she had been falling for. She couldn't have been more wrong. Everything he'd ever said to her had been a lie. A ruse to get into her pants. She'd been a complete and total fool.

Swallowing past the hard lump in her throat, she set her coffee mug down on the side table, bunched her fists at her sides and stood up. He was at least four to six inches taller than her, and Juney was no slouch at five-foot-eight, so she had to tilt her head up to look at him. But she did it with grace and poise, angling her chin just right and clenching her teeth until she no longer felt the need to cry.

"No, Rowan," she started, hating the slight quaver to her voice. "It wasn't a pity offer. It was a genuine offer. I like your food. I like you and thought it could work. Even if we weren't sleeping together, and I was matched with Will or Austin, I probably would have still offered you the job. Your food is delicious. As for desperation . . . " Her lip turned up into a snarl. "I'm not desperate at all. In fact, I'm desperate for nothing. I can and I *will* achieve everything I want, and I'll do it on my own. You could have called it *hope*. But not desperation. You see, I am at the top of my game. I'm a best-selling author, an award-winning vintner, and a successful entrepreneur. I'm not desperate at all, I *have* it all. But you, you're a fucking unemployed chef who's shot his mouth off one too many times and is *desperate* for work. And now, you've lost the opportunity to run your own restaurant, to fulfill *your* dream. And now it would seem you've also lost the girl."

She turned away, ready to head down the hall, but then vengeance, running hot through her blood, caused her to turn back. "You know, I don't think *Rowarn* needs a girlfriend after all. I think *Junica* will do just fine on her own. Maybe I'll cut out his character altogether or kill him gruesomely. Toss him out the castle tower window down into the town square or have him mauled by rabid wolfenboars." She grinned wickedly at him as emotion clawed at the back of her throat. "Yeah, torn limb from limb by a pack of wolfenboars. I like that idea. *Rowarn* is dead to me."

Her lip trembled slightly on that last bit. Despite her attempt at being cruel and hurting him the way he'd hurt her, she just didn't have it in her to be mean. She was in too much pain to be mean. But she managed to keep those tears at bay long enough to say what she needed to. So, with one last steely glare as her heart slowly shattered, she spun on her heel and stalked off down the hallway, willing her body to cooperate and keep the emotions in check until she was behind closed doors. She grabbed her doorknob, and a lone tear trickled down her cheek. Desperate? Yeah, Juney was desperate not to let this man destroy her heart, but she was beginning to think it was too late.

F*uck*! Rowan was an idiot. A moron. A dumbass. What had he done?

Probably ruined and alienated the best thing that has EVER happened to you, you jackass.

She'd offered him a job, named a fucking character after him, opened up her HEART to him, and he went and stomped all over everything. Let his pride get in the way. Who the fuck did he think he was? Gordon Ramsay? Hell, even Gordon Ramsay would probably be telling Rowan what a giant fuck-up he was being right now. Then he'd tell him that he'd overcooked his scallops and needed to do them again.

Go after her!

Shaking his head to release the fog, he made his way down the hallway. It'd only been a few minutes, but even that could have been too long. What if she was beyond the point of forgiveness? He really couldn't blame her if she was, he'd been so cruel. Pity? Desperate? That was his anger at himself coming out. Anger at his situation. That he was jobless . . . again. After being overlooked at work . . . again. He'd gone and shot his mouth off, and now he had no job *and* no girl. But Juney had offered to change all of that. She'd offered him a job and her heart and instead he'd stomped all over both *and* her country. Would he forgive her if the roles were reversed? He wasn't entirely sure.

His fingers came up, and he rapped on her door, nostalgia from four nights ago swamping him. He'd been just as nervous that night, but for different reasons. Now he wasn't only nervous, he was terrified.

"Go away," she said through the door. The faint sound of sniffles and tissues being drawn from their box made his chest tighten.

"Juney, can I come in? I'm really sorry. I . . . Can I come in, please?"

The door swung open a second later, and there she stood, with a tear-stained face and puffy red eyes. Both fists held wrinkly wads of tissues. A few others were strewn about the bed. "You come to tell me my books are crap, too?" she snapped, but her quivering lip told him she was seconds away from fresh tears. Tears he'd caused. Fuck if it was the last thing he did, he would never be the cause of Juney's tears again.

He pushed his way inside and shut the door. She took a few steps back, eyeing him suspiciously, bracing herself for more vitriol.

He fell to his knees. "Juniper, I am so, so sorry. I . . . " Inching forward until he was directly in front of her, Rowan grabbed her tissue-filled hands. "I honestly don't even know what came over me. There's no excuse. Everything I said, my reaction, my behavior, it was all wrong."

She pulled her hands free and glared down at him. "Stand up, you jackass."

He deserved that.

His lips bunched as he pushed himself to his feet, using the end of the bed for leverage. "I'm angry with myself, and I took it out on you," he started to say. "Angry that I haven't made it in the business despite how long I've been in it. Angry at constantly being overlooked, underestimated. Told that my food isn't good enough to make it onto the menu. And that I'll probably never get to run my own restaurant."

"So you decided to spit on a job offer to have all of those

things? While subsequently calling me desperate and making me feel like complete garbage?"

Shit!

She wasn't going to be easy to win over. Here he'd thought a simple knock on the door and a Canadian-y "I'm sorry" would do the trick. Was there something Canadians said besides "I'm sorry" for when they really fucked up?

I'm really, really sorry, my maple syrup queen?

Say that out loud and we will cut out your tongue with that St. Maurice Lefebvre knife.

He swallowed. "Juney, I am so, incredibly, genuinely, truly sorry. If I could take it all back, I would. None of what I said was true or a reflection of my real feelings. I was . . . shocked. You hardly know me and yet, you offered me a job."

She lifted one shoulder. "I like you, and I like your food. I go with my gut in this industry, and not once has it led me astray. I know wine, I know food and . . . "

"You thought you knew me."

She pursed her lips. "I thought I was starting to."

He took a step forward and reached for her hands again. She let the tissues fall to the floor and allowed him to lace their fingers. "You *do* know me. Probably better than a lot of people. I've . . . I've never been happier than I have in these last four days, Juney. I've been a workaholic for years. Miserable and desperate to get ahead."

Her head snapped up to face him.

"Yes, I'm the *desperate* one. Not you. Me. I'm desperate to have the kind of success you have in your field, in my own. Desperate for acceptance from my culinary peers. Desperate to have people love and rave about my food the way you do. The way I love and rave about your books. I'm the desperate one. Not you. And right now I'm desperate for you to forgive me. You are my match. Without a doubt. And even if the job offer is now off the table, and you go and have *Rowarn* brutally murdered, I still want to be with you."

Bright azure-blue eyes, still red-rimmed and glassy, shone back at him. She was gorgeous. Stunning. Even in goofy red and white candy cane pajama shorts and a red tank top, the woman was breathtaking. And, God, how he hated himself for how badly he'd hurt her. Even if Juney forgave him, he wasn't sure he would ever forgive himself.

"It would mean you'd have to move to Canada," she whispered, a smile in her voice and then a small one spreading on her lips.

Slowly, the vice around his heart released. "Haven't met a Canadian I didn't like. And your healthcare is better."

Her eyes took on a wicked gleam. "So, it's the universal healthcare that's sealed the deal, is it?"

Boldly, he swept his arm out and gathered her around the waist, pulling her tight against his chest. "No, it's the sexy, perfect little blue-eyed goddess offering to make all my dreams come true that has sealed the deal. All I have to do is not piss her off, and we should be golden."

She beamed, her arms floating up to rest on his shoulders. "I'll write up a proper contract, but for now, I believe a verbal contract should suffice."

"Verbal shmerbal," he purred. His hand came up, and he moved his fingers through her dark waves as he slanted his mouth over hers. "We seal this deal with a kiss."

CHAPTER FIFTEEN

Austin's whole face ached as he woke up the morning following Boxing Day. No. Ache was the wrong word. It throbbed. Pulse after pulse of throbbing agony gripped his face as he fought to open his eyes. Damn, even those hurt. Why did his face hurt? Probably because he'd been scowling all night. Eventually those muscles in his eyebrows and mouth had atrophied, and he ended up staring blankly at Hunter's butt. But now those muscles were getting their sweet retribution.

He groaned as he finally fluttered his lashes open and took in his dimly lit room. Thank God for blackout shades. What time was it? Was the trip over yet? Had he slept December 27th away? A part of him hoped he had. He grabbed his phone off the nightstand.

Shit. Nine-forty on December 27th.

He still had over twenty-four hours to go. One more day. One more day of this, and then he could return home to his boring, Hunter-free, fun-free, friendless life. One more day.

He swung his legs over the side of the bed and went to sit up. Black spots clouded his vision, and a small but loud and vivacious marching band picked up their instruments to start playing his high school homecoming song over and over again inside his head. The pain behind his eyes doubled, throbbing. He closed his eyes and trust-fell back into the pillows, rubbing his thumb and forefinger over the bridge of his nose to relieve the pain. Blurry images of the previous night flashed through his head like some trippy time travel scene in a movie. Jesus Christ, could things have gone *any* worse?

Hunter, as a last ditch attempt to be his friend, or more, had put down an Arkells song for her karaoke pick. And when her turn came, she'd turned to Austin, and with a sexy smile that had made his throat close up and his dick jerk in his pants, had asked him to join her.

Ah, hell no!

Hunter or not, Austin was terrified of public speaking or being in front of a crowd. He'd shaken his head and looked back down into his beer, deciding when the waitress came over that tequila was necessary. He was going to drink until he couldn't feel how big of an ass he was being. Until he was numb.

He figured she would just drop it and either go up alone or pass on the idea altogether, and it had looked as though she was about to, something that made Austin's guts spin and twist inside him. He hated seeing her so upset. But then Rowan grabbed her hand and pulled her up on stage.

"I'll sing with you, Hunter," he'd said. All smiles and a toss of golden hair. Austin had sat there glaring at him. The two hadn't sung exceptionally well. Hunter was better than Rowan, but neither of them could hold a tune to save their lives. But that wasn't what had killed him. What had destroyed his very soul was the look Hunter gave him while she was on stage. It was a look of defeat, slowly replaced by resolution as the song went on. And when Rowan wrapped his arm around her and planted a kiss on her temple, Hunter's eyes had flashed revenge at him. And she'd done just that.

For the rest of the night after her duet with Rowan, Hunter was a social butterfly. She'd danced with multiple guys, several times with that Hank twat, laughed and giggled, and smiled at every compliment and ounce of attention thrown her way. She hadn't even glanced at Austin again. But he'd watched her. She was all he saw. Every time Hunter danced with someone or laughed at their stupid joke, accepted a drink or smiled at a suitor, Austin did a shot.

He'd been heavy-lidded and hallucinating in the booth by the time Will and Rowan tossed his arms over their shoulders and hauled him out of the bar. He didn't even remember the walk down the hill to the cabin. All he remembered, and he still couldn't be clear if it was a dream, a hallucination or reality, was when Rowan and Will tossed him onto his bed, he still felt the presence of someone there, heard a voice, a soft, sweet voice. But that voice was frustrated. Even through its melodic hum, there was disbelief and anger in the tone. His boots were removed, as was his coat, all by the light and delicate touch of a sweet-smelling angel. Then that angel drew a blanket up and over him before turning out the light.

He wasn't sure if he'd mumbled anything or not. His head felt fuzzy and his mouth a sewer, but the gasp and then click of the door were the last things he clearly remembered hearing. Neither of them gave him any comfort or eased his drunken pain.

It wasn't until sometime later that morning, perhaps a few hours, so maybe it was lunchtime, that Austin finally felt a little less like death and managed to pry both his eyelids open and his sorry ass out of bed. He still had a killer headache determined to tear off his prefrontal lobe, but at least now he didn't see spots every time he moved faster than a geriatric sloth.

A shower, shave and brushed teeth did wonders, and by the

time he finished the last button on his black shirt, he wasn't feeling horrible, just . . . guilty. He'd behaved like a giant asshole. Probably to everyone, not only Hunter, and now he had to go and face the music.

He put his ear to the door.

Nothing.

Opened the door a crack.

Nothing.

Took a couple of steps down the hallway toward the main living area.

Nothing.

Where was everyone?

He noticed a note taped to the kitchen counter as he wandered in and poured himself some coffee.

Gone to visit Daisy's parents.
Be back soon.

SHIT! Hunter was over visiting Sam. The steaming coffee in his festive painted mug was no match for the blood that bubbled hot through Austin's veins. The handle on the mug snapped off at the image of Sam taking Hunter by the hand and leading her off to a quiet corner, where lo and behold, a mistletoe hung overhead as he confessed his true, hidden feelings for her. Austin looked down at his hands to where one held the mug and the other held the handle.

Holy shit.

He turned into The Hulk when he got mad.

He had to get a grip. But he couldn't get that picture out of his head now that he'd put it there. Hunter and Sam in a heated lip-lock under the mistletoe. Finding their Christmas happily ever after.

"No!" he said, not realizing he'd said it out loud until he heard his voice echo back to him in the cavernous, empty log cabin. Shaking his head, he switched mugs, grabbing a new one from the cupboard and putting the other one, the broken one, on the counter. He would see if he could find some Super Glue and try to fix it.

Should he toss on his boots and head to the Wrights' house, too? Stake his claim? Would that be weird? Yes, it probably would be. Especially since he wasn't entirely sure but would beg to guess that he'd not only ruined his chances from here to eternity with Hunter, but he was no longer on speaking terms with the others. He'd probably done something or said something to make them all mad at him. Or the women were rallying with Hunter and taking her side. Either way, he was happy for the solitude.

"How's your head?"

Austin spun around. Amber was coming in from the garage, all sweaty in nothing but a sports bra and tight black capris.

"Did you go for a run?" he asked before realizing how stupid a question it was. It was a blizzard out there.

She shook her head and walked behind him to the cupboard, where she grabbed a glass and then proceeded to fill it with water from the tap. "No, I found a stationary spin bike in the garage. A good quality one too. So I hopped on for an hour. I'm not used to this idle lifestyle. I'm always moving, always busy. I'll be sedentary when I'm dead."

Austin shook his head and added a splash of eggnog to his coffee from the carton. He ran when he could, did crunches and push-ups at home most evenings before bed, but he was enjoying the downtime. He didn't care if he put on five pounds this week, it'd been great to just de-frag. He mentally slapped himself.

De-frag, my ass. You're more fucked up now than when you came.

"You okay, there?" Amber asked, giving him a lone quirked eyebrow. "Trying to figure out how to free Tibet or something?"

"Or something," he muttered.

"Can I ask you something?" She pitched one hip into the side of the counter before draining her water. She filled it again, then stood waiting for his answer.

He nodded. He knew where this was going. She was going to ask him about last night. About Hunter. About his behavior. He had it coming. He deserved it.

"Does it bother you that Will isn't doing anything around here?"

Wait, what?

"W-what do you mean?"

She lifted one sweaty freckled shoulder. "I mean you take care of the fire, the driveway, the porch, the firewood. Rowan and Juney are constantly in the kitchen. Hunter and I do dishes, sweep, tidy. We've even put in a few loads of towels since we've been here and done laundry. But Will hasn't done anything. Nothing. Hasn't lifted a finger. Does that bother you?"

"It obviously bothers you," he said.

She nibbled on her lower lip and looked away before speaking again. "Yeah . . . a little. I mean, I'm not even sure he's conscious of it."

"I did notice you invited him to do the dishes and cleanup with you on Christmas and he declined before wandering off to go call his aunt or something."

She grumbled. "Yeah, I did. And yeah, he did."

"He's used to being the boss at work. Maybe he just doesn't know how it looks."

"Perhaps." She took a sip of her water. "Let's talk about last night, shall we? What the fuck happened?"

Austin groaned. Amber tilted her head and suggested they both go sit down in the living room. He followed her in and took a seat on the couch. The blankets were all folded and neatly set on the arm; he couldn't help himself and brought one up to his nose. This was Hunter's favorite, and it smelled like her. She'd glommed onto it the first night, claiming it as "hers," saying she loved how silky-soft the cashmere was. Whenever she was in the living room, it was draped around her in some way.

"Boy, you've got it bad," Amber said blandly. "Smelling her blanket. Jeez, what, did she lock her room so you couldn't go in there and do it to her pillow or panties?"

He dropped the blanket like it had just caught fire and glared at her. "No!"

Amber laughed. "Relax. I'm kidding. When Will gets up to pee in the morning, I roll over and sniff his pillow." Her gaze flew over to the front door and then back at him. "Tell a fucking soul I just told you that and I'll make sure you never see another Christmas."

He swallowed and nodded. Jesus Christ, the tiny redhead was scary when the possibility of her having any emotion besides indifferent or mildly entertained was about to be revealed.

"Let's talk about last night. Fuck, let's talk about this whole trip. What the hell is up with you and blondie?"

He shook his head before letting his gaze fall to his lap. He was a coward. Unable to even look Amber in the eye. Hunter was too good for him. "She's out of my league. So far out of my league. She's successful, beautiful, experienced, social. All things I'm not. It wouldn't work, and I don't want to lead her on. That's what I did to the last women I was with, even though I didn't even know it. But I won't do that to Hunter."

"How did you lead them on?" She took a seat on the leather ottoman.

"They seduced me. I slept with them. They asked to come

over again. I slept with them again. When they asked if we were together, I said 'yes,' not really knowing what to do or wanting the sex to stop. But then I never called them, never asked them out, never pursued the relationship past the second time we had sex. I did this three times."

"Why?"

"If I knew *why,* I wouldn't be doing it."

"Dude."

He rolled his eyes, but he still was unwilling to look at her. Amber had this disconcerting way about her. She was definitely in boss-lady mode. "What?" he finally snapped, glaring at her.

"Talk to me."

"What's there to talk about?"

"Why you're afraid to even talk to Hunter. Start there."

"I told you why."

"Okay then, start before you came up to the cabin. Tell me about school, about growing up this super-genius kid who's destined to change the world."

"See," he said petulantly, "you're exactly like everyone else. All you see is the brain."

"And there's more to you?"

"Yes."

"Ah."

He let out a sigh and ran his fingers through his hair before crossing his arms in front of his chest. "I skipped four grades. Four, five, seven and eight. I went to private school and took mostly AP classes in my senior year, and those classes allowed me to skip the majority of my freshman year in college. I pretty much started out as a sophomore when I was barely fifteen. Do you know how hard it was being the baby in the class? Not to mention the *smartest* person in the class?"

"No, I do not."

"It fucking sucks. Eventually the professors just started deferring to me and posing their questions directly at me. I didn't even put my hand up to answer. I wasn't this eager-beaver brown-noser. But everyone thought I was."

"Tough to make friends, then?"

He scoffed sarcastically. "Uh, yeah. You could say that."

"And being the younger person, you probably weren't as mature as the rest."

"Nope. Smarter but not more mature. I was still just a baby. At first, the teachers thought I'd play catch-up and follow my peers. That they would inspire me to mature quicker. My parents knew better. They were on the fence about me skipping grades, but the school pressured them. Said I was disruptive in my current classes because I was bored. I don't think I was. I've always been a pretty easygoing kid. I think it was all about the school and how good it would make them look. Who cares how it affected me emotionally, psychologically, socially or otherwise."

"So now you're this socially awkward genius, Sheldon-type guy? Who has only been laid a handful of times because he has no idea how to act around women, because when all his classmates were twenty-year-old co-eds banging in the dorms, he was fifteen with his nose in a book?"

"You got it. Toss in some cystic acne, gangly limbs, a squeaky voice and big thick glasses, and you've got yourself one giant geek."

"Hmm." She drained her water, then put it down on the coffee table before drawing her bottom lip back between her teeth and nibbling away on it in thought. "That's dumb."

"Excuse me?"

"You're using these reasons and excuses as a crutch. Take the fucking crutch away. Break that bastard. Chuck it in the motherfucking fire. You're twenty-seven years old and you've been using this 'socially awkward' label for years. Have you done anything to change it? Asked a girl out? You're with your peers now. We're all the same age. You have to have caught up by now. The acne's gone, your voice is deep, you've put on muscle and clearly went and got contacts. You're twenty-seven on the outside but still sixteen on the inside. Cut the crap, man, and grow the fuck up. You've treated Hunter like shit all week."

"I know."

"Then do something about it."

He looked back down at his knotted hands. "Did I . . . Did I do anything to offend you or Juney last night? I—I don't remember much."

She made a dismissive noise at the back of her throat, then stood up. "Nope. You were fine. Kept muttering under your breath that you were going to put a hit out on Hank with the money you'll make from this super-secret project you and Reginald Carruthers are working on. But that's about it."

"Oh, good." He let out a weighted sigh, his shoulder slumping as a few of the invisible dumbbells slipped off.

"Though you did tell anyone at the bar who would listen that your super-secret project is for Audi."

He could still hear her laughter down the hallway as he sat there staring out the window, his mouth open and his eyes unblinking. He was never drinking again.

CHAPTER SIXTEEN

By the time Hunter and the rest got back to the chalet, they were all stuffed full of Mrs. Wright's gingerbread cookies and a wee bit tipsy from Mr. Wright's hot toddies. Rowan and Juney wandered into the kitchen as if drawn by an invisible magnetic force.

"I'm not even hungry," Juney said. "And yet for some reason I feel the need to cook."

"My passion rubbing off on you?" Rowan asked, joining her in the kitchen and pulling out a cutting board and his new knife.

"Must be." She grinned. "Though with you, I think it's more of an *obsession*."

"Gotta impress the boss with my culinary skills. Whip up some spectacular dishes so she doesn't take back her offer. I've already started working on my *Canadian* accent. Don't worry *aboot* it, *eh*. I'll help fix your *chesterfield* and buy you a new *toque*, *eh*. Sorry. Sorry. Sorry."

Juney shook her head and smiled. "We *do not* sound like that."

"Left my *Marrs bar* in my *caarr* and it melted." His body shook as he struggled to contain his laughter. "Am I fired?"

"Damn straight." She giggled. "Though I seem to remember a contract of sorts. So, consider this a stern warning."

He came up behind her and spun her around, his big hands cradling her slender frame. "Do I need to remind you of our *binding* contract?" he purred, dipping her low. He gripped the back of her neck and angled her head up so she was looking straight at him. But her gaze shifted from his to directly above his head. Rowan looked up, too.

Was that mistletoe new?

Jesus, that shit had been popping up all over the place. Hunter figured it was Juney sprinkling it around when she and Rowan woke up early in the morning. A bubbly elf trying to make everyone else just as happy as she and Rowan were. Fat chance of that. At least for Hunter.

Rowan and Juney smiled at each other. He lowered his head and brushed his lips against hers. Juney let out a faint whimper as she wrapped her arms around his neck.

Hunter grimaced, followed by a groan.

"Gross," she said under her breath.

Amber and Will chuckled from their spot on the couch.

"Look, I'm happy for you guys and all," Hunter said. "But come on."

Rowan helped Juney to her feet. "Sorry, I just can't help myself when I'm around this woman."

Hunter glared at him. "I hate you." Then she stalked off toward her bedroom, happy that Austin was nowhere to be seen. He was probably out chopping wood. The man seemed to have found his inner lumberjack this holiday and looked for every excuse on the planet to leave the group and go outside to either replenish the firewood or shovel the driveway. Was he doing it to avoid her? Or did he actually enjoy it?

Fuck. It was probably both.

And after the clusterfuck from last night, it was almost definitely avoidance. When he'd turned her down for karaoke, her last-ditch attempt at getting him to give her the time of day, Hunter had gone into full-on mean-girl mode. She'd flirted and danced with other guys, let them buy her drinks and laughed at every stupid thing they said. Meanwhile, deep down all she wanted to do was sit in a corner booth with Austin and chat quietly about their hopes and dreams. Fantasize about a trip to Cambodia or plan a dinner date before the Arkells concert. But no, he'd turned her down, so she got drunk and did her best to make him jealous.

He'd been a mumbling, delirious fool by the time they were all ready to head home. Will and Rowan were forced to carry him down the hill, as Juney, Hunter and Amber led the way through the falling flakes. Rowan and Will had heaved him onto his bed muttering "good riddance" or something equally bitter before grabbing their women by the hand and leading them to bed. Hunter had stood there for a moment and just glared at Austin. How dare he do this to her? She was a CEO, for Christ's sake. She ran her own company, was the big boss, didn't take shit from anyone. And yet for some reason she took it from Austin. Let him be a jerk. Why?

Her big heart betrayed her brain, and she peeled off his jacket and boots before tugging a blanket up over his prone, snoring body. He shifted and hugged his pillow.

"I like you, Austin," she whispered. "And I wished you liked me." She turned to go but stopped and held her breath when Austin hummed and turned again on the bed.

"Hunter."

"Yes?" It came out as a squeaky whisper. She swallowed a couple of times to coat her dry throat.

"Hunter, I like you. Fuck." His words were so garbled she

had a hard time making them out. "Jesus. I like you. You're so pretty. I'm so stupid."

She swallowed. Was he dreaming? Or was he trying to have a legitimate conversation with her? She couldn't tell.

"You're too good for me. I'm not worthy."

"What? Austin, no." How could he think that? Of course he was worthy of her.

"Not worthy," he practically wailed, his face scrunching up as if he were in pain. "You deserve better."

She still couldn't tell if he was sleeping or not, but she had to ask. "Why are you being so mean to me?"

"Have to." He bunched his pillow case in his fist and winced.

"Why?"

"Don't want you to waste your time with me."

Her throat clogged up, and tears pricked the backs of her eyes. "It wouldn't be a waste."

"Waste your time. Waste of time," he mumbled again, followed by a ridiculous giggle. "Waste time. Waste. Time. Time." She was losing him; he was passing out completely. Shit. She wanted to smack his cheek and get to the root of what he'd just been saying, but a soft snore rumbled through the room, and his chest rose and fell in even deep breaths. He was out.

Giving him one last look of longing, she turned off the light and slipped out, letting the door softly *click* closed behind her.

But that was last night. She wanted to banish all memories of last night out into the blizzard. "Stupid Austin," she grumbled. She approached her bedroom door with heavy footsteps and an even heavier heart. The sound of happy couples in Christmas bliss, cackling and canoodling in the living room, propelled her forward. What did he mean, she was too good for him? What the hell was wrong with the guy? He had degrees up the wazoo. If anything, he was too good for *her*.

She gasped as she approached her bedroom door. What if

that's what he meant? What if in his drunken state he got confused, but what he really thought, what he meant to say, was that he was too good for her? He wanted a smarter woman, one with an education. Her heart hit the pit in her stomach. That had to be it. He'd just been confused last night.

Then just as quickly as the melancholy gripped her, fury replaced it. Fuck him. If he wasn't interested in her romantically, couldn't they at least be friends? Friendly? Couldn't he pretend to be nice to her for a few days just to make the group dynamics a little less uncomfortable? Or did all of his friends have to have a string of letters behind their name, too? Fancy diplomas and degrees. Certificates and awards.

She went to grab the doorknob and stopped. There was a small brown envelope wedged in the doorjamb. She grabbed it, turned the knob and walked inside, shutting the door firmly behind her and plopping down on the bed in a huff. It wasn't sealed.

DEAR HUNTER,

I'D LIKE to apologize for my behavior. Though, I'm guessing it's too late. Understandable. I've been a complete and total ass to you —to everyone, and if you stopped reading now and crumpled up my note, I wouldn't blame you one bit.

Still reading? Thank you. There's no excuse for my behavior. None. But I just want you to know that I really like you. I find you immensely successful, incredibly beautiful, intimidating, and so far out of my league, I can't even begin to imagine or believe that someone as wonderful as you could ever be interested in someone like me. And if you were, it would only be fleeting. I wanted to save us both the time and embarrassment of even trying to be your "match," because in my mind, we're not. You'd be wasting your time with a guy like me. You deserve so much better. You're too good for me.

I know it's probably too late, and again, I'm very sorry. But if you'd like to be friends, I'm willing. I can't say I'm a very good friend. I don't have many to use as references. But based on how I've treated you these past few days, you at least deserve that. You deserve so much more. You deserve the world.

I'm sorry.

—Austin

HUNTER SAT THERE FOR A MOMENT, reading and re-reading the note. Read it again and again and again, until she memorized it. Burned it into her brain forever. Only then did she get up and fling her door open and fly back down the hallway to the living room.

"Did you know about this?" she asked, stopping directly in front of Amber, waving the note in her face.

"Know about what?" Amber leaned back in the couch. "Get that thing out of my face. I don't want to get a paper cut on my nose."

Something inside Hunter snapped back into place, and she pulled the paper away, bringing it down to her side. "Sorry. But did you know about the note Austin wrote me? Did you say something to him while the two of you were alone here?"

Amber nodded slowly. "We talked, yes. But I had no idea he was going to write you a letter. What does it say?"

Hunter handed her the note. Will was cuddled up next to Amber, and the two of them read it. Juney and Rowan wandered over behind the couch and read over their shoulders.

"Short and sweet and to the point," Will said.

Hunter nodded. Her skin tingled as if she'd jumped into the

hot tub after rolling around in the snow. "What did you say to Austin?" she asked, turning back to Amber.

"I told him he's being an idiot. Behaved like an even bigger idiot last night and that he can't keep using the whole 'socially awkward' label as an excuse not to talk to you. He's used it as a crutch for so long. He was always the baby in school and work, never able to relate to his peers, so he's struggled socially. But now he's twenty-seven, with his peers and needs to start playing catch-up and acting like a decent human being."

Everyone was nodding.

"Sound advice," Juney said. "I said a few similar things when we were out on the chairlift. But I think last night's antics were the tipping point for him. He was a jackass."

"A huge jackass," Will said with a grunt. "I'm still not happy about how much fucking tequila he ordered."

The corner of Hunter's mouth crooked up. He wouldn't be nearly as pissed if he hadn't lost so badly at pool and been left with tab. By the end of the night, the bill had been over a thousand dollars. Not that Dr. Colson couldn't afford it, but still.

"What should I do?" she asked as her pulse thudded in her ears. He liked her. He didn't think he was better than her. How could she convince him she wasn't out of his league? She was a normal girl and wanted a normal relationship with a normal guy.

"Are you willing to forgive him?" Juney asked.

Hunter sucked on her bottom lip for a second. She had always been a very forgiving person. Maybe it was growing up in the system or just a part of her genetic makeup, but she always tried to see the good in people. Give them second, sometimes even third chances. No one was inherently bad, were they?

"I think so," she said slowly. "I mean, even if nothing romantic happens, I'd like to be his friend. He's willing to be friends."

"Then go out there," Will said with a snort, shaking his head as he wrapped his arm around Amber and pulled her close. She went into his embrace willingly, looking up at his face, beaming.

"And do what?" Hunter asked, fighting an eye roll.

"Go put on a sexy skirt, your ski jacket, and demand that he take you up against the woodshed." Amber grinned. Her hand fell to Will's thigh and gave it a gentle squeeze.

Will's eyes went wide, as did Rowan's.

"Yeah! Do that!" Will said finally with a big nod. Rowan nodded as well. "Do that. Go put on a skirt and demand he fuck you."

"Or at the very least *kiss* you," Juney joked.

Will nodded again. "If the guy turns you down after that, then write him off. I mean, I like him well enough, but come on, you're fucking hot and into him. Unless he's gay, a eunuch or saving himself for marriage, he's got to be fucking insane not to want you."

Amber's eyes flew back up to Will's face. But he placated her quickly with an ephemeral kiss to the temple. "Don't worry, you're the only woman here who I want to take up against the woodshed."

"Damn straight," she muttered.

"He likes you." Juney smiled. "He just needs a bit of a nudge."

"Or a big nudge, like you in a short skirt, no panties, and a ski jacket." Rowan snickered.

Will and Amber both laughed. Juney rolled her eyes. Hunter gave them all a steely glare, followed by a childish foot stomp and a big exasperated huff.

Were they right? Would that push Austin to reveal his true feelings? She'd never put herself out there like that before. Sure she'd had partners and been adventurous over the years, but Hunter hadn't had to work at getting the attention of a guy, never had to throw herself at a man to get him to notice her. This was uncharted territory.

The other four were still laughing as she stalked off to her room.

Bunch of twitterpated fuckers, having found their match the first night, fucked the first night, and been having holly jolly orgasms for the last four days. They would have someone to kiss on New Year's Eve and most likely a new budding relationship to start off the new year.

And all Hunter had was the female equivalent of blue balls.

She flung her bedroom door open and started ransacking her suitcase.

Fine!

One last-ditch effort to get Austin to admit he wanted her, then she was throwing in the towel, tossing on some snowshoes, and heading the twenty-one miles back down the mountain to her car. She'd had enough of this Christmas cheer, happy fucking couples, and talk of new beginnings. She wanted her own new beginning, and if Austin wasn't going to take a stab at their match, then she was done with him. Friendship *smendship*, she had enough friends. Hunter was lonely. Tired of dating jocks and meat-heads. She wanted brains, she wanted heart, she wanted love — she wanted Austin.

She pulled out her indecently short skirt. It was red and black plaid, with a belt around the waist. She normally reserved it for kinkier nights with whatever man she was currently getting frisky with, but during the holiday season, when paired with black tights and a bright red sweater, it actually looked quite nice. She drew her yoga pants down her legs, peeled off her underwear, and slipped into the skirt. An involuntary chill ran up her backside from the sheer thought of going outside with her bare ass hanging out. But she was going to try. When she and Austin talked when they had their moments alone, she was drawn to him; she liked him.

Why is this so hard?

She stuffed a condom into her coat pocket, pulled her black toque on her head, and headed out the door, deciding to go through the garage rather than having to walk back through the kitchen and living room, parading her ass in front of the dopey lovebirds. They were probably having a high school makeout party on the couches, anyway.

Wrapping her arms around her body, she made her way down the cobblestone steps. Austin had been very diligent shoveling several times a day, making a clear path to the hot tub and woodshed, down the driveway. He was no slouch or freeloader, that was for sure. She heard the faint sound of wood being stacked, mixed with the odd male grunt of exertion.

Hunter bit her lip, took a deep breath through her nose, and rounded the corner.

"Fuck!" Austin said with a snarl, grabbing a big piece of wood and slamming it down on the pile in the wheelbarrow. "Fucking fucker!"

Had she read the note yet? Did she think he was an even bigger ass? Probably. He would never be enough for Hunter. He knew that much. But he owed her an apology, and he owed her civility. He'd been ignoring her for days, and she'd done nothing wrong but wind him with her beauty, amaze him with her success and humble him with how down-to-earth she was. Only all those things just made her all the more intimidating. Not more approachable.

Stop hiding behind the label. Listen to Amber. She's right.

Austin heard the back door close followed by the quiet

stomping of booted feet making their way down the cleared path. At least he was pulling his weight around the place. He may not be pulling a girl, but he was pulling his weight. Unlike Will. Was Amber going to talk to him about it?

He spun around to put another log on the stack, and there she was, standing in front of him, an amber-eyed vixen. The wind whipped her hair around her like golden flames, while tanned and toned legs peeked out from beneath her big ski jacket. Was she in a skirt?

"Hi."

Hunter ran up to him, her eyes bright and her cheeks flushed.

"Do you like me?"

He swallowed.

"Do. You. Like. Me?"

He nodded.

"Then why won't you kiss me?"

"Hunter, I—"

She cut him off and lunged at him, wrapping her arms around his neck and slamming her mouth against his, capturing his words, his gasp, his excuses. Then something happened. Something inside Austin clicked or snapped or finally woke up. This woman wanted him, and unlike the other women that had thrown themselves at him, he wanted her just as much, and he was willing to risk revealing his lack of experience, risk her tiring of him quickly, just to get a taste.

He opened his mouth against hers, welcoming her tongue and encouraging her to explore. She hummed a response and pressed her body against him. His hands instinctively made their way down her torso to her butt. She was naked!

He pulled his mouth away from hers. "You . . . You don't have any underwear on!"

She grinned, pitching forward and tracing his bottom lip with her tongue. "And what would you like to do about that?"

Austin's eyes went wide. "I'd like to fuck you senseless."

Hunter's gaze was challenging as she dug a hand into her coat pocket. "Here." She passed him the condom. "I need you to know that I'm not too good for you, or out of your league. And getting to know you is not a waste of time." She bit her lip before speaking again. "I want you, Austin. I like you. I hate that I've had to throw myself at you, but if that's what it takes . . . "

He took the condom from her, his eyes roaming across her face. He'd never seen such a mix of emotions painted across such beauty before. There was lust, of course, but also fear and embarrassment, maybe even a touch of anger. She was frustrated with him, and rightfully so. But had she also been worried, afraid he would turn her down? Probably. And she was probably embarrassed that she had to resort to accosting him in the woodshed wearing nothing but a miniskirt. Fuck, he was such a moron. He'd forced her into this, he'd forced her to throw herself at him.

He shook his head. "No more throwing. I'm sorry. I've been an idiot. I want you too, so fucking much it hurts. I just . . . I haven't been with many women. I'm not *kinky*, but I'm willing to try. I *am* curious." The strain of his erection against his jeans was painful. The way this woman made his pulse race was enough to make him think he was having a heart attack right then and there.

Her eyes were wide and beseeching. "I don't care about any of that. We can learn together. I'm not *that* kinky."

"Learn together," he said, a smirk tugging at the corner of his mouth. "I'd like to learn everything about you. Every square inch."

Something above them caught Hunter's eye, and she looked up. His gaze followed hers.

Holy shit!

More mistletoe.

Their eyes locked, amber to green. Finally, they understood

each other. Finally, he would let his body do the talking rather than that stupid big brain of his.

Without another word, Hunter went to leap up on to his hips, but he stopped her.

"Can I at least do one thing *properly?*" he asked, giving her a small smile. He wasn't going to fuck this up with her, at least not more than he already had.

Her throat bobbed on a heavy swallow as she nodded.

He released her hips, and his hands traveled up to cup her cheeks. Gazing into her eyes, those beautiful, deep, soulful amber eyes, he leaned in and gently brushed his lips against hers. "I know this isn't the first kiss," he whispered, his lips coasting across her cheek, then to her temple, only to retrace his path to the other cheek. "But I—"

She shook her head and pulled away slightly to look at him, her eyes bright. "No, it's perfect."

Austin let one hand drift down to her waist, and the other cupped the nape of her neck. His fingers wove their way into her silky golden tresses. Dipping her low, until all she could see was his face above her and the gray sky, he ducked his head again and kissed her. He'd never wanted to be romantic with the other women, never wanted to please them and make them feel special. They'd been orgasms offered up on a silver platter. He'd been too stupid, too young, too consumed with work to even attempt a relationship with any of them. But Hunter, Hunter was different. The light had finally come on inside his brain, and he wasn't about to turn it off. He wanted to give her everything. Even if it was only for a short time.

She blinked up at him when he pulled away, her eyes so full of wonder and contentment. She was happy. He hadn't seen this look on Hunter since that first day, and he was the cause. He'd caused her to shed her smile, shed her happiness. Well, not anymore. Snowflakes fell on her lashes and sweet little nose. He continued to look down at her. She was perfect. And for some crazy reason, she wanted him.

Heat and need whipped into a froth inside him. Before he knew what he was doing, he hauled her up, and with a flick of his wrist, lifted her up onto his hips. Then with the force of all his pent-up self-loathing and years of frustration and social awkwardness, he ploughed her over and up against the wall. His hands kneaded her tight, cold butt while his mouth crashed down on hers and his tongue demanded its way past her lips. She groaned against him, her fingers working their way into his hair, pulling him down to her. One of his hands made its way around to the front of her body between them. He ruffled up her jacket and skirt, searching for her heat. Was she wet for him? Oh God, just the thought of Hunter wet made Austin rage against her, pushing her back harder against the unforgiving, unfinished wood wall.

His fingers continued to search. He growled low in surprise and appreciation when he found her hairless. She chuckled against his lips and bucked into those fingers, encouraging him to explore. Austin pulled his mouth away from hers and let it travel down along her jaw and throat until he found that sweet spot where the shoulder meets the neck. He nipped her lightly until she crooned, riding his fingers as they drew delightful little circles around her wet and swollen clit.

His pulse raced hot and fierce as his mouth feasted on her flesh, licking and nipping her silky-soft skin. The erection in his jeans pressed eagerly against her bare cleft. Hunter tipped her head back against the cold wood wall of the lean-to shed, and Austin took that as an invitation and tucked his head in tighter, nibbling and sucking, licking and nuzzling her slender neck. She smelled fucking fantastic. Like spice and heaven. He hardly knew the woman, and yet nothing else had plagued his thoughts the way Hunter did. He craved nothing else but her lips, her body, her heat since the moment he'd met her. She consumed his every thought in some form or another, most of those thoughts dirty.

They were so much alike.

Two lost souls searching for a purpose, for adventure. Why hadn't he seen it before?

He'd been too busy thinking he wasn't enough for her. Well, he could be enough. He wanted to be enough. He had to be enough.

"Yes," Hunter sighed when he slipped one finger inside her, finding her hot, wet and ready for him. She squeezed her muscles around him and began to bob up and down, mewling when his thumb worked her clit and his teeth grazed her neck.

"Hunter." Austin growled low in his throat, making sure her thighs were safely wrapped around his hips and her back firmly against the wall so that he could move his free hand from her butt and inside her coat. "Oh, God, Hunter . . . " One hand slipped into her tank top.

Oh fuck, she was braless too.

He groaned again when a diamond-hard nipple pricked the pad of his thumb. The woman had perfect breasts, big and full, rounded mounds, creamy and soft. Since that first night when she'd taken off her sweater and sat playing games in the living room, wearing nothing but a tight white T-shirt, he'd been a goner.

"Austin, c-condom," she stammered.

Lifting his mouth from her neck, he paused his hands and looked at her.

One blonde eyebrow lifted up half an inch. "Condom?"

He shook his head. "Oh. Oh yeah, right. Uh . . . " He started looking around on the ground. He must have dropped it. "I, uh, I must have . . . *Shit*. Uh . . . " Finally, his eyes landed on the little black and gold foil packet lying in the snow, half-buried by new flurries. Shit, how was he going to get it without dropping

Hunter or letting her go and pulling himself from her decadent heat?

She laughed. "It's okay. Get the condom." Instead of motioning to slip off his hips, she squeezed him tighter with her thighs, wrapped her arms around his neck and tilted her head toward the ground. "Use your legs, not your back." Her giggle made his cock grow longer and thicker by the second, and the sweet and spicy smell of her was driving his senses wild.

He smirked before slowly moving them away from the wall. Still attached, he gently bent down in an awkward squat next to the condom and snatched it up, only to rush them both back over and against the wall in less than a second.

"Sorry about that," he murmured.

She blinked a few stray flurries off her lashes and shook her head, more sweet and girly giggles bubbling up from her ample chest. "Don't be. It was funny and dorky and sweet."

Dear God, the woman was fucking incredible. Her cheeks and nose were a rosy pink, and her amber eyes shone bright and eager at him, welcoming him to make the next move, encouraging him to show her he felt the same way.

Swallowing hard, he quickly tore open the condom, doing some serious sex ninja moves, where he kept her pinned against the wall but still managed to get his zipper and belt undone. He pushed his pants and boxers down to his ankles, rolled on the condom, then grabbed her, sheathing himself to the hilt immediately. He'd wasted enough time dodging Hunter's advances, ignoring his feelings and making excuses. He wasn't wasting any more time now. He had to have her, and he had to have her *now*.

Hunter's eyes flashed wide from the impact. She let out a grunt of pleasure when he hit her deep and hard. His hands came up under her arms inside her coat and around her ribcage, the pads of his thumbs brushing her nipples overtop the thin fabric of the tank top, her dusky areolas visible beneath the sheer white.

He needed them in his mouth. He needed to bite and suckle her, feel her squirm and moan as pain and pleasure commingled inside her body. He needed to make the woman lose all control because he'd already made her wait, made her make the first move. But no more. Now he was going to make the moves, and all Hunter had to do was sit back and enjoy.

Dipping his head low, he used his cheeks to push her jacket open. His hands drew her tank top up past her belly to expose her breasts. He tugged one crimson bud into his mouth and flicked it with his tongue, then he took it between his teeth and pulled. She inhaled from the bite of pain, and he grinned with her nipple still in his teeth, all the while continuing to buck into her, desperate to be deeper, to possess every inch of her.

She whimpered next to his ear, her hands unwilling to release his hair. "Oh, God, Austin." Her moan was the sexiest thing he'd ever heard in his life. His cock grew harder from the husky tenor of her voice. She sounded like a fucking porn star.

Grabbing her fingers from his hair, he clasped them together and brought her arms above her head and pinned them there so she couldn't move. His hips slammed into hers until all she could do was balance on his waist and take everything he gave her. He was all over her. Hands on her body, mouth on her body, cock inside her. He needed it all. He'd gone to bed the last four nights dreaming of nothing but taking Hunter in every way, in every position, and now that he finally had her, he didn't want to disappoint.

She tensed in his arms and her breath hitched. She was close.

Yes.

Pinching her eyes shut, she tossed back her head and let the orgasm break free of her body with a rattled gasp and a sharp cry.

"Yes, Austin . . . Oh God, yes."

He couldn't remember the last time he'd felt such pleasure. And not just from how good it felt to be inside Hunter, because the woman was incredible, so tight, so sweet, her skin was like silk; but the way she threw her head back, called out his name, wriggled against him, he was on Cloud 9.

"Hunter," he groaned as she clenched around him. God, he loved her name. Loved saying it. It was so strong, so powerful, so *her*. He wedged his free hand between them, still keeping her arms pinned above her head with the other one, hips still bucking wildly. He flicked his finger back and forth over her engorged clit, loving how wet and swollen she was for him.

She was exquisite. The flush of pink on her skin, her long lashes feathered out against her cheeks as she perched on his cock with her eyes closed, exhausted from his lovemaking. He'd graduated top of his class with each and every degree, been given countless awards and honors, and yet nothing compared to the elation of knowing he was able to make Hunter come so hard. He may have made her scream, may have made her lose her mind, but he'd lost his heart to her the moment she found him out there in the snow. He couldn't wait to spill himself inside the beauty he'd been too afraid to kiss, too afraid to touch. Well, those fears were no more. The way she reacted to him, squeezing his cock, milking him, welcoming him. He was going to take Hunter as often as she would let him, make up for lost time and the days he'd wasted letting his head do the thinking.

HUNTER's entire body was on fire. What the fuck had he been talking about—little experience? Not kinky? The man was a fucking sex machine. It'd been ages since a man had made her feel this good. Made her skin prickle and flames dance along her arms and deep in her belly. Sweat misted her brow as Austin continued to ram into her, the look of pure passion and masculine triumph etched across his face in a surly scowl and pinched brows. He was concentrating fiercely on the task at hand, the way his body molded to hers, his lips searing hot on her skin. His touch made her cry out for more. He was a prodigy in *every* sense of the word. They were going to be fine.

"Austin," she whispered again, another orgasm brewing in her core with every harsh plunge of his cock.

Her clit and channel still hummed from the first climax. It had been intense. Incredible. Life-changing. And he still wasn't through with her. The man was insatiable. Her pussy quivered and squeezed him on each draw as he swept past her walls, only to slam back in, deep and ruthless.

"I'm close again."

Unable to recall the last time an orgasm this big threatened to unleash inside her, and even though climaxing consumed nearly every thought at that moment, she was also a tad frightened. It was going to be huge, bigger than the last two, she just knew it.

"Oh fuck," he groaned against her nipple, his tongue swiping across the tender bud before he clamped down with his teeth again and pulled.

"Fuck. I . . . I can't. I can't hold on. Oh . . . Oh Jesus . . . Oh fuck!" She strained against him as he hammered her into the cold wall of the shed, her entire body going rigid with the brutality of her release. Snow continued to fall around them, the wind whipping flakes into their faces and against their bodies inside the shelter of the lean-to. But the snowflakes melted on contact from their heated skin. Both flushed. Both on fire. She arched her back and pressed her breasts into his face, desperate for more, to prolong the pleasure, prolong the orgasm. Austin responded and took the other nipple into his mouth and sucked, ferociously striking it with his tongue until she silently pleaded for more.

Every muscle, every nerve ending, every cell in Hunter's body was a full-on inferno as the orgasm continued to pinball around inside her. From the tips of her hair and down to her curling toes, the pleasure just unfurled and unfurled over and over again, rolling right into another before she even had a chance to come down from the first. It hit her like a sniper bullet, from out of nowhere, without warning and right on target.

"Fuck. Austin..."

Holy mother of God, I'm going to pass out.

But he continued driving into her, his pelvis a battering ram against her clit, his hand holding hers captive above her head and his lips tirelessly roamed across her scorching flesh.

"Austin," she whispered again. "Please come. I think I'm going to pass out if I come any more."

He buried his head between her breasts, his words a mumble that made her gasp. "No. More. You need to have more."

"Aust..." Her head lolled to the side, and she tensed around him one more time as the last orgasm unraveled. Lifting his face from her chest, he kissed her hard, shoving his tongue into her mouth, challenging her to a duel. Languidly, she stroked his tongue with hers, but she was exhausted, sated, completely and utterly gone. Too tired to open her lips, to move her tongue more than just back and forth. She pulled away from his mouth. "Aust..."

"One more."

She shook her head. "No. I can't."

"You will." Before she could blink, Austin pulled out of her, set her bare bum down on a pile of wood, spread her legs wide, crouched down, and dove in face-first.

She gasped, inhaling the surrounding scents: fresh snow and yellow cedar, with the faintest but most divine smell of Austin. He smelled minty fresh but also manly. She laced her fingers in his hair and pulled on the ends, loving the way he groaned and responded to the pain by just giving her more pleasure.

His tongue was hot velvet against her tender flesh, and the way her body ignited to new life had her moaning and bucking into his face. He drew her sensitive clit into his mouth and tugged before sucking viciously and twitching his tongue over the hood.

She wriggled on the cold wood. The bark was rough under her buttocks, but the chill was welcome on her searing skin. "Oh fuck. I—I'm close again. Inside m-me . . . NOW!"

The man didn't even have to touch her, and that smile, that primal growl that rumbled at the back of his throat would have been enough to catapult her over the edge. His eyes were hooded with feral need, and as he gripped her hips again and lifted her up on to his waist, Hunter was gone. She was Austin's for as long as he would have her. He rammed his cock inside her, and she let go one last time.

"Oh my God!"

"Hunter!"

"Austin!"

His teeth found the soft spot of skin in the divot of her collarbone, and he clamped down hard. She sucked in a breath through clenched teeth and groaned, her pussy tightening from the bite of pain. He let out a grunt against her skin, stiffened and then let go. The pulsing of his release against her walls was divine, but Hunter was too exhausted to coax out another orgasm. So instead, she tightened and released, tightened and released, drawing him deeper inside her to heighten his orgasm.

His breath was warm against her skin as he finally let out a sigh, his body going lax with the end of his climax.

Hunter giggled. "I'm not sure what you've been worried about."

Austin's shoulders lifted and then dropped, his lips traveling lightly along her neck and chest before he finally lifted his head and he looked her in the eyes. "Me either. I'm so sorry. I . . . You're unbelievable, and I just . . . I just didn't believe I could ever be enough for you."

"But you are," she said softly, loving the feel of him holding her, inside her, close to her.

"God, Hunter, I've wasted so much time, too much time being afraid that I wouldn't be enough for you. Thinking you were out of my league."

She pressed her finger to his lips. "Shh. Don't dwell on it. You've smartened up now, and that's what matters. We've got all night and tomorrow morning. And then . . ." she trailed off, not wanting to assume too much or count any chickens.

"And then I'll do it properly and take you out on a date once we're back in Seattle. Do you like the Arkells? I have tickets to their January concert. The seats are pretty good."

Her chest tightened, and a smile that could melt snow erupted onto her face. "I'd like that."

Austin leaned forward and rubbed his nose against hers. "And I like you."

CHAPTER SEVENTEEN

You could have cut the sexual tension in the living room all night with a broadsword. Since their feral coupling in the woodshed earlier that afternoon, the air around Hunter and Austin sizzled and sparked with the desire for more. They (Austin) had wasted far too much time already not in bed, and they (Austin) needed to make up for lost time. He needed to continue to apologize for his stupidity. Win Hunter over once and for all. Hear his name, her pleas for more, her appeals to a higher power and crude profanities spill across her succulent lips as he drank her down. Watch her grip the sheets until her knuckles turned white and her toes curled. They'd all hopped briefly into the hot tub, and finally, Austin and Hunter had cuddled up together. It'd nearly killed him not to bring her to orgasm right then and there. Lord (and everyone else too) knew there were nefarious things going on beneath the bubbles, and the way Hunter ground her pelvis into his fingers told him he was doing all the right things. But he wanted to keep her climaxes for himself. Those were Austin's and Austin's alone.

Once back into the house for the night, everyone ducked

away to their rooms. Rowan and Juney nipped off to her room, while Will chased Amber down the hallway, the little redhead skipping and giggling as the big doctor prowled after her with a dark growl.

"I'm going to shower quick," Hunter said as they approached her bedroom door. "I hate the smell of chlorine, and the chemicals irritate my skin if I don't wash them off. I wake up all red and blotchy and itchy. Do you mind?"

Did he mind what?

Panic swamped him. Was she sending him to bed? Calling it a night? Shit, was that it? One searing hot tryst in the woodshed, some hand stuff in the hot tub, and they were done for the night?

"Uh, no?"

Her giggle made his cock surge to life in his damp shorts. "I'll only be a few minutes." She sucked on her lip before asking, "Your room or mine?"

Oh, thank frickin' God.

"Uh, yours?"

She nodded. "All right. I'll be quick."

Austin opened Hunter's bedroom door, immediately feeling like an intruder. This was her room, well not *her* room, but it was the room she had been sleeping in *alone* for the last four nights while he slept alone as well. Thinking, dreaming, imagining nothing but Hunter and her perfect body tucked beneath the crisp red sheets. Did she sleep naked? Did she pack any of her kinky toys? Had his petulant behavior forced her to use any of those toys?

The bedside light with it's red lampshade was on, and it lent the room a romantic hue. Sitting down on the bed, he gave it a couple of quick test bounces, then stood back up and wandered around. Hunter's suitcase was perched in the corner on the luggage rack, open, while the clothes inside were all neatly rolled up. Her hair and beauty products sat neatly on the vanity, and when he inspected further, he realized they'd been organized according to height.

Huh.

He'd just learned something new about his lady-love. She had a few quirky little OCD tendencies. They were *definitely* a match. He snorted and smiled to himself, catching a glimpse of his happiness in the mirror and only snorting again because of it, followed by a headshake.

He was a moron.

Why did he wait so long?

Thank God, Hunter had more sense than he did. He ran a finger gently over the perfectly organized bottles; wouldn't she lose her mind to see his medicine cabinet at home? He had a legend on the inside of the door. Everything was color-coded and organized not only by height but also by frequency of use. Yeah, he was Sheldon all right. And he'd finally met his match.

The shower across the hall came alive, and he pictured Hunter inside, dripping wet as the heated water sluiced over her perfect skin. Her nipples tightening to pebbles and her perfect pussy softening as she ran her soapy hand down her body and flicked her clit. His cock sprung up again inside his shorts, and he adjusted himself before sitting down on the bed. He closed his eyes and hummed softly at the thought of Hunter covered in soapy bubbles.

Opening his eyes at the sudden epiphany that struck him, he whipped out his phone and started to Google. Even if he wasn't experienced, he knew how to research and learn better than anyone. And as soon as he read something once, it was committed to memory for life. He brought up the site he'd been searching for and went to task.

Engrossed in what he was reading, while also trying to do the moves inside his mouth, he didn't hear the door open.

"What's so fascinating?" Her husky voice drew him out of his trance and made all the blood leave his brain and flood to his groin.

Illuminated by the hall light, Hunter stood like a white-toweled angel. She'd worn a one-piece into the hot tub earlier, a sexy little red number with cut-outs at the waist and a plunging neckline. Her cleavage alone had made Austin pitch a tent before they even slid into the hot water. She looked drop-dead stunning, of course. But now, somehow, without makeup and wrapped up in nothing but a towel, with her damp hair curling in thick clumps around her shoulders, she was more beautiful than ever before. A natural goddess. His to pleasure. His to obey. Moisture flooded his mouth as he flicked his phone off and stowed it on the nightstand.

"Hmm?" she hummed, lifting one eyebrow as she stepped off the threshold and inside. "What were you reading? More work stuff?"

He shook his head, his eyes fixated on the towel and how badly he wanted her to ditch it. He'd felt her, tasted her, but he'd yet to see her. "No. Not work," he replied. "Studying."

"I didn't know you were back in school. Can you *go* any higher than a PhD?"

He stood on wobbly legs. The woman made him weak in the knees. She made him weak, period. But no more. Their time in the woodshed had turned on the light bulb, galvanized a need so fierce, so primal, so all-consuming that he was determined to be the man Hunter wanted, the man Hunter needed. No more of this insecure *Sheldon* doofus bullshit.

No.

He would prove to her, to himself, to *everyone* that he wasn't this socially awkward little puberty-plagued freshman they all thought he was. That *he* thought he was.

With each step, more newfound confidence pumped through his veins and, before he knew it, he was next to her as she stood in front of the vanity and liberally applied some cream beneath her eyes.

She gave him the side-eye and smiled. "You want some retinol for those purple bags? I could stow my entire summer wardrobe in them, they're so big."

"Maybe later," he purred, grabbing her by the elbows and turning her to face him. The tube of cream dropped to the floor, and her eyes flashed wide at him in surprise. "Right now I want to see you." He reached for the top of her towel as she let her arms float down to her sides, watching him. He pulled the ends away and let the terry cloth plop to the ground. She was magnificent. Toned and tanned, curvy and feminine. What sculptors and artists, photographers and fashion designers envisioned when they thought of a *woman*. Sensuous and strong. The epitome of sexuality and all things erotic. A muse.

"You're incredible," he said quietly, his eyes slowly, so very slowly traveling the length of her. Imprinting every curve, every freckle on his brain for eternity. The woman was a masterpiece.

She swallowed hard and a sweet pink tongue darted out between her lips, running invitingly along the crease. "Austin," she sighed.

"I was such a fool."

"You were."

"A moron."

"A big one."

"I'm sorry."

"You should be."

"I'm going to apologize properly."

"That could be fun."

He gently trailed a finger down her arm and then across her torso beneath the curve of her ample breast. The only betrayal of her nerves was the rapid rise and fall of her chest; otherwise, she appeared calm. Was she normally a top or a bottom? Something told him Hunter was a bottom who liked to switch now and then. He would pull up his bootstraps and research more on being a top. Since hearing about her Curiously Kinky company, he's been researching BDSM every night and had learned a lot. He wasn't sure he had it in him to be a true "top," but for Hunter he was willing to try anything.

"I want to worship you, Hunter," he said. "Hear you scream. Watch you lose yourself as I pleasure you over and over again."

She let out a nervous little huff. "You nearly fucked me until I blacked out in the woodshed. I have no doubt in your skills."

He grinned. That'd been such a thrill. He'd never done anything like that before, never even gone down on a woman before, but something inside him, something visceral, something primitive had taken over, and the need to feel her come again and again and again had manifested into an obsession for him. An orgasm for each day he'd missed out. For each day he had been too caught up in his own brain, in his own shortcomings and made Hunter feel as though he didn't want her.

He looked up at her. He'd been watching her nipples harden right in front of him. Gorgeous little red peaks, tight and screaming at him to be licked, to be sucked, bitten, tugged, twisted and tweaked. "On the bed, on your back," he said softly but with an edge of command in his voice. If Hunter wanted a dominant in the bedroom, he was going to give her whatever she wanted.

With the grace of Aphrodite, she strolled over to the bed and eased herself on, letting her hair fan out around behind her like strands of spun gold.

"Fuck me, Austin," she said, lifting her arms and reaching for him. "Take me, please."

Oh God, how he loved the sound of her voice. Begging him to fuck her.

He shook his head and climbed onto the bed, positioning

himself above her, his arms on either side of her body, their eyes locked in a fiery gaze. She let her arms rest on his shoulders, applying a bit of pressure to pull him down to her, but he resisted, instead dipping his head and capturing her mouth with his. It was a sweet and sensual kiss. A kiss that said, "I'm not rushing a damn thing tonight."

He flicked his tongue out and gently pried open her lips, slipping it inside her mouth and massaging her tongue. She met his dance and pace, step for step, joining him, following his lead.

She tasted like heaven.

Like perfection.

Like Hunter.

Groaning against his mouth, she lifted her hips up off the bed and thrust into him. He was painfully hard, so he let his own need take over for a moment and pushed back into her, allowing her to rub against him. The heat between her legs, the smell of her, her little moans and the way she grappled for him was too much. He was going to lose it and either explode in his shorts or strip and take her hard and fast, and neither of those were part of the plan. The plan was to please Hunter. Make Hunter come so hard, come so much he would ruin her for other men. He wanted to be all she would ever need. All she would ever want.

"Take me," she panted against his lips as he lifted his head and nuzzled her neck, inhaling her intoxicating scent.

"Not yet."

"Please . . . " Her plea fled her on a sigh as he ran his tongue up along the vein in her neck.

He groaned in self-inflicted agony and lifted his head from her neck, gazing down into her beautiful eyes. Bright amber blinked back at him in confusion.

"Not yet. Right now is about you. Just . . . " He planted a kiss to her lips and then one to her chin, another to her neck. "Lie back and . . . " More kisses down her chest and to the swell of each breast. "Enjoy." He laved a scarlet peak, and she moaned above him as she arched her back. Drawing the bud into his mouth, he lashed it with his tongue, then pulled hard and sucked. She inhaled quickly. He shifted it to his teeth and bit down gently, tugging just a tad, just enough. Her eyes flashed wide, and she mewled. He delivered the same attention to her other breast while his hand came up and his fingers twisted and tweaked its twin.

"Austin . . . "

Releasing her nipple, he continued on his descent, swirling his tongue around her navel. Her perfect little pierced navel. The ring was a shiny barbell with a small flower of diamonds or crystals or something hovering just above. He flicked it with his tongue, and she gasped.

Kissing her mound, he sank down low onto his belly and spread her legs. Was she wet for him? Looking beneath her, he noticed a small patch of dampness on the sheet.

Fuck yes. She was fucking saturated.

"You're so wet," he said with a purr.

"Austin."

He dipped a finger between her slippery folds, and her hips left the bed. Up and down he explored, loving how bare and pink and perfect her pussy was, how soft. He pushed his finger into her channel, and she rippled around him, gripped him like a fist with her strong muscles. He chuckled to himself as he used his other hand to spread her wide.

"You asked what I was *studying* earlier." He hummed.

"Yes."

"I was reading the seven best techniques to eat pussy."

"Austin . . . you don't . . . oh God."

He drew his tongue up her slit and then flicked her clit.

"You don't need to research anything. You know what you're — Holy Mother of God."

He drew her clit into his mouth and pulled hard.

Her head came up and her back bowed on the bed. "Holy fuck!"

He tugged again and then sucked even harder, his finger pumping slow, languid strokes, until he found the spot inside her he'd been seeking. "I'm going to eat you all seven ways tonight, Hunter," he said, taking a quick break and sweeping the flat of his tongue up through her cleft. "And you're going to come each and every time."

"Oh, my God." Her head thrashed from side to side on the pillow when he pressed up hard on her G-spot. "No . . . I c-can't."

"You can and you will."

"Aust—"

Her gasp cut her words at the knees as he suckled her clit hard again, feeling the nub swell between his lips. Her hands bunched in the sheets and her head continued to toss as her hips bucked up into his face. He loved that he could make her lose control. Make her beg and demand more, ram her pussy hard into his face, because she wanted him to devour all of her.

"I'm going to come," she whispered. "Austin . . ."

Her clit hardened and grew in his mouth as he continued to suck, all the while still pressing hard on the spongy tissue inside her. She tensed around his finger, squeezed tight and let go. A warm gush raced over the back of his hand as her climax unfurled. Her body bowed, then sagged on the bed as she panted and moaned, cried out and cursed.

When she melted back into the bed and pillow with a contented sigh, he lifted his head from the apex of her thighs and glanced up at Hunter. Her eyes were closed, and a small, placid smile clung to her lips.

Hunter.

Her lids slowly opened, and she looked down at him. She appeared content but also exhausted.

"That's one," he said. He only caught a glimpse of the surprised look on her face before he got back to work.

"HOLY FUCKING GOD!" Hunter screamed as she hinged at the hips, her entire upper body lunging off the bed as orgasm number six speared through her like a freshly sharpened machete. Sweat misted her forehead and chest, and her brain was complete mush. She didn't have an alarm clock on her nightstand, but if she were to guess, it was somewhere around one-thirty in the morning.

Austin's head continued to bob between her legs, his brows pinched in a tight V of concentration as he diligently feasted on her sensitive flesh, lapping up her wetness with the fervent hunger of a starved man. But then, perhaps he *was* starved. He'd said he had limited experience with women. Maybe it'd been a while? Either way, his incessant dedication—which in Hunter's opinion had quickly morphed into an obsession—had her seeing spots, nearly blacking out, and she was pretty sure on orgasm number four she heard the sheets tear from how hard she gripped them.

Sinking back into the bed, she let out a loud sigh as the last remaining bits of the climax disbanded. The man was relentless. He'd actually gone and read the seven best techniques to eat pussy and was determined to dine all seven ways tonight. She hardly recognized him from the man four days ago. Unsure of himself, quiet and reserved. And yet now, here he was being all dominating and assertive. Confident in his prowess and topping her like a badass. Did he know she was a good little bottom who would take any punishment doled out like a dutiful submissive? She'd wear his bonds, bend over and take his lashings if he demanded it. Would he ever demand it? She hoped so.

She popped one eye open and gazed down at him. Those

sexy golden-green eyes pierced her soul, ravishing her, cherishing her, owning her.

"You don't have to make it to seven tonight," she said, her brain and libido battling it out inside of her. She wanted all the orgasms, wanted everything Austin had promised her and more, and yet she wasn't sure she had the energy, had the mental capacity to go one more round. She was afraid that one more might make her brain short circuit, everything would suddenly go dark and she would wake up hours later not knowing who she was. Besides, the man looked exhausted. His lips were sexy and puffy, and his chin and freshly shaved cheeks glowed from her releases. Even if she couldn't get off again, she wanted Austin inside her, wanted to feel him find his release, hear him groan her name as she drained him, made him feel just a fraction of how good he was making her feel.

He paused for a moment, his face expressionless, besides that lone eyebrow that was half an inch higher. Challenging her. Daring her. *Scolding* her. "I said seven."

Holy fuck, who was this man?

He put his head back down, spread her wide and blew cool air onto her throbbing clit. Jesus hell, he really was going for seven. Could she? She certainly hoped so. She prepared herself for the long, decadent sweep. The flat of his tongue drifting erotically, slowly up from her perineum to her mound, hitting every square inch of her pussy and making it quiver, before he plunged his fingers inside her and scissored. But there was no sweep. No plunge. No scissoring. Instead, he flicked her clit with the tip of his tongue. Back and forth, back and forth. The move was so small, so minimal, and yet it made her insides quake as another orgasm began its climb.

She bucked into his face and groaned, needing more, wanting more.

Or did she?

Her body was a maelstrom, a cyclone building momentum, gaining force and ground before it burst forth from its confines and ransacked her body to shreds. And all from the delicate flick of his tongue. The rhythm was quick and repetitive. It was all she needed. She was going insane from just a flick. A flick would do it. A flick would pitch her over the edge that one last time.

How did he know?

No one had ever eaten her out this way. No man had ever simply lain there and given her seven orgasms, using a different technique each time. No man had ever used just one move, over and over again. They'd all mix it up, and she would get there eventually, she always did. But this, this was exquisite torture. Diabolically wonderful torture.

She brought her hands to her breasts and cupped them, smashing them together, then letting her thumbs rub the tender pearled nubs. She pinched and pulled, loving how each tug, each bite of pain sent a shard of pleasure careening through her, landing hot and heavy in her clit. She was ready. So ready. So close. One more time. She could do it. She would do it. For Austin.

Pulling on her nipples even harder this time, because Hunter liked a little pain with her pleasure, she thrust her hips up into Austin's face and let go. Her toes curled as the twister unraveled inside her and the orgasm took hold. She shut her eyes, tilted her head back and cried out his name. Cried out for God, cried out for more.

Seven. Seven. Seven. Seven!

Moments later, Hunter's head hit her pillow, and she let out an exhausted sigh. Had she really come seven times? Plus, the four in the woodshed. This was a new record. She felt the bed shift, and Austin got up, inching himself forward up the bed until he was next to her. She opened her eyes and turned to face him.

The smile on his face, on his wet and hungry lips was enough to stop her heart and make it burst.

"That was . . . " she trailed off, unable to find the words. So instead, with the last bit of energy she could muster, she sat up, grabbed a condom from the nightstand, unzipped his jeans, slid them down his waist and straddled him. "I can't guarantee I'll come an *eighth* time. But I want you to come. Take as long as you need."

He took the condom from her, tore the wrapper and rolled it on. The sight of Austin handling himself, taking his thick length in his palm and rolling down the translucent rubber was hypnotic. He made sure it was down to the base before looking up at her, his gaze avid as his Adam's apple bobbed heavy in his throat. "Not trying to brag or anything here, but I'm about ready to explode." His lip turned up at the corner into a dashingly bashful smile.

Suddenly all Hunter wanted to do was lick that corner.

"My balls ache."

She chuckled softly as she lifted up, hovering above him, his crown pressing at her wet and swollen entrance, demanding sanctuary. "Then let's do something to fix that." Then she sank down low, squeezing him the whole way.

CHAPTER EIGHTEEN

Amber let out a satisfied sigh and rolled off of Will. "Well, Happy December 27th."

His laugh was deep and throaty. "Happy December 27th to you, too. Is it a day for celebration?"

Closing her eyes, she stretched like a cat in the sun with a belly full of cream. "No, but I'd say what we just did right there was pretty celebratory."

He rolled over onto his side to face her. "Oh yeah?" His husky whisper kissed the skin on her face, and she felt an inner grin grow from how happy it made her.

"Mhmm."

"So," Will started, "how are you getting back to Seattle? Seeing as your brother dropped you off here?"

Amber opened her eyes. "I dunno. I guess I planned to hitch a ride with Daisy. My truck is in the shop. Some lame-ass buffoon backed an excavator into the back of it on a job site."

"Lame-ass indeed," he said, followed by a yawn. "Well, you could always come back with me."

Her smile faltered. "Really?"

He lifted one chiseled shoulder, the sheet slipping further down his body and exposing those delicious lines that ran diagonally across both hips. She licked her lips and swallowed.

"Why not? We both live in Seattle, makes sense."

She nodded. "Okay . . . thanks."

"No problem."

Pursing her lips, she let her eyes fall down to the small empty space between them on the bed, the need to ask him something itching at the nape of her neck. But she was nervous. Despite the fact that the man had just been balls-deep inside her and made her come harder and more often than any man she'd ever been with, she still didn't know him that well. How would he take her question?

"Uh . . . "

Will lifted one eyebrow in an oddly sexual way. "What's up?"

"How . . . How come you're . . . Why . . . ?"

Do it like a Band-Aid, woman!

She cleared her throat and started over. "Why aren't you pulling your weight around here?"

He sat up straight, his back against the headboard. The sheet fell even further down his body, revealing the light dusting of hair on his pubic bone. "Excuse me?"

She swallowed. Shit, that had come out all wrong. "Well . . . " Fuck, she was the boss at work, why was she cowering under his intense gaze? She never cowered, and she wasn't going to do it now. Exhaling, she started, "Well, Rowan and Juney take care of the meals. Austin brings in the firewood and takes care of the fire. He also shovels the driveway and front stoop. Hunter and I do the dishes, tidy up and sweep the floors, put on laundry, et cetera. What do you do?"

"Has everyone been talking about me?" he asked, the tenor of his deep voice clipped and defensive. His glare fell on her.

She shook her head. "No. Not everyone. It's more of a joke than anything. *Will's the big boss man, but he doesn't do much.*"

"I never asked to be 'the big boss man,' " he snapped.

Amber sat up against the headboard, but instead of letting the sheet slip down her body, she pulled it up across her chest and tucked it under her arms. "I know you didn't. But somehow you've become the leader. You're the oldest, the biggest, the one who screams alpha-boss-man the moment you walk into a room. It's hard not to defer to you. And that's coming from me, who is also a big boss."

A muscle ticked along his square jaw. "So everyone is making fun of me and calling me a freeloader, then?"

She shook her head. "No. No one is saying that. I'm simply curious why you're not pitching in. You pour us all a scotch, pour yourself several, and that's it. I don't even think Hunter or Juney drink scotch. They always go back to wine. But you've never bothered to ask anyone what they drink."

"You think I'm an alcoholic?" His tone was starting to alarm her, and Amber, who had never been one who shied away from confrontation, found herself shifting an inch or two away from him.

"No. I never said that."

"Fine. I won't have another drink for the rest of the trip. Just to prove to you I'm not an alcoholic."

She had to stop herself from snorting. They left tomorrow at noon. He didn't have to abstain for long.

"My job is stressful," he went on. "I'm always on call, so I'm not allowed to drink. So, on the *off chance* I get a few days to myself, I like to indulge. Is that such a crime?"

She shook her head again. "I never said you had a problem. You're taking this way, *way* out of context here." She sighed. Crap, this had turned south fast. "Forget I even said anything, okay? Let's just go to bed." She went to turn out the light.

Will's brows narrowed; he swung his legs over the bed. "Yeah, well, you're not perfect either. You're a fucking emotionless robot. Would it kill you to take a brick down from your wall once in a while? Have an emotion? Have a feeling? God, if I didn't know any better, I'd have thought you were a fucking dude . . . or a psychopath or something." He pulled his white boxer briefs on and made a "humph" sound. "Jury's still out on that last one, I guess. I'm staying in my own room." With that, he opened the door and left, leaving Amber sitting up in bed, her eyes wide and her mouth wider, staring at the closed door in awe while a lone tear slowly slipped down her cheek.

WILL COULDN'T SLEEP. He was furious. How dare she call him a freeloader. He was anything but. He worked his ass off for the greater good. He saved lives. He worked twenty-four-hour and forty-eight-hour shifts, often not sleeping more than a few hours the entire time. He was the antithesis of a fucking freeloader. This just proved it, Christmas was terrible.

Pacing back and forth in his room, he ran his fingers over his head, wanting to scream, but knowing he couldn't or else he might wake up the house. He needed a drink. He wanted a drink. But he'd just promised Amber he wouldn't touch a drop, and he was going to keep that promise. He wasn't an alcoholic, he simply enjoyed good scotch.

Deciding he would eat his feelings instead, he stalked down the dark hallway to the kitchen. There had to be a bag of chips around here somewhere. He'd already devoured his Christmas present chips from Amber. Those hadn't lasted twenty-four hours. Only when he turned the corner, he found another soul eating their feelings as well.

"Hey," Hunter said, reaching into a drawer and pulling out

another spoon. She passed it to Will. She took a big scoop out of the tub of Rocky Road before handing it over to him. "What's eating you?" She licked the spoon provocatively. Was she doing it sexily on purpose? Or was that just how she ate ice cream, like a porn star?

"Am I freeloader?" he asked, putting the full spoon in his mouth.

"Yup!" She nodded.

He gaped at her. "I . . . I'm sorry." Suddenly, all his built-up heaps of self-righteousness came thundering down, sending him into a smothering avalanche of doubt. That wasn't at all the response he was expecting. Was he really that big of a freeloader?

She lifted a shoulder cavalierly. "No biggie. None of us *really* care. It's more funny is all. Why? Did someone say something?"

"Amber."

"What did she say?" She accepted the tub back and took another big spoonful.

"She asked why I'm not pulling my weight, why I'm not pitching in."

"And?"

He went to open his mouth, but nothing besides air came out.

"Why aren't you pitching in?"

"I hadn't really thought about it. I don't know." He took the tub back from her and scooped out more ice cream.

"Let me ask you this," she started. "Do you do your own cooking, laundry, cleaning, grocery shopping at home? Do you mow your own lawn? Shovel your own driveway?"

Holy shit.

No. He didn't. Slowly, reluctantly, shamefully, he shook his head. "No. I have a housekeeper who does most of those things, and I live in a high rise."

Hunter nodded, and a yawn followed. "Hmm."

"Hmm?"

"And what about your childhood?"

"Well, *Dr. Freud*," he said snidely. "My father left us when I was eight. He was a doctor as well. He's been through a slew of wives and is pretty much just a womanizing jackass. I was essentially raised by a single mother."

"And did your mother do everything for you?" She took another sexy lick of her ice cream. Will could only imagine that if Austin were here right now, he would be having fifty fits about how erotically Hunter was behaving. That boy had fallen hard for the cute little blonde, and his jealousy with any attention she received from either Rowan or Will was palpable.

"Yes."

"Why is that?"

"Fuck, do you want me to go lie on the couch over there? Stare at some ink blots, so you can figure out I'm secretly in love with my mother and want to kill my father?"

She cocked an eyebrow and asked, "Are you? Do you?" before sensuously licking the spoon.

He scratched the back of his neck.

"Why did your mother do everything? Why did you *let* her do everything?"

"Jesus Christ!" He sighed, scrubbing his whiskery chin and fighting the urge to stomp his foot. "Fuck, I don't know. Because she wanted to. Because she felt guilty, and she spoiled me, doted on me. I was a genius in school, so she let me get away with pretty much murder as long as I promised to get good grades and go to college. Which I did. And now that I'm loaded, I take care of her. I'm not a complete asshole, you know."

She took the ice cream tub back from him. "I never said you were. I don't think anyone said you were."

"Yeah, well, apparently everyone *thinks* I am."

She shook her head slowly, her blonde hair shimmying around her narrow shoulders. She was cute, damn cute, with a smattering of freckles across her nose and cheeks and a cute little button nose. He could definitely see why Austin was mad for the girl. But Will was attracted to Amber's strength. He didn't doubt Hunter was a ballbuster and strong, you'd pretty much have to be given her childhood, and had Amber not caught his eye, he definitely would have made a move on Hunter. Tiny blondes had become one of his favorite flavors. But this new flavor, ginger and spice, was throwing him for a loop and rocking his world. And now he just went and called her a psychopath. *Fuck!*

"No one thinks you're an asshole," Hunter said. "You're just used to being taken care of. Used to going to work, saving lives and then coming home and not having to worry about dusting or sweeping or doing laundry."

He shrugged. She'd hit the nail on the head.

"Nothing wrong with that. But here, here you need to pitch in. We're not your mother, and we're not your hired hand. So, tomorrow, make the freaking coffee, okay?"

He looked down at his feet. She was definitely a ballbuster. She probably ruled her little empire with an iron-plated, hemp-infused fist. He nodded. "I . . . I think I messed up."

"Yeah? What did you say to Amber?"

"How did you know?"

"You're not in her room screwing her brains out. Call it a lucky guess."

He huffed. "I called her an emotionless robot and a psychopath."

Hunter's eyes went wide. "Yeah, dude, you're in the doghouse."

"No shit." Truth was Will knew there was more to Amber. He knew she had a big heart and a sweet side. He'd noticed it from the very beginning. Not to mention she was the little Christmas pixie hanging mistletoe up everywhere. Yeah, she was a sweetheart all right, and he was a bonehead who's gone and screwed everything up by calling her a psychopath. *Fuck!*

"You know she's the boss of like twenty guys, right?" Hunter said, snapping him out of his reverie.

He nodded and took back the ice cream. There was only enough for two more bites. "So?"

"So, women aren't allowed to have emotions and feelings when we're the boss. And especially not when we're in charge of men. They won't take us seriously, will question every decision and say we're only allowed to make executive decisions twenty-five days of the month. Because the other five we're irrational, bleeding nut jobs."

Will's jaw dropped. Hunter scoffed. She took the last bite of ice cream before wandering over to the sink to rinse out the tub. "You want some tea or something?" she asked.

"Sure, but I can make it." He brushed past her and reached for the kettle out of the top cupboard.

A smile tickled her lips. "You know she's got three older brothers too, right?"

"Yeah." He hip-checked her out of the way so he could fill the kettle at the sink.

"And she's a tomboy. And she's the boss at a construction company. Where on earth has she ever been allowed to be emotional or show her feelings? She's been trying to be 'one of the boys' since she was practically a baby."

"She's told you all of this?"

She shook her head. "No. Not all of it. A lot of it I just discerned from her behavior and what she's told all of us. We've chatted here and there. She, Juney and I talked a fair bit on the walk back to the cabin last night when you and Rowan were carrying Austin. She said that even though she loves her job, she doesn't always enjoy having to be the boss, especially to men."

"You know, I don't have any siblings, but you'd be a pretty

cool little sister," Will said with a chuckle, plugging in the kettle and then bringing down two mugs from the cabinet. "I mean, you're cute, but you're not my type." That was a big ol' lie, but for some reason he felt like he needed to say it.

"You're not my type, either. The chip on your shoulder can be seen from outer space. No thanks! And what the hell is with your hatred for Christmas? I could never be with someone who hates Christmas."

Well, that stung. But it was the truth. Just like Amber, Will had an enormous chip on his shoulder. And that chip had gotten in the way and ruined *a lot* of relationships. Relationships that probably would have lasted if he wasn't such a selfish prick.

His lip twitched as he turned around to face her again. "Yeah, it is pretty big, isn't it?"

"Uh-huh."

"Ah, well, shitty things just seem to keep happening to me on Christmas. My dad left, my wife left. I don't exactly have the fondest of memories when it comes to this particular holiday."

She rolled her eyes. "And you think *I* do?"

Crap, he'd done it again. Here he was complaining about his dad leaving when Hunter didn't even know who her dad was. She'd revealed that tidbit a few nights ago. At least Will could put a face and name to his "sperm donor."

He was about to say something, even though he wasn't quite sure what, when she cut him off. "I'm not looking for your pity. I had a fine childhood, better than most who ended up in the system. All I'm saying is, you're a bit of a Debbie Downer being all anti-Christmas, and all because not every single one of your thirty-seven Christmases were chock full of kittens in fuzzy hats and people singing carols around a baby grand piano. Get over yourself, doc. It's exactly like your Christmas cracker said, 'not every flat stone is going to skip the same distance.' Not every Christmas is going to kick ass. Some are going to kick *your* ass.

Just because I've had the odd crappy boyfriend, do you think that means I should write off men completely? Three shitty relationships mean that all men are shitty and I should become a nun or start dating women?"

He crossed his arms in front of his chest and shook his head. "No."

"You've kind of sucked this week, being all anti-Christmas the whole time."

"But what about Amber?" he started to say. "She's anti-Christmas too, and you're not harping on her."

She tucked her hair behind her ears and gave him a look that reminded him an awful lot of Juney. It was motherly. It was annoyed. It was preparing to lecture. "We're not talking about her right now. We're talking about you. And she's not *anti-Christmas*, she's feigning disinterest, if you haven't noticed. You can't look at a snow globe the way she looked at the one you gave her and *not* like Christmas. Hell, I'd go as far to say the woman probably loves it. But that's a whole different kettle of fish that I'm not interested in getting into right now. You can sort that out with her yourself. But you, you're being an ass. You were an ass to her, and you've been behaving like an ass all week. Stop being an ass."

His lips twisted before he spoke. "You said I *wasn't* being an ass."

She shot him another Juney-esc look. "I believe I said you weren't being an ass *hole*. But you're most definitely an *ass*. As in *jackass*."

He looked down at his feet. "You're right."

She shrugged. "I know. I might not have a fancy college degree or a bunch of letters behind my name, but I'm no dumb bunny."

"I never said you were."

"Humph."

He needed to change the subject. Things were getting

heated, and the last thing he needed was *two* women in the house out for his blood. "So, what brings you out here at this hour? You and the leader of Mensa get into a fight or something?"

She shook her head. "No, nothing like that. How many women do you think he's slept with?"

"Who? Austin?"

She nodded.

Will shook his head. "No clue. He's decent enough looking, really smart, probably up in the high teens or twenties or thirties."

Hunter shook her head again. "That's what I had thought too. But his number's not very high. Not as high as I would have thought, anyway."

"All long-term relationships?"

"Nope. He was a prodigy. Skipped grades, started college early. Says he was always the *kid*, and that made him socially awkward. He was intimidated by me, or at least that's what he says. That's why it took him forever to make a move. And in the end I was the one who made the first move."

Will had to hand it to the guy, that was pretty brave admitting something like that. Most men, Will included, would have simply shut down or feigned some other excuse. Admitting intimidation was admitting fault, admitting weakness. But it was also brave to do it.

"Was he intimidated by your number?"

"No. He has no idea of my number. I didn't disclose that. Not yet anyway. He was intimidated by the fact that I own the Curiously Kinky at home romance party company and that I'm loaded and successful. He didn't think he would be enough for me . . . in bed or in life."

"Was he?"

A wicked glint shone in Hunter's bright amber eyes. "And then some." She moved over to the drawer that housed all the tins of tea and opened it. "I mean we haven't done anything kinky yet, but so far the man has been a freaking sex savant. And he said he's willing to try stuff, that *he's* curious. But he's not the first guy to run once he finds out what I do. I should never have said anything the other day."

"Then tell him that. Tell him you really like him, and that you're willing to teach and go slow. And if he's as smart as he claims to be, he won't run. You're quite the little package."

Averting her gaze, Hunter ran her fingers along the tins of tea, while her cheeks flushed from his compliment. Will poured the steaming kettle into two green mugs, and then Hunter dropped a couple of chamomile teabags into the water. Picking up her mug, she wandered over to sit in the living room. He followed her.

Snatching her favorite blanket off the back of the couch, Hunter curled up on the couch and tucked her legs under her. Cradling her mug in both hands, she pressed the rim against her lips and inhaled. "Do you think Daisy's algorithm was correct with Austin and I?" she finally asked.

"Yes, I do." He sat across from her on the other end of the couch, his eyes focusing on the reflection of the beautiful tree in the big picture window. "You guys are *a lot* alike."

"We are?" Curiosity stole over her face.

"You don't see it?"

Her lips scrunched, and she looked down into her mug, lightly shaking her head. "I thought maybe at first we were. But I'm not so sure anymore."

"You're both lost. Have reached the top and don't know where to go now. Or at least, that's how I see it. More you than Austin. But with Austin I see a lost little puppy who grew up way too fast because of his big brain, but he really doesn't know the real world. Hasn't done any traveling or had any wild experiences. And I'm guessing based on your life, you were forced to grow up faster than normal, too. No?"

She set her mug on the high table behind the couch, her jaw dropping as the flush of pink continued to travel up her neck and cheeks and into her hairline.

"Hit the nail on the head, didn't I?"

"Uh, yeah. I've always been mature for my age. And I hitchhiked and backpacked all across the states as a teenager, but I haven't really been anywhere else in the world. I want to travel. I want to travel so badly. And Austin hasn't been out of the country, either."

"You're lost."

Hunter continued to nod. "Totally. Lost and blocked. I mentioned earlier I haven't had a new design or business idea in ages. That's not normal for me."

"Then go travel. Find yourself, find your passion and drive again. Hell, go travel together. And, if things go south, then part ways. I took a semester off years ago and went backpacking with a college girlfriend. We broke up on the trip, but you meet loads of other travelers. You just glom on to a new group and travel with them."

She made a rather unladylike noise in her throat before she put her lips to her mug again, blowing on the steam. "You broke up? Well, that gives me *all kinds* of hope."

He shook his head dismissively and blew on his own tea before gingerly taking a sip. He hadn't realized until that moment that he was wearing nothing but white boxer briefs. His eyes fell down to his lap and then quickly darted around the room, looking for a blanket. Hunter picked up on his vibe and snatched another cashmere throw from the back of the couch and tossed it to him.

"I'm not interested, just so you know." She laughed.

"I'm cold."

"Sure. Why'd you and your college girlfriend break up?"

"We broke up because we finally had the kids talk. She wanted them, and I didn't. Still don't. And neither of us planned on changing our minds, so we didn't see the need to continue on with the charade as if we did. We broke up in Laos. She went on to Vietnam, and I went to Malaysia."

"You make it sound so businesslike."

He shrugged. "Kind of was."

"So, what, you think Austin and I should sit down with the tablet tomorrow and plan a trip to Southeast Asia together, having known one another for all of four days?"

"People have done stranger and wilder things."

She was quiet for a moment. Was she mulling it over? He certainly hoped so. Backpacking had been one of best decisions Will had ever made. Seeing the world, experiencing new cultures, meeting new people. He wasn't always the broody, overworked man he was now. He used to know how to have fun, how to party.

"Yeah, maybe," she finally said, rolling her bottom lip between her teeth.

"And as far as the kinky shit goes," he went on, bobbing his eyebrows up and down a few times. That earned him an eye roll and a half-smile. "Just talk to Austin. Most guys, most *normal* guys are into experimenting and getting a little raunchy. And tell him he's enough . . . if you think he is. *Show* him he's enough. Hell, I've tied up, been tied up, spanked and been spanked. Though I definitely prefer to be the one *doing* the tying up and spanking. But, there *is* something sexy about a woman who likes to be on top once in a while. Power is hot."

Hunter laughed. A creak in the floorboards behind them had them both turning around and looking down the dark hallway.

Amber stood there at the front of the hall, her body cast into a shadow by the dim nightlight that illuminated the narrow corridor. Her petite, fit frame was slow and hesitant as she padded barefoot toward them.

She came to stand next to him where he sat on the couch, her eyes taking in the scene of him sitting happy and carefree, drinking tea with Hunter. He could practically see her hackles start to rise.

He swallowed. "Hi."

"W-what's going on?" she asked. God, the woman looked tinier than ever. Her strength, confidence and big personality ordinarily lent Amber a commanding presence that made up for her lack of height. But at the moment she seemed smaller and more fragile than ever. And it was because of Will.

He made a strangled noise in his throat while Hunter made to get up off the couch, draining her tea in the process.

"We were just having some chamomile tea, as neither of us could sleep. And Will here pretty much convinced me to ask Austin to go backpacking with me for a few months. I think I'm going to go do that now. Whip out the tablet, close my eyes and whatever country my finger lands on . . . that's where we're headed." With that, Hunter took her mug to the sink, then made her way back down the hall.

Amber strolled past him toward the big window. The moon was out and practically full, and it made the gully of snow-quilted trees shiny and shimmer like diamonds. It was eerily beautiful, serene but also deadly quiet and lonesome-looking. She stood in front of the window looking down into the forest, her arms wrapped around her body as she trembled slightly from the chill that swept through the house.

Will got up, and in less than five strides he was behind her, draping the blanket over her shoulders. "I'm sorry for what I said. You're not an emotionless robot or a psychopath. And I am a freeloader, you're right. I'm also an asshole."

She didn't move or say anything.

"I—I'm used to being in charge," he went on, not waiting for her to reply. "And I'm used to being taken care of. Nurses and hospital staff at work, a housekeeper at home, and my mother when I was a kid. Besides a scalpel or a pencil, I rarely have to lift a finger. But I'm going to do better. I promise."

She still didn't say anything.

"And . . . and you're not a robot. I get that coming from a family of brothers, and with the job you have, you can't really express your feelings. You've been forced to bottle everything up, because you have to. But you know, with me, you can let your guard down. You can remove some bricks."

Finally, she moved and spun around to face him. There were tears in her eyes, and a few rogue drops trickled down her cheeks. Will's chest tightened and, at that moment, he vowed to never be the cause of her pain again. He never wanted to be the reason Amber cried.

He brought his hands up to cradle her face and used his thumbs to sweep away the tears. She looked up at him, big soulful hazel eyes blinking behind unshed tears. Her lip trembled slightly. She swallowed, then crumbled against him, her whole body suddenly shaking with pent-up emotion that was finally being set free. And Will only held her.

Several long minutes later, she lifted her head from his chest, using the blanket to wipe her eyes. "I'm sorry."

He shook his head. "Don't be."

"I—I don't even know what I'm crying about."

"Not getting that doll you wanted when you were seven? You've kept things bottled up for a while, haven't you?"

With a small snort, she ran the back of her wrist beneath her nose and nodded. "Yeah, I guess it's been a while. But no, I never played with dolls. I liked tool sets and trains. I was all about the Legos."

He tilted her chin up with his finger. "I really like you, Amber. And I don't want to fuck this up. It's been a while since I found a woman who challenged me the way you do. Wants the same things I do. Who's strong and powerful and doesn't take shit from anyone, even me."

"I—I like you too."

"I want to see where this goes. I want to date you when we get back to Seattle. Properly. Go out for dinner. The movies, a Seahawks game."

Her eyes went wide, and she nodded. "I love the Seahawks."

"See, you're perfect for me. No other woman has ever gone starry-eyed when I mentioned going to a football game."

She grinned. "I'd much rather cuddle up under a blanket at CenturyLink Field and watch the Hawks beat the Packers than go to a basket-weaving class or a couples paint night." Letting the blanket slip to the floor, she stood up on her tippy-toes and nipped his chin. Her arms drifted up to rest on his shoulders. She pressed her lithe body against his. His reaction to her closeness pressed hard and eager against her hip. "I forgive you. Call it a . . . Christmas miracle." She traced his bottom lip with her tongue and pushed her pelvis against his.

A low, primal growl rolled through Will's chest as the smell of Amber, the feel and heat of her enveloped him. This woman had him under her spell, and there was no turning back.

Fuck.

He'd never cared about anyone's feelings as much as he did Amber's. His heart physically ached knowing he was the reason there were tears in her eyes. And yet, here she was, forgiving him. It truly was a Christmas miracle, and certainly not one he was going to take for granted.

He wanted to ravish her, take her in his arms and apologize properly. But a bigger part of him wanted to know the woman he was falling for. Help her take down those bricks, tear down the wall she so carefully put up around herself, and let him in. Gently he put his hands on her shoulders and held her away from him.

"Tell me something that makes or made you happy. And then tell me something that makes or made you sad. I want to know you, Amber. I want you to feel comfortable enough to be yourself with me. I want to feel your emotions right along with you. Tell me."

She released a big exhale. "Something that makes me happy . . . well, I love Christmas. Like seriously love it. *Obsessed* is probably a better word. It's my favorite time of year. I love everything about it. The music, the cheer, the togetherness, the gifts, the tree, the cookies. I love it all. And you're the first person I've ever told that to. And I thought we were a match, but you . . . you hate it so much, and . . . " she trailed off. A hiccup snagged in her throat as more emotions threatened to bubble up.

He shook his head. "Why do you feel you can't tell people you like a holiday?"

"Because it shows weakness and vulnerability."

"It shows that you're human, and for the record, I don't *hate* Christmas. In fact, I'd say I might actually like Christmas, that is, if you'll give me another chance?"

She nodded and smiled, but no light, no happiness flickered in her eyes. She wasn't convinced of anything yet. "Something that makes me sad," she hummed. "Well, I know that I don't *want* children, but I also actually *can't* have them."

His eyes widened, but he didn't say anything.

"I had cervical cancer a few years ago. Not from HPV, if that's what you're wondering. Just good old-fashioned cervical cancer. They removed the cancerous spots, but based on a few things the doctors said after I recovered, they don't believe I'll ever be able to conceive, even if I want to."

Will's pulse thumped wildly in his throat. "And that made you sad?"

She nodded solemnly. "I've never wanted children. Not ever. But for a long time I thought that would change when I met the right guy, things would just *click,* you know? But I've always been content with my choice. Because it was *my* choice. But to have that choice taken away from me, for Mother Nature to say to me that I *can't* have a child . . . it didn't sit well. It was as if one day, if my feelings ever switched, Mother Nature had already decided that I was unfit to be a parent and took that from me. I was angry for a while. And then sad. Now I'm indifferent about it, because I don't want children. But . . . "

"But you still want it to be because *you* choose not to."

More tears welled up in those big, beautiful eyes. "Yeah." An awkward laugh simmered up from her chest as she used the hem of her T-shirt to wipe away her tears. "I'm sorry."

Will brought her chin up with his knuckle so they were eye to eye again. "Don't be. I asked. I want to know you. Thank you for letting me in. Telling me more about yourself. I really appreciate it."

She exhaled again, her shoulder slumping as her chest shook. "Thank *you.* I needed that."

His head dipped to the crook of her neck, and he bit her gently. "I can be whatever you need. I want to be what you need. I know I've only known you for four days, but when it's right, time doesn't really matter. You're my match."

She looked up at him. "Make love to me, Will," she whispered, her hands traveling down his torso and cupping him. "That's what I *need.*"

With a low growl, his hand circled around her waist, and he drove her backward until her back was pressed up against the cool glass of the window. She leaped up onto his hips and pulled his mouth up to hers. They were suddenly all teeth and tongues, hands and frantic, driven passion. It was a good thing Amber was in no more than an oversized T-shirt and had neglected underwear, because in seconds Will's cock was drawn through the front hole of his boxers and probing her core.

"I--I don't have a condom on me," she said, breathlessly.

He grunted and then muttered "fuck" under his breath.

"I'm clean . . . and I can't—" Her words caught in her throat. He wanted her more than anything. Wanted only her. He could trust her with the truth. She trusted him with her truth. "I've had a vasectomy, and I'm clean."

She paused and looked him square in the eyes. "Holy shit, you weren't kidding when you said you don't want kids."

Will grew very serious and met her stare. "No, I wasn't. I don't want children. Ever."

She swallowed, and fresh tears welled up in her eyes. "Me either."

Finally, someone just like him. Someone who understood. If he ever married again, he would be the best damn uncle in the world, but he didn't want to be a father, and Amber didn't want to be a mother. Fuck Mother Nature. This was their choice and one they both agreed on.

Smiling at him, she sank her hips down until he was buried balls-deep inside her, squeezing her muscles the whole way, feeling every hard, thick, vein-roped inch of him.

"Oh God," he groaned, his hands coming up under her shirt and cupping her butt as he surged forward and began to pound her into the glass.

Amber's head tilted back as Will's teeth ran along her jaw and down her throat, grazing her, nipping her, marking her. She moaned softly. He loved it. Loved claiming her, branding her. Loved knowing that tomorrow she would have bite marks and tiny bruises from his savage passion. The thought of it, of seeing those marks on her creamy white skin, just turned him on more and made him ram into her harder.

His teeth clamped down on her shoulder. He gave one hard, bone-crushing thrust into her against the cool, unforgiving glass, and she let go. Will continued to pump, seeking his own release but loving how uninhibited his Little Red was. The way she came was beautiful. Her lips parted, her eyes shut, and a soft peachy heat crept up into her freckled cheeks.

"Yes . . . more," she said with a sigh, clawing at his back.

His whole body raged hot and wild, like gasoline on a bonfire. He snarled against her skin, stilled, dug his fingers into the plump flesh of her ass and detonated. He went up in a beautiful, enormous flame of glory. Every nerve ending, every cell, every synapse fired as the orgasm soared through him. She tensed around him again and cried out as another climax tore her apart.

Yes. Yes, Little Red. All your orgasms are mine.

She squeezed her hot, tight little pussy around his throbbing shaft as he came. He bucked into her a few more times, hitting her clit with his public bone and getting her deep inside, and when she finally sighed and opened her eyes, Will knew right then and there he'd finally found his other half. Christmas, of all holidays, had finally brought him peace, his match, and happiness.

They stood under the light of the Christmas tree for several moments. The sound of their heavy breathing and beating hearts was the only noise in the quiet living room. Slowly, he set her down on her bare feet. He spied a box of tissues on the side table and snatched a few, then crouched down and cleaned her up. When he stood back up, his smile placid and carefree, his eyes drifted up over her head.

"When did you put this one up?" he asked with a soft laugh, reaching up and batting the hanging mistletoe.

Her gaze followed his, and a sweet little O formed on her mouth. "It's not mine," she said matter-of-factly. "Mine are all real. This one is plastic."

A warm flash of goosebumps chased across Will's sweat-kissed skin at the idea of Christmas magic. Did it really exist? Were there elves or unexplainable things of wonder happening, bringing all these lost and wounded hearts together? Amber caught his look of awe and smiled. She linked her hand with his.

"Christmas magic," she said sweetly, "it really does exist."

Perhaps it does. It—or crazy Daisy— brought me you.

"Come on, my little red *elf*," he said, scooping her up. "As much fun as sex against a window is, I'm just as happy screwing you in a bed. One more and then we'll call it a night." And with that, he stalked off toward the bedroom, the two of them giggling softly as Will softly hummed "Jingle Bells."

CHAPTER NINETEEN

Hunter crept back into her bedroom, unsure if Austin would be asleep or not. Their last discussion hadn't exactly been heated, but it hadn't been great, either. A night of mind-blowing orgasms, and even though they were both exhausted, they'd lain awake and chatted for a while, cuddled up under the covers, facing each other in the dark. She was finally seeing the normal Austin, the man with a heart nearly as big as his brain. He was interesting and funny, sweet and nerdy, and she really liked him. Only he'd also confided in her why the last four days had been a nightmare. Why he'd been so distant and confused, and his words had really jarred her. Despite her fatigue, she'd been unable to sleep. So instead of tossing and turning and possibly waking up the man in her bed, Hunter headed to the kitchen. Had this been Seattle, she might have gone to her home gym and run on the treadmill to clear her head, but they were in the mountains, and ice cream would have to do as an adequate substitute. But Will's advice had helped. It'd helped a lot.

The idea of backpacking around Asia for a while was very appealing. And she'd always wanted to see more of the world, make new connections with distributors and find new organic and eco-friendly fabrics and new design inspirations. More than anything though, Hunter needed to get out of her funk and find her passion again. And now that she and Austin had found *their* passion, why not head off on a grand adventure together?

The light was off, and Austin's body lay huddled under the covers, his chest rising and falling with each deep and even breath. She gently pulled back the covers and scooted onto the mattress, not wanting to disturb him. But she couldn't sleep, not now. Her body had flickered to new life, and the idea of throwing caution to the wind, leaving the company to her general manager for a few months, and hopping on a plane bound for Cambodia seemed more and more appealing by the second. Would Austin be into it? He said he wanted to visit Angkor Wat, see the ruins. This was his chance.

He rolled toward her when she pulled the blankets up to her chin, a moan escaping past those talented lips. Was he going to wake up?

"Hey," he mumbled, his long lashes fluttering open. "Where'd you go?"

"To eat my feelings," she said softly.

Groggily, wiping the sleep from his eyes, he sat up against the headboard and flicked on his bedside table lamp. "Huh?

She let out a big huff and joined him at the headboard, propping a couple of big, fluffy pillows behind her. "I hate that you still don't think you're enough for me. That you think I'll one day get bored with you, or think you're not adventurous enough. We've had sex all of twice, Austin . . . and in that time, I've had eleven orgasms. No man has ever done that to me. And even if that is the case, and we aren't a true *match*, don't you at least want to see where this could go?"

He knitted his fingers together and studied the pattern on the bed spread. "Yes."

She ground her molars to keep herself from saying something she might regret. She had come in here to either sleep or talk about traveling. She needed to stay on course. But his behavior was beginning to piss her off. When they were having sex, he was confident and wild, demanding more orgasms from her than she thought she could muster. Taking her body to heights and places she had never reached with another man before. But yet the moment the endorphins left him, he was back to being unsure of his prowess, self-deprecating and lacking confidence.

She reached for her tablet on her nightstand. "I'm going backpacking in the new year, I've decided. I'm going to tie up some loose ends, prepare my general manager for all possible calamities, and then I'm taking off for a few months. I need inspiration. I need to find my passion again. Find my drive. I've been wandering around in a fog for nearly a year and it's starting to scare me. I've never been this unproductive."

Austin's gaze snagged hers. "S-so you're breaking . . . " he trailed off.

"I'm not breaking up with you, if that's what you were about to ask. Though two fucks, eleven orgasms, and half a night spent in the same bed *doesn't* really classify you as my boyfriend. But no. I want you to come with me. You said it yourself, you've never been anywhere outside of the U.S., and you want to travel. Come with me. Let's get to know each other as we get to know the rest of the world. See, explore, experience and learn."

The screen of her tablet flicked on, and within a couple of seconds, Hunter was typing away into Google Search.

"We'd definitely start in Cambodia." She turned to face him. "Fulfill the dream, right? And then I'd like to do Thailand, Vietnam, Laos, maybe Malaysia. Head over to Indonesia and do Bali and maybe Jakarta or Sumatra. I've heard great things about batik from Indonesia. I might try to meet with some wholesale distributors there. Silk in Thailand of course. Plus, the beaches in Thailand are phenomenal. See?" She held up a picture of a beach, with big rock formations sticking high up out of the water. It was that quintessential postcard image. Blue sky, bluer water, white sand. Paradise in a four-by-six frame. "I'd also love to get my dive ticket. Daisy and Riley do a ton of diving, and she's been harping on me for years to get certified. I'll definitely do that, too. What about you?"

Hunter's pulse was racing as she checked flights and visa requirements, Googled hotels and dive companies, silk and batik distributors. Within a matter of ten minutes, she had over a dozen tabs open on her desktop. Austin still hadn't said a word.

"So?" she finally said, her chest heaving from excitement. "What do you think? You in?"

Austin shook his head. "I—I can't."

An invisible arrow pierced her heart, and it immediately began to wither and seep. Her jubilation from earlier drained faster than it came on. "Oh."

He let out a big sigh. "I mean I *want* to. But I can't. I have work. And we're trying to get this project finished. And then Reggie probably has another project. The man always has new contracts and projects. He never stops. And he needs me. I can't abandon him. I can't abandon my job."

She swallowed hard. "Oh, okay. I get it."

She pulled the cover of her tablet back over the screen, then sank down deep into the covers, pulling them up to her ears as she turned away from Austin and put her head down on her pillow.

Fine.

She understood the importance of work, the importance of deadlines and being accountable to your staff. But practicality aside, she couldn't deny the deflation and disappointment that surged through her, the feeling of loss and defeat that squeezed around her heart until hot tears trickled down her cheek and on to the pillow.

Seconds later the light flicked off, and she felt Austin move in the bed beside her, shuffling down deep into the covers. The bed jostled a bit as he struggled to get comfortable, then all was still, all was dark, all was quiet. Silence reigned. Hunter pinched her eyes shut, clenched her teeth, and prayed for sleep.

———

Austin knew he had blown it with Hunter. Again. The look on her face had shattered him. Torn his beating heart from his chest and stomped it to smithereens on the floor. And yet he didn't know what else to say. It had been the truth. He couldn't just pick up and take off. He had a responsibility to Reggie, to their project, to their clients. And yet the pure heartbreak on Hunter's face had made him want to quit his job right then and there and follow her to the ends of the earth and beyond. But he couldn't. He just couldn't.

She had still been asleep when he awoke the following morning, the image of his head between her legs as she slowly regained consciousness driving him mad. That was how he *wanted* her to wake up. That was what he had envisioned. But no, he'd gone and broken her heart last night. He was surprised she hadn't kicked him out. A part of him thought that might have been better, but instead she'd just shut down, and it'd destroyed him. It'd taken him forever to fall asleep again. He kept rolling over to stare at the back of her head, her hair fanned out like a beautiful golden veil behind her on the pillow while her back moved slightly with each breath. He wanted to wake her up and apologize. But somehow, he knew that wouldn't be enough.

Slowly, trying not to wake her, he slipped from the bed and headed to his own room. He'd vowed to power down for the week, but something inside him made him turn his phone on. He hadn't gone this long without talking to Reggie in ages. It felt weird.

Ten missed calls. Six voicemail messages. Thirteen emails.

He checked to see who the majority of the calls were from, and sure enough, they were from Reggie. Something had to be going on with the Smythe account. He needed to call him.

"Hey, *Sheldon*, mah boy!" Reggie answered, his British lilt heightened by his excitement. Reggie had always been an eccentric and larger-than-life kind of guy, but something in his tone was different. He not only sounded happy, he sounded . . . relaxed.

"Hi, Reggie. Merry Christmas."

"Happy Christmas to you. Are you having a nice break?"

"Yeah, it's been pretty great. Nice to de-frag and decompress, you know?"

Reggie scoffed on the other end, followed by a chuckle. "You're telling me. This has been the best week of my life."

Austin couldn't stop the squeaky tone of surprise that took over his voice. "Really?" Reggie was a workaholic. The fact that the man practically *ordered* Austin to take some time off had come as a total surprise.

"I'm in love, mah boy. Absolutely, head-over-heels in love."

"W-well . . . that's wonderful," Austin stammered, nerves prickling beneath his skin. Something was up. Reggie, although a great guy and full of pep, was never gushy, never whimsical, and right now his entire tone was laden thick with whimsy and cheer.

"Isn't it? It's bloody brilliant. We got married on Christmas day."

"Wait . . . WHAT? You got married?"

"That's right!" Reggie cheered.

"How long have you known this woman? What if she's after your money?"

Oh, shit. Filter, Austin, you socially inept fucker, filter!

But fear that poor Reggie was going to be fleeced of his millions by some gold-digging harpy who flashed him a smile, some leg and sat through one of his many long-winded explanations about wind energy verses solar energy shit-kicked any form of social grace. He was looking out for his friend.

Reggie chuckled on the other end. "Since I was eight. She's my childhood love, *Sheldon*. The love of my life. Her husband left her for a chippy half his age, and now Rita's got his millions. She called me up a few weeks ago, told me her story, said she should never have done as her father demanded and married the miserable Lord of *Who Gives a Rat's Ass*, and married me instead. We met in Barbados for Christmas and got married."

Austin caught his reflection in the mirror. His head was shaking so quickly, he looked like one of those ridiculous bobbleheads or a hula girl on the dash of a car.

"Married?" he continued to say. "You're married?"

"Mhmm. And it's the best feeling in the world. Something more important, more incredible, more fulfilling than work, money or success. It's love!"

"B-but . . . how?"

"When you know, you know. No sense wasting time. We wasted over forty years. We're not wasting another second. We're taking off on an *extended* honeymoon."

"But what about the company? What about the Smythe account, the project for Audi?" Austin was starting to panic. Did he have a job to go back to? All his hard work, hours and hours spent trying to figure out the new biofuel eco-efficient engine . . . he'd been eating, sleeping and breathing this thing for nearly two years.

"We'll finish all of that, don't worry."

He let out a heavy sigh. Thank God. At least he still had a job. At least Reggie hadn't fallen completely off his rocker.

"And then we're done. You can have the company or I'll sell it, or dismantle it. But once the current contracts are done, once we figure out this engine bullshit, then we're done. Rita and I just bought a sailboat, and we're going to sail around the world."

"Do you even know how to sail?" *Fuck, filter!* "What I mean is, Reggie, are you sure about all of this?"

"One hundred percent. I'm in love. Best feeling ever. I have my millions, Rita has hers. I'm done working. I'm sixty-three years old. I have no children and nothing but a lifetime of work and incredibly successful and world-changing inventions to show for it. I want more. I want the exhilaration of waking up next to the woman I love every day. I want to be able to wake up and ask her, 'What do you want to do today, honey?' And for her to say, 'Whatever the fuck we want, dear. We're retired and rich.' And then we make love, drink kombucha on the bow of our boat, then go scuba diving and spearfishing for our supper."

Jeez, the man painted one hell of a picture, that was for sure.

"I want you to find love too, *Sheldon*. We'll finish the project, and then if you want the company, it's yours. But we'll be making enough from Smythe and Audi that you'll be set for some time. The check will be millions."

Austin had to grab the phone with both hands. *Millions.*

"I think you should take off for a bit. See the world. *Travel. Fuck. Experience.* Spend some of your millions on frivolous things. I wish I had at your age. Now I'm sixty-three and having to play catch-up."

Austin swallowed. *Travel. Fuck. Experience. Millions.*

"Anyway, *Sheldon*, I just wanted to wish you a Happy Christmas and tell you the good news. I've been trying to call you for a couple of days now. You getting laid, too?"

Austin made a garbled noise in his throat. "Yeah. Good news."

"Oh, for fuck's sake, congratulate me! I'm married."

Fuck.

"Right. Uh, sorry. Congratulations, Reggie. Rita is a lucky woman, and I can't wait to meet her."

"That's better." Reggie laughed loud and carefree. "Maybe next time you say it, it will sound like you actually mean it."

"Sorry."

"Don't be. Think about that glitch with the wiring, and when we meet in a few days, hopefully we can hammer out the problems and wrap this puppy up. We set sail for the Baja on Valentine's Day!" He chuckled again, and then the sound of a woman's voice followed by what could only be described as a seductive growl filled the receiver. "I've got to go. The wife is needy . . . if you know what I mean? Happy New Year, *Shelly*. Cheerio." Then, without waiting for a fare-thee-well from Austin, Reggie hung up, the final sound on the other end being the high-pitched girly squeal of a woman before the line went dead.

Austin tossed his phone on to his bed, staring at it wide-eyed, his head continuing to shake. *Married. Millions. Travel. Fuck. Experience.* The words continued to rattle around and around and around in his head. *Millions. Travel. Experience. Fuck. Married.*

He ran his hands through his hair, then caught his reflection in the mirror. He was smiling. Grinning. From ear to goddamn ear, he was happy.

He had to tell Hunter the good news!

"WHAT THE HECK?" Rowan said with a yawn as he wandered into the kitchen, Juney right behind him.

Will looked up from where he stood at the counter. He was busy whisking eggs in a bowl while bacon sizzled on the griddle next to him. "May have taken a couple of days, but I got the hint.

Sorry, guys. Breakfast *and* cleanup are on me today. Just sit back and enjoy."

Amber, who was also in the kitchen, was busy cutting up some strawberries. She grinned over at Rowan and Juney before giving them a wink and putting her head back down.

"I like a little Tabasco in my scrambled eggs," Rowan said, wandering over to pour himself some coffee. "And maybe some jalapeno jack grated on top."

"Yes, Chef!" Will said with a big smile.

"What'd you do, fuck the cantankerous freeloader's brains out until he's now no more than a happy helper?" Rowan asked, wrapping an arm around Juney as she sidled up next to him at the bar, thanking him for her coffee.

Amber laughed. "Yep, pretty much."

"All night long," Will added with a smug smile.

A *scuff-scuff* sound from down the hallway drew everyone's eyes, and Hunter, with a messy bun and pillow creases on her cheeks, schlepped forward, wiping sleep from her eyes and yawning wide.

"Well, this is a lovely sight," she said dryly. "Giving back to the little people, are we, Dr. Colson?"

Will snorted. "I'm pretty sure you make more than I do, Miss Kingsley, so I'm not sure who you're referring to as *little* people." He placed a cup of coffee on the bar, and she sat in front of it. "So, you and Boy Wonder going off to paradise? What did he say?"

Hunter's face pinched tight, and she looked down into her coffee. "He said no. Said work was too important. And I get that. I respect that. Doesn't mean it still didn't hurt."

Juney reached over and rubbed her back.

Hunter looked at Rowan and then Will, blinking several times. Her eyes were glassy with unshed tears. "I'm still going to go, though. I emailed my general manager this morning, told her my plan, and when I get back to the city, I'm going to get the ball rolling. You said it yourself, Will, it's okay to travel alone. You find people who are like-minded, and you travel with them. That's what I'll do. I'll find my match abroad." She attempted a smile, but the struggle to turn up the corners of her mouth appeared to be too much, and her eyes still held shadows of pain.

"Hunter?"

All heads swiveled to look down the hallway to where the sound was coming from.

"Hunter?"

"In here," she called.

Just then, like a cyclone of plaid pajama pants and enormous smiles, Austin came careening down the hallway. "Hunter!" he hollered, even though he really didn't need to. She was only a few feet in front of him. "Hunter, there you are!"

"I'm here. What's wrong?" she asked calmly. Rowan couldn't blame her for not feeding off of Austin's excitement and smiling. The man had kept her waiting all week, then when everyone thought he'd finally come to his senses, he'd hauled off and broken her heart again.

Austin shook his head. "Nothing! Nothing is wrong. Everything is right! For once, finally, everything is right."

"What?" she asked.

"I'm coming with you. To Cambodia. To Thailand. To Bali. I'm coming. I want to come. I can come. Can I come?"

Finally, a smile. Hunter's eyes lit up as she took a step off the barstool and stood in front of Austin. "What do you mean? Last night you said you couldn't, you said work was too demanding and you didn't want to abandon your boss. What's changed in the last few hours?"

"Everything!" he said, his chest rising and falling as if he'd just sprinted down the hallway. Maybe he had. "My boss . . . Reggie, I just talked to him on the phone. He's retiring. After we wrap up this project, we're done. He got married to his childhood love over Christmas, and they bought a boat. He's either selling the company, or he said I could buy it off of him. But either way, I can come with you. I *want* to come with you. I want to travel, explore and see the world. . . with you. *Travel. Experience. Fuck. Millions.*" He was gasping for air now. The rest of them stared at him, and Rowan wondered if he was having a stroke or possibly drunk.

Hunter opened her mouth to say something, but the flash of the television on the wall above the hearth had all eyes pivoting from the drama in the kitchen to the cozy sunken living room.

"Hello!" came Daisy's voice over the surround sound. "Anyone there?"

Slowly, everyone made their way into the living room. Amber and Will settled on the couch, Juney and Rowan in the love seat, and Hunter and Austin stood next to each other behind the couch. Daisy's beautiful face appeared up onto the screen a second later, big smile and bright eyes flashing wide and happy. Cat-eye sunglasses were pushed up into her strawberry-blonde hair, and a turquoise bikini peeked out from beneath a white beach wrap. She looked tanned, content and gorgeous.

"Hi, guys!"

Everyone murmured, unsure if they should respond. Was she live?

"I'm live, and there's a camera on the top of the television, so I can see everyone. How was your Christmas?"

Juney's head bobbed. "Great!"

Rowan smiled next to her and wrapped his arms around her shoulder. "I'd say it's been one of my best Christmases ever."

"Mine too," Amber added.

"Hands down," Will agreed, pulling Amber closer to him and planting a big kiss on her temple. She nestled in more tightly to his embrace.

"Hunter? Austin?" Daisy asked, one faint blonde eyebrow drawing up in equal parts curiosity and maybe even a little motherly concern.

Will, Juney, Rowan and Amber all craned their necks around to look at the other two. Waiting. Hunter hadn't given Austin an answer yet. She hadn't forgiven him or welcomed him to join her on her adventure again. And if she didn't, the only person to blame would be Austin. He'd toyed with her emotions enough this week. If she was ready to call it quits, she had every right.

Hunter took a step to her right and laced her fingers with Austin's. The look he gave her could have set the house on fire. Scorching hot. Lust, passion, conviction. It was all there. This boy was a goner. He'd never say "no" to Hunter again.

"Wonderful Christmas," Hunter said with a smile. "Austin and I are going to the Arkells concert, and then we're taking off to go and backpack Southeast Asia."

Austin pulled her into his arms and kissed her. "And that's only the start of it," he said when they came up for air. "Hunter's made me *curious* about everything, and I can't wait to explore. We're going to see the world!"

Well, holy hell, where'd this bit of bravado come from? Rowan shook his head and chuckled to himself. Mr. Mensa finally found some *cojones* and was ready to be worthy of little Hunter. Good.

Daisy's eyes scanned each couple again, and she hummed methodically. "This is very interesting. I'm happy for everyone, of course, but, well . . . hmmm." She waved a piece of paper in front of the screen, then pulled it away and waggled her eyebrows up and down salaciously. "Are you at all curious to see if you found your match?"

Austin shook his head. "No, thanks. I know I did."

Hunter beamed at him and wrapped her arms around his neck. "Me too."

Will agreed with a big grin. "Me too."

"I know I did," said Amber.

"Me too," said Juney.

Rowan nodded. He didn't need a piece of paper or some fancy algorithm to tell him Juney was his perfect match. He felt it in his heart, knew it in his very bones that she was the woman for him.

Daisy continued to smile. "Well, good. As long as you're all happy, that's what matters. And now for some bad news. I'm afraid with the snowstorm and the fact that a couple of big trees have fallen down across the highway, the shuttle is unable to come and get you guys today. The weather is just projected to get worse for another few days, and they're not sure they can get the trees cleared until at least the first. Are you guys okay sticking it out a few more days? There should still be enough food. The freezer in the garage is loaded with food, and besides maybe milk for your coffee, you should be all right."

Will pulled Amber into his lap. He grabbed her ponytail and tugged until her neck was exposed to him, and he leaned in and nipped her. "Oh, I think we'll be quite all right, Daisy. *Plenty* to do."

Rowan hauled Juney into his lap as well, until she was straddling him. She draped her arms over his shoulders, her fingers twirling around the hair at the nape of his neck. He glanced around his lady love to the woman on the screen. "Loads to do, Daise. Don't you worry about us."

Juney giggled as his hand made its way up her torso and he squeezed her breast. "Rowan's right, Daisy, we're all good here."

"Yup!" Hunter laughed. "Ring in the new year in a log cabin, someone to kiss at midnight. New friends. Sounds perfect to me. Nothing to worry about. Enjoy your time in the Caribbean with Riley."

Rowan let go of Juney's waist for a moment and reached for

the remote from the table behind the couch. "I think we're all pretty content with the bad news. In fact, it's not bad news at all. But if you don't mind, Daise, I think we're going to say Merry Christmas, have a Happy New Year, and goodbye. We all have some *celebrating* to do."

Daisy chuckled. "All right, guys. Happy New Year."

"Happy New Year," they cheered.

"Turn the television off, Rowan," Austin said. As he glanced up, he noticed the piece of mistletoe hanging above him. Then he smiled, dipped Hunter low and finally made a move.

EPILOGUE

One year later...

"Wow!" Amber said, the whirr of the boat motor finally dying down as it pulled up alongside the dock.

"I'll say," Juney hummed.

"This is so cool!" Rowan exclaimed as he jumped off the boat, his sandals making a big, heavy clomping sound on the wooden dock.

"To be a millionaire . . . " Juney said wistfully glancing out into the endless sparkling turquoise water. "Though knowing millionaires with their own tropical island in the Caribbean is pretty fantastic as well."

"I thought it'd be bigger," Will said, helping Amber up on to the dock, her red hair flying in a frenzy across her face. With an irritated sigh, she quickly gathered it into her hand and spun it into a ponytail at the nape of her neck. A few rogue wisps escaped, but for the most part, the fire had been contained.

"Aren't you glad I didn't say the same thing when we first

met?" She chuckled, pushing her sunglasses off her face onto the top of her head.

"Nothing *is* bigger, baby," Will said with a growl, tugging her into his side and planting a big kiss to the top of her head. "I'm a freakin' mandingo."

Amber snorted a laugh. He was such a goof.

"Hey, guys!" Hunter said with a big grin, her blonde hair in a beautiful, loose French braid over her shoulder. Her peachy-pink maxi dress trailed behind her like a jet stream. "Welcome to paradise. A far cry from the snowstorm we experienced a year ago, wouldn't you say?"

Austin was right behind her, pushing a big luggage trolley. He greeted everyone warmly, then helped Rowan and Will load the suitcases onto the cart.

"Much better," Juney agreed. "Though . . . " She rubbed her belly, a small bump beneath her black tank top, "I can't say I'll be enjoying this heat much. I might spend ninety percent of my time in the water." She made a sickly face. "Or barfing."

"What are you now, like four months?" Hunter asked.

"Almost five," she said. "But I already feel like a house."

"A beautiful, sexy house," Rowan said, coming up behind her and wrapping his arms around her waist. "A house I'd like to live in every day for the rest of my life."

A peaceful smile coasted across her face, only adding to her already beautiful pregnant lady glow. "Thank you guys for having us here. Ever since the wedding last month, it's been go-go-go. We've been booked solid at the restaurant, doing Christmas parties and other weddings. It's nice to get away and enjoy some time together and with friends."

"You're welcome," Hunter beamed. "We're happy you guys could make it."

They all fell in line and followed their hosts down the dock toward a small cluster of buildings painted in bright yellows and aqua blues with white shutters and wraparound porches. There were at least three cabins, what looked like a big tool shed, and another more open-concept building with a pitched roof and columns but no walls. Inside was a big long table and what looked to be a grill, fridge, and counter.

The men took off toward the cabins, Austin pointing out which couple was in which building as Will and Rowan tipped icy cold beers back and wiped sweat from their brows.

"I can't believe you and Austin own an island," Amber said, taking a beer from Hunter. She was in awe of the beauty, the tranquility. Initially she'd grumbled at the idea of spending Christmas in the tropics, away from her tree, from the snow, from the whimsy. But as the sun overhead kissed her skin and the scent of warm sand, salt air and fresh fruit coasted past her, she couldn't deny the sudden feeling of contentment. She and Juney followed Hunter away from the outbuilding and out onto the beach in the shade of a few swaying palms. Half a dozen lounge chairs sat in the sand, and they each took one.

"And in Belize, no less," Juney added. "It's absolute paradise."

Hunter let out a contented sigh as she kicked off her flip-flops and buried her crimson-painted toes in the warm sand. "I know, me either. But to be fair, you can buy an island here for less than a high-rise back home."

Juney shook her head and rubbed her belly. "It's beautiful."

"Hard to believe it's only been a year," Hunter said. "And now you and Rowan are married and expecting a baby. Will and Amber are engaged. And Austin and I own an island and are getting married in three days."

"A wonderful, whirlwind year," Amber said.

Hunter nodded. "Absolutely."

"You have enough space to accommodate everyone?"

Amber's head swiveled around to see if she could see any more cabins. Though, if push came to shove, she and Will could always go wander off down the beach and just sleep on a blanket under the stars. Ever since their impromptu snow-shoeing tryst, she had quite the insatiable hunger for outdoor sex. They'd done it all over Seattle: in parks, on hikes, on the beach. Hell, they'd even done it at a Seahawks game.

"We have four cabins that sleep five to six each, and then there's another island about twenty minutes away by boat that has a bunch of cabins we've rented for the week. James and Emma Shaw own an island not too far from here. They're from Canada, and we've met them in Belize City a couple of times and on the plane to and from. They rent out their bungalows year-round when they're not using them and said we could have them for the week."

"Oh, you millionaires and your millionaire friends and their islands," Amber scoffed with a smile.

"It's going to be a beautiful day," Juney said.

Manly laughter and banter filled the air as the men strolled forward. There was some back-patting and big cocky grins as Rowan looped his arm around Austin's shoulder and pulled him in for a bro-hug. "Hard to believe this guy is getting married," he said with a laugh. "Why this time last year, you were a trembling little field mouse, afraid that the sexy blonde lady wouldn't want your winky."

"*Filter*, dear," Juney said with a groan.

Will was full-on belly laughing beside them. It warmed Amber's heart to see him so carefree and happy. He'd been excited to take some time off work, see their friends again, and celebrate Christmas. He'd even confided in her that he couldn't wait to give her his gift. Knowing Will, it was probably another snow globe and some kind of sex toy. They'd joined the VIP membership club of Hunter's company, and each month the "toy of the month" arrived on their doorstep in a discreet little package. This month it had been a riding crop with red and white candy cane stripes.

Austin smirked. "Well, she wants my *winky* now," he said blandly. "Right, baby?"

Hunter got up from her seat and went to stand next to him. "Until death do us part."

"You guys sticking around here for your honeymoon?" Juney asked.

Hunter and Austin shook their heads.

"No, we'll stay here until the new year, and then we're taking off for two months to go and backpack Eastern Europe," Hunter said.

"That's right!" Austin added, pulling her close. *"Travel. Fuck. Experience. Millions."*

Everyone gave him a curious look.

He shook his head. "Wise words once said to me. They rattled my cage and made me realize that I was pissing my life away with work, especially when my real life, my *world* was standing there in front of me asking me to join her on an adventure. Asking me to sing karaoke with her."

Hunter wrapped her arm around his waist. "And we've been on just one big adventure ever since."

"And duet partners." He smiled.

"To adventure, friendship and love," Juney said, raising her bottle of San Pellegrino.

"To finding your match," Rowan added, meeting her drink in the air with his beer.

Hunter lifted her beer into the air, too. "To Daisy."

"To snowstorms and setups." Austin grinned, knocking his betrothed's bottle with his.

Will and Amber's eyes met as they lifted their beers to the middle. "To Christmas."

**Curious about Sam and whether he gets his own happily ever after? Check out Hot Dad.
Available Now.**

IF YOU ENJOYED THIS BOOK

If you've enjoyed this book, please consider leaving a review. It really does make a difference.

Thank you again.
Xoxo
Whitley Cox

Here's a sneak peek of Chapter 1

Hot Dad

SNEAK PEEK OF HOT DAD - CHAPTER 1

Harper

I FUCKING LOVED MONDAYS. No, seriously, I loved them. I know most people hate them, bitch, moan, snivel and complain about Mondays. People can have a "case of the Mondays" but not me. I loved them. Why? Because Monday was the day I saw my people. My coven. My mom posse. Well, moms and one hot, unobtainable dad. A dad I'd been secretly lusting over for six months but have had no more than half a dozen conversations with in that time. Monday was the day I took my toddler to playgroup at the rec center a few blocks away.

It was a day that for two glorious hours I engaged in a coffee- and chocolate-infused bitch-fest with my nearest and dearest as we ogled Hot Dad from afar and drooled over his ass when he spun around. My posse was filled with women just like me who were operating on far too little sleep and hadn't peed alone in years let alone remembered the last time they washed *and* conditioned their hair. It was the one day of the week when I wasn't made to feel guilty for plunking my kid down on the floor and letting her battle it out over the toy trains with another child, while I sipped my overpriced latte and had some much-needed adult talk.

But it was an ugly Monday. January was ugly. A West Coast baby to my very marrow, I loved nearly everything about living in Vancouver—except January. January weather was the worst! It held the kind of wet cold that slipped past all the layers of clothes and embedded itself deep in your bones. Rain, sleet, snow, wind. Like a sucker-punch to the kidneys, it made the whole city buckle, whine and wish for spring. Enough of this winter bullshit; bring on the flowers. This January was particularly nasty. We'd been hit with the snowfall of the decade on Christmas day, but by the new year it had warmed up just enough to melt the majority of it, leaving nothing but slush in the streets, brown patches, and clumps at the corner of people's driveways and where kids had braved the chill to build snowmen or forts. But they were calling for another blast of cool weather from the north, so more snow was inevitable.

Great!

I finished the email I'd been writing on my laptop in the kitchen, hit send, then glanced through the wall cut-out at my happily playing child. Her bucket of dinosaurs sat between her legs as she methodically shoved each plastic reptile down the front of her loose-fitting tucked-in shirt. She insisted upon these kinds of shirts for this very reason.

"Two minutes, Carly," I said as a warning. "Two minutes, then we're going to get ready for playgroup."

Not even a glance my way.

Ignoring her rudeness, I went about getting myself ready. Wool socks, waffle-knit long-sleeved gray T-shirt, black hoodie, yoga pants. Check. Check. Check. Check. I placed my dark purple Hunter rain boots by the front door, then pulled on my raincoat and grabbed Carly's boots and jacket before wandering into the living room to go wrestle my toddler.

I crouched down to her level so we were face to face. "Come on, baby, we don't want to be late for playgroup."

Still not even a jerk of the head or a flick of her eyes. Fighting back the rush of frustration inside me, I gritted my teeth and took a couple of deep breaths. My sweet, agreeable little girl had embraced "two" like it was a new fashion trend, the toddler's version of a man-bun or an electric bike.

I pulled her into my lap and sat down on the couch to slip on her boots. "It's time to go. We don't want to be late."

"No booooooots!" she wailed, squirming in my lap before arching her back until she was as straight as a two-by-four. "No booooots!"

"Carly Elyse! We are going to playgroup," I said with an exasperated sigh. The child had been up before the birds (not that there were many birds out in January), climbing out of her toddler bed and throwing my bedroom door open at five-forty screaming "bottle" at the top of her tiny lungs, only to then toss all of her plastic dinosaurs on my face.

But *I* needed to go to playgroup. Probably more than she needed to go. It was my sanctuary. My place of peace. My safe space where I could wear my ratty ponytail, my torn and pilling yoga pants, feed my caffeine addiction all without judgment while gossiping and commiserating with all the other sleep- and sex-deprived mums. Only their sex deprivation was due to lack of sleep and not because they didn't have a man to share their bed. My sex deprivation was because I hadn't gotten laid since the night Carly was conceived.

It was a masked, drunken tryst in the dark break room at the New Year's Eve party of an art gallery downtown. I never even saw his face, never saw much besides an orgasm and a good time. But apparently, he'd been handsome, because my kid was gorgeous—thank God. My fiancé of three years had just dumped me on Christmas Day, less than two months before our Valentine's Day wedding, and I was looking for hot and dirty rebound sex with a stranger.

I'd found it.

I'd gone off the pill in early December as Vance and I had planned to start trying for a family right after the wedding, but my masked lover had used a condom, and yet I still managed to get pregnant. And at thirty-two, I was getting a little desperate. I wanted children. The circumstances just weren't ideal. But now here I was three years later, with a perfect, healthy two-year-old, living in my sister's basement suite in the heart of Vancouver and making a modest wage with my home-based business. Not ideal, but things could certainly be worse.

I pulled her other boot on, then reached over to the arm of the couch for her coat and toque. Zipping up her coat, I paused at the sound from the child on my lap. Her little chest lurched. Panic flooded me.

We all knew that sound. The deep throat convulsing sound. It was probably most recognizable when being made by a dog. I kept saying they should make alarm clocks with that sound. People would never hit *snooze* if they woke up to that noise. But even coming from a toddler, it was distinct, and before I knew it, I found myself pitching forward and running for the kitchen sink. It was closer than the bathroom, and even if we didn't make the sink, the laminate was better than the carpet.

Cheerios, apple, and scrambled egg all mixed with milk splattered to the kitchen floor as Carly started to heave in my arms.

"Oh no!" she cried. "Uh-oh!"

"It's okay, sweetie," I cooed. "It's okay."

Ah, shit! I knew she was going to catch something from her cousins. Preschool and kindergarten were even bigger cesspools than playgroup.

Lillian and Emmet were both sick upstairs, having come home from school on Thursday because they'd lost their biscuits. They'd stopped puking by Saturday, but apparently Carly spending time with them Wednesday was enough. I looked at the calendar on the fridge. Yep, five-day incubation time. That's exactly what my sister had said. *Crap!*

"Arly barted," she whined, unable to pronounce the C in her name and deeply immersed in the third-person phase of her speech development. She referred to herself as *Arly*. And, of course, "barted" was her toddler butchering of "barfed."

"It's okay," I said again. "Are you all done?"

"Yeah."

I set her little feet down on the floor, then turned her to face me. An up-chucked Cheerio clung to her chin. I fought the urge to vomit and instead picked it off and tossed it into the sink. Her coat was covered in chunks, and the light-brown strands of hair that she refused to let me fix into a ponytail or clip were dripping with stomach carnage.

Surveying the damage, I tried to keep my face as neutral as possible. A sensitive soul and easily spooked, she would get upset if she noticed I was anything but calm. Her big brown eyes stared back at me, watery and confused.

"Arly okay, mama?" she asked.

I nodded. "You're okay, baby. But we're going to stay home today. No playgroup. We're going to go have a quick shower, then cuddle up in our pajamas, watch movies and play dinosaurs. Sound good?"

Her eyes went wide and her smile even wider. "Dinosaurs!"

But then fear stole her glee, and before I knew it, I was holding her over the sink again as she tossed up more breakfast.

I guess I have to wait until next week to check out Hot Dad's butt.

A SHORT WHILE LATER, after what felt like hours of playing dinosaurs, watching a dinosaur documentary on the Discovery Channel and coloring in dinosaur coloring books, my toddler was asleep. Though of course not in her bed. We'd tried, but she'd barfed. Now her sheets were in the wash and she was in my bed with me, her head on my lap as I stroked her hair and worked on my tablet.

I'm a virtual assistant, and damn good at it too. If you're an author, an artist, an actor, a politician, a business person of any sort and need help organizing your life, your schedule, your social media or whatever, you come to me. Some kids used to play house or trains when they were growing up; I used to play secretary and wedding planner. I'd been organizing things and making schedules since I learned how to pick up a pencil, a ruler and make my own calendar. And I'd gotten very good at my job. Currently sitting with eighteen clients who all paid me handsomely to run their lives, I managed to make my own schedule and stay home with my kid, all while making a decent wage doing what I love.

But despite all that, it still wasn't enough to afford a house in Vancouver. I'd have to sell Carly and my kidney just to manage the mortgage on a loft apartment downtown.

No thanks.

So instead, we lived in my sister Quinn's basement suite, while she, her husband, Rick, and their two kids lived upstairs. It was a nice place, with lots of windows, a backyard and small garden. And what was best about it was my daughter got to grow up with her cousins, and I had my sister there to babysit when I needed a break.

Carly stirred in my lap, her body bunched into the fetal position and her face contorted into one of pain. I halted my finger on the touch screen and waited for her eyes to open. They didn't. Her face relaxed, and her thumb found her mouth. She rarely sucked her thumb anymore, usually only when she was sick. This was not a good sign.

I continued on with work, typing out an email to Mr. C.J. Forrester, the grumpy but brilliant wildlife photographer and nonfiction writer. He had me managing his newsletter and calendar, but true to form, as a man not used to someone telling him what to do, he'd gone and double-booked himself for two exhibits in two different cities without coming to me first. I managed to move one to a later date, because I'm a freaking miracle worker, but now I had to touch base with him to make sure he knew where he had to be and when.

My phone vibrated next to me. I glanced down at it and then at my kid. She was still asleep, sucking away on that thumb. Her long, dark lashes feathered out against her rosy cheeks. She was deep in dreamland. If I answered, I might wake her. It continued to vibrate. I didn't recognize the number.

Fuck.

It might be work. No matter how many times I told my clients that text and email were preferred as it put everything down in writing, left a paper trail and was less likely to wake up my kid, some still just had to talk to me in person.

Grumbling several "for fuck's sakes" under my breath, I hit the green button then cupped the receiver.

"Hello?" I whispered.

"Hello?" a manly voice replied, mimicking my tone and volume. "Is it nap time?"

"Yes."

"Is she *on* you?"

Okay, who the hell was this person? That was a weird question. Accurate, but still weird. I considered hanging up but then thought better of it. Most of my clients had their own kids, and they knew how devoted I was to Carly, even if none of them had ever met her.

I decided to play along. "Yes. On my lap. Who is this?"

"Is this Harper?"

"Yes. *Who* is this?"

"Sam."

Sam? Sam who? I don't know any ... WAIT!

"Hot—" I stopped myself before I said the whole thing.

Thank God.

"From playgroup. You probably know my kids better. Gemma and Landon?"

Fuck! Why the hell was Hot Dad calling me?

He paused for a second before he asked, "This is Harper from the Monday playgroup, right? Your daughter is Carly, the one who loves dinosaurs?" Hesitation colored his voice.

"Y-yeah. That's me. That's her."

"Oh, good. Thought I might've had the wrong number."

"Uh ..."

His chuckle warmed my skin. It was as if he, his breath, was right there and not miles away. "How are you?"

"F-fine."

"We missed you at playgroup today."

What the fuck is going on right now? Am I dreaming?

I'd missed loads of playgroups before, but never had Sam called me afterward to say he *missed* me. But then again, he didn't say *he* missed me. He said *we* missed me. Who was *we*? Who was he speaking for?

"Gemma had the dinosaurs all to herself. She was happy but confused all at the same time."

Oh, right! His kids. Jesus Christ, Harper, get ahold of yourself.

"Sorry. We meant to get there. Boots were on, toques and coats, the whole nine yards. And then barf happened."

"Yours or Carly's?"

"Oh God, mine! No wait, sorry. Carly's, not mine. Fuck!" Carly wriggled on the bed, and I held my breath. She was a bloody mynah bird these days, so with my luck, she would pick up on my blasphemy in her sleep and be chanting it when she woke up. Her dinosaurs would no longer say "rawr" but "fuuuuuck!"

Dear sweet lord, this man flustered me. Why was the man I'd been hard core crushing on for the past six months calling me out of the blue? And how on earth did he get my number? Waiting with bated breath, I watched as my sick and dozy toddler spun like a log on the bed and repositioned herself with her head no longer on my lap but instead down by my knee. Her feet kicked up toward the pillows. She always was a squirmy worm. Couldn't keep covers on her to save her life. But her eyelids remained fully shut; I finally exhaled.

"Sorry, what?"

He was laughing now. "I didn't say anything. You just cursed like a sailor, and then I thought you'd hung up. Everything okay?"

Prying myself off the bed with ninja stealth, I wandered into the kitchen so I could speak above a hush. "Yeah, sorry. I thought I'd woken Carly up. My sister's kids came home from school last week with the flu, and it looks like Carly caught it."

"Oh, no. How do you feel?"

My insides began to buzz and hum from his concern.

"Okay so far. Though I wash my hands and tend not to lick the walls or furniture, so fingers crossed I manage to avoid it."

"Aw man, I love licking the coffee table. Next to the ottoman, it's my favorite thing to have my tongue on."

Whoa! Now all I could think about was Hot Dad's tongue and the various places *I'd* like to have it. Had that been his intention? Was he talking dirty? Why was he talking to me at all? Thoughts and images, questions and giddiness much too extreme for my age cannoned around inside my head as I paced my kitchen. I needed to do something. I needed to occupy my hands. As if answering my cry for help, my stomach gurgled, and I snatched a banana from the bowl and peeled it.

"You still there?" he asked.

Oh crap, how long had I been silent?

"Yup," I said with a mouthful.

"What are you doing? You sound funny."

"Eating a banana."

Now it was his turn for silence.

"Seriously?" he finally asked.

"Yeah."

"Whole, or did you cut it up into pieces first?"

Holy freaking frack, he's flirting with me!

"Nope."

His chuckle swept over my skin as if he'd just licked each and every inch of it. Divine heat pooled between my legs, and I felt my nipples tighten against my bra. I resisted the urge to reach up and cup them to relieve the sudden strain of their weight.

"What are your plans this weekend, Harper?"

"Um ..."

"Banana in your mouth?"

I swallowed and blinked.

"Mhmm. Sorry."

"It's okay. Swallow."

Holy Mother of God, him telling me to swallow ... my heart nearly leaped clean out of my chest.

"I guess I should probably double-check first that you are in fact single. That you're not seeing someone but just haven't bothered to let your friend Amy know."

Amy! I could kiss that meddling little woman.

"Yes. Yes, I'm single."

"Good. Me too." I could practically see that sexy smile of his it came through so clearly in his voice.

"Well, Harper, would you like to go out with me this weekend?"

I nodded and then did a little hop. My pulse was racing and my brain was struggling to keep up. I was planning a date with Hot Dad! "When? What time?"

"How does Friday around seven sound?"

Yes, woman. Say YES!

"You can think it over if you need some—"

But I cut him off. "I'd love to!"

"Great! So, Friday at seven?"

"Absolutely!"

"Perfect. Text me your address, and I'll swing by to pick you up. How does dinner and a movie sound?"

"Sounds great!" Oh shit, my voice was getting higher. Had he noticed?

"Awesome. I'll see you Friday. Don't get sick."

I swallowed again. "Okay."

"Bye, Harper."

"G-goodbye, Sam."

He hung up.

I stared at the phone and his number. Hot Dad just asked me out on a date!

Hot Dad.

On a date!

I brought up the number for Amy, my sister from another mister and my favorite mom in my mom posse, and texted her.

HARPER: Umm, why did Hot Dad just call me and ask me out on date? What were you two talking about today at Playgroup? About how sad, lonely and sex deprived I am?

· · ·

She texted back almost immediately, as I knew she would. She had Mondays off and usually spent the afternoons with Henry at home or out and about. I checked the time. It was nearly four. She was probably prepping supper.

Amy: Bahahaha. Yes. He knows you're horny as a rabbit in the spring. Get on that, little bunny. He and I were the only two parents who brought their kids today to playgroup. We started talking, I found out he's a single Hot Dad. I thought the two of you might hit it off. He's hot, you're hot. Be hot AND sweaty together. Are you going out with him?

Smiling, I texted her back. Amy was a gem. Feisty, petite and a true friend. We'd met on the first day Carly and I joined playgroup. She'd offered me a piece of chocolate from her pocket. She normally kept her stash hidden and slipped a square into her mouth when no one was looking. But based on the way I'd entered the joint, with a tear in the bum of my brand-new yoga pants, a screaming toddler, and hair caked in oatmeal and banana, she figured I needed the sugar. And we've been friends ever since. She brought me into the fold and made me one of them. There was no bashing, no judgment, just support. And even though I loved all the women at the playgroup, Amy was my person. I could always count on her and she on me. If I didn't have Quinn as a sister, I would have wanted Amy. I texted her back, my pulse thundering in my veins as I replayed my phone conversation with Sam over and over in my head.

H: Duh!? I'd be stupid not to try to hit that. I've been trying to figure out a way to hit that for months.

. . .

A: Ha-ha! Yes, I'm well aware of your six-month love from afar. You deserve this. Good luck and let me know how it goes :)

H: THANK YOU!!!!!!!!!

I SENT her a photo of me blowing a kiss, then tossed my phone onto the counter and started the most epic dance party of my life, all to the tune of the music in my head.

**Read on for Chapter 1 of *Love, Passion and Power: Part 1*
Book 1 of The Dark and Damaged Hearts Series**

LOVE, PASSION AND POWER: PART 1 - CHAPTER 1

Kendra

"Whoa-ho-ho, just take a look at Mr. Mega-Bucks who just pulled into the parking lot. All perfect hair and over-priced sunglasses."

I glanced up to where Damien was indicating. Sure enough, there was a Mr. Mega-Bucks, albeit also a Mr. *Super-Sexy* Mega-Bucks, stepping out of a gunmetal gray Aston Martin DB9. The slick paint job and clean rims glistening like freshly polished silver in the warm May sunshine.

"Well isn't he a delectable little piece?" Manuel added, coming up behind me and resting his elbows on the counter, settling his stubbly chin on his interlocked hands. "Who do you think he is?"

"He's Justin Williams, and he's going to be working with you, Kendra. He's been referred by his physician, and you're to give him the works," Lacy said, looking up at me beneath her feathery lashes.

"Lucky girl," Manuel whined playfully. "I'd certainly like to give him *the works!*" Then he elbowed me in the ribs before heading to the back to see to his massage client.

I rolled my eyes. Yes, lucky me indeed. I get to work with this pompous ass. Who probably has more money than brains and better hair than most women I know. Lucky me indeed. I watched as he sauntered toward the front door and opened it, the sun behind his head giving him an almost biblical glow as he removed his sunglasses. He tucked his shades into the neck of his baby-blue polo shirt, and graced the foyer with his presence.

And despite my usual indifference toward someone with more money than brains, because clearly, that was the case with this guy, I couldn't help but feel myself get a tad winded by his looks as he strode toward us. Light brown hair fell just so over his forehead with messy windswept abandon, while eyes, as blue and bright as the Caribbean Ocean, sparkled above youthful rosy cheeks. Boyish and innocent Hollywood — not that there is anything innocent about Hollywood and there probably wasn't anything innocent about this guy either.

But when he smiled at Lacy — Jesus Christ! I just about swallowed my tongue. Big, straight white teeth on that million-dollar grin, to go along with what I can only assume were his millions of dollars. His swagger was practiced and carefree, but it also exuded cockiness and confidence. And the heavy sway of the bulge in his khaki shorts said he was well practiced in bringing a woman to her knees and keeping her there — willingly!

"Hi," he said, all smiles with a coquettish wink at Lacy who was eating it up with both hands. She batted her eyelashes and flipped her platinum shoulder-length hair around her head as if there was a giant fan in the corner. "Justin Williams. I'm here for a consult. Dr. Ernest referred me."

I turned my back on them, too embarrassed by the ridiculousness of my co-worker to continue watching. Instead, I busied myself with the file in my hand, straightening papers that didn't need straightening and reading things I didn't need to read.

"Yes... yes, Mr. Williams. We've uh... we've been expecting you." Lacy's words fumbled and fell out of her mouth like marbles in a teaspoon. Get it together woman; he's just another pretty face. "Uh, Kendra...?"

I turned to her, taking great care not to look at the sexy God-like creature standing on the opposite side of the reception desk. "Yeah, wuzzup?" I instantly cringed inside at my overly cavalier attitude. I never say 'wuzzup.' Nobody says 'wuzzup' anymore. It's been thirty seconds, and already this man has me acting like a complete fool.

"Are you free to take Mr. Williams into the back for his consult and orientation?"

"Sure. Mr. Williams, if you'll follow me please." I gave a vague and disinterested smile to *Mr. Williams,* motioning for him to follow me. He gave another flashy grin and wink to Lacy, which sent her into a fit of giggles and snickers like a moon-struck schoolgirl, her hair flying in a completely unnecessary tailspin around her bobble head.

We traveled down the hallway in silence, but the fact that I couldn't see him didn't mean I wasn't fully aware of the eyeball-sized holes he was boring into my ass — the man was an incorrigible pig.

"In here. Have a seat, and we'll get started." I gestured, holding the door open to the office I shared with other personal trainers on staff.

The room was empty. Damien, Cheryl, and Tim were all out with clients, and with that emptiness, I felt a sudden awareness of this man and his big — I'm guessing six-foot-three, two-hundred-pound body — being only inches from mine as he crossed the threshold. And of course, he smelled magnificent; a heavenly mixture of aftershave, coconuts, and soap.

His eyes traveled up and down my body in slow appraisal and, although I had clothes on, the way he was looking at me I could have been wearing nothing at all. Instinctively I squirmed under his gaze as I propped open the door and walked around the desk to take my seat.

"So, Mr. Williams, let's start off with you telling me a little bit about yourself and why Dr. Ernest referred you to our facility."

I opened his file and scanned it briefly, slowly lifting my head to meet his gaze; it was penetrating. His head was slightly cocked to one side, and a bemused half-smile danced across his sensuous lips. I raised my eyebrows slightly to prompt a response and show him that, contrary to popular belief, he didn't have the same effect on *all* women. I wasn't about to lose my shit or my cool simply because he'd smiled at me and undressed me with his eyes, all the way down to my toe-ring.

He leaned back in the chair and crossed his left leg over his right, resting the ankle on the knee, took a deep breath and then exhaled loudly. I didn't move, fidget or respond. I just waited.

"Well, what can I say? I'm a workaholic who eats shit, doesn't exercise, barely sleeps and takes prescription drugs to stay awake. Some of these drugs are not exactly 'legal.'" He used air quotes. "In Canada... And according to my doctor, all this caused me to have a heart attack a few weeks ago... albeit a mild one."

A faint buzzing sound permeated the sudden silence in the room. Immediately he put his foot down on the floor and leaned forward. Pulling his phone out of his back pocket, he slid his thumb over the touch screen and then it was as though I didn't exist. That we weren't in the middle of a serious conversation and that I wasn't sitting across from him, four feet away.

I watched as he continued to fiddle on his phone, his face in a pent up scrunch, lines that I hadn't noticed before etched deep on his otherwise youthful face. Suddenly the phone buzzed again, and he held a finger up to me indicating silence or that he needed a minute, either way, it was rude as hell.

"Williams!" He snapped into the receiver. "I don't care right now John, just liquidate and pull out. I don't need the hassle right now. Pay them fucking overtime for all I care, double-time if we have to, it'll still be a savings in the long run. Just get it all out of there... good... Call me when it's done." And without a farewell, he did the less-than-dramatic red-button press and hung up on "John."

"Sorry about that." He looked up at me and shrugged sheepishly, adding a wink to his grin to try and soften the blow. "Business."

"Mr. Williams, we have a strict 'no phone' policy in the facility. For future reference, you are to turn your phone off or onto silent mode and either leave it in your locker in the men's change room or check it at reception with Lacy."

His eyebrows shot up in surprise, and that same quirky smirk played across his full pouty lips. "Is that so? Well, I am *never* without my phone... but I'm up for the challenge. Would you like it now?" he asked as he put it on the desk and mimed sliding to across to me.

"We won't be in here long. You can hand it off to Lacy when we pass reception."

"Very well... I, uh... I get the feeling... Miss...?"

"Kendra, Kendra Black," I snapped, eyeing him up and questioning where this was going.

"Miss Black, I get the feeling you don't like me very much. Is that correct? Have I done something to offend you?" His head cocked to the side again as he leaned forward, clasping his hands and resting them on the desk.

I sighed heavily and leaned back in my own seat gauging him warily. "I don't know you, Mr. Williams—"

"Justin, please call me Justin." Humor and mischief danced in his eyes.

"Justin, fine, I don't know you at all... *Justin*, but I will tell you this. I have zero, *zero* tolerance for recreational drug use or abuse of prescribed pharmaceuticals. If I find out you're using again I will drop you as a client faster than you can blink, are we clear? This is a center of rehabilitation for the body and mind. People come here after they have had surgery, an injury, a heart attack like you, a stroke or other kinds of serious trauma or setbacks. But we are *not* a rehab facility for addicts. Got it? Secondly, I don't know who you are, or, better yet, who you *think* you are but don't think you can charm me like you charmed Lacy. I'm not impressed by money or power. You're the client, and I'm your trainer, and the sooner you realize and accept that the better this relationship will be."

I caught my reflection in the sunglasses he'd hooked in the top of his shirt. I looked pissed off. Why was I so pissed off? I needed to cut the guy some slack. I didn't know him, and he'd just had a heart attack. I berated myself for my earlier bitchiness and corrected my scowl. I could still maintain professionalism and also be nice. I *was* a nice person.

I watched him as he processed my comments, his eyebrows dancing up and down on his tanned forehead while his lips twisted into a tiny pout. It was a cute look for him, I must admit, but I couldn't let myself get distracted. Nice didn't have to mean flirty either.

"Well, Miss Black, I assure you I'm clean and plan to be for the foreseeable future, so you don't have to worry about that. And as far as the charming goes... well, it's up to you to be strong enough to resist my charms. I'm just being me." A satisfied and wry little smirk caught on his mouth.

I huffed a laugh and then reached for my pen. "Very well, Mister... Justin, if you don't mind, I'm going to ask you a series of questions so I can get a better idea of your lifestyle. To understand how we can best help you here. Is that all right? I see you completed our online in-depth new client form, thank you, that saves us some time."

"Ask away, lady. I'm an open book." He leaned back and crossed his ankle onto his knee again.

"All right, well it says here that you are thirty-four, is that correct?"

"Yes."

"How often would you say you exercise per week and what does that exercise consist of?"

"I don't work out. At all."

"Oh, okay." I scribbled a big line through the section concerning workout routine.

"And your diet. What does a typical day's diet look like for you?"

"Six cups of coffee, two in the morning, four spread out over the rest of the day, a microwave breakfast burrito if I remember to eat breakfast that is. Maybe a burger, or a slice or two of pizza for lunch and probably the same for dinner or maybe a steak if I have to go out for dinner with clients. And I love potato chips. I usually eat at least a bag a day while at work in my office, salt-and-vinegar or all-dressed, those are my faves. Sometimes I don't have time for lunch, so I just down a bag of chips before a meeting. And then I finish the night off with a six-pack of beer or two or three doubles of scotch, usually."

"Wow, I'm surprised you're not four hundred pounds."

"A fast metabolism runs in my family."

I tapped my pen against the desk. "Yes, well, just because you're not overweight doesn't mean you're healthy. Now tell me about your personal life. What do you do to relax and have fun?"

"I don't. I work. All. The. Time. I socialize for work purposes, drinks with clients or potential clients, golf to schmooze. I have friends, but besides James I barely see them, we're all too busy."

"Is James your... uh, partner?"

"No," he said flatly. Purposefully not giving me any inclination into his sexual orientation. Though by the way he flirted with Lacy and had been blatantly raking his eyes up and down my body, I'd bet he was as heterosexual as they come.

"Romantic relationship status?"

"Nothing significant."

"So, single?"

"Yes."

"How do you relieve stress?"

"Sex. Or copious amounts of masturbation."

I looked up at him from beneath my lashes, determined to look professional and let him know that his comment, although meant to startle me, hadn't fazed me in the least.

"That's it?"

"Yep. Oh, and I like to read comic books."

"Okay then. And how about your relationship with your family?"

He lifted one shoulder. "*Meh*, it's all right. I mean it's not strained. I love my parents and my brother and sister, but we're not what I would call 'close.' I've got a good relationship with my dad, but he lives in Hawaii. My mum, step-dad and half-sibs live in Montreal."

"And have you taken the leave of absence from work your doctor advised?"

"No."

I tilted my head and lifted an eyebrow. "Why not?"

"Too busy. I'll do everything else he's making me do, but I'm not leaving work."

I decided to ignore this as it was ultimately going to get me nowhere and chose to move on. "Okay. So, I see here that Dr.

Ernest has recommended you take up yoga for stress and that I set up a fitness routine for you. Something that you can manage and fit into your life so that it is maintainable once we're through. I'm also going to set you up with a nutrition plan to help change your diet. After all, changing your body for weight-loss or fitness is *thirty* percent exercise and *seventy* percent what you put in your mouth. Are you okay with all of this?"

He lifted one shoulder arrogantly. "Yeah, sure. I mean I don't want to have another jammer and die."

"No of course not. I don't want you to have another *jammer* either. So, I think today what we'll do is do a fitness assessment, get your body mass index, body fat content, your body age. I already have the blood work that the hospital sent over, so that's good. And then I think we'll do a yoga session for the last hour to de-stress, so we finish on a high note. Did you bring other clothes?"

"No."

"Well, I think we'll be able to find you something here."

"Here," I said, throwing him a pair of basketball shorts and a loose, white t-shirt. "These should suffice for today." I grabbed two yoga mats off the rack and led Justin down the hallway toward the studio while pointing to the men's room on the left. "You can change in there if you want to. I'll set up in here."

"Ah, I should be okay."

Following me into the yoga studio, he removed his shorts down to his, The Incredible Hulk boxers, and kicked off his running shoes and socks. Then he pulled his shirt off over his head, while I busied myself laying out the mats. I tied my long and frustratingly thick dark, red hair back into a ponytail and secured the whispies with a thin black headband I keep wrapped around my wrist. All the while desperately trying not to watch him in the giant floor to ceiling wall mirrors, but it was difficult, especially since *he* was watching *me*. Our eyes locked for just a second, then that smirk was on his face again. I rolled my eyes and kicked my flip-flops to the side while unzipping my white hoodie.

He had a nice body considering how little he took care of it. I studied his arms and torso, looking to see where I could add definition and toning. We'd definitely have to lift some heavy weights to build up his delts, traps, and pecs, they were virtually non-existent, but he had nice toned legs and from what I could see a taut little ass.

"You're going to put me in an early grave with those sexy yoga pants and hot-pink top Miss Black. Are you trying to give your clients a heart attack? Or in my case *another* heart attack?"

I rolled my eyes again and ignored his come-on. "All right let's begin with some deep breathing. Stand in the center of your mat, feet together facing the mirror, hands in prayer position in front of your heart."

I watched him walk over, his big masculine feet with a light dusting of hair on the tops and toes making small imprints on the cobalt blue mat. Big feet, big... My mind wandered for a second and his eyes caught me staring, which of course earned me another large playful grin. But despite all that he followed my orders and we managed to make it through a full hour of yoga. His flexibility was paltry at best and his sense of balance laughable, but I had to give the man credit: he tried every position without a grimace and didn't roll his eyes or ask to stop. And every time he lost his balance he'd get right back up and attempt it again.

"So, will this work for you then?" I asked as I handed him the proposed schedule that Lacy had printed out. It had us seeing each other five days a week for two hours a day, and four hours on Mondays to allow time to set up his meal plan for the week.

"Yes, uh, I think this should work. Sooooo, I guess I will see you on Monday then. Thank you, Miss Black."

He extended his hand, and I shook it, our eyes locking again, a small squeeze of his fingers sending a jolt of awareness to my very core. When our hands separated, he offered me a very genuine and surprisingly small smile before nodding at Lacy and turning to leave, placing his sunglasses back in front of his eyes.

"Hey, babe."

I turned around to see Alexa as she walked up behind me. And without thinking, I immediately grabbed her by the neck and planted a kiss on her lips. She was surprised at first but didn't pull away. Instead, she deepened the kiss as her hand grazed my hip affectionately. When we came up for air from our more-than-a-peck lip lock I noticed Justin standing just outside the open door; his sunglasses were pushed down onto the bridge of his nose, his mouth open in surprise like an octopus. Smiling, I pulled Lex closer and captured her mouth with mine again, sliding my hand around to cup her perky butt.

"Do you want to go out tonight?" Lex asked as she turned into the liquor store parking lot.

I loved looking at her. She was absolutely stunning: her tanned almost muted copper skin glowed vibrant and youthful, while wild, jet black hair fell in thick, voluminous waves down her back, and big, soulful, dark brown eyes held wisdom far beyond her years. We're not what you would call a "couple," we're best friends and roommates who also happen to occasionally sleep together and have threesomes when we feel like it. She's my safe place, my rock, my family. And when I find a guy I'd like to sleep with Lex is always there too, making sure nothing bad happens.

I climbed out of her sleek little red Miata. "I don't know," I said. "Do you want to?" My own Jeep was in the shop, so Lex, who's the head pastry chef at a cute little bakery and is usually off work by three, had come to pick me up.

"Well, I just got a text from Chad saying that a bunch of them are going out to The Fig for dinner, and they want to go dancing at that hot new nightclub up the street afterward. Want to do that?"

I nodded and fought off a sudden yawn. "Yeah, could be fun."

"So how was work?"

We walked into the liquor store, and immediately male heads and a few female ones turned and took in the vision that is Lex: all big breasts, rocking ass, long legs and curves that won't quit. And the worst and the best thing about her is that she's the most down-to-earth and least vain person I've ever met. Truthfully, she has no idea how gorgeous she is.

"It was pretty good," I said. "I have a new client. He's handsome as hell, super rich and is a serious playboy. He can't help but hit on anything and everything that walks. I practically caught him delivering pickup lines to a lamppost until he realized it wasn't just a really thin woman."

"Dear God, is he stupid too?" she asked with a throaty laugh, picking up a bottle of red wine to read the back label.

I shook my head. "No actually, I don't think he is. I thought that he might be. You know, a rich boy spending all of Daddy's money without a care or concern in the world. But I actually think he's self-made and pretty smart. He's an investment banker who owns a bunch of buildings and a few clubs and restaurants in town as well. But he's one of those guys that just can't turn it off. You know? He's just always on, always joking around, but at the same time, he's attached to his phone like it's another appendage. He answered it three times during our session and was constantly texting and checking his emails even after I asked him to give his phone to the front desk. I can't figure him out."

"So is that why you sucked my face off when I picked you up?" she asked, giving me the side-eye as she scrutinized the wall of beer.

I managed a rueful smile. "I just needed to send him the message that I wasn't interested. Thanks by the way."

She shrugged. "Anytime. How about vodka? Hey, let's get some Galliano and orange juice and make Harvey Wallbangers!"

"Yeah sure, whatever..." I trailed off, my thumb wedged sideways between my teeth as I wandered aimlessly up and down the aisles. "I just can't figure this guy out. You know? He doesn't work out, eats shit and has no stress release besides sex... what's his deal?"

"You also can't stop thinking about him. Or talking about him. Maybe his other stress release is humor? Should we grab some beer?" She tucked the bottle of Galliano under her arm and wandered back over to the microbrew section.

"What?" I chased after her. "I'm not thinking about him, or his stupid hair or stupid blue eyes..." She gave me a wry look. "But you make a good point about him being constantly *on*."

She rolled her eyes at me. "Come on, let's go pay for our booty and head home to change. I want to wear my new dress, but I need you to help me accessorize."

ALSO BY WHITLEY COX

Love, Passion and Power: Part 1
The Dark and Damaged Hearts Series Book 1

Love, Passion and Power: Part 2
The Dark and Damaged Hearts Series Book 2

Sex, Heat and Hunger: Part 1
The Dark and Damaged Hearts Book 3

Sex, Heat and Hunger: Part 2
The Dark and Damaged Hearts Book 4

Hot and Filthy: The Honeymoon
The Dark and Damaged Hearts Book 4.5

True, Deep and Forever: Part 1
The Dark and Damaged Hearts Book 5

True, Deep and Forever: Part 2
The Dark and Damaged Hearts Book 6

Hard, Fast and Madly: Part 1
The Dark and Damaged Hearts Series Book 7

Hard, Fast and Madly: Part 2
The Dark and Damaged Hearts Series Book 8

Quick & Dirty

Book 1, A Quick Billionaires Novel

Quick & Easy

Book 2, A Quick Billionaires Novella

Quick & Reckless

Book 3, A Quick Billionaires Novel

Hot Dad

Lust Abroad

Snowed In & Set Up

UPCOMING BOOKS

Quick & Dangerous
Book 4, A Quick Billionaires Novel

Hired by the Single Dad
The Single Dads of Seattle, Book 1

Dancing with the Single Dad
The Single Dads of Seattle, Book 2

Saved by the Single Dad
The Single Dads of Seattle, Book 3

Living with the Single Dad
The Single Dads of Seattle, Book 4

Lost Hart
The Harty Boys Book 2

ACKNOWLEDGMENTS

There are so many people to thank who have helped me on this daunting journey to becoming a published writer. First and foremost, my friend and editor Chris Kridler, you lady are a blessing, a gem and an all around amazing human being. Thank you for your honesty and hard work.

Jeanne St. James for doing the first beta-read for me, your notes, brutal honesty, insight and ideas were so helpful. You really are my sister from another mister. Thank you, Shannyn Leah for your beta-read and encouraging words, you're such a wonderful person. Thank you, Justine and Krista for your beta-reads as well. I love that I can hand you the rough, unedited stuff and you'll read it and give me your feedback. Thank you.

Tara at Fantasia Frog Designs, your patience with my indecisions when it comes to covers is appreciated. You never disappoint.

My Romance Writer's Behaving Badly Blog crew, I love being part of such a tremendous set of inspiring, talented and supportive women. Thank you for letting me learn, lean on and join the team.

My street team, Whitley Cox's Curiously Kinky Reviewers, you are all awesome and I feel so blessed to have found such wonderful fans.

The ladies in Vancouver Island Romance Authors, your support and insight have been incredibly helpful, and I'm so honored to be apart of a group of such talented writers.

And lastly, of course, the husband. My rock, who proposed on Christmas because he wanted to be able to remember the date. It was the best Christmas present EVER. You are my other half in every way. Thank you for your unwavering support and love. I love you.

JOIN MY STREET TEAM

WHITLEY COX'S CURIOUSLY KINKY REVIEWERS
Hear about giveaways, games, ARC opportunities, new releases, teasers, author news, character and plot development and more!

Facebook Street Team
Join NOW!

DON'T FORGET TO SUBSCRIBE TO MY NEWSLETTER

Be the first to hear about pre-orders, new releases, giveaways, 99cent deals, and freebies!

Click here to Subscribe
http://eepurl.com/ckh5yT

YOU CAN ALSO FIND ME HERE:

Website: WhitleyCox.com
Twitter: @WhitleyCoxBooks
Instagram: @CoxWhitley
Facebook Page: https://www.facebook.com/CoxWhitley/
Blog: https://whitleycox.blogspot.ca/
Multi-Author Blog: https://romancewritersbehavingbadly.blogspot.com
Exclusive Facebook Reader Group: https://www.facebook.com/groups/234716323653592/
Booksprout: https://booksprout.co/author/994/whitley-cox
Bookbub: https://www.bookbub.com/authors/whitley-cox

ABOUT THE AUTHOR

A Canadian West Coast baby born and raised, Whitley is married to her high school sweetheart, and together they have a spirited toddler, a brand new baby and a fluffy dog. She spends her days making food that gets thrown on the floor, vacuuming Cheerios out from under the couch and making sure that the dog food doesn't end up in the air conditioner. But when nap time comes, and it's not quite wine o'clock, Whitley sits down, avoids the pile of laundry on the couch, and writes.

A lover of all things decadent; wine, cheese, chocolate and spicy erotic romance, Whitley brings the humorous side of sex, the ridiculous side of relationships and the suspense of everyday life into her stories. With mommy wars, body issues, threesomes, bondage and role playing, these books have everything we need to satisfy the curious kink in all of us.

Manufactured by Amazon.ca
Bolton, ON